*Totally Bound Publishing books by Sandra Carmel*

**The Cure**
Capture
Discover

I0691674

# The Cure

# DISCOVER

SANDRA CARMEL

Discover
ISBN # 978-1-83943-842-4
©Copyright Sandra Carmel 2019
Cover Art by Erin Dameron-Hill ©Copyright October 2019
Interior text design by Claire Siemaszkiewicz
Totally Bound Publishing

# DISCOVER

# Dedication

For those who remember to treasure the memories.

For those who appreciate tannin water.

And to Bastian and Merlin, my warm gorgeous babies, for your unconditional love and support and adding your own special words to my story.

# Chapter One

## The Ring Cycle

*Sub Rosa basement lab, Hobart, October 1965*

"Help! Help us!" Eva screamed, but no sound came out. Her breath caught in her throat. She had to be dreaming.

*Wake up. Wake up!* She closed her eyes, opened them again. *No!* She was still in the Sub Rosa basement. In hell...but not the biblical fiery type. It was stark and sterile, lab-like, the pungent odor of bleach stinging her nostrils.

*We'll find a way to get out of here*, she wanted to tell her husband, but she couldn't. They had an audience, a black-radiation-suited audience, their shielded inhuman-looking eyes peering at them — studying, analyzing, deciding whether to keep them alive.

*Do I know them?*

*Does my husband?*

None of the frightening figures had said a word.

The one in charge held up a fluid-filled syringe that glinted in the grim light. Her gaze darted between the man and the needle. The man and the needle. The man and the... He squeezed out a drop and she gulped down frenzied gushes of air. In one swift move, he stabbed the syringe into her IV. *No no n...*

She roused. Still a prisoner, strapped down to a stone-cold gurney. She should be petrified. It had to be the injected drugs that dulled her fear.

Adrenaline lay dormant in her system, her heart droning on and on and on. *Thrump. Thrump. Thrump.* Her circulation slowed, shunting her lava-like blood through her veins and clouding her brain.

Hazy, scattered thoughts swirled about, mostly out of conscious reach. She tried to open her eyes, the lids hanging heavy, almost immobile, as though each lash were weighted with a ten-pound dumbbell.

Artificial calmness enshrouded her, further dulling her sense of reality—not bad, but not good. Floaty, relaxed...but she was trapped, with no way to escape.

She tried to turn to see the love of her life and her body slammed against the steel table. "Ugh," she groaned. Thick black rubber bands encircled her chest, hips, knees, ankles and wrists, holding her in place, keeping her prisoner.

Craning her neck only got her a glimpse of her husband's golden-brown hair. The agency had made sure of that. They'd made sure to sever the connection to her soulmate.

Her husband, Richard, had discovered stuff—things, sensitive information and now...

He wasn't at fault. He'd tried to do the right thing and had convinced her to join him, but they'd gotten intercepted.

They hadn't been married long. The twenty-third of July 1965. Three, short amazing months. They were still in the honeymoon phase.

Mesmerized by Richard's light green eyes, his tender passionate lips, his sexy whispered words, she'd made love with him day after day, night after night. And each morning, she would wake up snuggled into him, safe and secure in his strong arms.

But he wasn't just a wonderful lover, he was a romantic, considerate man, frequently leaving her a sweet sentiment or poem in different spots—on the notepad by the phone, on her bedside table, on a coaster, on her dinner napkin, pinned to the fridge by a fluffy cat magnet and even on the steamed-up mirror for her to see when she got out of the shower.

Just when she thought he'd run out of places to hide them, he'd find a new one. Richard—always so thoughtful, loving and full of surprises...

His slurred words jolted her out of her drowsy state and she snapped her eyes open to brightness. Interrogative-spotlight intensity. She squinted, furiously batting her eyelids in an attempt to adjust to the glare.

She'd been moved, and her precious heart engagement ring, wedding band and gold marcasite watch were gone. Would she and her husband be disposed of next?

She sucked in a sob-like breath, choking on noxious air, and her womb cramped. Still sore, stripped, raw, she tried to focus her blurry, tear-filled eyes on Richard's handsome face. He lay only a few feet from her, but she could hardly make him out. If this formed part of Sub Rosa's torture plan, it worked a thousand times better than any physical suffering.

If only she could reach out and touch her husband, tell him she loved him, reinforce that she didn't blame him for any of this and they'd make it through. They'd be together again, stronger than ever. However, she struggled to form words in her head, let alone speak them, her tongue numb, heavy, defective.

The same black-suited man walked over and prepared a syringe with a blue liquid. "Nooo! Pleease don't dooo this... Leave him alooone!" she pleaded, her words slack and slurred.

The faceless man jabbed the syringe into her husband's drip. Tears sprang from her eyes and a burst of adrenaline kicked her heart into overdrive, frantic beats thrashing against her ribcage.

Within seconds, Richard's eyes fluttered and he went as limp as a puppet with slashed strings. She strained at the obstinate ligatures, desperate to break free to reach her lifeless husband, but the man approached and stuck the same needle into her IV.

Black.

Bright.

Black, bright, black, bright, black, bright. The flickering fluorescent lights blacked out and her pulse plummeted, her scream barely a whisper.

# Chapter Two

### A Sense of Reality

*Hobart, June 2010*

Eden Freberg and her best friend, Grace, stepped out of the cinema and onto the dimly lit street after seeing *Eclipse* for the first time. They walked to the car, the steady clip-clop of their shoes echoing against the pavement.

"Oh my God, Edward is so perfect, isn't he?" Grace gushed, almost tripping over her restless tongue.

"Yeah, if you think a hot-looking vampire is a good catch. He only has to be hungry one night and suddenly you'll look incredibly appealing...in a food type of way."

"Very funny."

Eden grinned. "Seriously though, let's say I hooked up with a 'vegetarian' vampire like Edward in real life. How would I ever explain it to you? You'd think I'd gone insane, and don't say you wouldn't."

"I might think you're slightly insane, but if the guy's as hot as Edward..."

"You're a shocker!"

Grace smiled like Eden had given her a compliment.

Eden shook her head, her hair tumbling over her shoulders. "If you ask me, I think Stephenie's letting all us girls know that the probability of finding a man like Edward is as likely as finding a vampire sweetheart."

"You just have to ruin my little fantasy, don't you?"

"Well, I don't think it's positive to fantasize about something that's impossible. There are too many books and Hollywood blockbusters that do that to women already. It just sets all of us up for failure."

Grace rolled her eyes and sighed. "Ugh. Eden, it's just a movie. No one takes it seriously. Honestly, you're no fun sometimes."

"You're the one who always says we should be realists."

Grace stopped and turned to her, her chocolate-brown eyes probing. "That's right, when it comes to real life. And speaking of real life, why don't you go talk to that guy?"

"What guy?" Eden resumed walking, the icy breeze cooling the burst of heat in her cheeks.

"You know exactly who I mean."

The man in question had been watching Eden for weeks and it hadn't taken her long to notice. With his cool rock style and good looks, he'd stood out, even in the dark club. She'd had a few opportunities to initiate a conversation—getting a drink at the bar, walking to the toilets, heading to the dance floor—but she lacked the confidence to take that first step…especially after what had happened with those other gorgeous guys.

Unlike her friend, Eden wasn't a one-night-stand woman and, instead, remained focused on finding a decent man, the *right* man. When she'd said that to

Grace during one of their nights out, her friend had laughed and said, "What are you doing here then? This place is a meat market!"

Months earlier, Grace had confronted her during their lunch break at work.

*'Come on, Eden. There has to be at least one guy in the club you like. You've been single for ages. It's not right.'*

Eden had stabbed at her rare beef salad. *'I'm fine.'*

*'No, you're not. You're looking desperate, desperate for the right guy. And how are you going to know if he's it, if you don't talk to him?'*

Eden had shoved a forkful of pinky-red meat into her mouth. *'I suppose...'*

*"Just because you talk to someone doesn't mean it has to go any further. Think of it as experience for when you meet the right guy."*

The next time they'd gone out, Eden had plied herself with a couple of liquid icebreakers and strolled over to a good-looking guy at the back bar, who Grace said had been eyeing her.

He'd been talking to a couple of other men until one of them nudged his arm and he'd turned around. The cheerful surprise on his face had made him look like he'd just won first prize in the lottery.

Eden had taken a few deep breaths and forced the most radiant-looking smile she could muster. "Hi, I'm Eden."

"Hi Eden, I'm Finn. Nice to meet you."

"Same. I haven't seen you here before." Her voice had wavered. Thankfully, the loud music had helped to disguise it.

"Probably because it's my first time to Tasmania. I only got in this morning."

She'd shifted her weight from one foot to the other. "Oh, where are you from?"

"Melbourne."

"So, are you enjoying yourself?" She'd leaned on the bar to try to stop herself from shaking.

"I am now."

Eden had averted her eyes from his steadfast gaze. "Um…how long are you staying?"

"Only until Monday…unfortunately."

She'd glanced up at him. "Oh, that's a shame."

"Sure is. So, do you live around here?"

"Yeah, about five minutes away…by car."

His eyes had lit up like he'd selected the one-night-stand prize of a lifetime. "Really?"

She'd repositioned her slipping, sweaty hand on the bar to regain some traction. "Yes. What brings you here, business or pleasure?"

"Business originally, but —"

"But?"

"There's more pleasure here than I anticipated," he'd said with a suggestive smile.

She'd swallowed the beach ball of nerves in her throat. "I see."

He'd edged in closer, his dark brown hair falling across his forehead, tempting her to reach out and flick it away. "Anyway, would you like a drink?"

The combination of her previous alcoholic beverages and the scent of his aftershave had created a heady, intoxicating mix, though not enough to appease her anxiety. "Oh, um…yes. A house champagne would be nice. Thanks."

He'd ordered their drinks, handed her a glass of champagne and led them to a quiet table in a dark corner. She'd taken a seat and he'd slid in beside her.

They'd sat so close she could almost hear his heart beating.

She'd gazed into his intense, azure-colored eyes and her pulse had shot through the roof, Burj Khalifa style. Maybe Grace had been right. Maybe hot men out there were interested and she'd only needed to approach them to make things happen.

Finn's gaze had moved between her eyes and her lips and he leaned in. He'd covered her mouth with his, but instead of excitement, she'd felt drained, anchored, like his saliva thickened into setting concrete, dragging her down.

Shock had disabled her lips and tongue, as though paralyzed by anesthetic. *Stop, stop, stop!* She'd pulled back and stared at him. The guy had been physically attractive, friendly. How could the kiss have felt so wrong?

The hungry, I-want-to-taste-every-bit-of-your-body look in his eyes had confirmed that he'd gone from interested to turned on. Eden had frowned. *How can that be?* Unless he was a selfish, delusional sociopath.

*Escape.* She'd needed to escape...and quickly.

She'd surveyed the surrounds. If only she were a shapeshifter, she could have disappeared into the drift of scented smoke floating in front of them. But she wasn't. *Shit, shit, shit!* She'd jumped up, thanked him for the drink and chat then taken off in search of Grace.

Eden had stepped between her friend and a man, bursting their flirt bubble. "We need to go. *Now!*" she'd said, her tone packed with panic.

Outside, someone had grabbed Eden's arm, pulling her to a stop. Her stomach sank. *No!*

"What the hell's going on?"

*Grace.* Eden had breathed out hard. "I'll explain in a minute. Can we please just go?" she'd said, her words wobbly, and she'd yanked her arm from Grace's grasp.

Once inside the car, Eden had explained the stressful situation.

"Don't worry about it. It's no big deal." Grace had brushed off her concerns like coat lint. "You guys probably just didn't have the right sexual chemistry. You can't give up based on just one experience. Promise me you'll give someone else a go."

Eden had reluctantly agreed, and two weeks later, she'd tried again with a lovely, hot-looking man from Sydney...with equally disastrous results. She couldn't understand it. "Maybe there's something wrong with me," she'd said to Grace on the drive home afterward.

"No, I think it's because your expectations are too high."

Eden had stared out the passenger side window into the blackness. "I like them before they touch me, though."

"I know. But obviously what you're expecting to feel isn't realistic."

Eden had shrugged. "Maybe. I don't know. Though I should feel something even a little bit nice, especially if I find them attractive."

Grace had stopped at a red light. "You're right. You should." Her I'm-an-expert-on-this stare had met Eden's eyes. "Honestly, I think you've set up this ideal in your head of how things should be and feel, and no man is ever going to live up to it."

Eden had looked down and focused on her ringless wedding finger, her vision blurry with brimming tears. "You're probably right. But I need to feel a certain way to pursue anything or else it's never going to work."

The light had turned green and Grace continued down the road. "Only you can decide what's right for you. I just don't want to see you miss out."

"I know. Thanks." With her repeated lackluster experience with men, Eden had begun to believe she'd be single...forever.

# Chapter Three

## The Second Beginning

Thornton sprang onto Eden's lap for some loving, his purring tapping into a meditative frequency in her brainwaves. Her mobile phone alarm went off and she jumped, Thornton's claws clinging to her track pants and scratching her thighs.

"Ouwch!" She nudged him off and he curled up beside her on the couch. The time had arrived to get ready for her weekly Wednesday ritual.

"Hump day," Grace said each time, and, with a twinkle in her eye, added, "and hopefully hump night!"

After reviewing her wardrobe options several dozen times, Eden slipped into a blue-violet halter-neck dress and appraised herself in her full-length, white-rose-framed mirror. A plump of cleavage, curve-enhancing. *He won't be able to resist me.* A nervous laugh stumbled from her lips. *Fingers crossed!*

Grace picked her up, and ten minutes later they were inside the nightclub. They went straight to the bar and Grace ordered them champagne. Drinks in hand, they wandered upstairs and down, nodding acknowledgment to the regulars as they passed. Eden scrutinized every patron, every dark corner, but hadn't seen any sign of *him*...yet.

The cool, two-story club flashed with disco lights, and strawberry-scented smoke hissed out of smoke machines in sync with the music. The owners promoted the place as Hobart's pint-sized answer to Studio 54.

Downstairs, they found a space on the dance floor near the front bar. Seconds later, *he* appeared, standing in his usual spot by the back bar. A smile spread across Eden's lips.

She threw herself into dancing, injecting sensuality into her moves, emboldened by the couple of drinks she'd had, combined with his sexy, libido-spiking stare.

Eden stole another glance in his direction and his eyes locked on hers. Her heart thundered and she looked away.

"He's here again." Grace's voice boomed in her ear.

"Sorry?" Eden danced away from her.

Grace shimmied forward, eyebrows raised. "That guy. The gorgeous guy who stands at the bar and eye-fucks you every week."

"Oh, him."

"Yeah, him. Just go over and talk to the poor man. Please!" she begged.

Eden shook her head and looked down. "I can't."

Grace sashayed in. "Of course you can. Forget what has happened in the past. This is a new guy. Just go and have a chat to him. It's pretty obvious he's interested. He can't take his eyes off you. It's like no other woman exists."

Eden stared into her friend's eyes, searching for answers. "If he's so interested, why doesn't he approach me?"

"Maybe he's shy?"

"Well, I'm shy too..."

"Well, someone's got to make the first move," Grace said, shaking her hips to the loud, thumping beats.

Eden crossed her arms. "I just don't see why it has to be me."

"Do you like him or not?"

"Well...yeah, he is kind of cute. And there is a weird, intense sort of flirtation going on..."

A strobe light flashed across Grace's face. "Then don't just stand there. Go speak to him. You've gone up to guys before. It's not a big deal. What's the worst thing that can happen?"

"I'll feel like a cement truck has parked itself in my mouth...again."

"At least you'll know he's not right and you can move on to someone else."

Eden stared at her blue-violet patent-leather pumps. "I don't know."

"You're twenty-seven. Let your hair down. Have some fun — or you're going to be single your whole life. Is that what you want?"

Her gaze collided with Grace's. "No, of course not. But I have to go with how I feel."

Grace moved away and put her hands up. "Fine. It's up to you. I'm just trying to help."

Eden forced a smile. "I know. Thanks."

"Okay, I'm going to the bar. Do you want anything?"

"No thanks."

Grace walked off and Eden resumed dancing. She snuck another peek over to where the guy always stood, but he'd vanished. Her gaze darted to the back bar then toward the toilets. *Where has he gone?* Under the UV lights, his white shirt glowed like a beacon, so he shouldn't be too hard to find.

After five minutes of searching, Eden stopped. He had to have left. Her heart slumped. *Damn.* She forced herself to continue dancing to one of her favorite tracks, Chris Raven's *I Know You Love Me Too*, the van Bellen remix, while waiting for Grace to return.

Her friend usually never left her on her own for this long, not without an explanation. Eden glanced up, ready to take off in search of Grace, but a big, sexy body blocked her vision. *His. The guy* stood right in front of her.

Eden sucked in her breath and froze. She stared up into his superb, angular face, her mind became a jumble of surprise, joy and angst. He had to be over six feet tall, given that her skyscraper stilettos shot her up to five foot nine. He didn't say anything, just kept staring as though she'd captured his gaze and held him spellbound.

His eyes were the most amazing light green she had ever seen. *Magnetic.* Her stare stayed locked on his, and she drifted closer until their bodies almost touched. They began moving in sequence, mirroring each other, as though dancing a choreographed routine.

Their unspoken communication continued, his lips closing in on hers. She moved up to meet him...and the song finished, breaking the trance. His gaze remained glued to hers.

After a few long, staring seconds, he leaned in. "Would you like a drink?"

His hot breath against her ear, combined with his sexy, deep voice, sent her heart rate skyrocketing. Something about his musical, tenor-type tone had a familiarity and friendliness, and that, in conjunction with his musky, masculine scent, rated him eleven out of ten on the allure scale.

"Yes, thanks. That would be nice," she said, her voice straining above the blaring music.

He led her to an empty booth near the back bar and gestured for her to have a seat. "What would you like?"

*You.* "Just the house red, please."

He smiled. "No worries. I'll be back in a minute."

He sauntered over to the bar, his blue jeans and white, fitted shirt emphasizing his lean, toned body. She still couldn't believe he'd chosen her out of every female in the place. With his style and good looks, he could have anyone.

Eden scanned the club and spotted Grace, standing at the front bar, talking to a guy. Before she could make eye contact, *he* returned, handed her a glass of red wine and slipped into the other side of the booth.

"I hope merlot is okay."

"Perfect. I love merlot."

He stared into her eyes and raised his glass to hers. "Me too. Cheers."

"Cheers."

They both took a sip of their drinks, without breaking eye contact. She swallowed and dropped her gaze to his Johnny Depp-esque small moustache and goatee. Normally she hated facial hair on men, but not on him. It totally suited his rock-bohemian style and blended in perfectly with his balanced, masculine face.

He placed his glass down on a promotional beer coaster. "I would ask if you come here often, but I know you do. Anyway, I'm Rick, and I have to admit, I've wanted to speak to you for ages."

Her toes curled in her towering heels and she smiled. "Nice to meet you, Rick. I'm Eden."

"As in 'Garden of Eden'?" He raised his eyebrows.

"Yes. Hopefully I won't lead you astray like poor Adam," she said, joining in with his joke. His bible reference didn't surprise her, given the cross necklet and ring he wore. He seemed almost too perfect. Something had to be wrong with him. Maybe he was a bible-thumper type. *Heaven forbid.*

A roguish grin slid onto Rick's lips. "I don't know…that might be fun."

She laughed. *Definitely not a bible thumper, thank God!*

He looked down, as though to get his thoughts in order, then locked his eyes on hers. "I've seen you around Sub Rosa and have been trying to find a way to introduce myself, but…"

*He works at Sub Rosa?* How had she never noticed him?

A shy smile pressed at the corners of his kissable mouth and he shrugged. "What excuse does a simple researcher like me have to speak to a stunning PA like you? You are the PA to the Organizational Culture Senior Manager, right?"

Her boss had been dubbed 'Ms. Caramel' by Grace for her always perfectly slicked-back caramel-colored hair. A strange twinge of familiarity seized her stomach. "How do you know so much about me?"

Rick grinned. "I do my research."

An arrow of desire shot down between her legs. "Oh…" Heat radiated in her cheeks. Either he really liked her or he was a possessive stalker. Her response to him combined with her rarely-wrong gut instinct suggested the former rather than the latter. *Fingers crossed.*

Rick chuckled. "Seriously, it's not as dodgy as it sounds."

So he realized it sounded bad too. *Good. A good sign.*

"A few weeks ago, I pointed you out to a work friend of mine who's had some dealings with you. He's employed as a researcher, like me, and is a bit of a computer whiz as well. Apparently he stopped a computer virus from going viral across the organization about two-and-a-half years ago. His name is Simon, Simon Fidelis."

She had a sip of wine. "I know his name. We've exchanged a couple of work emails. He seems nice."

"Yeah, he's a cool guy. Anyway, he told me where you go out. You see, he overheard you and a colleague talking about it when you were leaving work a few weeks back. He suggested coming here with me for moral support, as well as to suss out your friend, but unfortunately, he's been rostered to do a lot of odd hours lately. So here I am, on my own. Is that a bit freaky? I hope you don't think I'm some weirdo."

"No...well, not yet, anyway," she joked.

Rick smiled and his shoulders relaxed. "I'm glad. I just really wanted to meet you. That's all."

"So why did you wait until tonight, then...and why here?"

Rick took a couple quick swigs of merlot and put his glass down again on the coaster. "Good question. I wish I could give you a good answer. Ultimately, I went with my gut. For some reason, it felt wrong coming up to you at work. I needed a reasonable segue into asking you out but I couldn't think of one. And even if I could, I didn't want to risk you possibly rejecting me in front of an office full of people. That would have sucked. Plus, I guess I just needed some time to psych myself up."

He shifted in his seat. "You're such a beautiful woman... I wanted to see if I had even a remote chance first. I had to check if you seemed interested. After watching your response to me over the past few weeks, combined with our conversation tonight, I'm assuming you are. I hope I'm right. Am I?" He searched her eyes for an answer.

Eden looked down and fiddled with the rose-topped, gold key pendant hanging around her neck. "Oh, um —"

"That's okay. I won't put you on the spot...yet. I'm just happy to finally talk to you. So, anyway, do you live around here?"

Eden met his gaze. "Yeah, not too far. It's about a five-minute drive. How about you?"

"It takes me about twenty-five minutes...and it's totally worth it."

She smiled and stared at her fidgety hands, her heart racing at seven-shot-espresso speed.

Rick finished his drink, propped his elbows on the table and leaned in. "Unfortunately, I have to get going, but I'd really like to see you again...outside of here, so we can talk some more. So, ah...can I get your number? I'll give you a call tomorrow."

Eden polished off her wine, her hand trembling as she placed her empty glass down. "Oh, um...yes, it's —"

"Hang on..." He grabbed his sleek black phone out of his jeans pocket. "Okay, go ahead."

"Zero four one nine, three nine one, nine double four."

He tapped her number into his mobile and read it back to her.

She nodded.

"I'll speak to you tomorrow then."

A bevy of butterflies swarmed her stomach. "I'm looking forward to it." Hopefully she didn't sound too desperate.

"Me too." He stood and smiled, showing perfect, straight white teeth. "Goodnight."

*It certainly has been.* "Goodnight, Rick."

Within seconds of him leaving, Grace plonked her handbag on the table and slid into the booth beside Eden. "Oh my God! I can't believe he finally came over. What did he say?"

"That he's wanted to talk to me for ages — and he asked for my number."

Grace's large, chocolate-brown eyes stared into hers. "And?"

"Well, I gave it to him and…ah…he said he's going to call me tomorrow."

Grace bounced on the spot, a giant smile dominating her glossy pink lips. "Really? This is so exciting! Make sure you find out if he's got a good-looking, single friend for me."

"How about I suss him out first?"

"Nah, if he's got a hot friend, introduce me. I'm not as picky as you," she said with a wicked grin. "I still can't believe we were just talking about him and, out of nowhere, after weeks of staring, he finally decided to make a move."

"Yeah, I know. If you weren't here, I'd wonder tomorrow whether it had really happened."

"If I hadn't seen you two together, I don't think I'd have believed you." Grace flicked her long, chestnut brown hair to the side, slung her handbag over her shoulder and stood up. "Now that he's left, shall we get moving?"

"What about that guy you were talking to?"

"All sorted. We're catching up Thursday night. Come on. Let's go."

Eden wriggled out of the booth. "Okay, okay."

Her friend looked her in the eye. "You better tell me if he rings you."

A dreamy smile floated onto Eden's lips. "Definitely. He really is gorgeous, isn't he?"

Grace hooked her arm through Eden's and they walked toward the exit. "Yes. Beyond gorgeous. And so are you. You guys looked perfect together."

# Chapter Four

The Norway Experiment

The elevator dinged, announcing Rick's arrival at the thirtieth floor. The doors opened and he followed the signs leading to the Sub Rosa conference room.

Extravagant floor-to-ceiling windows showered the space with blazing beams of sunshine. Squinting, he stepped through the doorway and hesitated while his eyes adjusted to the onslaught of light. *Where are my sunglasses when I need them?*

A long, shiny mahogany table ran down the center of the meeting room, with comfortable-looking black leather chairs surrounding it. A projector whirred, displaying a series of shots of a Norwegian snowscape and what looked to be a compound.

*Deception Point* by Dan Brown popped into Rick's head. He shivered then laughed at himself for being so paranoid.

"Hey, mate," Rick said, and took a seat next to Simon.

Only a handful of other research staff were in attendance. Andy Falon, Sub Rosa's Chief Executive Officer, sat at the head of the table at the far end of the room. An older, distinguished-looking man, he always appeared cool, calculated and confident—and as though he wouldn't take crap from anyone.

Although he clearly attempted to exude charm and approachability, the guy had an edge of darkness. Goosebumps prickled on the back of Rick's neck. He'd make certain he steered well clear of the wrong side of the CEO.

The Manager of New Projects—a metrosexual man around Rick's age with the latest haircut and attire—going for a creative vibe but coming across as a try-hard—sat to Andy's right. Mr. Right Hand Man was his nickname, given the physical and brown-nose position the guy always took.

One of Rick's colleagues pressed a button on a small black remote control, activating the shutters above all the windows. They slowly descended, blocking out the penetrating sunlight, and he focused his attention on the brightly lit screen.

The brief Rick had received leading up to the meeting explained that the Norway Experiment had commenced in the 1930s and aimed to perfect a form of justifiable genome cleansing.

At first, Rick had thought he'd be working on eradicating a faulty gene within the human population. It had shocked and fascinated him to find out that it extended beyond that, into the realm of fantasy and myth.

His yes-man, middle-aged manager, who stood alongside the PowerPoint presentation, adjusted his white shirt cuffs and cleared his throat. "As you should all be aware, two clans of vampires exist—Violets and Jades, so named because of their telltale eye color. The

Violets have vibrant, violet eyes, while the Jades have a deep, jade-colored version.

"Due to their physical strength, speed and need for blood, they pose an ongoing threat to the human race. The major concern is not only that humans will be used as their main food source but also that those not killed may be changed, creating more vampires and setting humanity on a course for possible extinction."

Tuning in to the mundane man's project history overview posed a challenge. His monotonous voice didn't help retain attention, driving Rick to doodling 'Eden' on his notepad, in his best left-handed calligraphy.

"Luckily for us, neither clan gets on with the other, which stems from a civil war that broke out in the Middle Ages. Their unresolved differences led to Violets telling us the whereabouts of Jades and vice versa, in an attempt to save themselves from capture.

"Not that it gives them any real bargaining power, because we detain them anyway. Then, once captured, the clans refuse to work together, hence reducing their chances of developing an effective escape plan. Keeping them segregated helps reinforce the animosity," the manager said with a smirk in his vapid tone.

"In the early days, various barbaric methods were used to control and attempt to genetically alter the vampire test subjects, including withholding food, twenty-four-hour sunlight exposure in the top end of Norway during summer months, trial of harsh experimental drugs, abortion of and experimentation on mixed-caste fetuses and housing Violet and Jade clan vampires in squalid conditions."

Rick jolted his head up. *What the fuck kind of place do I work for?*

His manager coughed into his loosely fisted hand and rubbed his crooked nose. "However, let me assure you that it has all changed. The brutal treatment of captives has now ceased, and all processes are aboveboard and ethical, in line with modification of the original aim to 'finding the cure' for vampirism. However, the ultimate goal is the same. Finding the cure is for the good of all, to preserve the human race."

Relief washed over Rick. No matter how great the job opportunity, he couldn't have kept quiet and condoned inhumane practices. He refocused on his notepad and continued his gothic design, adding his name and entwining it with Eden's, while his team leader went on a big spiel about how Sub Rosa supported diversity within humans.

"However, in this case, it's a matter of finding the cure to prevent propagating of the persistent, faulty gene in order to thwart serious long-term ramifications," Andy interjected, his imposing voice commanding everyone's attention.

It got to six p.m. and the whole-day brief was nowhere near finished. Obviously Rick's idea of a whole day and theirs had two completely different definitions. He tapped his fingers on the table. *Come on!*

At eight-forty-five p.m., the meeting wound up. The team members were warned not to discuss the Norway Experiment with anyone outside the project staff and to commit to at least one full-day briefing per month, if they planned to remain involved in the project.

Desperate to leave, Rick didn't protest. He needed to get home...and call Eden. That was all he could think about.

\* \* \* \*

All day, Eden could barely concentrate. Every ten minutes, she checked her phone, just in case she'd missed Rick's call. It got to seven p.m. and still nothing, not even a text message.

She flopped down onto one of the dining chairs at her small, round kitchen table and tucked into reheated Mongolian beef stir fry from the night before. Her mobile phone sat silently to the right of her bowl.

The screen lit up. She stopped mid-mouthful and stared at it. "Fill Grace in." Great, a reminder that he still hadn't called. Eden poked her fork at the remaining grains of rice and vegetables.

Maybe he'd just said he'd call when he had no real intention. Maybe when he woke up, he'd realized he'd made an alcohol-fueled, impulsive decision he no longer chose to pursue.

After dinner, she showered and slumped onto the couch in her pajamas, trying to immerse herself in her favorite television program, *Spooks*.

Her phone rang. She glanced at the clock—nine-twenty-nine p.m. With a quivering hand, she snatched her mobile off the coffee table. There was no name, just a phone number, definitely not anyone in her contacts. Could it be *him*? Her heart hammered against her breastbone and she pressed the green 'Receive Call' button. "Hello?"

"Eden? It's Rick. I met you last night. Sorry to call so late."

She gulped, his voice sounded even more alluring than she remembered. "Hi, Rick…"

"I hope I didn't wake you."

"No, not at all. It's a bit early for me to be in bed just yet. I was watching TV."

"Anything interesting?"

*B-r-e-a-t-h-e.* "To be honest, I didn't take much of it in." Thornton roused and rubbed himself against her thigh.

"I see... Um...are you doing anything tomorrow night? I thought maybe we could go out for dinner? If you're free."

She swallowed back a squeal. They had chemistry, though maybe they shouldn't do dinner yet, maybe something more...low key. Ease into things. Make sure they suited. "Um...how about a coffee?"

"Oh...yeah, sure."

Rick's tone sounded heavy with disappointment. But she scarcely knew the guy. What if he turned out to be a loser or a player or, even worse, a psycho? *No.* He seemed way too sweet—however, at this early stage, it made more sense to be cautious, to stay on the safe side. "I finish work at four-thirty, so we could catch up straight after that, if you'd like?"

"I've got a meeting off site that's supposed to finish around that time. How about I meet you at Café Destino at five p.m.? I'll text you if I'm running late."

Eden curled her legs up and hugged them to her chest. "Okay. I'll see you then."

"Great. See you tomorrow."

As soon as they hung up, she saved his mobile number into her phone. Then, as promised, she sent a quick text to update Grace.

*Guess who's going on a date 2moro!*

**\* \* \* \***

33

Eden's day plodded along at a sedated-slug pace. She kept eyeing the clock, but it didn't speed up time. When her lunch break finally arrived, Eden, Grace and a handful of colleagues made their way to one of their favorite local haunts. Eden remained too distracted by her impending date with Rick to partake in the conversation.

"Eden, are you okay? You've hardly said a word."

She plastered a polite smile on her face. "I'm fine, thanks."

"Come on. Fess up!" Grace said.

Eden stopped nibbling at her rare beef salad sandwich and glared at her. Grace just didn't get it. She might be happy to blab about every guy she met but Eden didn't want to. She didn't want to jinx anything. It didn't make sense to discuss Rick until she knew he had serious potential.

Grace ignored her. "She's got a hot date straight after work tonight, so I'd say her mind is on *other* things."

"Ooh!" the rest of her colleagues said at the same time.

The new girl gestured along the length of Eden's black dress with lush red cherry print. "I wondered why you were all dressed up."

"Anyone we know?"

"Maybe. His name is Rick and he's a researcher. He works downstairs," Grace said, making eye contact with each woman in turn.

"The name sounds familiar…"

"You have to tell us how it goes," an older colleague said.

With each comment, the heat spread on Eden's cheeks, most likely creating deep red splotches.

"Yeah, we want goss," Grace chimed in.

"Grace!" Eden hissed through clenched teeth.

A sassy grin spread across her friend's face.

Thankfully the conversation wound down and changed direction while they finished their meals, then they all returned to the office. With each passing hour, Eden's excitement grew and grew and grew.

By four-twenty-five p.m., Eden wasn't just chomping at the bit, she was chomping at the whole bridle. Friday afternoon, the last day of her working week, and soon she'd meet up with a hunky man, as well as celebrate the long weekend ahead of her. She went to shut down her computer, and an email came through from Grace.

*Big night…*

*Ooh, it's nearly time! Are you nervous? ;-)*
*Better go. Ms. Distressed is cracking the whip ;-)*
*You better give me a full update tomorrow!*

Eden ignored the post and logged out, desperate to get ready and leave or else she'd arrive late. She didn't want him to think she'd stood him up.

In the ladies' room, she retouched her makeup, reapplied some antiperspirant, sprayed herself with her favorite perfume then undertook the brisk, ten-minute walk to the cafe.

She arrived at four-fifty p.m. and looked around for a seat. Near the window, Rick caught her attention with a discreet hand wave. Eden walked toward him, her heart racing like a prize horse bolting out of the starting gate.

His red fitted shirt and black pants matched the colors of her own outfit. *Freaky.* Around his neck sat the black leather necklet with the cool, gold and black cross, and on his right ring finger he wore the matching cross ring he'd had on when they'd first met.

Rick smiled and pulled out a comfortable-yet-heavy-looking armchair. His close proximity radiated heat, and that, combined with the aromatic, woodsy scent of his aftershave, played havoc with her senses. He pushed the chair in behind her and she sat, without them making any physical contact.

"Thanks," she said, impressed by his chivalry, and placed her bag on the floor between her feet.

Rick returned to his chair, his black velvet jacket hanging off the back. "You're welcome."

"You're early," they both said at the same time, then laughed.

"What would you like?" he asked. The sunshine lightened his hair to a rich, warm brown with natural golden streaks and made his light green eyes even more magnificent.

*Alcoholic intervention.* It would help calm her jitters so she could relax and enjoy their date. "Is it too early for a liqueur coffee?"

A playful smile curled onto his lips. "I don't think so. It *is* nearly dinner time."

"In that case, I'll have a long black with a shot of Baileys, please."

"Mmm...sounds nice. I might join you. Would you like anything else? A cake? Muffin? We could share something...."

"That lemon meringue looks pretty good, but I can't eat it all on my own. Do you like lemon meringue?" Something about the lemony delight screamed *share me with Rick*, like they'd done it before.

"Yeah, I do. I've been eyeing it since I walked in. So, are we decided?"

She nodded, the strange connection with him sticking in her brain like food on a worn-away Teflon pan.

While he went to place their order, she tried to slow her breathing. Being close to him in broad daylight felt much more intense, yet thrilling and familiar.

Rick rejoined her and rested his taut forearms on the table. "How was your day?"

"Not too bad. How about yours?"

"Okay, though the last few hours kind of dragged. I found it a bit hard to concentrate."

She propped her elbows on the table and leaned in. "Oh, is everything all right?"

His intense stare drew her in, like a homing beacon. "It is now."

Eden gulped.

Rick's gaze didn't waver. She'd swear he didn't even blink. "The truth is, I felt a bit nervous about seeing you tonight."

"Really? Me too."

He smiled, then went to speak and stopped as though weighing up what to say. "I'm sorry if I keep staring. It's just...your eyes are amazing. I didn't notice just how beautiful they were the other night. They're like a blue-violet color."

"Oh, um...thanks." Eden glanced down, heat rising in her cheeks.

"I know this is going to sound weird and probably make no sense whatsoever, but I've never seen anyone with eyes like yours and yet they're really familiar to me."

Her head swam with vague, jumbled-up images—a man's face in her mind's eye that she couldn't quite make out, yet he seemed recognizable. He kissed her, then she lay strapped to a gurney, trying but failing to reach out to him. Anxiety scrambled through her system and her breathing rasped in her chest.

Eden attempted to rein in her wandering thoughts and make sense of the unsettling vision. Had she relived some kind of dream...or nightmare? Unsure of how long she'd been quiet, she grabbed the jug of water on the table, her hand shaking.

"Did I say something wrong?" Rick asked, clear concern in his voice.

Her gaze met his. "No. Not at all." She filled their empty glasses with water.

"Please tell me if I'm making you feel uncomfortable. Believe me, it's the last thing I want to do. It's just... I find you so incredibly endearing that it's hard for me to think straight when I'm around you. It's like the overwhelming feelings are flooding my brain and overriding my usual ability to filter and inhibit what I say. See what I mean?"

His concern was so damn adorable. "Don't worry. You're not making me uncomfortable. In fact, I think you seem very thoughtful and honest. It's really refreshing, though a little confronting. I guess I'm just not used to hearing men speak in such a truthful and upfront manner. In the past, I've found guys tend to be over-complimentary and charming...with only one thing on their mind."

The coffee crowd had slipped out and the noise along with it, leaving the soothing sounds of gentle love songs crooning through the speakers.

Rick reached across the table, stopping his hand within centimeters of hers. "I'm definitely not one of those guys. I don't just give away compliments. I say things because I mean them, unless I'm mucking around. But you'll know when I am...hopefully. I would never put on the charm just to get something in return."

She edged her hand toward his. "I know…"

The waiter appeared and they retracted their hands. He placed their coffees, a piece of lemon meringue pie and a spare spoon and plate on the table. "Bon appétit," he muttered mechanically and headed toward the kitchen.

"You do the honors," Rick said.

Eden shook her head. "No, you go ahead."

"Ladies before gentlemen."

"Not in this case. Have you seen the thickness of that crust? I think you'd better cut it. I don't want to be responsible for sending half of it flying across the room!"

He chuckled. "If you insist. But I can't promise I'll do any better."

"I trust you."

"Thanks, no pressure or anything," he joked. Rick picked up the knife lying on his napkin and expertly sliced the lemon meringue into two equal portions, placing one piece on the spare plate and divvying up the cream using his dessert spoon.

"Nice work. I'm impressed." She cut herself a small wedge, dipped it into the side serving of thickened cream and placed it in her mouth, the tangy flavor zinging her taste buds. "Mmm…this is delicious."

Rick looked at her with an I-want-to-taste-you stare. "I agree."

The lust flowing between them created a crackling current zipping through the air. She squeezed her thighs together to stem the ache of desire between her legs. "How long have you worked at Sub Rosa?"

His heaped spoon hovered in mid-air. "Nearly two months now. I started in May. I can't believe how quickly the time has gone. How about you?"

"Nearly five years." She couldn't quite believe she'd been there that long. She shook her head and had another mouthful of pie.

"You must like it. Most people are lucky to stay in a place for more than eighteen months these days. It's not like forty years ago."

Eden had a sip of coffee. "Yeah, then people would stay in a place nearly their whole working life."

"I've heard one of the senior managers has been around about that long."

"The distressed-looking older guy," they said in stereo, and laughed.

"What attracted you to working at Sub Rosa?" Eden spoke over the light chatter from the influx of the dinner crowd.

"I'd finished my Master of Science degree at Uni and needed a break. While I looked for jobs, I kept myself active and did some construction work. Nothing spoke to me until I saw the Sub Rosa ad for the research opportunity of a lifetime — my dream job, really — and I had to apply."

He hesitated, as though debating what to say next. "This is probably going to sound a bit weird" — Rick leaned in, keeping his voice low, though loud enough for her to hear — "but I felt drawn to Sub Rosa beyond their high standing in the research field. Something in my gut told me I had to work there to succeed." He had another mouthful of cake and coffee, and his gaze reconnected with hers. "And now I've met you. It's all been so perfect."

Scorching heat burned her cheeks and she stared at her half-eaten dessert as though it represented a stress-eliminating elixir. Her pulse pounded, making her a little lightheaded. She really should have ordered decaf.

"What are you doing tomorrow?" His sexy voice slipped under her defenses.

"Um...I've got nothing planned at this stage." She sliced another bite of pie and coated it in cream.

"How would you feel about...spending the day with me?"

The spoon dropped out of Eden's hand and clanged onto her plate. "Oh...um..."

"If you don't want to, that's totally fine. I'd rather you be honest with me."

She looked him in the eye. "No, it's not that. You just took me by surprise is all. What did you have in mind?"

He smiled. "Well, I thought I could pick you up at, say...nine-thirty, and we could have some breakfast then a wander around Salamanca market, maybe go for a drive and have a late lunch or early dinner. What do you think?"

"That sounds really nice."

"Does that mean you're in?"

"Yes, definitely."

A delighted grin filled his face. "Great."

"Oh, I suppose you need to know where to come to get me, huh?" Eden rummaged around in her bag for a blank piece of paper and a pen.

"That would be helpful," he said, a cheeky lilt in his tone.

Unable to find a pen or paper, she scribbled down her address—7 Swan St, Sandy Bay—on her napkin, using her favorite pink lipstick. She handed over the faint, glossy details. "I hope you can read it…and my writing. I struggle myself at times."

Rick laughed, a deep, husky sound infused with pure, raw sexiness. Then he read it back to her, neatly folded the napkin and tucked it away in his wallet. "You know, it's already six-thirty. We may as well stay and have some dinner. I don't know about you, but I really can't be bothered going home to cook now."

Eden reached between her legs and pulled on the long, thick strap of her handbag, as she considered his proposal.

Rick's eyes urged her to accept. "Come on…unless you don't want to."

"It's definitely not that…"

"I hear a 'but'. You've already got plans."

She shook her head. "No."

"Then?"

Eden had no good reason, just some dumb rule she'd made up in her head about the correct dating procedure. If she really liked him — which she did so far — why shouldn't she stay? It wasn't like she'd invited him back to her place late at night for a 'coffee'…yet. And she had agreed to spend the whole day with him tomorrow. One meal should be a cinch in comparison.

"Let's stay and have some dinner," she said.

"What an excellent idea," he said with an impish grin.

They didn't end up leaving until eight-thirty. Rick insisted on walking her to her car, waited until she sat safely inside and bid her goodnight. He hadn't even attempted to kiss her, yet he seemed so keen. *Strange, but sweet.* Maybe there still were true, young gentlemen living in 2010?

The whole drive home, Eden's mind switched gear into high-speed, Rick-centric. How things could change in just three days. It all seemed too good to be true. *He* seemed too good to be true.

# Chapter Five

Jade versus Violet — The Legend of the War

*Norway, 1231*

"I'm burning! Help me. *Help me!*" David screamed, his face contorted with pain. Flames licked his body inside and out and he writhed in agony, each fiery breath scorching his windpipe, each swallow singing his esophagus.

Out of the window was breathtaking Norwegian fjordland, with snow-capped mountains lined up like a parade of cold soldiers. He imagined himself as a snowman, with the sleet raining down but rage still rose inside him. *How can I possibly still feel so hot?*

Then it stopped. He lay on a single bed, tangled up in white sheets, in a tiny room surrounded by strangers. A tall, hefty, older man explained that they were his new family. Then he remembered.

*The blizzard.* He had only just turned twenty and had been trudging through the powdery snow, trying to find his way back home. Every way he turned had stretched out in endless, disorientating white.

Frostbitten, he'd shuddered and ached with cold and his hand color had changed to purple-blue, the blood freezing in his veins. His feet had gone numb and he'd stumbled and fallen. Buried in the mounting snow, he'd been sure he would die.

When he opened his eyes again, his new mother was sitting by him, her long, flowing raven hair hanging forward, dabbing his brow with a cold cloth.

"How long have I been...ill?" David asked.

"Three days, though that's normal following the feverish, burning phase of the transition." Her deep violet eyes were kind and reassuring.

He did a quick mental check of his body. "I'm starving."

She smiled. "I can remedy that."

During dinner that night, they had freshly slaughtered venison blood. It tasted strange but not repulsive. Quite the opposite, actually. It totally satisfied him, along with the accompanying glass of special purple wine.

"This flavor is...wonderful. What is it?" he asked.

"Our version of alcohol," his new dad explained. "It still has an alcohol base but is mixed with animal blood and toadstool juice, which gives it that extra kick. Unfortunately, once you're changed, alcohol on its own doesn't have much of an effect."

"Then why even drink it?"

The man sucked on a bloodied piece of venison leg and licked his long, thick fingers. "I suppose it's like sleeping. We don't need that, either—however, sustaining some human rituals helps keep us on track and sane. Some might say 'civilized'. It's important not to forget where you come from and balance it with your new life, so your growth isn't restricted.

"Of course, there are those who are less traditional, less connected to their human past, and they tend to feed or hunt for sex at night. Be wary of them. It's easy to get caught up in a pleasurable, self-indulgent lifestyle, especially while you're still grappling with your new drives. But it's bad news in the long term. Change is hard at the best of times — and especially when many things that were taken for granted are suddenly taken away. Retaining some humanness will help you adjust."

"When can I see my parents?"

His new, burly dad sternly looked him in the eye. "Never."

"Never? But I need to tell them I'm okay. They'll be beside themselves!"

"I'm sorry, son. You can't. It's in their best interests."

David shook his head. "I don't believe that."

His father's violet eyes flickered, as though instigating a form of hypnosis. "You must understand... You're no longer human, and with that comes different needs and urges, which could put your family in danger."

*No longer human.* His parents used to tell him stories about 'the others' but he'd always thought of them as fables, their way of keeping him in line. Now he'd turned into what they had described.

"Surely I couldn't hurt my own family."

"You'd be surprised. It's best not to take that chance. Plus, you don't want to frighten them. You look different now and will remain forever frozen at twenty."

Over the next few weeks, his new family educated him on their culture and history. Two tribes had lived peacefully, side by side for centuries — the Violet clan, to which he now belonged, and the Jade clan. But each kept to themselves.

With only a vast coursing river separating the two communities, they knew of each other's existence, yet no one ever attempted to cross the divide. It remained an unspoken, mutually respected rule.

From what his new dad had explained, their society saw mixing as a precursor to trouble. No one knew what it could produce and no one wanted to take the risk.

The cold months of darkness and isolation didn't bother them. It benefited them. The remote, dark and freezing conditions suited the Violets' limited tolerance to direct sunlight and also meant that not many humans chose to settle in the area.

Six months into his new existence, his father took him hunting, solidifying his initiation into the community. He and his dad had been tracking brown bears for several days in the lush, green forest many, many isolated miles away from the settlement and getting closer to the narrowest border line.

A large, meaty bear drank from the small stream. David ran, ready to pounce on the bear, when a breathtaking, golden-haired woman and her daughter appeared on the other side of the water. He dug his feet into the earth and came to a halt on the edge of the bank. The bear started and loped away, disappearing in the dense forest.

David's gaze connected with the girl's bewitching, jade-green eyes and he couldn't look away. The impenetrable force of their connection filled his heart with a fire he didn't recognize.

Crackling heat consumed his body, drowning out the babbling of the flowing water and the resident willow warblers' intermittent bird calls. He went to speak, but his father slammed a beefy hand onto his shoulder, spun him around and pushed him away.

He glanced back. *I need to meet her.*

When they returned home a couple of days later, he quizzed his parents while his new siblings, Hugh and Beauregarde, sat, wide-eyed and silent.

His mother strode over from the kitchen, her hands dripping wet. "We don't know about them and we don't need to. Our parents and grandparents got by just fine keeping to themselves, and we will do the same. If you respect us, you will abide by our request."

However, the less he knew, the more he needed to know. He had to cross the river and find out more about the girl with the captivating, jade-green eyes. So, utilizing his human carpentry training, he got to work constructing a small boat.

The night of the July rose moon, just after what should have been his twenty-first birthday, he set off on his journey. He sailed across the uncharacteristically quiet, calm water. *A good omen?* Reaching the other side in less than an hour, he anchored his boat and set foot upon the new land.

Dense vegetation and thousand-year-old trees filled the steep embankment, the moonlight filtering through the gaps in the foliage. It took him twenty minutes to reach the plateau, and he followed a dirt path into the main township.

The similarity between the Violet community and theirs was astounding, given their ignorance of each other. Log cabin dwellings, similar in shape and size though more densely packed together, dotted the landscape.

It remained quiet, outside of a couple of well-lit places offering night-time entertainment. Mostly men jostled out, drunk and disorderly, trying to orient themselves enough to stagger back home. They didn't notice him standing in the shadows.

The sun rose, prompting him to return to where he'd docked his boat. *Gone.* It was gone. *I tied it securely, didn't I?* He darted his gaze along the bank to the right and left, but no boat. *Someone must have stolen it. Great. How can I get back?* Swimming wasn't an option. He'd never learned how.

The only other alternative was to get to the narrowest crossing point. *Shit.* That would take two days of non-stop, fast-paced trekking and his family expected him back in a couple of hours. Until he could find his only safe and efficient means of returning, he remained trapped.

He grabbed fistfuls of his hair and tugged until it hurt. "Argh!"

In among the overgrown green grass, he sat with his head in his hands. How long should he wait for his boat to reappear, if it ever did? He stamped his foot on the damp ground. *How could I be so careless?*

A gush of water squirted up the bank and splashed the toe of his laced-up boot. He looked up and *the* girl sat in *his* boat, making her way to the shore, right in front of him. *A dream? A vision?* She docked the boat and ran up the bank. The second she reached him, she threw her ethereal arms around his neck and pressed her fair cheek against his, confirming the soul-stirring reality.

"What's your name?" he whispered.

She pulled back and smiled, permanently etching a spot in his memory. "Oriel."

*A beautiful name for a beautiful woman.* "I'm David. I've been searching for you."

"Me too..."

He lit up. They spoke the same language. That should make things easier.

"Ever since..." they both said at the same time, and stopped.

She looked around and leaned in. "I've walked here every night since I saw you in the forest that day. My parents don't know."

"Mine either."

"What should we do?"

"Be together." He couldn't explain why or how he knew, but he'd never been as sure of anything in his life.

"We hardly know each other."

"I feel like I've known you forever."

She dug her shoe into the loose dirt. "What about your family?"

"What about yours?" David nudged the crumbling earth with the tip of his boot. "It's not going to be easy."

"I know."

They strolled along the water's edge, huddled up together, a shield from the frosty, biting winds—and to be close, as close as possible...for the moment.

After a long silence, she said, "You're going to stay, aren't you?"

His gut told him he should go, but he couldn't, not when she looked at him that way. "Yes. How can I possibly leave now that I've found you again?"

A beautiful, irresistible smile brightened her face. *So perfect.* Surely it would be impossible for his family not to love her.

They continued walking hand in hand until they reached the township.

"I'm going to introduce you to my family. Today. They need to know," she said.

"I agree. But before we do that, I just need to do one thing."

Oriel stopped and turned to him, the forest behind them and the city center ahead. He stared into her eyes and ran his thumb, feather light, over her parted lips. Gently nudging her chin up, he brought her mouth to his and kissed her with such a deep infusion of love and passion that their skin started to glow.

The kiss intensified, as did their incandescence, pulsating in rhythm with their breathing, until they were so luminous that they shone like a star fallen to earth, lighting up both sides of the river. The growing radiance of their skin prompted him to stop.

David looked at her then at himself, speechless. Seconds passed and the brilliance slowly diminished into diamond-like sparkles that refused to fade. A permanent reaction seemed to occur when they connected, forever changing them, eternally binding them together.

He kissed her cheek, leaving a brief, glowing imprint of his lips. As he pulled away, her seductive, jade-green eyes fixed on his and he wanted to make love to her right there on the riverbank.

David pressed a kiss to her forehead, fascinated by the slowly dissipating lip print that was sparkling in the low light. "I don't know of anyone who has done what we're doing, but I'm not going to let that deter me. The incredible reaction we have together can't be wrong. It just reinforces how close-minded our communities have been.

"They won't even try to step out of what they know to see if life could be better. Now that we can show them what is possible, hopefully they'll realize the stupid rules they stand by are based on fear and ignorance, and they'll give us a chance."

They entered the front door of her family home and she squeezed his hand. Oriel's eyes met his and her broad smile saturated his heart with love.

It only took a moment for concerned voices to travel down the stairs.

"Where have you been?"

"Anything could have happened!"

"We've been worried sick!"

"How could you do this to your mother?"

"What will people say?"

Her father arrived first, his narrow, disapproving stare clamping on their clasped hands, then David, then his daughter. "Get him out of here. Do you hear me?"

"But..."

"No. Don't you understand? He's not like us...and he can't ever be, can't ever fit in."

"*You* don't understand," she said. "We love each other and we want to be together. We *need* to be together."

"Since when?" Her father spat out the words as though they left a sour taste on his tongue. "You've never mentioned him before. You're only eighteen —"

"I'll be eighteen forever!" Oriel shouted.

Her father's jaw tensed and he pointed his finger at her. "Don't be smart with me. You're young and impulsive and you'll change your mind. Believe me. And when you do, there are plenty of eligible young Jade men you can choose from."

"I don't want any of them, and I *never* will!"

Her father thumped his fist on the dining table. "While you live under this roof, you must abide by my rules."

"Fine. I'm leaving then." She clutched David's hand and strode to the door. Oriel stopped in the doorway and turned to her father. "I really thought if anyone would understand, it would be you. You go on about fairness and equality, but what you really mean is fairness and equality within a select group. I can't stay and listen to that anymore. I refuse to be a hypocrite."

The whole way to the riverbank, Oriel stayed silent. David helped her onto his boat and kept hold of her hand. "He'll come around. He's just angry because he didn't expect it."

"No, I don't think so. I've never seen him like that before." Her voice trembled as if she were stifling a sob.

"Have you ever brought a man home?"

Her sorrowful eyes looked thirsty for shed-able tears. "No."

"How would you know what to expect then?" David caressed her cheek, her pearlescent skin as smooth as sculpted marble. "Let's give him a chance to calm down, and in the meantime, I'll introduce you to my family. Hopefully we'll get a better response from them."

"Hopefully." The corners of her mouth twitched with her attempt at a smile. He enveloped her in his arms until her body relaxed, then he paddled to the opposite shore.

David took her straight to his house, but no one was home. Holding her hand, he led her up the stairs to his bedroom and they sat on his modest single bed. He gazed into her eyes and leaned in to procure another kiss. She yielded willingly and he laid her back against his silk, checkerboard-pattern quilt.

In between kisses, he discarded his hooded reindeer-hide jacket, the electricity building as she moved her hands along and illuminated his bare torso. *No.* He couldn't get too carried away. He had to do things right. David pulled back.

The bright white light of their intimacy created an aura around her. "I don't want you to stop."

"I don't want to either…but we should." David rolled onto his side.

Oriel looked at him with a defiant glint in her eye. "Who cares what they say? They'll never understand. Let's do what suits us."

"I agree, though it would help if we had even one community on our side."

"What if we don't?"

"I'll take you away."

Her boldness deserted her with the cold, divisive reality. "What about our families?"

"We might have to choose between them and us."

Grief poured from her eyes. She had clearly chosen him over them.

David got up and walked over to the carved, wooden chest at the foot of his bed. He lifted the polished pine lid, foraged around until he found what he wanted, then with his hands behind his back, he kneeled before her.

"My great-grandfather made jewelry and created an engagement ring especially for my great-grandmother. My mother passed it down to me. My *real* mother. She always wanted a girl but instead got three boys, me being the oldest. I wish she could meet you, because I know she'd love you, especially once she saw how happy you make me. I love you so much. You will be my wife, won't you?"

A radiant smile lit up her ravishing face. "Yes, of course I will."

He opened his hand, revealing the antique gold-and-ruby heart ring, and slid it onto her wedding finger. It fit perfectly. "You're meant to have this."

She hugged him and vowed to be his for eternity.

He was still beaming when his family returned home. But his smile soon faded with the disapproving, you-defied-us reaction on his parents' faces. Instead of the congratulations he had hoped for, they reprimanded him and demanded that Oriel leave.

"If she goes, so do I." David held his fiancée's hand and strode out of the front door. They hadn't gone far before…

"Wait!"

*Hugh?* David stopped at the edge of the forest, a hundred feet from the house.

His brother Hugh stepped in front of them. "I don't agree with them. You two have a strong connection and you should foster it." He pressed his hand against his heart. "I can feel it. Most people are lucky to experience a quarter of what you have together. So, whatever you do, don't give in to their ignorance."

David looked him in the eye. "Thank you. Your support means a lot to me—a lot to both of us."

Hugh slid his hand into the front pocket of his jacket, his kind, encouraging smile exposing more of his gentle, old soul. "I'm not sure if I told you, but I've been dabbling in alchemy again recently and I've developed a unity ring. I know you're not into that kind of thing—however, I'd like you to have it, as a sort of good luck charm."

"That's very kind of you, but—"

Hugh grabbed David's right hand, and placed a black hematite ring with a diamond and ruby on either side of an intricately carved rose into his palm then curled his fingers over it. "No buts. I want you to have it, even if you need to trade or sell it to help you be together."

David went to put the ring in the front pocket of his pants.

Hugh grabbed his arm. "Uh-uh. Now that it has your energy, you need to give it to her, to bond you."

With a creased brow, he did as Hugh directed and slipped the ring onto Oriel's right ring finger.

Her big, beautiful eyes were full of gratitude. "Thank you."

David reached out and shook Hugh's hand. "I'll miss you."

Tears welled in Hugh's eyes and sat poised to spill over the rim. "I'll miss you too. Promise me you'll look after yourselves."

"We will," David said and hugged his Violet brother.

"Hugh, come back into the house!" their mother yelled.

Hugh stepped away. "I'd better go. I wish you all the best." Tears trickled down his pale cheeks and he turned and ran back to their mother, who stood in the front yard, her jaw clenched. Beauregarde loitered in the doorway with a monstrous sneer.

David grasped Oriel's hand and squeezed it. "Let's go."

"Where to?" A worried frown wrinkled her pretty face.

"To see the missionary. He'll marry us." *Or at least he marries humans.* David knew that from his mortal days.

Hopefully the man wouldn't reject them in their changed state.

They walked for three days through the forest, without food, before they reached the missionary's dwelling, perched on the edge of the land before it submerged into the endless ocean.

David and Oriel staggered up to the front door and set eyes on the old human. Since being reborn, David hadn't come face-to-face with one, and he didn't know what to expect. Saliva pooled in his mouth. Although the man had whet his appetite, David's drive to be married went beyond the need for food.

*Vampires.* The missionary's heart hesitated and his stomach clenched. *Should I welcome them into my home?* He'd been warned against it. But as a missionary, he had sworn to help others. Nowhere had it said that vampires weren't included.

He gestured for them to come in. "You look hungry. I don't have much, though I can offer you some sustenance and a place for the night, if you need it."

They each slumped onto a wooden dining chair. The male studied him, his violet eyes weary. "We're looking for someone to marry us. Can you help?"

"I can marry you — but only by human law."

*Good enough.* The relieved smile on the man's face said it all.

After he slaughtered venison for them for dinner, he started a small fire under the stars, cleansed their spirits and pronounced them husband and wife, providing them with intricately engraved, wooden wedding bands.

The spark in their eyes and luminescence in their skin flared when they touched and kissed, like nothing he'd ever seen before. They were perfect for each other, two halves of a whole.

"Thank you. We will never forget your kindness," David said, and led his jade-eyed bride back to the house.

The missionary remained by the crackling fire. He had allocated them the best room he had, overlooking the wild cerulean sea, lush conifer forest and snow-capped mountains — a window view into paradise.

A bolt of light flashed overhead. A shooting star? He went to make a wish... *What on earth?* The light hadn't come from the sky but from the honeymooners' bed.

Violet-jade sparks flew, the couple's passion and desire transforming from a state of feeling to a state of being. They merged, unifying on all planes — physical, mental, spiritual, emotional — like sparklers entwining. The missionary couldn't look away, mesmerized by the power of their union.

\* \* \* \*

The afternoon sun shining through the window warmed David's face. He could do with some more of his wife's warmth too. With his eyes still closed, he patted the bed next to him.

*Oriel?* His eyes flew open and he sat up. She appeared in the doorway, wearing a paper-thin white robe, her golden hair plunging over her shoulders.

She looked like an angel, a very sexy angel. The way she carried the tray of cow blood accentuated her every curve. Oriel placed it on the bedside table, and he sighed. Kneeling on the bed, he undid her robe and pushed it off her slim shoulders, revealing fair, smooth skin gleaming with permanent, youthful flawlessness.

She shot an arm across her breasts and the other across the honey-blonde curls covering his idea of paradise. "The door's open!" she protested.

He peeled her arms back, ran his hands over her body and nuzzled his nose against her pearl-satin neck. "So?"

"What if he comes upstairs for something?"

"He won't." David pressed her to him, and proceeded to make love to her — for the fifth time.

They kissed and cuddled until it grew dark, then got dressed and went downstairs. The missionary had already prepared a meal for them — warm rabbit blood.

The missionary had a twinkle in his eye. "You must be starving."

"Yes, ravenous!" David said, and in seconds he and his wife had demolished their dinner.

The missionary sat at the head of the table. "Will you stay a while?"

David mopped his mouth with a napkin. "I wish we could, but we've taken advantage of your hospitality long enough. We need to make a life on our own now."

The missionary had had a vision that they would come only for a brief time and change his life. A pang of worry shuddered through his stomach. Their lives had changed too, though not in the way they would be envisioning.

Would being together mean they'd always be on the run, searching over their shoulders? What sort of a life was that? They deserved to be settled and enjoy every moment together.

"Please don't feel you have to leave straight away. You're welcome to stay here as long as you'd like."

David smiled. "Thank you, but we're putting you in danger the longer we're here."

"Where will you go?"

"I'm not sure yet." David reached over and held his wife's hand. "Instinct has gotten us this far, so I trust it to take us to where we need to be."

The missionary looked from David to Oriel. "I will pray for you."

"Thank you," they said in unison.

"Before you go, I have something to give you." The missionary pulled a small purple pouch out of his pocket. "My alchemist father devised what he called 'the essence of togetherness'. It is in powder form and reacts with the elements.

"Your relationship has a fire-driven energy, so I recommend using it in this way... When you are sure that being together is no longer certain, sprinkle the powder in a circle around you and hold hands. The magic will eternally unite you as soon as there is the threat of separation. I have been waiting a long time for the right couple to give it to, and I know it is you. The potion is very powerful. Please use it wisely."

David accepted the purple pouch and held it tightly in his hand. "You are too generous. You have been good to us, more understanding than our own families, and we are extremely grateful."

\* \* \* \*

They left that night and followed the path to the nearest mountain. Using some supplies provided by the missionary, they set up camp and made love under the stars.

In the morning, they continued along the coast toward the Swedish border. When darkness descended, they sheltered in a large cave, the walls glittering with glow worms.

David held Oriel close and covered their naked bodies with a warm blanket. "Are you sure you want to do this?"

She lifted her head off his chest and looked into his eyes. "Yes. Are you?"

"Very."

The next night, they sat on a small, makeshift raft they had thrown together and sailed down Norway's southeast inlet.

A surge of foamy white swell slapped against the wood. David's gaze darted up and focused in on two specks floating on the horizon.

Oriel whipped her head around and grasped the sides of the raft "No! They've found us!"

David picked up his stroke rate, but he couldn't outrun the streamlined Violet and Jade vessels. Within the hour, the Jade boat hovered alongside them. Two strapping blond men reached overboard and yanked up Oriel. She squirmed and kicked and they lost their grip, sending her crashing into the river.

Her golden hair swirled to the surface and her head broke through the choppy water. She gasped, her gaze finding David's. "Keep going! Get out of here! We'll find another way."

The purple pouch smoldered like a hot rock in his pocket, as though rebelling against her words. He closed his eyes. *You can do this.* He teetered on the raft's edge, his muscles twitching. The Jade ship stopped beside him and the Violet vessel loomed behind.

Her eyes pleaded with him to go but he pointed his hands and dove in after her, breaking the ice-cold water barrier. Refreshing calm seeped through his body like a cleansing baptism. David put his arms around her and the Jades leaned over the side of their ship and reeled them in.

"You should have left me here," she whispered, her wet hair clinging to his shoulder.

He patted his pocket, the purple pouch now cool and soothed. "I couldn't."

The Jades took off, leaving their empty raft bobbing in the agitated water right next to the outwitted Violets.

Upon their return, David got charged with spying, kidnapping and rape and was sentenced to death. A horde of Violets crossed the border, shouting in protest and carrying flames that seethed on the walls of his Jade-manned cell. The unrest went on for weeks with countless fights breaking out.

Then one still night, when the rose moon high in the sky, Oriel snuck in and visited him. She discarded her 'angry Jade' disguise, and he grabbed the purple pouch out of his pocket and encircled them with its alchemic contents. A heady mix of rose petals, frankincense and myrrh wafted into the air.

The ground rumbled and shook with stampeding Violets and Jades storming the building. Oriel flinched and flew into David's arms. Both camps stopped within feet of them and turned on each other, their shouting punching the atmosphere.

One voice cut through the quarrelling. "What are you all doing?"

"Hugh?" David murmured and cast his eyes over the irate mob.

Hugh stepped forward out of the silenced crowd. "Don't you realize how ridiculous it is fighting over two people because they're in love? They've harmed no one. Go home and focus your energy on improving your own lives rather than interfering in others'."

"You're wrong. They've unsettled the community and ruined our peace. Now Violets constantly invade our land, steal our livestock, poach our women, fight the men and vandalize our town. They need to be brought to justice!" a Jade man yelled and charged toward them.

Oriel clung on to David and he held her close, his eyes boring into those of the fast-approaching, teeth-gnashing Jade. The Jade reached the perimeter of their circle and a ring of fire shot up, blasting the roof off the jail and throwing him back against the far wall.

Lightness and buoyancy pumped through David, and when the fire subsided, he levitated above the prison, looking down.

He scoured the area. *Where are our bodies? Did we shed them, releasing our souls into the night sky and uniting as one?*

When the flames petered out, Hugh penetrated the smoky, blackened circle, his alchemic ring and her engagement ring glimmering among the ashes. He bent down, picked up the surviving hematite band and dusted it off.

Where had they gone? Outside of the jewelry, no trace of them remained. Had his unity ring really worked? Had they found a way to make it out together? He stared at the circular ruby and a bright reflection beamed into his pupils.

Hugh squinted and glanced above him. A single star glowed like a beacon of Violet-Jade light. Was it their sign to him? His eyes welled up and one salty droplet dripped onto the ruby, transforming it into a tear shape.

A family of Jades advanced and he pocketed the ring for safe keeping, until the next soulmate couple needed it. The family stole away with Oriel's engagement ring, and became submersed in the sea of Jades and Violets grieving for their loss. The divided crowd began to turn on each other again and Hugh slipped away.

# Chapter Six

## An All-day Affair

*Hobart, June 2010*

Eden's stomach bubbled with anticipation. Rick would arrive at any minute. She took several slow, even breaths, checked her appearance in the en suite mirror — again — and sat on her two-seater couch in the lounge.

Thornton jumped onto her lap, eager for a pat, and curled into a big, black, fluffy ball. His rhythmical purring, a sort of vibrating cat ohm, eased the tension in her tight muscles...a bit.

She closed her eyes and massaged the top of his head, between his ears and under his chin. He bunted her stomach, readjusted his position, then licked the back of her hand with his sandpaper tongue.

*Ding dong.*

Eden jumped. *Rick!* Thornton sprang off her lap, and her gaze shot across to the wall clock — nine-twenty-five.

She stood and brushed the fur off her loose, crushed charcoal-gray top and black leggings. "Reliable and punctual."

Eden threw on her long black coat, grabbed her handbag off the hall table and opened the door.

Rick wore a cool black leather jacket over black jeans, sunglasses pushed back on his head and a warm, sexy smile. "Hi. Are you ready?"

*To jump you?* "Yes."

"You look great," he said, and led her to his car — a classic red MG with a black soft top — that he'd left running in the driveway. "As always."

*Snap.* He looked pretty bloody good himself. Heat seared Eden's cheeks and she turned away. "Thanks."

He opened the passenger door for her then went around to the driver's side and sat behind the wheel.

The old-school wood panel dashboard and black leather interior were immaculate. She ran her hand over the hot, sleek surface. A memory of a red car flashed into her consciousness and caught at the back of her brain. "Cool car."

"Thanks, it's my weekend, let's-go-for-a-lovely-scenic-drive car." He secured his seatbelt and swiveled to face her. "My normal car is just a 1995 Hyundai Excel. It doesn't drive that smoothly and it's cheap and old, though it's reliable. It's perfect for everyday use."

Within twenty minutes, they entered a trendy café in Battery Point, Hobart, with a heritage sandstone frontage. They sat at a quiet table in the corner with a window looking out onto a square bustling with café frequenters and shoppers. Once again, he pulled out a chair for her then seated himself.

"I don't know about you, but I'm starving!" So it wasn't just her, salivating over the scent of freshly baked bread, fried onions and honey-smoked bacon.

Eden devoured the menu. "Me too." The lush in her wanted to choose the Big Breakfast with rare steak, but she didn't want him to think of her as a glutton, a weirdo or a leech, taking advantage because he'd most likely pay...again.

He slapped his menu down onto the table. "Well, I'm having the Big Breakfast."

"Actually, me too."

"Ooh, a woman who enjoys her food. I like it."

"That's good, because I do love to eat." Was she flirting? Outside of the occasional hair flick, preening and stare-and-look-away, she never outright flirted.

He poured them each a glass of water. "I can't handle these women who just nibble on salads and call it a meal."

"Me, either. I know this probably sounds a bit extreme and hedonistic, but if I couldn't eat food I like, I don't think I'd get much pleasure out of life."

"I know exactly what you mean." Did he? Did Rick really understand where she was coming from, how much he affected her?

When the waiter came around, Rick ordered for both of them.

"And how would you like your steak?" the waiter asked.

"Rare," they said at the same time.

"And your eggs?"

"Poached," they both said together again.

Eden stared at Rick in disbelief.

"Any coffees or juices?"

Rick gestured to her. "Ladies first."

"Thanks. Um…I'll have a decaf long black, please."

Rick handed the waiter their menus. "And I'll have a short black. Thanks."

As soon as the waiter walked out of earshot, Rick met her gaze, eyebrows raised. "Decaf?"

"Yeah. I love coffee, but I can't have too much caffeine. Makes me a bit, ah…agitated." *And I'm nervous enough as it is.*

"Well, we definitely don't want that."

*Those eyes. That stare.* Anxiety-provoking, yet arousing. She squirmed in her seat. "You know, you're the first person I've met who likes their steak done the way I do."

"Same here. I've always loved red meat, whereas most people I know prefer 'charcoal'."

She laughed. "My experience exactly. What's your favorite meat? Lamb's mine but minced beef is a close second."

"Me too. You can't really go wrong with a lamb roast or a mincemeat dish… unless it's overcooked, of course."

She debated whether to confide in him or not. *Ah, go on.* Her kindred spirit would get it, so if Rick didn't, she'd be massively disappointed. Failing her test would throw a huge damper on their date.

Though, better to know earlier than later if boyfriend potential existed. "I know this is probably going to sound gross, but seeing you share my love of partially cooked meat, hopefully you'll understand. Every time I make meatloaf, I sneak in a few mouthfuls of the mixture before it makes it into the oven. The flavor is…delicious. I can't even begin to explain how much it hits the spot. Even thinking of it now makes my mouth water."

His green eyes sparked with desire. "You're making my mouth water as well."

*Whoa!* Did he mean the meat or her?

"Enough of this food talk, otherwise I'm going to start gnawing on my arm...or yours," Rick said with a roguish grin.

*Flirting. Full-on flirting.* What if he tried to kiss her? Would she let him? Eden's laugh wavered with stomach-strangling anxiety.

"So, do you have any family?"

*A reprieve.* She was safe from his tempting advances, for the moment. "No. Well, no living relatives that I'm aware of, anyway."

"Me either. I grew up in boarding school."

"Me too!"

"And let me guess—you prefer the cold, and dusk is your favorite time of day."

Surprise shocked her lips into an awestruck smile. "Yes...and yes. Are you psychic or something?"

He chuckled, deep and sexy. "No. I just had a feeling. Geez, if anyone heard this conversation, they'd think we were vampires."

"Too funny. But seriously, we do seem to have a lot of bizarre things in common. It's kind of weird...in a good way."

"No wonder I like you so much," he said with an I-want-you glint in his eye.

An image of them sitting down to breakfast, barely dressed, in a large room bathed in natural light, blasted into her brain. The incredibly vivid detail made it seem more like a memory than a daydream. However, up until a few weeks ago, she had never even seen Rick. And she hadn't ever been to his house. It didn't make sense.

*Why do I get these strange visions around him?* Could unmet desire for a romantic relationship do that? Sure, she craved a boyfriend, but not enough to set off hallucinations. *Right?*

Their food arrived, re-grounding her in the moment.

When the bill came, Eden went to pay — however, Rick plucked it out of her hand.

"Let me get it, please," she said. "You've covered everything else and you're driving me around all day. It's not fair. Unless you're made of money, of course."

"Unfortunately, I'm not made of money, though I am a bit old-fashioned when it comes to this sort of stuff. I asked you out, so I'm paying for everything. When you ask me out, you can pay for me." His impish grin created kissable crinkles at the corners of his eyes.

It was impossible to argue with such adorableness.

Rick held open the café door for her, and they headed to Salamanca Market. They drifted along the various rows of stalls, and Eden stopped at a jewelry vendor selling some unique items.

A black hematite ring with an intricately carved rose on the front drew her focus. A circle of tiny diamonds surrounded the rose, and below it hung a deep red ruby teardrop.

"You should try it on." Rick's hot breath caressed her ear.

"I don't know…" She didn't want to get too attached. It probably cost an exorbitant price, way out of her budget.

"Go on." His whispered encouragement sent a shiver of excitement skittering across her skin.

*Hmmm…I guess there's no harm in seeing how it looks on.* The enticing ring might not suit — or even fit her finger. "Okay."

Rick got the elderly stall holder's attention and pointed to the ring in the glass-topped display case. "Could we have a look at this, please?"

A surprised smile broke out on the lady's lips. "Of course." She finished rubbing some moisturizing cream into her hands, pulled out the ring and gave it to him.

He examined it, turned to Eden and placed it on her palm. "It's got a real warmth to it, both in temperature and energy. See what you think."

Heat burst through her hand and blazed through her body. Endorphins flooded her veins, swelling her heart with elation and love...for Rick. *Lust, yes, but love?* It couldn't be. She'd only just met the guy.

The stall holder made eye contact with Eden. "Legend has it that Eros gave Psyche a ring just like this. The story goes that as soon as Psyche entered his life, he knew she was the one for him but felt frustrated by his inability to accurately convey the depth of his feelings. His strong and pure love for her inspired him to make an eternal gift of it, something tangible she could carry with her always."

The lady regarded Rick with a gentle smile. "After three days of deep contemplation, the answer finally came to him. He needed to make something precious that represented the creation of pure love in its physical form, and what better way than through harnessing the building blocks of nature.

"He selected carbon to make diamonds, signifying strength, clarity and purity, oxygen and iron to make hematite, representing life's blood, and he added a sprinkling of chromium and titanium to the oxygen and iron to make a ruby, symbolizing love, confidence, loyalty and courage."

The stall holder paused and pointed to the emotive ring in Eden's palm. "Then he set about hand-crafting the diamonds, hematite and ruby into a ring, symbolizing everlasting unity, and as a final touch, he carved the intricate symbol of a rose on the front, signifying pure love and feminine beauty.

"When he next saw his beloved Psyche, he presented it to her and she responded with tears of joy, one of which fell onto the brilliant cut ruby under the rose and converted it into the teardrop shape you see today. As Eros slid the ring onto her finger, she vowed to cherish it forever."

The woman's kind, wrinkled eyes moved between Eden and Rick. "Then when the time came for her to leave her earthbound life and permanently join Eros in eternity, she gave the ring back to the earth, leaving their legacy of love behind for future couples to enjoy.

"Before parting with the special ring, Psyche infused it with a spell, ensuring only a woman truly in love would feel a connection to it, and once she wore the ring, she'd be forever bound by love to the man of her dreams. Ultimately, the ring signifies the sanctity of marriage between soulmates."

She stared into Eden's eyes as though she could see beneath her conscious and subconscious layers and read her spirit. "I've been selling jewelry here for over forty years and you're the first woman to even glance at it. So it appears, young lady, that you've found your perfect partner."

Eden's gaze dropped to the ring, throbbing in her palm. She slipped it onto her right ring finger and the elation and love escalated. It seemed the ring thought Rick was the one too, like it had soulmate selection powers.

"Ooh, it fits like a glove, like a jeweler custom made it for you. Everything about it really suits you — the colors, the style… It's the perfect choice," the woman cooed.

"We'll take it."

*What?* Rick hadn't just said that. He couldn't have. The ring would be way too expensive, not to mention that they were little more than strangers. "What are you doing?"

"You like it, don't you?"

"Yes, but —"

"Just say 'thanks'."

"Thanks, but you really don't have to buy me anything."

"I want to."

Eden squinted and shook her head at him. "You're very naughty."

He moved in close to her ear and whispered, "I know, but you like that."

Desire erupted deep down between her legs.

A mischievous smile slid onto his lips and he grabbed his wallet from the back pocket of his well-fitting jeans.

"That'll be two hundred dollars," the woman said.

Eden delved into her bag, searching for her purse. "Come on, Rick. That's way too much. Let me —"

The stall holder reached over the counter and stilled Eden's hand. "You two make a wonderful couple. I wish you both many years of joy and prosperity." The lady smiled, her face a weathered roadmap of life.

Eden swallowed so loud it surprised her that people at the next stall didn't hear. "Thanks." It was only her second date with Rick and even a stranger could pick up on their chemistry. Eden felt his gaze boring into her back but the bizarreness and intensity of the situation stopped her from returning his stare.

Deep in thought, she said nothing until they reached the car. "You didn't set that up, did you?"

His brow furrowed, creating a cute little cleft down the center of his forehead. "Set what up?"

"That whole thing with the jewelry-stall lady."

He laughed. "No. Why would you think that?"

"I don't know. It was weird. I thought maybe you'd done it for a bit of fun."

His eyes sparkled with mischief. "I can think of much better ways to have fun."

Heat rose in her cheeks at the sexual innuendo, and she stared at her feet, hoping he didn't see her thoughts detour down the dirty track. "Yeah, I guess so."

He opened the passenger-side door and stood silent until her gaze met his. "Look, Eden. Whatever I want to say, I'll say to you directly. You can count on that. I don't believe in playing games."

"I know, but I just wanted to double-check."

Rick's gaze flicked to her mouth and returned straight to her eyes. It was classic I-want-to-kiss-you behavior, according to Grace. Eden swayed toward him, like a flower toward the sun.

He leaned in until their bodies were almost touching. "It was a pretty good story though. I only wish I'd thought of it." Then, instead of making a move, he walked around to the driver's side and got in, leaving her in a state of sexual frustration.

\* \* \* \*

On the far side of town, Salvator answered his mobile phone. "Sis?"

"Hi, Sal. The oddest thing happened today. This lovely young couple came past the stall and the woman's eyes went straight to that ring you gave me all those years ago. Do you remember it?"

He slumped down onto his worn, faded living room couch. "How could I forget?"

They'd gifted it to him only a few days before everything had gone pear-shaped. He'd been whining about not being able to find his own soulmate and she'd handed the ring to him and said, *'I've found mine. I don't need it anymore. Hopefully, it will help you find yours.'*

The guilt for his part in their fate had weighed heavily on him and he couldn't keep the ring. Every time he looked at it, sadness, regret and helplessness tore through him, so he'd given it to his sister to sell in her jewelry stall.

Looking back now, he probably should have included it as part of his friends' exit wardrobes, as he had the rose key pendant that unlocked the black gothic desk drawer. But he hadn't really been thinking straight at the time. His poor decision had joined the long, seemingly ever-growing line of poor decisions.

"Anyway, I just thought I should let you know I sold it. I'm sorry, Sal. I know I should have asked first but it just seemed right. The woman had this look in her blue, almost violet eyes and the man with her seemed so happy to buy it for her. I can't explain it. Maybe the legend is true?"

Blue-violet eyes. It had to be *her…them*. A wave of relief rippled through his stomach. "That's fine. Don't worry —"

"The ring isn't worth much these days… I'll get the money to you as soon as —"

"I don't care about the money, sis. Just keep it." The main thing was that his friends were reunited with the ring and each other.

"Are you sure?"

"Of course. When are you going to come around and see me? It's been ages."

"Soon. I promise. I know things have been a bit quiet for you since you retired. I think we've swapped roles. I've been busier than ever over the past eighteen months, so busy I almost can't keep up."

"I've noticed."

"It's uncanny how things happen, isn't it? It's all about timing."

"It certainly is…"

As soon as they hung up, he clipped his mobile phone back onto his belt. Should he have asked what the couple looked like, just to be certain? No, it would've sounded too strange.

He'd just have to check it out, as subtly as possible, when his sister next visited. But even with the scant details, it sounded like *them*. He would almost bet his life on it.

\* \* \* \*

Eden angled the ring under the sunlight and it cast red and rainbow beams across the inside of the car door and dashboard. *Beautiful.* Something about the ring entranced her, had her behaving out of character like a flashy, materialistic type. Not only did she feel amazing wearing it, but also closer and more aligned with Rick.

It had to be the connection the ring created that captivated her, though something else was beneath it too, something she couldn't quite identify. Maybe the romance of the stall-holder's story?

The woman probably told the tale to everyone to help sell her jewelry, though Eden wished it held some truth. On many levels it made sense. Everything about Rick felt right, almost synchronistic.

Her mind continued to wander, while Rick embarked on the scenic drive up to the top of Mount Wellington. He seemed to tune in to her need to be silent and didn't try to engage her in conversation.

At the pinnacle, they got out, took some photos from the observation points then continued their journey into the countryside. Rick used it as his opportunity to start speaking to her again and, thank God, he didn't bring up the whole ring incident.

They needed to get to know each other way better before delving into such a serious talk about their relationship. Yet, she kept catching herself glancing at the ring on her finger and knew he noticed.

After a ninety-minute drive, they stopped at Woolmers Estate, took the heritage house tour then sat in the quaint café for a late lunch. Rick paid the bill and suggested a stroll through the picturesque grounds.

Eden agreed, eager to check out the continually flowering National Rose Garden Rick had mentioned during their meal. Given the winter season, it intrigued her to see the quality and variety of what was in bloom.

On their way outside, he explained in more detail about the All-Weather Rose project Sub Rosa had been working on.

"After years of rose lovers complaining about the barren look of their gardens when roses were out of season, Sub Rosa jumped on the massive gap in the gardening industry and decided to try and corner the market. Woolmers was kind enough to host the resulting test garden.

"The classic, fragrant English roses were the target crop, and staff assigned to the project have worked really long hours over the last eighteen months to develop a hardy, identical species that mimics the original in every way, except that it can withstand frost, snow and plenty of rain.

"So far there haven't been any detrimental side effects. If all goes to plan, they're hoping to be able to start selling them by spring. It's incredible how identical the genetically modified roses are to the originals, too. But don't just take my word for it. Go see for yourself."

Eden stopped and took in the barren rows of regular roses. "It sounds like Sub Rosa has their fingers in a number of research pies."

Rick chuckled. "Big time. They're becoming the *Jim's* franchise of scientific research."

Eden continued over to the experimental rose garden and drifted from one variety of rose to another, delicately grasping the head of each different flower and leaning in to inhale its glorious and unique perfume. "This is amazing! I can't believe it. They really are just like the real thing!"

He laughed. "You should see yourself."

She looked over and he stood still on the path, enthralled by his mobile phone screen. "Did you take a photo of me?"

A devilish grin slid onto his lips. "Maybe."

She strode over to him. "Let me see."

"Only if you promise not to delete it."

"Yeah sure, whatever." She lunged for his phone.

He held it just out of her reach. "Promise?"

"Yes. Hand it over."

He hesitantly lowered his hand and Eden snatched his mobile to study the snapshot. Bent over, her face was buried in and partially obscured by the scarlet-red rose she held in her hand, her hair and top blown back by the wind.

"Oh come on. You should have warned me. I look ridiculous!"

She handed the phone back to him and he scrutinized the picture some more. "No, you don't. You look magical, just like a nymph straight out of *A Midsummer Night's Dream*."

Eden had to admit, the angle of the photo combined with the elemental influences did make her appear to have wings, to be almost supernatural.

She shook her head and looked away, heat sizzling in her cheeks. When she glanced at him, he had a triumphant smile on his face. He'd noticed. *Damn it!*

In the gift shop on the way out, Rick bought a sparkling pinot noir and a merlot made by the estate vineyard and loaded them into the car. "We'll crack them open when you come over for dinner. I'll cook. How about tomorrow night?" he asked and started the engine.

"Tomorrow?" Had she heard right? He wanted to see her again already? *Yes yes yes!* Excitement exploded like celebratory fireworks in her stomach.

His gaze fixed on hers. "Yeah…only if you want to."

"Of course I want to," she blurted, her face scorching at her fervent disclosure. The more she saw him, the more she wanted to see him, and it seemed he felt the same about her.

An exultant smile adorned his sensuous lips. "Is there anything you don't eat?"

"You mean outside of inanimate objects and live animals?" she joked.

"I'm surprised. I thought for sure you'd be into chowing down on a live animal, followed by a pebble or two, just to clean the teeth and cleanse the palate. Hmmm…I'll have to change the menu now."

She laughed. Not only was he panty-melting hot, but also kind, thoughtful, generous and had a wicked sense of humor. In a competition for the perfect man, he'd not just be in the running, he'd be in the lead—far, far in the lead. "Okay, seriously, I'm not a big fan of asparagus and I hate garlic. It gives me heartburn."

"Me too," Rick said.

When they pulled up at her house, Eden hoped he didn't have to leave straight away. He turned the engine off and got out of the car, opened the passenger side door and walked with her to the front entrance. *So far, so good.*

She rummaged in her bag for her keys, her heart hammering in her ears. "Would you like to come in for a drink?"

"I'd love to, except I'm catching up with Simon tonight. He's been doing a lot of extra shifts on that rose project and it's his first night off in ages, so I promised him—"

"That's okay." She forced a smile, trying to hide her disappointment. "I guess I'll see you tomorrow then?"

"Yes. I'll send you a text with my address later. Sorry I have to leave straight away."

The hematite ring heated her finger. "Don't worry about it. Thanks again for today. I had a really nice time."

"Me too," he said, with a warm smile.

In the sexually charged silence, they drew nearer to each other, like some invisible, magnetic force was pulling them together. They stood so close that a hand would struggle to slide between their bodies. High-voltage electricity pulsed across the narrow divide, and she longed for them to touch to complete the circuit. Her heart leaped.

As though on cue, he leaned down, shifting his gaze between her eyes and her lips. Closer, closer…and he stopped, only a few millimeters away. He attempted to speak but nothing came out.

Finally, he stood up straight and found his voice. "Goodnight, Eden."

"Goodnight?" she said, her voice breathy with disbelief and unmet need. "Drive safely."

"Thanks." He smiled, teetering on the spot as though torn. "Umm…see you tomorrow." He hesitated then returned to his car.

Eden waved goodbye as he drove up the street, then she walked inside, her forehead wrinkling like a crinkle-cut chip. *Why didn't he kiss me?* He seemed like he would and she certainly hadn't discouraged him. If anyone had hesitated, it should have been her, given her disastrous kissing history.

During their two dates he'd had plenty of opportunities to hold her hand or brush her arm, and yet he still hadn't tried to touch her. It felt like he was avoiding it for some reason, which seemed incongruous with the rest of his behavior.

She fiddled with the ring he'd bought her. Surely buying her jewelry meant he was interested.

Eden flopped onto her living room couch, her brain still working overtime, trying to figure him out. "He did admit he's a bit old-fashioned. Maybe that's why he's holding back," she said, trying to console herself.

Thornton jumped onto her lap and meowed.

She patted him, and he settled down and purred. "Hopefully Rick will make a move tomorrow night."

# Chapter Seven

A Dinner Date with Destiny…

Eden opened her wardrobe doors and stood in front of the rack full of clothes. *What to wear?* She breathed out hard. What would encourage Rick to take that next step?

She picked through the hangers, pulling out and trying on dress after dress, but none took her fancy. After forty-five minutes, her bed had transformed into a colorful mound of castoff clothing.

She moved to the drawers, unfolding jeans and pants, shaking her head and hurling them onto the growing pile. Thornton crawled out from under a pair of jeans, the mishmash of outfits tumbling to the ground.

Eden fell back onto her bed and stared at the blank ceiling. "Argh! I've got nothing to wear!"

She sighed, pushed herself into a sitting position and started picking through the scattered, discarded pile of clothes on the floor, trying to find something suitable, something that felt right.

Thornton sauntered over to the open wardrobe and disappeared inside. "Meow."

"What is it, Thornton? Have you found me the perfect outfit?" She stared at him and laughed. "Come on, out of there."

He didn't budge, his amber eyes glowing in the darkness.

On hands and knees, Eden followed him deep into the closet, past the only material connection she had to her family — her grandmother's wedding dress, which was neatly preserved in a garment bag — and she stumbled across a black halter-neck dress with white polka dots that had dropped off its hanger.

Eden emerged from the cupboard and held the dress up in the sunlight. "When did I get this?" She racked her brain. "Obviously I've been doing too much shopping lately."

She tried it on and checked herself out in the mirror. The dress was figure-hugging on top and fell into an A-line style, finishing just above her knees. "Mmm...not bad. What do you think, Thornton? Do I look hot?"

Thornton slinked over and rubbed himself against her bare legs. She reached down and patted him, and he purred, loud and rhythmically.

"I'll take that as a 'yes'."

She rifled through her bedside drawer and selected the sexiest underwear she owned — black lace, *just in case*... She'd seen *Bridget Jones's Diary* too many times to be caught unaware.

She slipped on a pair of black patent leather stilettos and twirled in front of the mirror. "Perfect."

\* \* \* \*

*A sandstone mansion nestled up on the hill? Whoa!* It couldn't be Rick's place. Eden rechecked his text message then the number on the sandstone fence and her GPS.

It was definitely his address and not at all what she'd envisioned. She'd expected something pretty modest after his I'm-not-made-of money confession.

Open wrought-iron gates welcomed her into the property, and she proceeded up the sweeping driveway. Night lighting ran along the sides, illuminating the lush garden filled with ferns, mosses and lichen, as well as a range of tall Australian native and European trees.

"Beautiful," she murmured.

At the top of the driveway stood a central marble fountain with a carving of Eros and Psyche in the middle, and surrounding it were smaller, less conspicuous, cherub statues.

*'Deep inside the chambers of my cavernous heart lie secrets, truth and eternal love'* ran along the circular base, which was engraved with raised hearts and roses. She shivered at the coincidence—her ring, his statue. *Strange. Way too strange.* It felt like the whole universe aimed to get them together.

Eden parked her car next to his silver Hyundai Excel at the front of the house and surveyed the gorgeous grounds. The fountain bubbled away behind her, its steady flow, combined with the quiet, picturesque surroundings, stripping away all her pent-up anxiety.

She closed her eyes, and when she opened them again, the enormity and grandeur of the house felt almost confronting, yet oddly familiar. From where she stood, the garret appeared to touch the inky-black sky.

The intricacy of the gargoyles and the stained-glass gothic rose window only helped her fall more in love with the place. Eager to see Rick and what he'd done with the inside, she hurried up the steps, lit only by two black wrought-iron lanterns.

She grabbed the black-ringed door knocker and lightly rapped it against the grand oak front door.

"He's not going to hear that," she murmured, undertaking some last-minute grooming—tidying her hair and straightening out her dress—before knocking again.

The latch clicked and she stopped. The door swung open and Rick stood right in front of her, wearing a tight black shirt that emphasized his deliciously defined chest, blue jeans that clung to his lean, muscular thighs and a broad, inviting smile.

*Mmmm...* Her stomach went into freefall. His sleeves were pushed up, and he had on his signature cross ring and necklet, as well as a cool black leather wristband, featuring a cross motif.

"Hey, you made it. Did you have any trouble finding the place?" he asked.

"No, thanks to my trusty GPS."

Behind him, a long, sprawling passageway opened up into a flight of stairs in the distance, and amber light flickered on the walls, suggesting he'd lit a bunch of candles. *Very romantic. That's a good sign.*

"Please come in." He moved aside, and a fluffy, charcoal-gray cat appeared in the corridor. "Wow. I can't believe it. Usually he hides when I have visitors."

She waved a hand along the front of her body and flashed him her sauciest smile. "Obviously he has good taste."

Rick's gaze raked over her like a sensual caress. "Obviously."

Her nipples beaded beneath the fabric of her dress and she hoped he hadn't noticed her ravage-me response. She'd just walked in the door, for God's sake. She bent down to pat the cat and tried to breathe, controlled and steady. "What's his name?"

"Smokey. Original, huh?"

Eden laughed. It sounded forced, stilted, giving away her nerves. "Very. He's adorable." She stroked him and he purred and rubbed himself against her hand and legs. "He can probably smell Thornton on me. Did I tell you I have a cat as well?"

"No, you didn't. I look forward to meeting him. He must be rather dashing with a name like Thornton. Obviously you're a *North and South* fan."

She glanced up into his gorgeous green eyes. "Yes, he is, and yes, I am. How did you guess?"

"What girl doesn't love a bit of classic romance?"

"True. But that doesn't explain how you made the connection." She stopped patting the gorgeous fluffball and stood up straight.

"I plead the fifth on that one. Let me show you through to the lounge room."

He stepped in close enough to touch her, possibly even steal a kiss. Her pulse pelted in her ears. *Settle down!* "Mmm...something smells yummy. What's on the menu?" Eden asked, the aroma of marinated, roasting meat stimulating her appetite...nearly as much as he did.

"It's a surprise. However, I'll give you a hint. Many people picture these babies at night." A roguish smile slid onto Rick's lips and he started walking down the hall.

"Wait a sec..." She caught up with him and looked him in the eye. "What? That's not a hint. That's a cryptic clue. I've always been shockingly bad with those."

He laughed, deep, husky and hot. "The trick is to receive the information with an open mind then hand it over to your subconscious to piece it together. The harder you think about it, the less likely you are to come up with the answer."

"Hmmm…I think I might just enjoy being surprised."

He studied her, his gaze solid and supportive. "Come on. Don't give up. I have faith in you."

"Aren't we supposed to be changing the subject so I can let my subconscious work on this?" she said, her tone infused with cheekiness.

He feigned exasperation. "Okay, okay…" He turned and continued down the corridor.

The gothic vibe carried through to the inside of his home, though it had a more modern edge. High ceilings, with ornate cornices and just the right amount of furniture and artwork, solidified the theme. It had perfect balance, 'good Feng Shui', as Grace would say.

"Wow. Your house is amazing. I thought you said you weren't made of money? This place must have cost you a fortune!"

He stopped and faced her. "Not exactly. I inherited it. Though saying that, the renovations haven't been cheap. The way I'm going, I think it'll take the rest of my life to pay them off!"

Old houses like his had tremendous character, beauty and artistry, though they were a maintenance nightmare. She hesitated. *Hang on… Did he say 'inherited'?* "Um, sorry if this sounds like a dumb question, but if you don't have any family, who left you the house?"

"That's not a dumb question at all. It's kind of a strange story. Up until three years ago, I was a struggling uni student in Melbourne. Then, out of the blue on my twenty-sixth birthday, I received a solicitor's letter, telling me I'd inherited a property in Tasmania. I thought it was a scam, a joke, at first. Then I investigated further and confirmed it was legitimate.

"Apparently the property has been in my family for a long time and I'm the last known living relative. Before that, I didn't even know one thing about my family. According to the information and the state of the house when I moved in, no one had been living in it for quite a while.

"Then, when my uncle died, my name showed up in his will. I still don't know how he knew about me, seeing as I had no idea about him. Anyway, he nominated me as the sole beneficiary of the house and, so far, no one has come out of the woodwork to contest it."

A grateful smile brought out the fullness in his lips, lips she kept imagining on hers.

"I feel incredibly blessed and privileged. I mean, this place is fantastic. It's like a dream come true. I just wish I'd had a chance to meet the old guy before he passed away. But things don't always work out how you want them to, which isn't always a bad thing. I guess it's all part of the thrill of being alive...

"Anyway, what was I saying? Oh yeah, that's right. Sorry... I tend to go off on tangents sometimes. I keep trying to rationalize it to myself by saying I can't help it, that it's one of the downfalls of having a scientific brain. But it can be useful too. There I go again. See what I mean? I think I'd better slow down on the alcohol, don't you?"

Growing redness flushed his face—so likeable, desirable, lovable. "Nah, you're fine. You don't have to drive anywhere."

"True." He cleared his throat. "Ah…where was I? Oh yeah. When I first got here, the place was pretty run down and needed a lot of work. Even in that state, I knew how I wanted it to look. Have you ever been to the Forum in Melbourne?"

She shook her head. "No."

"Bugger." His gaze shifted up and to the right. "Um…let's see… How can I best describe it? Basically, the Forum used to be an old picture theater, then only a few years ago, the owners decided to refurbish it, making it into a concert venue, using contemporary design to complement the existing gothic-style architecture.

"And I reckon they pulled it off. As soon as I walked into this house, I knew I wanted to create that same feel, so I kind of jumped on their bandwagon."

The green of his eyes brightened with excitement, as though lit from behind by a high-powered torch. Clearly he was proud of what he'd achieved. And he should be. The place looked amazing. "Even though it's been expensive, it's also been kind of fun…and therapeutic. The house is a piece of me now. I can finally call it home. So your appreciation of it means a lot."

"You've done a great job. It's really beautiful. Instead of stark and cold, like many of those *Home Beautiful* featured places, you've been able to create a warm, cozy feel."

"Thanks." He led her into the lounge-dining area, a massive beaming smile on his face. "Please make yourself at home."

"Do you need a hand with anything?" she asked.

"No, everything's under control…for the moment. I might need help with the dishes later, though." He headed toward a door at the far end of the room, which she assumed led into the kitchen.

She walked over to the roaring fireplace, the smoldering timber casting out a rose-gold warmth. "No problem."

"I'm joking. I wouldn't do that to a guest. I have a dishwasher. Her name's Jean. But she's not due in until next Thursday."

Eden spun to face him. He'd stopped walking and propped himself against a dining chair, staring back at her. "Errr, you can't wait until then. After dinner, I'm helping you wash, and I won't take no for an answer."

"If you insist... All of a sudden I'm looking forward to it." The glint in his eye suggested his mind had wandered in the same sexual direction as hers.

She looked away and fingered the rose key pendant around her neck. "So, um...do you live here alone?"

"Yep."

With just the two of them there, anything could happen—and most likely would. Her whole body tingled with anticipation.

He smiled and continued through the far door and out of sight. The clang of cutlery and slam of drawers indicated further food preparation. He had made such a huge effort. Hopefully it meant a positive progression in their relationship.

"It must get pretty lonely, living in such a big house," she called out to him.

"Yeah, it can be sometimes. But Smokey keeps me company and I have my writing and my music." He slid open a panel in the wall that she'd thought was a fresco-style painting and stood behind a counter filled with a large platter, cutlery and a collection of containers.

*Wow. A camouflaged compartment. So James Bond.* Their gazes reconnected. "Do you write your own music?"

"No, not really. Though I play the guitar…badly. I like to think I'm better than I am."

She laughed. "What sort of music do you play?"

Rick spooned out some olives and pickled vegetables. "Mostly depressing indie ballads. Pretty cliché, huh?"

"No…actually, yeah it is. At least you can play an instrument, though. I'm hopeless, except with the recorder. Sad, I know."

He rolled up super-thin slices of cold meat and arranged them on the platter. "I used to drive everyone crazy practicing that damn thing."

"Me too. So, outside of your love of depressing indie ballads," she said with a sassy tinge in her tone, "is there any other stuff you're into?"

"Actually, I like all sorts of music. The only music I can play is depressing indie ballads."

She grinned. "Oh, right."

"Hey, I just realized I didn't put any music on. Sorry. I meant to do it before you got here but got caught up in the kitchen…" He moved out of view and a gush of water on metal told her he'd gone to the sink and turned on the tap.

"Don't worry about it."

"No-no, I'll go and put something on right now. Better late than never." He reappeared and strode over to the stereo. "What music do you like?"

"Just about anything except death metal, full-on rap and country… Hey, is that Bellini's *La sonnambula*?" she asked.

Rick stopped on his way back to the kitchen and stared at her with disbelief. "Yeah. I'm surprised you know it. I've never met anyone else who does."

"I saw the opera for the first time a few years ago, though I can't remember who I went with. All that sticks in my head is how much the performance moved me. Bel canto-style music is amazing. Anyone who knows and appreciates it, knows Bellini."

"Very true." Rick entered the kitchen, returned with a bowl filled with crackers and set them on the table.

"And you mentioned writing as well. What kind of writing do you do?"

He glanced up and met her gaze. "Poetry mainly, outside of writing research reports, grant submissions and the occasional research article for work."

*Not just intelligent, but also creative too.* "That's so cool. Not many straight men will admit they're into poetry. I'd love to read some of your work…if that's okay."

"Of course. Poetry is written to be read, right?"

"Right."

"After dinner, I'll do a little poetry reading for you. How does that sound?"

"Great. I can't wait." She took off her black coat and hung it over the back of the closest couch. "I wouldn't mind reading some of your scientific journal articles too."

"No worries. Apparently my work has been touted as the perfect cure for insomnia. So if you're having any trouble sleeping, it'll work a treat."

She laughed.

"Okay, what would you like to drink?"

"How about that sparkling pinot noir?"

"You read my mind."

While he poured their wine, Eden studied the two snapshots on the mantelpiece. A sepia one depicted a young man shaking hands with another man in front of what appeared to be the erection of Rick's home, and the other was a selfie of Rick and Smokey. *How sweet.* Only a man with a kind, loving heart would proudly display such a cute shot.

Rick joined her in front of the hot, crackling fire. "Your drink, milady."

They chinked glasses. "Cheers," she said, the bubbles rising up out of their champagne flutes, connecting and melding together.

"Thanks for coming. It's so nice having you here."

Heat scalded her cheeks and she gulped down two large mouthfuls of wine in quick succession. "Thanks for inviting me."

"Why don't you take a seat over here" — he gestured to the table, walked over to it and pulled out a dining chair for her — "and I'll bring out our entree."

While she sat, Rick collected the platter he'd made up earlier and placed it in the center of the table. Her mouth watered. Was she salivating over the food or him? Although a self-confessed foodie, she leaned more toward it being Rick.

He chose a chair opposite her, way too far away. Why would he select that spot when she had an empty seat right next to her? Was he keen on her or not? He kept saying things suggesting romantic interest, so why hadn't he tried to stay close...and touch her?

"If you don't like this stuff, I can get you something else," he said.

*Oops.* She snapped into action and stocked up her plate, mostly with cold meats. "No, I love it. Sorry. I got lost in my own little world there for a moment."

She started sampling the range of gastronomic delights, and he put a piece of rolled prosciutto in his mouth and lit the candles on the wrought-iron centerpiece.

"Sheep. I mean, lamb!" she said, blurting out the answer to the riddle he'd posed earlier.

"See? I told you you'd figure it out. Nice work." Rick smiled and glanced at his black-and-gold skeleton watch. "Ooh, speaking of lamb, I'd better go check on it. I'll be back in a minute."

Seconds later, the scent of roasting meat overwhelmed her senses. It smelled so incredible that she had to hold herself back from bursting into the kitchen to try a bit. She tapped her feet on the floor and looked around the room. Smokey had curled up on a nearby couch in front of the fire.

"Come here, Smokey. Distract me," she whispered. He jumped off the couch and sauntered over, circling her agitated feet. She bent down and stroked him—however, her mind didn't move from its raw, irrational animal craving for bloodied meat. Where did that fit on Maslow's hierarchy of need scale? She laughed to herself.

Smokey bunted her legs then lay at the tips of her toes. Eden stopped patting him, reached for her wine and guzzled down the rest.

Rick rejoined her, eyebrows raised. "Well, Smokey certainly didn't waste any time. I'm gone for two minutes and he's already snuggling up to you. Anyone would think he's trying to cut my lunch, or in this case, dinner."

Eden laughed. Maybe Rick should take a leaf out of Smokey's book.

He glanced at her empty wineglass. "Would you like another drink?"

"Only if you're having one."

"I am. Would you prefer another sparkling pinot noir or should we start on the merlot?"

"The merlot, please...if that's okay. Otherwise I probably won't get to try it. I still have to drive home, remember."

"You can crash here if you'd like."

Eden averted her eyes and fiddled with the rose key pendant around her neck. "Oh um...thanks, but...ah..."

He brought over the merlot and filled their glasses. "It's okay. You don't have to explain. It's entirely up to you. I just thought I'd give you the option." Rick put down the bottle and raised his glass to hers. "How about a toast? To sharing many more lovely evenings together, just like this."

She gulped. *Maybe he's going to make a move?* "Cheers."

Rick took another sip, put his half-full glass of wine next to hers on the table and hurried back into the kitchen.

*Nope.*

As he carved up the lamb, Eden did all she could to stay in her chair. Within five minutes, she had her plate in front of her and her legs shook, waiting for him to sit so she could start.

"*Bon appétit.*" Rick looked at her like she represented the prime dish on a sexual feast menu.

Eden tried to temper her spike in arousal and swallow the inordinate amount of saliva swamping her mouth. She picked up the fancy knife and fork and cut into the bloodied slices of lamb. *Mmmm...rare.* Just how she liked it. "This is delicious." She stifled a moan.

He chuckled. "I'm glad. That was the idea."

"Where did you learn to cook like this?" she asked between mouthfuls.

"Years of practice."

"There's still hope for me then?"

"I'll let you know after you cook me dinner." What a sly, impressive way of setting up for another date. Her heart swelled with delight at his enthusiasm to see her again. She definitely wanted to spend more time with him too. And it all hinged on whether they kissed tonight...and the outcome.

Once they'd finished, he cleared their plates and brought out their final course — brandy snaps stuffed with brandy-soaked mixed berries and cream on the side.

He watched her take her last mouthful like he wished she was his dessert. "What did you think?"

Eden wished that too. Her cheeks flared with renewed heat. "Very nice. My compliments to the chef. Thanks for making such a huge effort. I really appreciate it. But you could have made it a lot easier on yourself and ordered in. I wouldn't have minded."

He swallowed his last spoonful of dessert and stared into her eyes. "I know. It's not the same, though. Honestly, it was no trouble. I enjoy cooking. And I wanted to make something special for you, so I'm glad you liked it."

"I certainly did. The lamb in particular..." She sighed. "Exquisite."

"Does that mean you'll come to this restaurant again?"

"Definitely!"

A delighted smile spread across his face. "Well, shall we move to the lounge?"

# Chapter Eight

Moving Closer

"Oh, um..." Eden checked her gold marcasite watch, her pulse thumping. "I probably should head home. I've got a longish drive and I'm really tired."

"Oh, come on. It's still early. Please stay a bit longer."

She struggled to say no to him, especially when he looked at her like her leaving would make him miserable, like he never wanted to let her go. The same strong pull tugged at her heart—but she was scared.

Scared that the slightest touch, let alone kiss, could be a disaster. And she didn't want the night to end like that. She didn't want their relationship to end. "Don't you have work tomorrow?"

"Nope. I have a day off."

"Me too."

"Then there's no excuse for you to have to rush home." His persistence fanned rather than doused the flames of desire within her, encouraging her to stay and fight her fears.

"Actually, there is. I've been known to fall asleep at people's houses before—"

He stood up. "I'm sure I can cope with that."

*I don't know if I can, though.* She hesitated. "Don't say I didn't warn you."

He chuckled, strolled over and sat on the black leather double-ended chaise lounge, facing the fireplace. She continued past him and went to sit on one of the single seaters.

"What are you doing all the way over there?" he asked.

She turned to face him.

"Why don't you come and sit next to me?" Rick patted a spot to the left of him. "Don't worry. I won't bite…unless you'd like me to."

Eden laughed nervously and dropped her gaze. What if she sat there, he kissed her and it turned out like every other time? Or what if he didn't make a move at all? Should she ask him about it? No, she couldn't. That would be too weird. What would she say? 'Why haven't you kissed me?'

Though, like Grace had said, women equally made moves on men these days. Maybe he'd been waiting for her? No, too old school for that. It had to be something else.

Maybe he'd also had negative experiences in the past where the first kiss had been the kiss of death for the relationship? They had so much else in common, she wouldn't be surprised…

Smokey rubbed against her legs, jolting her back to the present. *Go sit down.* It was the least she could do. Rick had been nothing but sweet. And he did look pretty damn hot.

*Mmm…* She went and sat beside Rick, angling herself toward him but keeping enough distance to reduce the risk of accidental touch. Butterflies swarmed her full stomach, slamming into the small free space.

Rick smiled — bright, mesmerizing, memorable. "Your turn to tell me more about yourself. I feel like it's been a 'me-fest' so far tonight. No wonder you're tired."

"You crack me up. Honestly, I've had a really nice time. You're a very interesting person."

"And you're very mysterious."

She laughed, a nervous staccato stumbling from her lips. "I suppose I can be. I don't like giving too much of myself away —"

"You've been hurt before." His eyes searched hers.

She shook her head. "No."

"Ah...you're worried you will be."

She hesitated. "Yes."

"If it's any consolation, I'm worried about that too. But I feel unusually comfortable with you. It's like I can tell you anything."

Eden rubbed and twisted the soulmate ring Rick had bought her. "Really?"

"Yes. I've already done plenty of that, though. Now it's your turn."

She stopped, the building heat of the precious metal burning her skin. "Seriously, I'm not that exciting."

"Let me be the judge of that."

"Hey, how about that poetry reading you promised me earlier?" she said, desperate to change the subject.

He propped his elbow on the top of the backrest and leaned in closer to her. "Nice try. I'd like to hear a little more about you first."

"You're not going to let me get out of this, are you?"

"Not a chance."

*Damn.* "Okay, well, what would you like to know?"

"There's so much. Where do I begin?" He focused his eyes on her with sudden intensity, like all his thoughts had lined up and spat out the answer. "Ah, I know... Okay, I should warn you — my first question's going to be a tricky one, but I reckon it's a good place to start. The way a person answers a difficult question tells me a lot about them."

She stared at him, nerve-jangling adrenaline injecting her heart.

"Hmmm...how shall I ask this?" He tapped his fingers on his mouth. "Um..."

"Just say whatever words are in your head," Eden said, wanting to hurry up and end the interrogation. How would she explain the weird holes and inconsistencies in her memory? He'd think she was insane.

"Maybe I'd better not. Forget it. I'll go and grab my laptop and pick a poem to read to you instead." He went to get up.

"No. Just ask me now."

"You sure? I don't want to stress you out."

"I'm fine, really." Her tone sounded short and as sharp as a razor blade.

"All right then. What are your thoughts on...?"

"Mmm..."

"Blue and green. Do you really think they should never be seen?"

A relieved laugh burst from her lips. "You're so infuriating, you know that?"

"So I've been told." He grinned. "But I bet you're feeling more relaxed now, right?"

She shook her head, unable to stop smiling. He knew how to ease her stress. Well, except for the raging sexual tension. "You're too intelligent for your own good."

"I've been told that too. You still haven't answered my question."

She readjusted the fall of her dress against her less-shaky legs. "In all honesty, I believe blue and green can definitely be seen...depending on the outfit."

He chuckled. "Touché."

"Okay, seriously, I suppose I do feel more relaxed."

"Good. Does that mean I can ask you anything now?" A suggestive smile lit up his face with mischief.

"Of course you can. It doesn't mean I'll answer it, though." She took off her shoes and curled her legs up onto the couch.

Rick topped up their wineglasses and they sipped and chatted into the night.

He scrutinized her heavy-lidded eyes. "You know, you are actually starting to look a bit sleepy."

She yawned. "Probably because I am. I think you must have tired me out yesterday. I know I had all day to recover, but I hardly slept."

"Me either. I was too excited about seeing you tonight."

She dropped her gaze, her breath trembling in her windpipe. "Same here."

A short, sexually charged silence throbbed in the air.

"Shall I make us a coffee?" Rick asked.

Eden looked at him and smiled. "Yes, please." The safe answer. Her heart wanted him to kiss her — however, her head continued to worry about the possible ramifications.

She could kiss him, but fear of a negative outcome held her in her seat. What if they had no chemistry, like her experience with other guys? How could she politely excuse herself after coming on to him?

Rick got up and, with his back to her, she took the brilliant opportunity to perv on his fine butt. The moment he walked out of sight, Eden laid her head against the backrest and closed her eyes, picturing him in her mind's eye—his piercing light green eyes, his sexy smile and his mouth-watering, V-shaped body...

She sighed and sank further into the couch, the warm flickering of the fire lulling her into a drowsy state.

Floating in and out of consciousness, Eden fought against imminent sleep, but it overtook her mind like an LSD trip. A surreal sequence of lurid, nonsensical images flashed into her head, bombarding her with messages from her subconscious. Then the flow of pictures slowed down and began to take shape.

*A glowing fireplace at Rick's house, yet it looked different. Eden sat next to him on a shiny black porcelain couch, wearing a traditional white wedding gown, and Rick wore a black suit. They resembled the old-fashioned bride and groom figurines off a 1960s wedding cake.*

*He wrapped his arm around her and she rested her head on his shoulder. They relaxed into each other, and water started filling the room. She didn't worry at first, until it crept up to their knees.*

*She panicked. "Rick, we have to get out of here."*

*He remained cool and calm, assuring her everything was fine.*

*The water continued to rise, and Eden wound her arms around his chest and clung to him. She closed her eyes, hoping that when she opened them again, everything would be back to normal.*

*A sudden pop, the sound of fire consuming wood, startled her and she glanced at the fireplace. The water had engulfed it, as it slowly but steadily did them. However, although the yellow, orange and blue flames should have been drowned out by the flood, they were bigger and brighter.*

*Within no time, the icy cold water lapped at her chin, but out of the corner of her eye, the persistent, oddly comforting fire continued to glow. Rick remained composed and hadn't even attempted to move. His lack of concern was oddly reassuring and totally obscure.*

*She tried to speak – however, her mouth froze, thwarting their last chance to escape. She shivered, her teeth chattering, and used her last ounce of energy to lift her head and look into her husband's eyes...*

When Rick returned, Eden was asleep, with Smokey purring by her side. Mesmerized, he stopped and stared. *Beautiful. A beautiful, living, breathing china doll.*

As though on automatic pilot, he wandered over and whispered her name. Eden stirred and started to fidget and shudder. Should he comfort her? He didn't want to be too presumptuous.

Rick sat beside Eden and she seemed to settle. Without touching her, he moved in closer, using the opportunity to study her face. A faultless complexion, though her cheeks were a little rosy. Was it from the wine, the fire, her feelings for him or a combination of all three?

*Kiss her, kiss her, kiss her,* his mind screamed. *No, be patient.* He fidgeted and turned away. When would it ever be the right time? How would he know?

Eden's head nudged his shoulder and a hit of pleasure shot up his arm, like it'd been pumped full of endorphins. *Whoa!* He sat dead still, unsure what to do.

The overpowering sensation spread, gaining momentum from one synapse to another, like a crowd doing the Mexican wave at a huge sporting event. His breathing escalated into short, quick pants, and he uttered her name.

"Rick," she murmured, still dozy, and clutched onto him. The path of her hand across his chest scorched his flesh, yet goosebumps pricked on his skin. His nerve endings felt exposed and hypersensitive to her touch, setting his body ablaze with desire.

The intense, foreign sensation had his head jumbled full of *should I, could I, if I...* He didn't want to do the wrong thing, yet he felt compelled to touch her. Rick swallowed back his hesitations, gave in to temptation and gently stroked her face.

She roused and jumped back.

"Are you all right?" Rick asked.

"Yes. Um...sorry." *What the hell just happened?* Eden's heart pounded—and not only from the strange, creepy dream. Her cheek throbbed with ecstatic warmth, like a vibrating electric blanket lay beneath her skin. "I did warn you."

"Yeah, but I didn't realize you literally meant you'd fall asleep on me."

Eden laughed, the sound still husky with sleep.

A serious, I-*really*-want-to-kiss-you look shone in Rick's eyes. There'd been glimpses of it all night, but the intention in his eyes right now had amplified a hundred times compared to before. This time it would happen.

The hematite, diamond and ruby soulmate ring on her finger flared with heat and she shifted in her seat, her heart slamming against her ribcage. Either she made a swift exit or stayed and took a huge risk.

"Um...I really should head home. It's getting late and..." Eden looked around for her things.

She went to stand up and he grabbed her hand. "Don't go."

A rush of heat and electricity sizzled up her arm, and an overwhelming yearning blazed inside her core. Her mind buzzed. She stopped, still sitting on the edge of the couch, looked down at his hand on hers, then up at him.

His gaze shifted between her eyes and her lips. With his other hand, he reached up, caressed her cheek and leaned in.

The second his soft, inviting lips met hers, they melted away every hesitation, every rational thought in her head. The skin-on-skin contact seemed to set off a chemical reaction and ignited an untapped store of passion, her feelings rushing to the surface like an erupting geyser.

Eden's animal instincts took over, and she threw her arms around Rick's waist and crushed her mouth to his, her response matching his intensity and fervor.

When they finally pulled apart, they just stared at each other. Before now, she had never been lustfully out of control. Did that mean he was the one? Maybe he was just an amazing kisser?

Should she hang around and see how things panned out? *Tempting, but no.* She had to leave before she got too carried away and did something she might regret. Eden shifted forward on her seat.

"Where are you going?" he asked.

"Home. I think I should..." She couldn't look at him. She didn't want him to see her face burning up.

"Please stay. You're too tired to drive home. I'd never forgive myself if anything happened to you." He inched closer and held her hand. "It would be irresponsible of me to let you go. I'll set you up in the spare bedroom and you can drive home in the morning."

The tingles in her arm hummed, strong and persistent, like she'd been freed from a deep, numbing sleep. Eden's gaze met his and her breath hitched. *God, so gorgeous.* Was it possible for Rick to get more attractive by the minute?

"Look… It's totally up to you, but I'd prefer you stay for your own safety and…because I want you to. I promise I won't hassle you…much." That devilish grin on his face screamed dangerous. Disarming.

Smokey jumped down off the seat beside her and rubbed himself against her legs, as though trying to prevent her from getting up, like he was in cahoots with Rick.

Eden reached down and patted Smokey, while considering Rick's suggestion. She really should go but she didn't want to.

Had his kiss put a spell on her? Did he have magic saliva, sweat, skin? Being with Rick felt so right, yet how could she trust him implicitly when she hardly knew him?

It didn't make sense, yet emotionally it made perfect sense. So, should she go with her heart or head? *Heart or head? Heart or head…* "I guess I am pretty tired. Okay, I'll stay." *Heart, obviously.*

A brilliant smile broke out on his handsome face. "Great!"

Smokey slunk away, found a spot in front of the fireplace and started cleaning himself, with a focus on his private parts. She wouldn't mind Rick giving a bit of special attention to her private parts.

*No.* Her emotions must have multiplied way out of control, like some sort of mutating lust virus. That line of contaminated thinking had to stop or she'd wind up in his bed. Her body thrummed with need, her mind in conflict. Because their relationship was in the embryonic stage, she couldn't go there yet, shouldn't succumb to sex — or so her good-girl brain tried to convince her.

Rick sprang off the couch, keeping his stare fixed on her eyes, and squeezed her hand. "Come with me."

She smiled nervously, shivering with delight at the hot, throbbing bare skin contact. Every nerve fiber prickled and thrust against her flesh, as though desperate to get as close to him as possible.

She slung her handbag over her shoulder and stood. "Where are we going?"

He guided her toward the staircase. "You'll see."

Upstairs, the glow of candles lit their way, and he stopped in front of a closed door only a short distance down the corridor. Soft shadows danced on the walls around them, as though celebrating their new level of connection.

"Okay, here we are — your room for the night, milady. Not so sinister, is it?"

She laughed. "No. Well, not so far. But anything can happen to change that."

"Such as?"

"I think… No, actually, I'm *sure* you know exactly what I mean."

"Don't you trust me?"

Eden stared into the spellbinding green depths of his eyes. The way he looked at her, serious and unblinking, held undeniable truth. "Well, yes. I wouldn't have stayed if I didn't, but — "

"But?"

"We haven't known each other long so... I mean, I have no reason to distrust you but... Put it this way. I always try to give people the benefit of the doubt. Basically, I trust a person until they prove otherwise."

"I tend to do the same. Though my gut instinct is right most of the time, so I usually go with that."

"Me too."

He stepped closer. "So, what does your gut say about me?"

"That you're trustworthy."

And closer. "Anything else?"

*That you'll be amazing in bed.* She looked down, heat searing her cheeks and sizzling her core.

"I'm assuming that's a 'yes'. Would you like to elaborate?" His sultry breath stroked her forehead.

She shook her head. "No."

He rubbed small circles on the back of her hand with the pad of his thumb. "Come on. If you tell me one other thing, I promise I won't tease you anymore tonight."

With each labored breath, her hardened nipples brushed against her bra.

"Seriously. Cross my heart." He made the sign of the cross over his chest, his fingers barely a centimeter from her breast.

How was she supposed to think now? "Hmmm...okay. Well...um...you're intelligent — and not just with academic stuff. You're caring and very genuine. There, that's three."

His smile looked pleased, reaching-his-eyes sincere. "Thank you. They're three qualities I think are really important."

"I agree. And just so you know, I wouldn't have said them if they weren't the truth. I may get nervous and hesitant about answering your questions sometimes, especially when they relate to my emotions, but I won't lie."

"I know. Anyway, enough of the serious talk...for now. Let's get back to the practicalities. I'm assuming you didn't pack an overnight bag."

"You assume correctly. I didn't anticipate —"

"Me either. But I'm very glad things worked out this way."

If the sexual tension between them built any more, she'd combust. Eden averted her eyes and stared at the floor, her hand remaining in his.

"Some of my old T-shirts and pajama tops are in the bedside cabinet if you want to change into something else...to sleep in. I don't have any women's clothes. Sorry."

"I'm glad to hear it. Otherwise, that might have been slightly concerning. Frank N. Furter concerning," she joked, trying to ease the sexual static in the air.

He laughed, true joy etched around his eyes.

She gave his hand a gentle squeeze. "Seriously, thanks."

"No worries. You'll also find some toiletries in the en suite. Only men's stuff, unfortun —"

"Don't worry. It'll be more than fine."

"Let me know if you need anything else, okay?"

"I will. Thanks."

They stood awkwardly for a few moments, still hand in hand. Eden looked down and shifted her weight from one foot to the other. She took a deep breath, then another, and forced herself to regain eye contact. "Goodnight."

Longing beamed from Rick's eyes and he touched her face, his fingers gentle, entrancing, then kissed her tenderly on the lips. He pulled away and leaned in to her ear, his light stubble scratching her cheek and igniting her sex. "Goodnight," he whispered, paused, then moved to make eye contact.

An insatiable rush overtook her and, before she knew what she was doing, she locked her lips on his and wound her arms around his neck. Rick ran his hands along the sides of her body in a slow, sensual glide, bringing his palms to rest on her lower back.

He pulled her close, her chest and pelvis slamming against his, and she gasped. Rick's solid bulge showed how much he wanted her, sending a spike of desire between her legs.

After a few intoxicating minutes, he slowed things down, peppering her mouth with feather-light, adoring kisses. Rick rested his forehead on hers, lingered, then pried his face away and stared into her eyes. "I'll see you in the morning."

"Yes." Her voice sounded breathy, wanton.

He hesitated, his body still pressed against hers, then stepped back and walked away. A glimpse of her soulmate ring sparkling in the candlelight captured her attention. Maybe the ring story did hold some truth?

Rick stopped in front of an open doorway, partway down the corridor, and turned. His gaze penetrated deep, like he had X-ray vision and could see beneath her clothes. Her nipples strained against the fabric of her bra in an I-want-you-too display.

Her body seemed to have its own ideas about how far to go with Rick, blatantly rebelling against her brain. She clasped her hands in front of her pubic bone, a shy smile pulling at the corners of her sensory-overloaded lips.

A dashing grin flashed across his face and he disappeared into what must be his bedroom. Eden entered the spare room, closed the door and squealed. She replayed the past forty-five minutes over and over again in her mind, reliving every touch, every look, every word.

When their saliva had mixed, a molecular reaction of love and lust must have occurred, creating a strong bond between them. She couldn't stop smiling.

*Is he as excited as I am?* If she went by his physical response, it would be a clear 'yes', but how about on an emotional, mental, spiritual level? If she went with her gut, it would still be a resounding 'yes'.

However, a gut feeling didn't equal fact. What did their romantic encounter actually mean to him? Was it just a couple of kisses after a few drinks? No, it felt much, much deeper than that, going by the effervescent emotions bubbling inside her.

Eden switched on the lamp, sending a dim glow throughout the room. The sparse layout had simple décor compared to the rest of the house. The overall theme remained strongly masculine though, suggesting no women had had a significant presence, at least not while he'd been in residence.

There were no ornaments, just a plain, wrought-iron light fitting and only one abstract painting in white, black, charcoal and silver. A black, charcoal and white doona and pillows topped the queen-size, four-poster bed, and white chiffon draping hung from the wrought-iron frame and wound around the posts.

Above the spotless cast-iron fireplace hung a black wrought-iron mirror, and a black lamp sat on the bedside table. She dropped her bag beside the bed, bent down, opened the largest bedside drawer and searched through the neatly stacked piles of his clothes for suitable sleeping attire.

A black, gold and red paisley pajama top drew her focus. She lifted it out of the drawer, her hands shaking, and she swooned at its fresh, masculine scent. It smelled of Rick.

In the en suite, she opened the black silver-handled vanity cupboard and found a selection of men's toiletries, cleaning products and three fluffy charcoal-gray towels. "Ooh, he's neat and clean too. Another big tick."

Eden washed her face and brushed her teeth, then undressed down to her black lace briefs and threaded her arms through his pajama top. She did the buttons up to her cleavage and glanced at herself in the mirror. *Hmmm...kind of sexy in an understated way.* In the morning, she'd get *his* verdict.

# Chapter Nine

## Prodigious Proposition

Eden woke to the buzz of a text message coming through on her mobile. She patted around for her phone on the nightstand. *Not there.* She snapped her eyes open and sat up, her chest heaving.

Then it clicked. She wasn't at home. She was at Rick's place. She hadn't dreamed the events of last night. They really had happened.

Rick had kissed her, not just once — three times! She sighed, ran her tongue slowly over her lips then touched them with her fingers. "Hang on! I kissed him the third time. Oh my God. I can't believe I did that!"

The alarm clock clicked over to eight-o-three. She reached for her handbag on the floor beside the bed and grabbed her mobile. A message from Rick. *I miss you.* She clutched the phone to her chest, her heart aflutter. Then she read his words again — and again and again.

She had to go see him. It was *so* not a rational decision, so totally unlike her usual play-it-safe persona. For the first time, she would go with her heart. It felt too right to ignore.

Eden skipped into the en suite and checked her appearance in the mirror. Her tousled dark hair toppled over her shoulders but overall, she looked refreshed. She brushed her teeth, had a quick toilet stop and returned to the bedroom.

A folded-up piece of paper protruded through the gap under the door. *A note?* He'd only just sent a text not long ago. She made a beeline for it and picked it up. Sure enough, it was a message from Rick in blue, backward-slanted handwriting.

*Dear Eden,*

*I woke up early this morning, full of inspiration, thanks to you.*

*I figured, seeing as I didn't get to do my poetry reading for you last night, I owed you a breakfast recital at the very least! ;-) I don't like breaking promises.*

*Anyway, meet you downstairs at about 10 a.m.? I'm assuming you like bacon.*

*Love,*

*Rick x*

Eden's heart skipped a beat, then two, as she reread his words. She couldn't believe what had happened between them in such a short time. Only a week ago she'd never anticipated her life would become this wonderful. It really did seem too good to be true.

She folded the note, held it against her heart then filed it away in the front pocket of her handbag. Should she still go to his room? Maybe she should wait until ten, as specified. Maybe he wasn't ready yet. But what would she do with herself for an hour and a half?

Eden plonked down on the bed, fidgeted, got up and paced. *Stuff it!* She needed to do something impulsive for a change.

Her initial strides toward his bedroom were swift and confident—however, she slowed down the closer she got to his door. *What am I doing?* If she knocked, would that lead him on? Would he think it meant she wanted sex? Because she did, more than anything.

Grace would be so proud. But should she go there yet? Shouldn't she really get to know him a bit more first? She hadn't even known him a week. What if they just had incredible chemistry with no substance? She needed more than that.

Eden fingered her rose key pendant. What should she do? If she went by the pulsing warmth of her soulmate ring, she wouldn't hesitate. But she didn't want to look desperate.

*Just knock. Yes. Just knock and see what happens.* She could always stop things if he went off the gentlemanly course. Though, what if she couldn't? What if… *Stop it! Come on.* He definitely wasn't the groping sleazy type…right? Before she had a chance to change her mind, she rapped on his bedroom door.

*Footsteps.* Moving in her direction. Eden's breathing caught and ratcheted along her airway. The door eased open, revealing Rick in just low-hanging pajama pants that matched the top she'd chosen.

*Oh. My. God.* How hot could a man be? Her gaze snagged on his generous package. *Eyes up, eyes up.* Heat flared in her cheeks, and she couldn't make eye contact.

Around his neck hung the familiar cross necklet, the bottom of it dipping into a sprinkling of soft, golden-brown hair that spanned his chest. Her gaze drifted to his washboard stomach and lower to the golden-brown trail leading down from his navel.

Eden's mouth watered. A trip down there would be beyond paradise. She squeezed her fingertips into her palms, itching to reach out and touch him.

"Obviously you got my text...and my note. Though I'm pretty sure I said ten, didn't I?" Rick asked.

*How do I explain myself now?* "Yes, sorry, um..."

"I'm mucking around. I hoped you'd come and see me first. So, thanks."

She lifted her gaze to meet his stare. "Thanks for your messages. They were so... I've never felt... You're very thoughtful."

Rick smiled and grabbed her hand. "Come and sit with me," he said, and led her to his unmade bed.

His hand felt electric, yet so snug and secure that she didn't even think twice about going with him.

The giant room looked huge, even with a king-size, four-poster bed eating up the space. And the overall gold-and-black-themed décor provided greater warmth than the cooler silver and black tones in the spare bedroom.

On the left, a door led into an en suite, and on the right, an entrance led to what appeared to be a study-cum-private library. Inside, a black gothic desk was bathed in natural morning light and the walls were lined with books, standing to attention like rows of faceless, multicultural soldiers.

"You look really sexy, by the way," he said, checking her out.

"Oh...um...thanks." Her cheeks burned at his overt approval. "You don't look too shabby yourself."

He chuckled. "Thanks."

They sat on his bed, right beside each other, their thighs connecting like an induction stove top. Rick stared into her eyes for what felt like an eternity, then he looked down, let go of her hand and stood.

He took a few steps, stopped, then a few more and came to stand right in front of her. "I thought, seeing you're here, that I could do my little poetry reading for you now instead of waiting until breakfast. What do you think? Aren't you glad you came early?" he joked.

Eden laughed. *Came. With him.* If only... "That would be nice. And yes, I am."

He smiled and sucked in a deep breath. "It's only short, but heartfelt. And the extra benefit is that I won't bore you. Well, hopefully I won't. Okay, here goes... It's called, *Private Connection.*" He cleared his throat.

*"Night fell*
*a cloak shielding*
*Truth*
*that can't be spoken*
*Except between each other..."*

Eden closed her eyes and tuned in to his exquisite words, intermingled with his deep, seductive voice. Her heart swelled to bursting. His poem sounded familiar, as though he'd spoken those words to her before, like they'd had a loving, longstanding relationship.

It added to the string of déjà vu moments since they'd met. It had to be fragments from a dream...or possibly another sign, reinforcing they were perfect for each other.

*"Love, a connection*
*between two hearts*
*and minds*
*Matching desire."*

He stopped speaking and watched her, as though trying to gauge her response.

Tears welled in her eyes. "That was really beautiful. Thank you."

Rick smiled, but a small, nervous twitch tugged on one corner of his lips. "I'm really glad you like it." He fidgeted with the poem in his hand, rolling the edges, up, down, up, down, up, down.

"Um…" He headed over to the closest bedside table, spread the poem out flat, then retrieved something from the drawer. "This isn't the way I envisaged doing this, but I need to go with how I feel and, bizarrely, this feels right."

He stood in front of her, his hands behind his back. "It took me ages to get to sleep last night. I couldn't stop thinking about things…about you, until I made a decision.

"I kept trying to convince myself I shouldn't rush into anything, but I can't help it. I've never met anyone like you before. I've never connected with someone as deeply as I have with you…on every level. We just hit it off so well. We're so in sync. I mean, check out what we're wearing. I think it's a sign. We're meant to be together."

He'd said exactly what she thought. They were so aligned that it was uncanny. But his speech couldn't be traveling down the proposal path. Not yet. *Could it?* Eden stared at him, her heart in her throat.

"I know you'll probably think this is a bit premature and probably crazy…" He dropped down on one knee and locked his eyes on hers. "I love you, Eden. I'm in love with you, and I want you to be with me every day, every night. I want you to be my wife. Will you marry me?"

"Yes!" she said, without thought, dizzy with joy and disbelief.

A huge smile spread across Rick's face. He gently grabbed her hand and slid an antique gold and ruby heart ring on her wedding finger. "According to my research, this betrothal ring originates in the Middle Ages, and it looks like it's been in my family for generations. I hope you like it."

"I love it! It's beautiful!" Her eyes welled up again. "And it fits perfectly. I feel like Cinderella." She sniffled, a joyous droplet spilling out of her eye and rolling down her cheek.

Rick reached up and caressed her face, wiping away the slowly descending tear. "So, obviously, I'm Prince Charming."

She threw her arms around his neck. "Obviously."

Rick kissed her mouth, nose, forehead, love and excitement infused in his every touch. Then he sought out her lips again and leaned her back against his bed.

He slid his hands over her curves. "It's so hard to resist you." His hot breath scorched her skin.

"Then don't." Eden threaded her fingers through his golden-brown hair and brought his mouth to hers. She lifted her bare leg and hooked it over and around his waist so they were intimately intertwined.

He pulled back and chuckled.

She pouted.

Rick looked into her eyes and stroked her hair, which did delicious things to her scalp and right down to her sex. She never would have dreamed the two would be sexually interconnected. Then again, it seemed no matter where Rick touched her, her body sang.

"There's no hurry, is there? We're already rushing things enough as it is. Don't you think?"

*What?* Since when did a guy slam the brakes on sex? "I can't believe you just said that. Shouldn't that have been *my* line?"

He chuckled again, in an I've-got-a-real-nymphomaniac-on-my-hands kind of way. Wouldn't most guys be pleased, excited, jump at the opportunity? But no, not tame, controlled, do-the-right-thing Rick.

Eden's smile faded. "Don't you want to…?"

"Of course. More than anything. I'm sure you can feel that pretty strongly at the moment," he said with a wicked grin. "It's just… I know it sounds old-fashioned, but I'd like to wait. Not for ages. I promise I'm not repressed or anything. It's just…I've never been like other guys.

"It's not that I don't crave sex. I do. I just want it to be more than a physical act. Not that physical pleasure isn't good, it's great. It's just… I want the experience to be deeper than that. If I'm only after a bit of meaningless pleasure, I can always do it myself, right? Sorry if that's a bit crude, but it's the truth."

Rick smoothed her hair and drew long, soothing lines along her spine. "The thing is, if I'm sharing the experience with someone else, then I want it to be a celebration of the love, loyalty and devotion we have for each other.

"I want to share that experience with the woman I marry, the woman I choose to spend the rest of my life with. I want to have something a little extra special to look forward to on our wedding night, something we can celebrate together, just us, commemorating our unique union."

*So much for Grace's claim that sweet, masculine, gorgeous men didn't exist in contemporary society.*

He propped up on one elbow and kissed her temple. "Don't worry. I'm not a fundamentalist Christian either. I'm not even religious. It's just the way I feel. These days most people can't understand or relate to it. That's why I've always felt like I should have been born in another time."

"Me too... Umm...if you're not religious, what's with all the cross jewelry?"

"Good question. I inherited it with the house. I found the necklet and ring in among a whole heap of junk in the attic. Luckily, I didn't accidentally toss it out. I swear, it was like a hoarder's paradise up there. I even found the engagement ring I gave you and a pair of gold wedding bands. I know they're only material things, but they're special to me. They're the only connection I have with my family."

She understood all about grasping on to tenuous connections and sentimental value.

"As soon as I laid eyes on the cross ring and pendant, I developed an affiliation to them. I can't explain it except to say I feel right with them on. They're like my little security blanket, like a lucky charm. I feel protected, for want of a better word. I know I probably sound insane—"

"No, you don't." She kissed his sultry lips. "You sound intuitive and passionate, and I love that."

He kissed her forehead, the tip of her nose, her mouth. "Thanks. I can't tell you how good it is to finally meet a woman who I'm not only incredibly attracted to on every level, but who also doesn't find my quirks too confronting. You might have noticed I can be a bit full on at times. It's just that...when I know what I want, I give it my full attention and energy."

*Definitely a keeper.* "It's a good philosophy to have. I admire it. Unfortunately, I tend to get consumed by uncertainty and fear, especially around men. Thank goodness you were focused and persistent when it came to us. If we'd had to rely on me to get things happening, we'd still be eyeing each other at that nightclub...till we were forty, assuming you hadn't given up on me by then. I'm hoping to absorb some of your strength by osmosis."

He laughed. "You are so adorable."

"Thanks." Eden tucked his hair behind his ear. "Can I ask you something?"

Rick lay back down and tightened his arms around her. "Ask me anything you like."

"If you knew you had feelings for me, why did it take you so long to act on them?"

His glorious, green eyes gazed into hers. "This is going to sound weird, though you're probably used to it by now, seeing I've been saying that all night. Every time I've tried to have relationships with women in the past, they've gone nowhere.

"Things always seemed fine at first until I touched or kissed them. Then I felt nothing. Seriously, nothing. Only their scent still held some appeal. It's as though all the attraction suddenly ceased to exist. It left me feeling guilty about telling the girl I'd lost interest, because strangely, her attraction to me seemed to have grown. Heaps.

"It felt like the women extracted and absorbed every ounce of my desire, leaving me emotionally empty." He shook his head, as though trying to erase the building torment.

"Seeing the hurt and disbelief in their eyes... It was awful. I felt like a total prick. But I couldn't pursue a romantic relationship if the woman's touch no longer turned me on. So I got all nervous and hesitant about being intimate with you because I worried it would work out the same way, and I really didn't want that to happen."

He brushed a few loose strands of hair off her face and she leaned into his touch. "This is probably going to sound stupid, but I thought if I invested my time in getting to know you and developed strong feelings, it would override everything else. That's why I held off. Don't get me wrong. It wasn't easy. Many, many times I wanted to touch you, kiss you, but the possible negative outcome made me too afraid to even try.

"Instead, I focused on giving us the best chance of connecting first. And even though my instinct pushed me to cross the physical divide, I would have held off longer if you hadn't fallen asleep on me. As soon as you touched me, I knew it was right."

*Incredible.* Their experiences were almost identical. They really were two soulmate peas in a pod. "That doesn't sound stupid at all. You're right. It does sound weird, though not in the way you think. You see, I've had the exact same experience with men...until you.

"That's why I reacted how I did after you kissed me the first time. The emotions you stirred up overwhelmed me, took me by surprise. I didn't know how to respond. Like you, I'd never had those feelings before, but I knew they were right. I knew that's how things were supposed to feel."

"Exactly." Rick held her face between his hands and planted a kiss on her lips. "What I feel for you is so foreign, so opposite. I just can't seem to get enough of you..."

His I-want-to-fuck-you-into-next-year look talked straight to her sex and she squeezed her thighs together to stem the sensual ache.

"Anyway, I think we'd better change the subject before I get carried away again..." He took a deep breath. "So, are we just going to sit around in my pajamas all day or shall we do something?"

"Hmmm...I wouldn't mind you getting carried away again," she said and rubbed against him.

He laughed. "And here I was thinking you're a good girl."

"I am, normally. You're obviously a bad influence."

Rick smacked his hand against his heart. "Me? No way! I'm a good boy. I think we both know who the naughty one is around here," he said, and slapped her bottom.

"Ouch!" She laughed, and wriggled against him.

They slipped under the covers, and Rick lay on his back while Eden rested her head on his shoulder and nestled the full length of her body against his side. She caressed his chest, playing with the smattering of golden-brown hair, still trying to get her head around what had happened. *Please don't let it be an elaborate dream.*

"I love you, Eden," Rick said, and kissed the top of her head, reinforcing everything was real.

Her stomach somersaulted and she angled her head to look into his eyes. "I love you too."

He stroked her cheek, his smile broad and seductive, then leaned in and kissed her lips.

Eden pressed into him, the kiss heating up. With the tip of her tongue, she licked along his neck, then bit down and sucked on a patch of skin below his jawline, creating a hefty red love bite. "Oops!" She laughed. "Looks like you might need to wear a scarf."

"Thanks for the heads up, but I don't mind showing it off. You might, though." Rick's lips curled up in a roguish grin. "Everyone will finally know you're not the nice girl you appear to be."

"Surely you wouldn't damage my reputation."

"I think you've done that all on your own."

"I have not!" She playfully punched his arm.

"You do realize you've set a precedent now." His stare devoured her as though she represented a rare Wagyu steak. "Hmmm…shall I make a matching one or try another spot?"

"You wouldn't…"

"Pick a spot or I will," he said, with a teasing twinkle in his eye.

"Um…"

"You better hurry…"

"All right, all right. How about here?" Eden traced the top inner curve of her left breast.

"Mmm…very nice choice." Rick kissed the designated spot, sending tingles deep into her core.

He slid his hand along her thigh and bit and sucked on her milky-white flesh. She gasped. Sharp pain contrasted with his soft, cushiony lips and warm, moist tongue. She wanted to rip off her clothes and feel his mouth all over her body, but she refrained, given his virtuous speech earlier.

He moved lower, his hot breath blowing on her pubic bone, then her inner thigh, and he bit and sucked on the new section of skin. Pure, irrational desire pumped through her and she reached down to shed her underwear.

He stopped her hand and she whimpered and arched against him. Then he moved back up, and their lips reconnected.

"That's enough," he murmured against her mouth.

"No. Come on!" She kissed every sensitive spot on his neck, trying to manipulate him into submission.

He shivered, his body betraying his words. "Uh-uh. You know, teasing you is so much fun."

"Ugh." Eden groaned. She'd just have to keep working on him until he fell off the edge of decency and succumbed.

"We're going to have a great time a month from Friday."

*What?* Her eyebrows drew together. "A month from Friday?"

"Yep. If you have no objections, I thought we could get married up at Cradle Mountain on that Friday afternoon."

So Rick was closer to caving than she'd thought. They'd be making love in a month. Just thinking about it got her sex all soaked.

"Unless you think it's too soon. It's the quickest we can get a marriage license. But we can wait longer if you want. That's totally fine with me."

"No. It's perfect. But how are we going to get time off work on such short notice? And don't we need witnesses and a celebrant? And who's going to look after Smokey and Thornton?"

Rick touched his index finger to her lips. "Leave it to me. I'll get everything sorted. All you need to do is decide on an outfit and turn up."

She stared into his fathomless green eyes, as though they held the secrets to a joyous journey together. "I'm going to ask Grace to be my bridesmaid."

"I might ask Simon to be my groomsman then. I have a good feeling about those two. I reckon they'll hit it off really well."

She snuggled into him. "I guess we'll soon see…"

\* \* \* \*

*Sub Rosa basement lab, Tasmania, December 1965*

Weightless, hovering in the depths. Snippets, flashes of fractured memories floated in and out of X1944's mind. *His* thick, golden-brown hair, *his* playful light green eyes. So tender, loving. Though who was he? Who was *she*? Would she ever know again?

Dark and floaty and fluid, she felt like a baby in a womb waiting to be born. But when and how? With no sense of time or the length of gestation, she should be anxious. But she experienced no stress, just calm.

It had to be her chance at a new existence…assuming she hadn't died. Maybe she'd already reached heaven. This buoyant space couldn't be hell. It was too relaxing, though way too limbo-like to be a final resting place.

Did a fetus experience these sensations? Not that she was a fetus. No way would *he* feature so prominently in her memory if she hadn't had a life.

How did she end up in this cool, barren place? And what had happened to *him*? Had they been together? Or was he a figment of her imagination—a dream, a vision, a wish? Her flimsy memory felt like it had been hole-punched, leaving a stack of unreadable gaps.

Hope, fear, delusion or plain naivety, she sensed in her waters that she would get out of here…eventually. And when she did, she needed to find *him*, the man with the magnetizing green eyes, and be with him.

Maybe they could make sense of this weirdness together.

# Chapter Ten

## The Wedding Plans

*Hobart, June 2010*

Rick took Eden's hand and led her out of his bedroom on a tour of the rest of the house, ending at the conservatory. The extensive windows looked out into a rambling back garden full of Australian native and English-cottage-garden-style plants, the sunlight breaking through gaps in the dissipating fog.

Misty tendrils, like wisps of cotton wool, weaved around and draped over leaves and branches, unraveling as the sun's rays injected them with concentrated heat.

He turned to her and said, "Let's eat breakfast out here. If you're cold, I can turn the heater up —"

She squeezed his hand. "It's perfect."

He smiled. "Good. I'll go get breakfast started. I don't know about you, but I'm starving."

"Me too. I'll come and help you."

Rick kissed her forehead. "No. I want you to just relax. Even though you're officially my fiancée, you're technically still a guest, and I like my guests to just take it easy."

"What are you saying? After we're married, I'll have to start slaving away like a good little 1960s housewife?" she joked.

"Yeah, pretty much." With a cheeky grin, he leaned in, brushing his lips against hers, then kissed a slow, sensual path to the pulse point at the base of her neck. "Mmmm…you smell delicious."

"Must be the men's toiletries."

He chuckled, his hot breath teasing her skin. "What would you like to eat?"

She dropped her head back and to the side, encouraging him to discover her throat's most sensitive spots. "I believe you promised me bacon."

His slow, open-mouthed kisses drove her to the edge of decorum. "I did. What else would you like with it? I've got eggs, mushrooms, tomatoes and I can make toast."

"What? No hash browns?" She feigned disappointment, trying to divert her attention from ripping off Rick's clothes.

"Sorry, all out. I'll drive you through Maccas later though, if you're a good girl." He kissed his way back up to her mouth and swiped his tongue across her bottom lip.

She whimpered. "I suppose that's reasonable." *More reasonable than tugging down your pajama pants with my teeth.*

He let go of her hand, slapped her bottom and headed toward the kitchen.

"Ouch!" Eden rubbed her throbbing behind. It didn't actually hurt. The smack surprised her, especially the way it inflamed her desire.

"Take a seat…if you can." His laugh loitered in the cool, open space. "I'll be back soon."

"I'd like my eggs poached, please," she called after him, still recovering from his kisses and sensual spank.

"No worries."

"And I'll have mushrooms and tomatoes too, if it's not too much trouble."

"It's the least I can do."

Eden remained standing by the window, lost in a rabbit-hole of thoughts and lingering lust. The relationship between them felt easy and comfortable, like they'd known each for ages. Add to that the look and feel of his house. It rang bells in her mind…with no clear memory attached.

She searched her brain for a connection. Only snippets of familiarity surfaced, intermingled with blankness, like scenes cut out of a roll of film. His arms winding around her waist snapped her back to the present.

He skimmed his feather-light lips along her neck and she sighed.

"We should eat before the food gets cold." Rick's voice vibrated against her skin and longing reverberated through her body.

"Yes," she said, but didn't move.

Rick held her hand and steered her toward the wicker and wrought iron, glass-topped table. "I forgot to ask what you'd like to drink."

"Is it too early for champagne?"

"It's never too early for champagne…or celebrating. I'll grab you a glass."

"Seriously, a juice is fine."

He returned with her drink, sporting his signature gorgeous grin, and sat opposite her. "So, have you decided how you'd like to spend the rest of the day?"

*In bed, with your hands and mouth all over me.* Furnace-hot flames shot into Eden's cheeks and she had a sip of juice to cool her sex-crazed thoughts. "Actually, yes. If it's okay with you, I'd love to hang out here and have a stroll in your beautiful garden while we fine-tune the wedding plans."

"Excellent idea."

After breakfast, they both showered, separately, and Eden dressed in her clothes from the night before. When she came out of the spare room, Rick was leaning against the intricate balustrading, his hair damp, and looking scrumptious in a cream V-neck jumper and black cargo pants.

His gaze wandered over her. "You know what I'd love to do right now? Press you up against that wall, slip my hand under your dress, slide it along your thigh until it reaches the edge of your panties and —"

"Rick!" A throbbing ache pounded, hard and persistent, between her legs.

"Don't you want to hear how it ends?"

*Yes, yes, yes!* "I think I have a pretty good idea."

"And would you like that?"

She shuffled from foot to foot. "Maybe."

"I think it's more than 'maybe', given your behavior earlier." *God, that sexy voice.*

Her faced burned. He could read her like an open, transparent book.

Rick interlaced his fingers with hers. "Anyway, shall we head out to the garden?"

They ambled in the glorious sun for a while then sat under a white gazebo in the far reaches of his backyard.

Birds twittered and chirped, as though rejoicing in their union.

Rick tilted her chin up and stared into her eyes. "I don't want you to go."

"I don't want to go either, but I have to. I have to feed Thornton and get my clothes ready for work tomorrow…"

Dejection infested his face and he slumped his shoulders.

She knew the feeling. "Hey, why don't you come and stay at my place tonight?"

Hope enlivened his eyes. "Really?"

"Yeah, definitely. You can pack what you need, get Smokey sorted and follow me back in your car. We can spend the night together, all very innocent of course," she said with a cheeky smile, "then go into work, have dinner and afterward you can drive home…or stay again. What do you think?"

"Hmmm…it's very tempting, but—"

"Oh, come on."

"I don't know. I should warn you. I sleep naked. Is that going to be a problem?"

*If he wants us to keep our hands off each other until the wedding, yes!* "Oh…um…"

"I'm only joking. Actually, no I'm not. I always sleep naked."

She shook her head. "You're shocking."

Rick lifted her onto his lap and held her tight. "That's why you love me."

# Chapter Eleven

## A Violet Tale

*1939 – 1997*

Hugh stumbled through the Norwegian forest, barely able to lift his feet. Where were all the elk? He salivated and collapsed in a crumpled heap on the pine-needle-covered ground. Four days had passed since he'd last eaten and his energy levels had faded…fast.

Faster with each minute that ticked by… His stomach had gone beyond growling to the verge of starvation and, just like in humans, it only meant one thing — death. *What a horrible way to go.*

The familiar sting of tears pricked his eyes and a salty droplet slid down his cheek. He shouldn't cry, not now, but he couldn't help it. Curling up into a ball, he wept until he'd wrung himself out, dry as an empty husk.

A reindeer frolicked in the snow-covered undergrowth, the sky a clear cobalt blue. Hugh crept up behind it and pounced, the deer morphing into an injured, bleeding man. Hugh snapped his eyes open and sat up.

*Dreaming about food. A bad sign.* He inhaled. A hint of biting, salty air tantalized his taste buds. A trace of blood? His mouth watered. He hoisted himself up and followed the scent, like a nose-to-the-ground bloodhound.

Across the river, an anchored boat bobbed in the water. He dove into the clear, ice-cold depths and swam toward it, the frostbitten wind laced with potent blood. It had to be a haul of gutted fish.

*Where is the fisherman?* Hugh grabbed hold of the edge of the boat, heaved himself up and flopped into it. No fish. Instead, beside him, an unconscious man bled from his temple.

Hugh leaned in and sniffed the red trickle. He licked his lips and stared at the oozing, delicious redness. *I can't.* An inordinate amount of saliva filled his mouth. He tried to gulp it down but it kept flowing, like a broken fire hydrant. *Just a taste, a drop.*

He licked the stream of blood, saliva dripping down his chin, and swallowed, then he dove straight back onto the open wound, like a hungry breastfeeding baby. *What am I doing?*

*Zap!* Intense heat shot through Hugh's neck and he fell to the side of the man, buzzing, shaking, paralyzed. A lumbering human stood over the top of him with a gun of some sort and a whopping sneer. *Caught by humans? A first time for everything.*

The turning point, 1939, surely was a time of change. While men were lining up to die for their country, the Sub Rosa Corporation had started collecting vampire samples as he'd heard to save humanity. *Who'd have ever thought it possible?*

The man had taken him prisoner and confined him to a cramped, damp room, Hugh languished, awaiting sustenance, like a morphine addict desperate for his next injection. His body's trembling, aching need went way beyond a normal craving.

Twelve hours into his captivity, two different men arrived — one holding the stun gun and the other a bowl with a steak and vegetable stew.

"Is that for me?" Hugh asked.

"Who else would it be for?" The man with the gun scoffed.

"Thanks, but I can't eat that."

The man turned to his colleague. "Precious little vampire on a special diet, is he?"

Hugh stared into his eyes. "I guess you could say that. I need blood."

The gunman raised his eyebrows. "Are you asking one of us to sacrifice ourselves?"

"No, of course not. I only drink animal blood."

"That's not what I've heard," the unarmed man said.

"What you've heard is wrong. Only a small percentage of us prey on humans. They're the ones that give the rest of us a bad name."

The gunman patted his pistol. "Oh, really?"

"Yes, I swear."

"You can swear all you want, but actions speak louder than words," the other man said.

Hugh screwed up his face. "What's that supposed to mean?"

"You were caught sucking the blood from an injured man," the unarmed man explained.

Hugh thumped his forehead with his palm and sighed. He dropped his hand into his lap, clasped his hands together and regained eye contact with the men. "I was delirious with hunger. Trust me... If I'd wanted to make a meal of the man, I would have done it way before I got shot."

The gunman shrugged. "If you say so."

"Looks like you won't be needing this then," the man holding the bowl said, and wolfed down the watery stew.

The two of them laughed and exited the cell.

Six hours later they returned, this time with a mug of fresh-ish blood. They had listened...surprisingly. Either that or they'd laced it with something. Hugh drank in the earthy aroma. No poison, as far as he could tell, just rat. Rodents were far from his favorite, but better than nothing.

He snatched the cup out of the man's hand and gulped down every last drop. The hunger pangs eased within minutes, yet he remained unsatisfied. Animal blood kept him going, though it never really hit the spot. It was like trying to satisfy a morphine craving with cannabis.

"Don't think you'll be getting a treat like this every day." The gun-toting man snickered.

Of course not. They couldn't possibly kill enough animals to keep all their vampire prisoners fed on a regular basis. *I have to get out of here.*

That night, recharged from the blood and darkness, Hugh yanked at the heavy metal door of his cell, breaking the lock and bursting free. He got captured and escaped, along with many others, countless times over the years until Sub Rosa introduced the concentrated sunlight barricade system in 1986.

Instead of heavy metal doors, beams of sunlight streamed down the front of his and the others' newly-renovated cells twenty-four hours a day. The space appeared more open, comfortable and free, yet he and the rest of the vampires remained trapped.

The Sub Rosa research staff had finally worked out how to tap right into the Violets' and the Jades' main weakness. Their high level of white blood cells conducted sunlight. So how did Hugh and other vampires walk around in the daylight? With difficulty. But it was possible with good planning and practice.

They needed shade breaks, decent clothing coverage and regeneration at night to remain functional. The more vampire genetics, the higher concentration of white blood cells and hence the greater need for respite from the sun.

His hybrid compatriots had a bit more flexibility. Half-caste vampires had half white blood cells and half red, giving them double the sun exposure time. Quarter-castes were made up of three quarters red blood cells and a quarter white, allowing them to behave almost as though they were fully human — human with high sun sensitivity.

A familiar buzz. Seconds later, singed air scorched his nostrils. Another new captive must have run at the sunlight bars in an attempt to break out. The first night they had been installed, he'd done the same. He shivered, reliving the force of the electric shock that had thrown him from the bars of sunlight and smashed him into the wall.

\* \* \* \*

*The bleakness of light, February 1986*

Hugh crashed to the floor, like a swatted fly, convulsing, shuddering, jerking. It felt as though he'd been tasered with sunlight at a hundred times the strength. And he'd thought the stun gun experience had been bad. This was much, much worse, catastrophic.

When the shuddering stopped, he tried to get up and failed, his body fully immobilized. Panic frizzled his attempt to problem solve. Was his brain fried too? He lay on the floor for hours before he could wriggle his fingers and finally push himself into a sitting position, his skin still radiating with the potent light.

A massive clap of thunder penetrated the air and an arc of brightness, like a shooting star, shone past his cell. *A system malfunction already?* He stared at the scorching radiance. It seemed to be morphing into a person—or maybe his retina had been burned when he'd tried to beat the bars. The radiant person shook and flashed like a strobe light.

The brightness dissipated, and he recognized his Violet neighbor from two cells up, now a person-shaped block of charcoal. Staff ran up both sides of the corridor with Taser guns drawn.

They neared the ashen vampire, flakes flying into the air, and he cleaved into millions of embers and disintegrated. By the second night, everyone had stopped trying to escape, except the occasional, desperate new captive.

As the prison filled, Sub Rosa staff could no longer manage the food demands and several vampires died from starvation. The absence of ingested red blood prevented absorption of required nutrients to support the function of their white blood cells and give them energy.

The prominence of white blood cells gave them their pale appearance and allowed accelerated healing. But without consumption of red blood, the white cells deteriorated, resulting in death.

Experimenting on corpses and malnourished vampires would have only yielded limited results, so the staff had to make changes. Using technology developed to prepare food for astronauts travelling into space, Sub Rosa introduced a Clayton's meal — an astringent supplement, a liquid multi-vitamin for vampires that contained the essential nutrients of red blood.

It gave some sustenance, and very basic nutrition, like comparing the smell and taste of banana lollies to real bananas. It was chemical and artificial, but lifesaving.

\* \* \* \*

*Interview with a Vampire, August 1996*

Hugh chugged down the mouth-puckering supplement and removed the small plastic vial from his mouth, a drop falling on his tongue. *Ergh!* He screwed up his face and coughed.

"Still no improvement, eh?"

Hugh smiled and turned toward the open door. "Salvator, please come in." His visitor reminded him of a stereotypical graying researcher — scraggy build, lopsided bow tie, crumpled, ill-fitting suit.

Salvator looked him in the eye. "I've spoken to them about the taste and smell and they assured me — "

"I don't doubt you. Somehow, I don't think it's a high priority for them to make changes." Hugh raised his eyebrows. "Anyway, have a seat," he said, and threw the small, empty container into the metal bin under his desk.

Salvator chose the same chair every time — a tapestry manual recliner. *And humans think vampires are territorial.* Hugh sat opposite him on the matching two-seater couch. "What did you want to talk about today?"

"ESP?" Salvator chuckled. "I was just about to ask you the same question."

Hugh grinned. "You know what they say? Great minds think alike."

"They do, they do..." Salvator grabbed a note pad and pen out of his blazer pocket. "So tell me, wise one, what would you like to enlighten me about this fine morn?"

Hugh swished his hand through the climate-controlled air. "Where do I start?"

"How about with your past? I'm sure I could learn a lot from your experiences."

Hugh swallowed the lump of raw emotion in his throat. *Don't cry.* "Do we have to talk about that?"

Salvator put the pen and pad down on the coffee table and looked him in the eye. "No. But I'm curious. I'll be honest, Hugh. You fascinate me. I enjoy spending time with you. There's something about you that's very calming. On the few occasions we've met, I've left feeling soothed and relaxed and have gone on to have an incredibly restful night's sleep. I haven't experienced peace like that in a very long time."

Hugh smiled. "Well, thank you, though your fascination is more likely linked to my innate vampire wiles than anything else. From what I understand, it's a genetic survival trait we have to draw in potential prey."

"I think it's more than that."

"Wow, my allure is stronger than I thought," Hugh joked.

"Seriously, if it were purely that then I'd feel it with all the others I've been interviewing, but I've only truly connected with you and one other from the Jade camp."

Hugh crossed his legs and leaned forward. "Really? Interesting. Tell me more..."

Salvator shook his head. "I'm here to learn about you."

"Given it's my session, don't I get to choose?"

"I suppose..."

"Good. It's settled. Before I disclose anything more about myself, you need to share something about you."

Salvator stared back at him, a flash of fear in his eyes. "What would you like to know?"

"Why are you really here?"

Salvator glanced down, his leg shaking. "For work."

"Your main driver is something else, though—something you won't talk about with anyone. But you should. It'll help. Part of your problem is you've tried to keep it buried and, instead, it's snowballing in your mind."

"You're very perceptive." Salvator wrung his olive-skinned hands in his lap. He coiled and uncoiled, coiled and uncoiled, coiled and uncoiled his fingers. "I've played a part in hurting two people close to me." Salvator hesitated, but continued. "I originally met them thirty-one years ago." He'd dialed the sound down on his voice to barely audible. "They also worked at Sub Rosa and volunteered to trial a soulmate serum I developed, based on an ancient alchemic formula.

"Anyway, they ended up being perfect for each other and got married almost straight away. They even asked me to be best man at the ceremony. We all just really hit it off. Then three months later, everything changed. *He* had found evidence linking Sub Rosa to unethical practices and misappropriation of funds and planned to go to the authorities. Before he could, he and his wife were detained and a senior manager directed me to dispose of them. I didn't realize who the detainees were until I arrived."

Salvator grasped his creased shirt, where it covered his chest. "My heart nearly stopped when I saw them. I had to find a way to save them—and quickly. The only workable solution I could think of was to use them for experimentation." He picked his pen up off the coffee table and flicked the button at the top. *Click click, click click.*

"Saying it aloud makes it sound even worse. You see, Sub Rosa had been trying to get ethics approval to do human testing of memory eraser and filler drugs, as well as assess the effects of freezing humans in their new, million-dollar cryogenic storage unit—however, it had been held up by bureaucratic red tape.

"It was the perfect opportunity to utilize my two friends." Salvator's remorseful gaze reconnected with Hugh's eyes. "I didn't want to suggest it, but if I hadn't, they would have been killed—and me along with them if I'd have refused."

Hugh edged forward in his seat, his stare glued to Salvator. "What happened to them?"

"Management at the time agreed to my proposal and my friends are still in cryogenic storage as we speak."

"I see. And are you sure they're still alive?"

The pen clicking stopped. "Yes. I monitor them closely."

"Even from here?"

"No, not from here. I left behind two experienced research staff to work with them and give me regular updates."

"When will you be able to let your friends go?"

Salvator hesitated. "I'm not sure. I can't have anyone recognize them, so I'm in a holding pattern until staff who knew them leave or pass away."

"It's getting to you, all this waiting and uncertainty. That's why you're here, isn't it? To escape."

Salvator sighed. "I needed to find a way to feel useful and engaged, to speed up time and stop the nagging, regretful thoughts."

"But it's not working as well as you'd hoped," Hugh probed.

The pen clicking resumed. "No. I've been trying to immerse myself in my work here, but... I thought if I could just find a way to help others—"

"It would act as a sort of atonement for your actions."

Salvator's hazel eyes were moist with remorseful tears. "Yes. I can't tell you how bad I feel, how ashamed I am. But what other choice did I have? It was the only way to keep them alive."

"Was it?"

Salvator put his pen down and squirmed in his seat. "I suppose I could have found a way to free them, though it would have been a huge risk for the three of us. If they had been caught and their escape tracked back to me, we would have all been killed. I chose what I thought was the safest path."

Hugh studied Salvator's sad eyes. Sincerity lingered there—and regret, but it sounded like he'd done the best he could at the time. "For what it's worth, from what you've told me, I think you did the right thing."

Salvator breathed out hard. "Thanks. That's what I keep trying to tell myself. It still doesn't excuse what they've been put through. If they... *When* they make it

out alive, I don't think I'll ever be able to face them."
He buried his face in his hands.

Hugh reached forward and touched the man's bony
shoulder. "You're stronger than you think."

Salvator glanced at Hugh's hand on him, his eyes
glazed. "Being in your presence, I can almost believe
anything is possible."

Hugh patted Salvator's shoulder and dropped his
hand. "Because it is. I never give up hope of getting out
of here permanently and meeting my soulmate, even
though it seems impossible at the moment."

Wishing his Violet vampire brother, David, and
David's forbidden Jade fiancée, Oriel, good luck and
farewell flashed into Hugh's mind. "I made a special
unity ring once, using an alchemic formula, with the
intention of it linking me with my soulmate. It wasn't
too dissimilar to your interest in developing a soulmate
serum, I suspect. However, the ring's purpose lay
elsewhere. Soulmates at risk of separation were drawn
to it and it helped them stay bonded."

"Where's the ring now?" Salvator asked.

"I've lost track of it. My one consolation is that it will
stay where it's most needed. So that leaves me with
only my mind and intuition to guide me on my quest.
But I'm not worried. I've learned you can harness the
power within yourself. What you believe positions you
where you need to be to make things happen.

"Things don't always work out in the way you
anticipate, but you need to remain focused and patient.
There are no specific timelines attached to reaching
your end goal. You're here for a reason, as am I. It's part
of both our destinies."

Salvator grabbed his pen and notepad, scribbled
something and glanced up. "Have you thought of

doing the motivational speaking circuit? I think you might even give Anthony Robbins a run for his money."

Humor. A hurting man's attempt at coping, escaping reality. "Ha-ha. If you look really closely at any situation, you can usually find some positive in it, even if it's only heightened self-awareness so you can make better decisions in future."

Salvator's breathing slowed and the pain and tightness in his face fell away. "You really are quite inspiring. Thank you for being non-judgmental. I feel like a ten-ton weight has been lifted off my chest."

"I'm glad I could help." Hugh couldn't delay any longer. Salvator had held up his crushing end of the bargain. "I suppose it's my turn now."

"Yes," Salvator said with pen poised. "Tell me about yourself, from the beginning, from when you were still human."

"How do you know I wasn't born a vampire?" Most humans assumed it was an option.

"You understand humanness and human frailties too much. Then there's the scientific practicality. If being a full vampire freezes a person at that age, then a conceived, full vampire embryo would remain an embryo, and I imagine would naturally abort."

"Excellent deduction. In terms of full vampires empathizing with humans, I'm sure you're aware not all of them share my thinking. There are some who, although they've been human, have retained no compassion for humanity."

"Yes. But they were probably always opportunistic, self-centered types."

"True…"

Salvator flicked over to a blank page in his notepad. "So...how old are you?"

"I was born in 1206."

Salvator's head shot up and his pen dropped onto the tiled floor. "Whoa! I had no idea."

"Yes, we full vampires hold our age well." Hugh grinned.

"You don't look a day over twenty-five." Salvator picked up his pen and repositioned himself in his seat.

"Funny you should say that. I turned twenty-five the year I got changed."

"What happened?"

Hugh took a deep breath and exhaled slowly. It had been centuries since he'd spoken aloud about his life. But he could do it, and hold the tears at bay...hopefully.

"I worked as a fisherman. As an only child, my parents relied on me to provide food and a living. My father had groomed me from birth to follow in his footsteps. Even if I didn't make much money, at least we could still eat.

"My parents had had me late in life and were no longer fit enough to manage on their own. I didn't mind the added responsibility. In fact, I considered myself fortunate. Most of my friends' parents had already passed, so I worked really hard to hold on to mine as long as possible.

"Although I enjoyed fishing, if I'd had a choice, I wouldn't have chosen it as a career. My real passion was alchemy, and in the little free time I had, I hung out with the best. They did amazing things — turned rocks into gold, quartz into diamonds, hate into love.

"I wanted to join them — however, the inconsistent pay would have prevented me from providing for my parents in the same way. So I relegated alchemy to a hobby and focused on practicalities." Hugh paused and gathered his thoughts.

"Things were going well, for the most part. I had dreams of finding a wife and having a family..." The familiar burning prickled behind his eyes. *Not now.* Hugh swallowed, and forced a smile. "I still remember my last day as a human. Most of my human memories have faded over the years, but this one is still quartz-crystal clear, as though somehow etched into my brain."

Salvator leaned forward and stared, his eyes eager for information.

"When I left home, the conditions were sunny and calm, perfect for bringing in a huge haul. I could hardly contain my excitement. Within an hour, I reached my favorite river mouth and had only just dropped my net into the water when the weather changed.

"The sky became an ominous black and the water raging and choppy, tossing me about and making me horribly seasick. I'd never gotten seasick and it scared me. It meant the conditions had turned dangerous. I used all my energy to try to steer the boat to safety, yet I only moved where the wild winds and water took me."

The memory of the rough water, of bouncing around in the small boat, roiled Hugh's stomach. "Even though I knew the area well, I became disorientated. I decided the safest thing would be to wait until the conditions settled rather than waste all my strength fighting something beyond me.

"I sat, shivering, with my eyes clamped shut and my teeth chattering, holding tight to the boat. I'd been caught in inclement weather many times before, but nothing that bad. Then just as quickly as it had started, it stopped. Everything went unnervingly calm.

"It took me a few moments to sense the peace. My waterlogged hair was plastered to my face and my cold, drenched clothes clung to my goosebumped skin. I inhaled as deep as my constricted lungs could stand, the icy cold air stinging and making me cough."

Salvator finished scrawling some notes and glanced up.

"When I opened my eyes, the sea rose, forming a giant wall of water only meters away and encroaching fast. Adrenaline kicked in and I tried to row myself out of danger, but I couldn't outrun the angry ocean. The enormous waves crashed down on me, destroying my boat and throwing me against the nearby rocks.

"I hit my head hard and cracked it open. My last moments of human consciousness were of being dragged down into the depths, my warm blood pouring out into the freezing water and swirling around me. When I woke up, I had been reborn into my new life. It all happened not long before the outbreak of the civil war between the Violets and the Jades."

Hugh's flesh burned with the memory. "At first, I couldn't believe what I had become. I'd heard stories about non-humans and had always thought they were folklore, born out of ignorance and fear. It didn't frighten me, though. I saw it as my second chance. It took three days for me to transform into a full Violet, and I focused on how to get back to assisting my parents, how to help them cope."

Had the climate-controlled air turned scalding? Not even a bead of sweat sat on Salvator's skin. No, it had to be him and the physical impact of reliving his story. "I'd been banned from visiting my parents, yet I was determined to find a way. I snuck back to my old home to check how they were, careful that no one saw me.

"I wanted more than anything to tell them I was okay, to show them I'd survived. It broke my heart seeing them grieve. I visited every day for a month and always came back tearful. I felt frustrated, helpless. I didn't know what to do or how to assist them.

"One day I got back early and my new family caught me crying. When I saw the shock on their faces, I thought I'd be punished...but no. They explained they'd never seen anyone who had been transformed retain that ability.

"Throughout my human life, I'd been a passionate, emotional person, so it didn't surprise me that I'd held on to that human trait. For a man, I'd always been highly attuned to my emotions, though not to a pathetic level. Although sensitive, I'd like to think I had...have...a reasonable amount of emotional intelligence."

Salvator furiously jotted down additional notes, his handwriting more hieroglyphs than English alphabet.

"My new family speculated over what my crying might mean. I just hoped one day my special ability would be able to help rather than hinder others."

Hugh paused, giving Salvator time to catch up. His ears had to be strained and his hand aching, trying to keep up with Hugh's soft speech. "Over the years, I've come across other Violets who reported having similar, yet different, experiences. One woman explained how her intelligence thrived and another said her vision not only allowed her to see clearly in the dark but also through solid objects.

"Going purely by anecdotal evidence, my guess is there are about ten percent of us who have these special powers. It's unclear how they occur. I'm assuming there's a genetic influence and possibly an environmental component."

Salvator stopped writing and rubbed his hand, his hazel eyes bright with possibilities. "I could arrange some testing to try to figure it out."

"I don't think you'll get too far. In fact, I doubt you'll get anyone else to own up to having any special abilities. We're already being poked and prodded enough as it is."

Salvator leaned back in his chair, sober realization flooding his face. "Sorry. Sometimes the scientist in me gets a bit carried away."

Hugh grinned. He'd had the same experience when in the midst of an alchemy experiment. "I can see that. If it's any consolation, you're not like the others. You seem to have a genuine interest in us and our culture."

Salvator put the notepad and pen down next to him and focused on Hugh. "I do. For me, research is about finding answers and improving things. It's not about taking advantage of or hurting anyone."

"And yet you work here."

Salvator leaned in close to his ear. "Only because my hands are tied, shackled really, and I'm still searching for the right key. I've thought about leaving many times, but I can't, not with the predicament I've put my friends in. I've even considered going to the authorities, like my friends had planned to. However, that would put me in danger—and them too.

"I just can't risk it. So, for the time being, I'm stuck here. And while I am, I'm focusing on making things as ethical, above-board and fair as possible."

Hugh studied him for a few moments. "I believe you."

Salvator smiled, like Hugh's opinion really mattered to him and not just because it gave him an experimental foot in the door. "Thanks. Any other interesting vampire facts you can share with me?"

"That depends."

"On what?"

"What you're going to do with the information."

Salvator propped his forearms on his knees. "Let me assure you that whatever you tell me, I plan to use to try to free you and all the others and get this place shut down," he said, his voice pin-drop soft.

Hugh stared into Salvator's eyes. "You really mean that."

"Yes."

"So I should trust you."

"I know it's a lot to ask, but yes."

Salvator's body language and words matched, which meant he was either telling the truth or was an expert at lying. According to Hugh's gut, he believed the former rather than the latter.

"All right. I'll give you the benefit of the doubt." Hugh edged closer and whispered, "Did you know there are magnetic properties in the vampire DNA sequence, subconsciously drawing us to one another?"

Salvator shook his head.

"Up until I started mixing more into human society, I hadn't noticed it. Any time I passed near even a quarter vampire, I felt at ease, a sense of belonging. It seemed almost like our DNA acted as a natural radar. I imagine it's a survival thing, to retain strength in numbers."

Wonder flashed across Salvator's face. "Wow. That's pretty amazing. I'd *love* to do a study on that. But, I know, it's useless trying to pursue it…at the moment."

He resumed taking notes. "I'm curious... Whatever happened to your parents?"

The dreaded question. Hugh swallowed back tears and retreated into the couch. "A few months into my new existence, I had an idea, a way I could let my parents know I'd survived without putting them in danger.

"So from then until the day they died, I brought them fish and a living like I always had, but in a quarter of the time. Being a full Violet made me stronger, faster, fitter and almost invincible.

"I can never forget the surprise on their faces the first time — and every time after. Even though it's been several hundred years since they passed, I still think about them every day." Hugh blink, blink, blinked to soothe the stinging in his eyes and stop the flow of tears before it started.

"Are you okay?"

Salvator's image morphed into a mishmash of color and the room became a blurry mess, like standing too close to an Impressionist painting. Cool tears trickled down Hugh's cheeks. "Yes, thanks." The tears wouldn't stop.

Salvator discarded his notepad and pen and moved to the edge of his seat. "Is there something I can do to help?"

"Not really. Sorry about this."

"Don't be sorry. I feel privileged I've had the opportunity to see your tears firsthand. Sorry if that sounds a bit...brutal."

Hugh sobbed and chuckled at the same time. "There's that scientist coming out again. Well, don't just sit there. Aren't you going to collect some samples?"

"Are you sure?"

"Of course." Hugh moved until his mouth almost grazed Salvator's ear. "As long as you use them for good, as you promised."

\* \* \* \*

*A tearful analysis*

Hugh carried a glass of special wine in one hand and an espresso coffee for Salvator in the other. "How many buckets did you say there were?"

Salvator sat down in his usual position, notepad and pen at the ready. "Three... And the tears glow in the dark, like they're alive. Did you know that?" His awe-filled eyes gleamed.

"I did. But don't ask me what it means." Hugh put his ornate pewter goblet and Salvator's short black down on the coffee table and took his usual seat, opposite him.

"Thanks," Salvator said, glancing up. "I'll definitely be checking that out."

"I'd be interested to know what you find." Hugh took a large mouthful of purple wine. "Oh, and thanks for pushing for us to have access to our personal possessions. It makes being here a bit more tolerable."

Salvator sipped his steaming hot coffee. "It's the least I could do."

"You know, I haven't had a crying episode like that for quite a while."

"What brought it on last time?" Salvator asked, pen hovering over his notepad.

"Someone asked about my parents. I still miss them, as you can see."

"How about your vampire parents?"

Nostalgia crowded his mind with memories. Hugh smiled. "They were wonderful too. They taught me a lot. They saved me, and I will be forever indebted."

"Where are they now?" Salvator asked.

"Unfortunately, they were killed in the civil war in the 1400s. Their home sat right in the middle of the war zone. They'd been in the same spot in Norway for hundreds of years and refused to flee, more because of my mother than my father. She had a sentimental attachment to the place. She used to say the only way she'd leave was in a wooden box. Unfortunately, her words became a self-fulfilling prophecy."

Salvator finished his note and regained eye contact. "That's really sad. But I'm curious... How is it you're able to speak about their deaths without crying?"

Hugh had another sip of the special wine. "Good question. Although I cared for and respected them, they had lived long, happy lives and had a choice to escape. They chose not to, though. My birth parents, on the other hand, were vulnerable and had circumstances thrust upon them that were beyond their control."

Salvator drained his cup and placed it on the saucer. "Other than your birth parents, what else brings on the tears?"

"The longest lasting, most intense episodes occur when I'm really sad and upset. But I've also been known to break down out of anger and frustration as well as joy."

Salvator tapped his chin, shifting his gaze up and to the left. "I wonder if the composition of the tears changes according to your mood?"

Hugh gulped down the remainder of his drink and placed the goblet on the coffee table. "I'm not sure, though the sad tears do feel thicker and taste saltier, more concentrated."

Salvator beamed like a little boy let loose in a lolly shop. "I'd love to get a range of samples."

"I'm sure you would, but I can't produce them on demand. The circumstances have to be right. However, if it happens while you're still on secondment, I'll collect samples for you."

"You would? That would be great."

Hugh could see the research cogs turning over and over in the scientist's mind.

Salvator tapped his pen on his notepad as though to refocus. "You mentioned before that your Violet parents saved you. How about others?"

"Yes, it's part of the culture. Contrary to popular belief, both the Violets and Jades are against killing humans for food. Instead, they've always hunted and farmed animals such as elk, deer, rabbits and bears. According to Violet laws, if any of us come across a badly injured, dying human, it's our duty to try to save them.

"If their vital signs are compromised, the human should be changed. That way, they can continue to exist as a person, just a different breed. However, there are rules around who can and can't be saved. Anyone under fifteen or over eighty-five would need to remain human, no matter how dire their circumstances."

Deep frown lines marred Salvator's forehead. "That seems very discriminatory. How were the ages chosen?"

"From drawing on catastrophic experiences over the years. It does sound heartless, choosing not to save a toddler, for example, but think of the long-term consequences. Once a human is changed, they will remain frozen at that age forever. Imagine a two-year-old vampire and the chaos they could cause.

"Children at that age are a law unto themselves. They'd be killing, feeding and transforming others without much thought. It would be a total disaster. I've seen a few cases over my lifetime and they caused incredible damage. One time, a sole toddler decimated a whole town."

"How was the toddler dealt with?" Salvator's contorted face and stiff body gave away his struggles with the concept.

"All sorts of behavior modification were trialed, but none were successful. So, the child had to be stopped."

Salvator's eyes widened and his mouth dropped open. "You mean...killed?"

Hugh hesitated, racking his brain for a nice way to say it. *Nope, no nice way to talk about enforced death.* "Unfortunately. Imagine being the person who had to do it."

Salvator shook his head as though to shake the offending information from his mind. "Awful, just awful. And how about the older folk?"

Hugh clasped his restless hands in his lap. "They start slowing down mentally and physically. Their decreased capabilities impact on their ability to feed and make the best all-around decisions. And just like in humans, a prolonged period without food leads to death. So, in the end, the community agreed the fifteen- to eighty-five-year window was the fairest, safest option for everyone."

Salvator's watch chimed. "Shit," he muttered, and collected his bits and pieces. "I'd love to continue discussing this, but I need to stop there for today. I have to get moving."

"Why so early?"

A cloak-and-dagger style smile spread onto Salvator's lips. "Let's just say I'm on the verge of a scientific breakthrough."

Hugh sat up straight in his chair. "Sounds intriguing. Anything you can tell me about?"

Salvator thought for a moment. "Not really. I wish I could, but—"

"It's classified. I understand."

Salvator stashed his notepad and pen in the blazer pocket of his creased brown suit and stood up. "Thanks again for being so candid with me. I'm hoping you'll soon be able to enjoy the fruits of my labor."

\* \* \* \*

*A break in the light, October 1996*

After dinner, Hugh reclined in his armchair, book in hand, when the sunlight bars flickered. He sat up and studied the streams of light. Three bars were missing on the far right-hand side.

A malfunction? Hugh jumped up to inspect the gap. Could he fit through it? He reached into the space and retracted his hand just before the sunlight beams blasted back into place.

*That was close!*

Salvator arrived early the next morning.

"Up with the birds today?" Hugh joked.

Disappointment shone on Salvator's face. "Something like that." His breath hissed, his face as deflated as a punctured tire.

"Is everything all right? You don't seem yourself."

Salvator slumped onto the couch opposite. "I'm sorry. I thought I'd finally made a breakthrough with that classified research project. However, the results aren't quite what I'd hoped."

"Oh, that's a shame. Do you think you're close?"

Salvator stared into his eyes, as though trying to communicate telepathically. "Very. If I can sort out the gaps tonight, then I should have the desired outcome by tomorrow morning."

*Gaps?* Had Salvator tampered with the sunlight barricade? That would explain his hesitation to talk about it. "I see. That's pretty exciting."

"If everything goes to plan, it's more than exciting. It's freeing," Salvator said with a Cheshire Cat grin.

For the rest of the day, Hugh focused on preparing to possibly leave, to get his head around the whole idea of freedom. What would that actually look like in current society?

By the evening, he'd started packing — light. *Wallet? Check. Fake passport? Check. Sunglasses? Check. Hip flask? Check.* Then he grabbed the novel he'd been reading from his small wooden bookshelf, sat on the couch and tried to reconnect with the story while keeping one eye on the sunlight bars.

After two hours he placed his book upside down on the coffee table and picked up his pewter wine goblet. *A little early for a nightcap, but what the heck.* He took a sip, the room temperature rabbit blood tingling in his throat. *Mmm…*

*Flash…flicker…flicker.*

His gaze darted to the barricade. *Five bars missing.* A grateful smile stretched his lips. He reached for a coaster off the coffee table and scrawled 'Thank you' on the back, his eyes filling with tears.

Hugh ran to his kitchenette and grabbed a clean glass out of the cupboard. *This will have to do.* He pressed it up under his right eye then his left, collecting the cascading salty droplets. Then he put it on the coffee table and placed the coaster on top.

Gritting his teeth, he tentatively shoved his hand through the sunless space. *No shock, no pain.* He slipped the rest of his body sideways through the gap and rejoiced. *I'm through!* Only a step away from his cell, and the sunlight beams shot back into place. He jumped. *Whoa! Talk about cutting it close.*

He scoured the area. No guards were in sight and his surrounding Violet compatriots remained trapped. He skulked down the dimly lit passageway, corridors of cells branching off to his left and right in a grid-type design, and followed the neon green and white exit signs. Up ahead, *Exit* glowed above a heavy metal door. Still no one around. *Must be skeleton staff. Perfect.* Hugh picked up his pace. Nearly there.

*Click clack, click clack.*

Footsteps. Hugh threw open the closest office door, slipped inside and peered through the pane of glass. A tall, muscular man and a petite, power-packed woman with holstered Taser guns in tow stopped in front of the window and looked around. Hugh couldn't get past them without being zapped, and he couldn't kill them. *Damn it.*

The woman stood on her tip toes and whispered in the man's ear. A cunning smile crept onto his lips. He grabbed her hand and reached for the door handle.

*Oh no.* Hugh dove under the desk, curled his knees up to his chest and held his breath.

The door swung open. *Don't turn on the lights.*

They shuffled across to the desk in the dark and stopped in front of the opening. The man unzipped his fly and the woman kicked off her flimsy panties. Then he lifted her up and plonked her down on the desk, her legs dangling over the side.

*Of all the times and places to have a roll in the hay.*

The man thrust into her, the desk squeaking and shuddering.

"Faster. Yeah, yeah, that's it." She panted. "Harder. Yes. Yes. Yes!"

"Aw yeah, baby!" The man grunted as he came, the desk rumbling like a train careening down the tracks.

Heavy breathing punctuated the stillness.

"You on for tomorrow?" She jumped down and slid back into her panties.

He sidled up to her and groped her behind. "Definitely."

They snuck out of the door, and Hugh sighed and dropped his head to the side, making contact with the timber. *Another close call.*

Once their footsteps had faded, he crawled out from under the desk, eased the door open and looked right and left along the corridor. *Empty.* As light-footed as a cat, he slunk toward the exit door. *Please don't have an alarm.* Hugh grabbed the handle, closed his eyes and pulled.

Silence. *Phew!* He breathed out hard. Everything looked pitch black outside...for humans. He scanned the area. A range of outbuildings dotted the sweeping field. Although things had changed, the area remained the same.

His eyes adjusted, like the focus on a camera lens, until he could see the clear drops of dew on the lush green blades of grass. *Night vision, how I've missed you.*

Hugh traversed the rickety wooden steps. Obviously they hadn't been part of the renovations. He ran across the paddock, the cool, damp grass refreshing against his skin.

*Freedom.*

* * * *

*Kismet*

Hugh stood in front of the bright departures screen at the airport. Trondheim, traveling with SAS to Copenhagen with transfers to Sydney, Australia, departing at six a.m.

He glanced at the time—three-fifteen a.m. Going by the usual Sub Rosa schedule, the staff shouldn't notice he was gone until after his plane had taken off. That would do perfectly.

He approached the ticket desk, and outside of the strange look he copped when he had no luggage to check in, all went smoothly. Ticket in hand, he strode to the gate and waited. He needed a fresh start somewhere new. Hopefully, Australia met his criteria.

The flight went smoothly and he took a taxi straight to the Sydney hotel he'd chosen near The Rocks. He checked into his hotel room and, once inside, cranked up the air conditioner, closed the blinds and collapsed onto the bed.

Surely such a large continent had cooler areas, more like home. He picked up the pile of travel brochures he'd collected off the bedside table and flipped through them.

Queensland—all beaches and sun. *Forget it.* The Northern Territory—remote, but hot. *Scratch that off the list.* Western Australia—too coastal and beachy. Victoria—more of a metropolitan cityscape feel. Great for hiding in plain sight but too busy. *No.*

Tasmania. A wave of excitement rolled through his stomach and his eyes teared up. It had to be the place...or so his intuition said.

Wilderness, mountains, lakes, lush green vegetation and, further south, colder. Perfect, except for one little thing—the Sub Rosa head office was in Hobart. Would that really affect him? He didn't plan on basing himself in the city, and even if he did, it didn't mean they'd find him.

However, staying hidden away in the bush would be best to reduce the risk. Plus, hopefully, he would get an opportunity to thank Salvator in person when he returned from his secondment. The man had risked a lot for him.

He smiled. *Decision made.*

Hugh spent the rest of the day on the phone, making arrangements, and early the next morning he left Sydney and traveled by small plane to the southwest corner of Tasmania.

By early afternoon, he'd checked into Lake Pedder Chalet, Strathgordon. His room overlooked the shimmering, dark tannin lake. The place was not only gorgeous but was also a fisherman's paradise, according to the tourism literature. *Those were the days.* He sighed.

Hugh placed his black overnight bag on the suitcase rack, took off his gothic black-and-silver buckled shoes and lay on the king-size bed. Just one thing was missing—his soulmate. Where could she be? He'd spent hundreds of years roaming the earth and nothing. Surely she had to be around the corner.

His eyes snapped open. It had gotten dark, except for his glowing violet stare like a dual laser beam against the white ceiling. *Dinner time.* He sprang off the bed, pulled the door open and froze.

A petite young woman with a mass of long, shiny caramel ringlets turned the corner pushing a trolley stacked with white bed linen, towels and miniature toiletries. Butterflies battered against the stiff walls of his stomach. *Beautiful.*

She started…then bit her lip. "Hello," she said, and glanced down. Her voice sounded like a chorus of angels.

Tears welled in his eyes. He smiled, a salty droplet trickling down his cheek. With the back of his hand he reached up and dabbed it away. *Hold it together.* "Good evening."

Her big, cobalt-blue eyes stared into his. A shy smile formed on her lips and she resumed pushing the trolley down the corridor.

*Don't let her go.* The words rang in his ears. He fidgeted, compulsion gnawing at his insides. "Wait!"

She stopped and hesitantly turned.

"Um…what are you doing tonight?"

She fiddled with the towels and toiletries. "Working."

"Oh. When do you finish?"

"Late. Why?" she asked, her gaze not quite connecting with his.

"I thought we could have a drink. Together." *What am I doing, flirting with a full human?*

Her cheeks filled with delicious redness. "Oh."

No woman had ever made him tear up, not in a romantic sense. It had to mean something. "Is that too forward? Sorry… I'm not good with this sort of thing."

She giggled. "It is a bit forward, but I don't mind."

"Does that mean you'll join me later?" *Please say yes.*

She shrugged. "I don't get off until two a.m."

"If it doesn't bother you, it doesn't bother me. I'm a night owl."

She started re-stacking the towels. "Okay, um…where will we meet? Everything will be closed."

"My room?"

Her eyes widened with obvious shock and…eagerness? "Your room? But we only just met."

Hugh stepped forward and stopped, leaving some space between them. "I don't mean it like that. I won't try anything. I promise."

She bit her lip and looked down. "I don't know…"

"How about you think about it, and if you want to come, come. I'll be here, waiting. But if not, I understand."

"Okay," she said without making eye contact — and continued into the next wing.

Possible alone-time with a full human meant dinner had to be decent to avoid temptation. Hugh ambled outside, unable to wipe away his huge smile. She'd seemed nervous, but instinct told him she would come. He kicked a pebble and it skimmed across the lake, creating a rush of ripples.

He shouldn't be so excited, as if he and a full human could ever successfully be together… The whole idea was crazy. They could never have a proper relationship. Food and cultural rituals were markedly different, and having children was almost out of the question, for God's sake. *I shouldn't lead her on.*

Hugh followed the path along the edge of the lake, the massive mountain looming in the background. How amazing it would look, snow-capped in winter. He hoped his stay would be a long one.

He reached a dense patch of bushland and stepped off the path. His nose pricked up. *Kangaroo. A delicacy.* He tracked the scent for over two hours and came to a plateau. In among the tussocks, a feast of gray kangaroos fed. Hugh licked his lips and pounced. Three slammed onto the ground, knocked unconscious.

Hugh sank his teeth into the first. Hot, salty blood spurted into his mouth and he sucked the carcass dry then moved to the second. When the animal went limp within his grasp, he stopped, his stomach distended. His gaze wandered over to the last kangaroo, its breathing shallow and labored. *I need to be sure. Just do it.*

He discarded the bloodless body, picked up his third course and drove his teeth into a large throbbing artery in the animal's neck, its mass of soft, gray fur brushing his face.

Once he'd drained every last drop of blood he pulled back and lay among the vegetation. "Ugh," he sighed, patting his stomach. He angled his wrist and checked his watch. Midnight. *Time to head back.*

Hugh ran the entire way, reaching his room in under an hour. He checked his appearance in the mirror, his glowing violet eyes lighting up the bathroom. "Rugged is good, but not disheveled," he muttered, laughing to himself.

He had a quick shower, tidied his hair and gargled with mouthwash. Then he went over to the teak bedside drawer, pulled out a couple of champagne glasses and put them on the small wooden table.

The complimentary bottle of champagne lay chilling in the bar fridge. He shuddered and screwed up his face. Sparkling wine tasted like carbonated dirt.

Hugh stared at his overnight bag. Inside, he'd tossed his empty hip flask on top of his clothes. Normally he'd use its contents to alleviate some of the disgusting flavor, but he'd run out of time to stock up. He'd push through and drink the vile brew for *her*, though.

Sitting on the king-size bed in the dark with the blinds open, he stared into the moonless night.

*Tap tap.*

Hugh jumped up, nerves skittering in his stomach, switched on the lamp and opened the door. She stood only inches away, oozing soft femininity. "I hoped you would come." *So much for not leading her on.*

She looked around, her damp hair hanging in clusters like caramel wafer rolls. "I shouldn't really be doing this."

*Me either.* "Doing what?"

"Socializing with guests," she whispered. "It's against the rules."

"Then why are you here?"

She lowered her gaze and shrugged. "This is probably going to sound really silly, but I had this overwhelming urge to see you again."

"It doesn't sound silly. I feel the same about you."

A coy smile crept onto her lips.

"Come in," he said, moving aside.

She hesitated, then walked past him and stopped in front of the window, her freshly washed skin the fragrance of sweet white roses.

He moved toward the bar fridge. "Would you like a drink? I'll open the champagne."

"That would be nice. Thanks."

"I'm Hugh, by the way," he said, and popped the cork.

Her eyes met his stare. "I'm Indigo."

Indigo…and he was from the Violet clan. It had to be a sign. Hugh poured the champagne and handed her a glass.

His hand brushed hers and she shivered. "Your skin is icy cold."

"Bad circulation." He held up his glass. "Let's make a toast—to the burgeoning of a long and lasting relationship."

"Relationship?" she echoed, nearly spilling her drink.

"Maybe that's not the right word. Please forgive me. As I said, I'm not very good at speaking to women, especially ones I'm attracted to."

Her gaze dropped to the bubbling brut, hot pink infusing her cheeks.

Hugh initiated chinking glasses, and they both took a sip. "Whereabouts do you live?" The fizzy dirt infiltrated his taste buds and his jaw twitched.

"Here. My parents own the place."

"Do they?"

She stepped in closer. "Just between you and me, I've been thinking about moving to Hobart, where it's busier and I can meet more people my own age, rather than cruddy old fishermen."

Old fisherman, ex-human—two black marks against him already. But were they deal breakers? *Hang in there.* He laughed. "When are you leaving?"

"I'm not sure."

*Good.* He still had some time…

She had another sip of her drink. "How long are you staying?"

"As long as I can."

Her cute little forehead furrowed. "What does that mean?"

"I have no set plans."

"Don't you need to work?" she asked.

"Not at the moment. I have savings." *Quite a bit of savings, in fact.*

A concerned expression crossed her face. "But that won't last forever."

Though it would come pretty damn close. "You're right. Is there any work going here? I could help out."

Indigo finished her drink. "Not paid work. Though, Mum and Dad might be able to waive the room rate and throw in a meal allowance. What sort of things can you do?"

"Cleaning, cooking, handyman work. Whatever's needed."

Her eyebrows flew up until they almost reached her hairline. "You've had experience with all that?"

He nodded. *And a hell of a lot more.* "Sure have."

She fiddled with the empty champagne glass. "How can that be? You don't look old enough."

"How old do I look?"

Indigo studied him for a few moments. "Mid-twenties, max."

He smiled. "Great guess. Let's just say I've traveled around a bit, so I've picked up a few things."

"Hmmm...how old am I?" she asked.

"Twenty."

She pouted. "How did you know?"

*By the scent of her blood.* It had a freshness rating. "Lucky guess. Please, take a seat."

Indigo sat on the single bed and Hugh topped up her glass. Then he placed the champagne bottle in a chill bucket and sat on the king-size bed opposite her.

Her gaze met his. "You have very unusual eyes. They're so violet and mesmerizing. Where are you from?"

He put his almost-full glass on the bedside table. "Norway."

"Are violet eyes a common trait over there?"

Hugh stretched his arms out behind him and leaned back. "I wouldn't say common, though they're very strong in my family."

"Wow. They're really amazing!"

He smiled. "Thank you."

She crossed her legs and took a sip of champagne. "What brings you to Lake Pedder?"

"I needed to explore somewhere new and different, and yet find a place that still feels like home. Does that sound ridiculous?"

"No, not at all." She leaned forward. "Does it feel like home to you here?"

Hugh shifted to the edge of the bed, his knees almost touching hers. "Very much."

She swilled the remainder of her champagne and smiled. Would she continue to smile when she knew what he was? He had to tell her. It was only fair. But when? How? Although their relationship was still hovering in the early-days stage, the tight ropes of tension in his stomach told him otherwise.

"Are you working tomorrow?" he asked.

She fidgeted and glanced at the ticking wall clock. "No, I have the day off."

"Would you like to spend it with me?" His insides buzzed. He was dying to see her again, greedy for her presence, her physical closeness, even though it meant he would have to confess.

She bit her lip, her cobalt blue eyes staring into his. "Yes."

A mix of joy and terror tore through him. "Great. Well, I suppose I should let you go. I don't want to get you in trouble."

Indigo stood, and he followed her to the door. She stopped and turned to him, her bright youthful eyes dancing with elation. "I know just the place to take you. How about I meet you at ten a.m., by the lake?"

It wouldn't have mattered what time she'd said. He wouldn't be able to sleep now anyway, knowing he'd be alone with her again soon, combined with the stress of what he had to do.

"Sounds perfect." Hugh leaned in and kissed her, his lips lingering against her warm, rosy cheek. His body zinged with euphoria. Hopefully there would be more intimate encounters to come.

\* \* \* \*

*A private exposition*

This time, Hugh would be fully prepared. He dug through his overnight bag and pulled out his engraved pewter hip flask. Stealthy as a shadow in the dead of night, he snuck into the woods, stalked and killed a rabbit then drained its blood into the flask, his mouth watering. *Have some control.*

He closed his eyes and took a deep breath. A waft of acrid bitterness stung his nostrils. *Fungi.* Hugh zeroed in on a sprouting of white-capped, tiny toadstools, hidden deep within the mosses and lichens of a gnarled old myrtle beech tree.

He picked the whole bunch, zipped back to his room and steeped them in boiling water for fifteen minutes.

Then he poured the warm, blue-tinged juice into his hip flask and shook it.

He glanced at his watch. "Better get a move on," he muttered, shoved the hip flask into his back pocket and headed outside.

Hugh stood by the lake and stared into the still water. Acting like a voluminous mirror, it reflected crystal clear images of the mountain, surrounding vegetation...and him. His telltale violet eyes were hidden behind black sunglasses and he'd chosen a hat, white linen shirt and pants to ward off the sun.

Today was the day. No matter what, he wouldn't allow himself to back out. Nerves scuttled through his stomach like a plague of invading mice.

"Hugh!" Indigo squealed.

He looked up, his gaze greeting hers. A huge smile lifted her lips almost all the way to her pretty little ears. She hurried toward him, carrying a wicker picnic basket, her white summer dress with colorful floral print flouncing about her tan-color legs.

Indigo grabbed his hand and led him to a small boat, bobbing in the water. "It's only a short ride across to the other side, then we've got quite a bit of a walk," she said and prepared the boat for departure.

When they reached the opposite bank, she jumped out and docked the boat, her stylish white walking shoes gleaming in the sunlight. Hugh grabbed the picnic basket and followed her up a steep, rocky path, surrounded by kaleidoscopic alpine flora.

After three hours of trekking, the path opened up, the sheer cliff dropping away to reveal a huge, iridescent lake. Hugh's mouth gaped open. "This is spectacular." It reminded him of a mini version of his native Norway.

"I know, right?" she said, in between puffs and pants.

They walked up close to the edge and found a spot in the shade, under a wind-weathered rock outcropping. Hugh took off his hat, pushed his sunglasses onto his head and opened the wicker basket.

He laid out the padded, red flannel picnic blanket, slipped off his sandals and sat cross-legged while Indigo dished out their lunch onto shiny white plastic plates.

"I hope you like rare beef salad," she said.

"Perfect." He patted his back pocket. *Well, close enough.*

"And I brought fruit and cheese and red wine too. I wanted today to be special." She glanced down, her caramel curls bouncing over her shoulders.

His mouth watered at her pure beauty. "It definitely is that."

Hugh forced in his meal, took out his trusty pewter hip flask and poured a nip into his glass of red wine.

"What's that?" Indigo asked.

*Um...* "Just a little concoction that helps me tolerate red wine." He swished the blood-red contents of his glass like a true wine connoisseur.

Disappointment dragged her mouth down into a lip-biting frown. "Oh, sorry. I didn't realize you didn't like it."

"It's not that, exactly. Red wine on its own doesn't really agree with me, but if I add a bit of this, it's fine." He smiled and washed the lingering, rancid taste of the picnic lunch down with his special red blend.

"What's in it? Can I try a bit?" She snatched the glass out of his hand, took a sip and spat it straight out. "Errr!" Her face screwed up. "That's revolting! It's so salty and bitter."

He took the glass from her outstretched hand. "I guess it's an acquired taste."

"Biggest understatement of the year!" She guzzled down the rest of her own drink, packed everything away and rejoined him on the picnic blanket.

Indigo looked into his eyes and clasped his hand. "We shouldn't be disturbed up here."

Hugh's gaze moved between her eyes and her lips and he leaned in, connecting his mouth to hers in a light, gentle kiss. He should stop and tell her about his heritage, but she was too irresistible.

Indigo pressed her parted lips against his, entwining their tongues, and he forgot about everything except the taste and scent of her sweetness. Hugh wound his arm around her and she grabbed his free hand and slid it over her breast and down, between her legs.

Animalistic adrenaline bombarded his body. *Mmm...so hot and moist...stop it!* He pulled back. "No."

Her eyes searched his and she bit her kiss-swollen bottom lip. "Did I do something wrong? Was I too pushy?"

Hugh grabbed her face between his pale hands and kissed her wrinkled forehead. "No, you did everything right." A survival-type urge tried to convince him to take her away, somewhere where they could be together without fear, without risk, without judgment...assuming she'd accept what he was.

"You're just saying that because you don't want to upset me."

"It's not that."

"Well, what then?" Her bottom lip trembled.

His chance had arrived to come clean. He should take it. "The truth is I like you too much and I don't want to hurt you." Well, it formed part of the truth, anyway.

Her eyes flooded with tears. "You're hurting me right now," she said, and ran out of their little love nest toward the lake.

"Indigo, wait!" He jumped up and chased after her. "Let me explain, fully."

She went to stop and her foot skidded on a loose rock, dropping her to the ground. Her body tumbled, and she slid straight for the edge of the cliff. "Help!" she screamed.

Hugh switched into high gear and reached her just as she catapulted over the side. He dove off the edge, pulled her flailing body into his arms and spiraled, head first, toward the earth below. She clutched onto him and cried.

"Close your eyes," Hugh said, his voice calm.

She squeezed them shut as they hurtled downward, her hair flapping against his wind- chafed face. Twisting in the air, he righted himself and landed on his feet in a cluster of tussocks right next to a small, clear tarn.

Indigo peeped through one eye, her heart pounding against his chest. "Are we dead?"

"No. We're fine," he said and carried her to a small rocky ledge overlooking the pristine water.

She wriggled in his arms. "How can that be? We must have fallen two hundred meters at least!"

Hugh placed her down and sat at her feet, his brain desperately searching for the perfect words to explain. He constructed a few thoughts and went to speak, but fear strangled his throat. "Um…" He coughed, in an attempt to limber up his constricted vocal cords, and squeeze out a few sentences. "I need to tell you something. I thought I'd have a bit more time to get the wording right but things have moved quicker than I anticipated... The thing is, Indigo, I have very strong feelings for you.

"However, to have the chance of developing the lasting kind of romantic connection, I need to be totally honest about who I am, even if it means I might lose you forever. It's because I care about you that I'll take that risk."

Worry perfused her big blue eyes.

He glanced at his fidgety hands, gathered his thoughts, then re-established eye contact. His stomach clenched hard, weighing down his insides like a solid clump of steel. "I'm just going to come right out and say it. The reason we didn't die back there is because I'm a vampire. We're not that easy to kill."

She baulked. "A vampire? Come on, Hugh. I'm sure you can think up a better excuse than that."

He ran his trembling fingers through his hair. "What I said earlier is true. I am from Norway. But...there's more. I'm part of a Violet clan, whose key traits are violet eyes and dark hair.

"I was originally born human in the Middle Ages and was changed at twenty-five by Violets who found me drowning. I used to be a fisherman. Just so you know, most vampires are humanists and would never prey on or intentionally hurt a human. We only feed on animals."

"Vampires don't exist." Indigo rubbed her forehead with her shaking hands, as though to erase the incomprehensible idea from her mind.

"That's what humans in positions of power want you to believe. They'd rather keep things hidden. They don't want the masses to panic."

Indigo peeked through her fingers. "If you're harmless, like you say, then no one needs to be scared."

He looked her in the eye. "I agree, but try convincing others of that. Where there's difference, there's fear. Plus, unfortunately, there are that small minority that give us a bad name."

"How do I know I can trust you?"

"You don't. Just like with human relationships, trust has to be built." *Please give me a chance.*

Indigo's large eyes darted between his and the surroundings. Was she trying to find a way to escape? His stomach dropped like a fired cannonball crashing to the canyon floor. She looked petrified...of him. Before he could stop them, tears burst from his eyes.

Anguish washed over her sweet face and she touched his cheeks, attempting to wipe away the wetness. "I'm not afraid of you," she said, as though understanding his sorrow.

He smiled through the still falling droplets. "I'm glad."

Indigo shifted forward, her hands saturated with his tears. "You frightened me at first. But now the fear has gone. In fact, I think I love you." She hesitated, as though surprised by her own words, as though his tears were a truth serum.

He swallowed back the last of the tears. "Indigo, thank you, but —"

She focused her eyes on his. "I know it sounds kind of crazy and impulsive, but that's how I feel. I don't care that I haven't known you long or that you're a vampire or even an ex-fisherman!" She giggled, then her facial expression turned serious again. "You're the kindest, most beautiful and loving man I've ever met. And you just saved my life."

Had his tears caused her about-face reaction or had her changed response stemmed from the rush of emotions following her near-death experience? Or both? Even though they'd only just met, the attraction felt almost palpable. But was it love or lust? "You don't owe me anything."

She reached for his hand and entwined their fingers. "I know. I want us to be together because we're right for each other."

If they both sensed it so strongly, it had to be real, legitimate. Didn't it? "I feel the same way, though I'm not sure it's fair for you. Our life won't be easy. For one, we won't be able to have a fully intimate physical relationship."

Confused creases lined her youthful forehead. "Why?"

"The risk of harming you is too high. Vampires are very strong, so I have to be careful how I touch you all the time. Humans are very breakable."

She edged closer to him. "You're always gentle with me."

"I try, though I only need to get the tiniest bit carried away and — "

"That's why you stopped things before."

"Yes..."

She joined him on the warm ground, her beguiling blue gaze locking on his. "You won't hurt me. I know you won't. You just need to trust yourself. *I* trust you."

Her words were so full of conviction that she made it sound possible. Or had his emotions skewed reality, wishing rather than knowing she was right? He had to be a realist, even though that's the last thing he wanted.

He kept hold of her hand and focused on her eyes. "But it's not just that. If we did make love and you fell pregnant, you wouldn't be able to survive the pregnancy. A vampire fetus is way too rough. It'd tear you up inside. I don't know one human female who has lived through the gestation period. I couldn't risk doing that to you."

"We don't have to have children."

Hugh swept a springy, caramel curl off her face. "If we make love, there's always a risk. You see, there's no safe form of contraception. Vampire sperm eats right through condoms and overrides any contraceptive pills."

"We'll find a way around it. We can make the relationship work—or at least give it a good try. I think it's worth it, don't you?" The look in her eyes matched the pleading in her voice.

Hugh stared at her. "I can't believe how open-minded and understanding you are. I thought for sure—"

"I'd run a mile? Why would I want to do that? You're the best thing that's ever happened to me."

Was he dreaming? What she'd said couldn't really be true, could it? After all these years, could he have finally found his soulmate? His eyes filled with tears. "Me too."

She let go of his hand and hugged him, the heat of her small hands and body seeping into his skin. "Let's talk about this more later. We should head off now before it gets too dark."

"I'll take you the short-cut way this time," he said with a wink and whisked her into his arms.

It would have been much easier if he'd fallen for a Violet—or even a Violet hybrid. But no, instead he'd found Indigo. Though, maybe she was right. Maybe it could really work out between them. They really were only a few shades difference.

\* \* \* \*

*Heart on the line*

*Knock knock.*

Hugh opened his eyes. *Still dark.* He glanced at the black-and-white clock on the wall—five-forty-five a.m. Had she had second thoughts? His stomach squeezed and his breath stilled. *Don't make any assumptions. Just let her talk.* He threw off the covers and answered the door in his underwear.

"Indigo, are you all right?"

Redness filled her cheeks and she averted her gaze from his semi-naked body. "Um…I've been thinking—"

"Come in." He reached for her hand and led her to his bed.

She sat down next to him and bit her lip. "I couldn't sleep. I couldn't stop thinking about everything."

He swallowed the growing lump in his throat. "And…"

Her eyes lifted to meet his stare. "I'm not sure the relationship works for both of us."

"Oh, I see." His eyes stung. *Not now. Let her finish.*

She squeezed his hand. "It's not what you think. I still love you. Yesterday, all I could think about was how to hold on to you. So totally selfish. You've waited a long time to find the right woman… You deserve a perfect relationship, one with no limitations."

"There's no such thing as a perfect relationship. There will always be limitations and compromises."

"But how can you be happy knowing you might never make love to your partner? Never have children? Then there's the aging thing. How would you feel about being with a wrinkly, eighty-five-year-old woman when you still look twenty-five?"

Hugh held her hand between his hands. "I've had a long time to think about all these things and they're not enough to deter me. I've come across many beautiful, lovely women in my time, though none have had the pull you do. From the moment I saw you, something resonated deep within me, and I became teary. Right then, I knew you were someone special. That had never happened to me with any woman before. Then there's your name, Indigo. And I'm a Violet. There are too many signs to ignore. Do I want to make love to you? More than anything. Do I wish we could have children? Absolutely. Would I prefer we grow old together? Of course. But are those things deal breakers? No. Not for me.

"Physical intimacy constitutes fifteen percent of a relationship at most and, of that, we can still participate in at least ten percent. When it comes to children, I only want them if my wife does, and it's possible and safe. As for the age issue, it's not the appearance that bothers me as much as the knowledge that I can't have you forever. But I'd still rather have you for seventy-plus years than not at all."

Her watery eyes searched his. "So you're sure then?"

"Very. You?"

"Yes!" She wrapped her arms around his waist and rested her head against his chest, her caramel curls soft and springy. "You're always going to feel this cold, huh?"

He caressed her back. "Yes, sorry. No warm, red blood coursing through my veins and all that."

* * * *

## A risky proposition, May 1997

Indigo squeezed Hugh's hand. "This place is amazing!"

"I made the right choice then. I had trouble deciding whether to go ocean or mountains."

"Ocean is perfect. It's different, so it makes it feel more like a holiday."

"And it's not far out of Hobart. I know how much you've wanted to visit the area." His stomach stiffened like an over-starched shirt. Should he really have chosen somewhere so near Hobart, given the proximity of the Sub Rosa office?

Probably not. Then again, they had no idea where he'd escaped to. They'd probably have bounty hunter staff on high alert for him, and other vampires, in most places with a cooler climate across the globe.

While on the run, nowhere was truly safe. Given that, he'd decided to take the risk. Indigo had her heart set on Hobart, and he loved making her happy. Plus, the accommodation ticked off all the requirements on his ideal list for what he had planned.

"You're such a sweetheart!" She hugged him. "So what's on the agenda for our two days?"

He held her close and pressed a kiss to the shell of her ear. "You time."

"Which means?"

He brushed a loose, caramel curl off her face. "Spending as much time with you alone as possible."

"But we already get a fair bit of that, don't we?"

"Yes, but it's not the same as being a couple in our own place and doing things in our time. Do you know what I mean?"

She bit her lip. "I do."

"So, tonight I thought we'd stay in, then tomorrow we'll sightsee around Hobart." *Very briefly.* "Any objections?"

She ran her hands up his chest and secured her arms around his neck. "No. But what about dinner tonight?"

"I've got something special planned."

As the day progressed, his nerves went from dry mouth to queasy stomach to constricted chest. He tried to hide it, but struggled to sit still, determined to make their evening together memorable...in a good way. No, a positive, life-changing way. Finally, he convinced her to have a relaxing shower while he organized their fateful meal.

Thirty minutes later, Indigo walked back into the living area, her hair wet and her feet bare, wearing only a robe tied at the waist. She looked like a sexy present, waiting to be unwrapped.

*Mmm...* He breathed out hard. *Concentrate.* "Take a seat. Dinner's nearly ready."

"Did you cook? What's on the menu?" she asked, and wandered over to him.

He stepped away from the boiling pasta pot and leaned on the bench, facing her. "Tonight, for your gustatory pleasure, we have beef ravioli in Bolognese sauce, followed by eye fillet and vegetables, with peanut butter and chocolate ice cream and mini cinnamon donuts for dessert."

"You've already done all that? I didn't think I was gone that long."

"You weren't. Super speedy vampire skills... Remember?"

"Oh yeah." She grabbed her hair with both hands and flicked it behind her shoulders. "What are you having? Or shouldn't I ask?"

He adjusted her terry toweling lapel. "Don't worry. There won't be any animal sacrifices at the table. I'm not a very neat eater," he said with a mischievous grin. "I'm actually having the same as you, with a special sauce on the side."

"Let me guess—your hip flask concoction."

He tugged her collar, pulling her body against his and pressed a tender kiss on her sweet lips. "Excellent deduction. You're not just a pretty face."

Within twenty-five minutes they were seated at the table and starting on the second course.

Indigo sliced a piece of steak and loaded up her fork with sweet potato and green beans. "First the delicious ravioli and now a melt-in-your-mouth steak. This meal is orgasmic!"

Hugh laughed, nearly choking on his food. "Thank you. What can I say? A product of years of experience trying to fit into human society."

They savored their meal and, once they were done, Hugh collected their empty plates and put them in the sink. "Now, for the pièce de résistance."

Indigo patted her bloated stomach. "I don't know if I can squeeze any more in. I feel like I'm going to explode!"

"Come on. Humor me. Just try a bit and you can finish it tomorrow."

"The problem is, if it's as good as the first two courses, I don't think I'll be able to stop."

Hugh carried over two plates, each with a rectangular slab of chocolate and peanut butter ice cream with three small cinnamon donuts laid across the top. "I have chocolate dipping sauce and thickened cream as well, if you'd like."

"Ugh," she groaned. "No thanks...unless you'd like to see dinner and dessert reappear."

He chuckled, sat down opposite her and poured some special purple sauce from his hip flask, over the top of his serving.

Indigo cut a sliver of ice cream and donut and popped it into her mouth. She closed her eyes. "Mmm..." she murmured. Then she went on to finish the entire plateful. "Irresistible."

"*You're* irresistible."

A flush of pink spread over every inch of her exposed skin.

"Now, roll on over to the couch and I'll bring you an espresso and a little nightcap to help you digest everything."

Hugh carried over a tray with coffee, a Norse ceramic bowl, two pewter liqueur glasses, a bottle of fortified wine and his pewter hip flask and placed it on the coffee table, not spilling a drop...which surprised him, given how much his hands shook.

Indigo lowered her feet off the cozy, chocolate-brown couch and levered herself up into a sitting position. "Today's been amazing. Thank you so much."

He sat beside her. "You don't have to thank me. I should thank you for allowing me to have you all to myself."

Indigo pointed to the small ceramic bowl. "What's in there?"

"Why don't you have a look."

She leaned forward and lifted the lid, a quizzical crease on her forehead. "A fortune cookie?"

"I couldn't resist."

She rubbed her belly. "I seriously can't fit any more in."

"Don't worry about eating it, just break it open. Let's see what the future holds for you."

Indigo picked it up and held it between both hands. "Wish me luck," she said and snapped it in half.

*Clang!*

"What the hell?" she muttered, searching for the fallen object among bits of broken biscuit. "Is this a fortune cookie or a Kinder Surprise?" she joked. She rummaged around on the tray and stopped. She glanced up at him, her mouth agape.

Hugh got down on one knee. "Indigo, these past six months have been the happiest of my entire existence. I've never felt so alive, so loved and accepted. I can't imagine life without you."

He paused, holding her hand between his, and locked his gaze on hers. "Having you as my wife would be an honor and a privilege, a dream come true. I've already taken the liberty of asking your father's permission and he consented. Now it's up to you. Will you marry me?"

Her blue eyes shone and she opened and closed her mouth a few times before she got any sound out. "You're so cute and romantic." She wrapped her arms around him and squeezed him tight.

"Yes, of course I'll marry you. It would be an honor and a privilege to have you as my husband. I love you so much, my thoughtful, old-fashioned knight in shining armor."

"I love you too."

Indigo pulled back and bounced on the seat, a smile stretching across her breathtaking face. "I can't believe this is happening!"

"Soon we'll be husband and wife, living in our own little cabin with picturesque views." He picked the ring up off the tray and slid it onto her wedding finger.

The brilliant-cut violet solitaire diamond-and-platinum ring sparkled in the dim light. "Hugh, it's breathtaking."

"It's a rare beauty, just like you."

She sniffled. "Now you've got me doing the whole joyous crying thing. It must be contagious."

Hugh's eyes moistened with barely contained happiness. "How about a celebratory drink?"

Without waiting for a reply, he poured them each a liqueur, topped his up with the blood and toadstool juice out of his hip flask and sat down next to her again. "To the most wonderful fiancée a man could ever hope for."

"To the man of my dreams."

They clinked glasses.

"I really am the luckiest girl in the world." She shot her drink and put the glass down on the tray. "Now, come with me. I've got a little surprise of my own," she said, with a twinkle in her eye.

Indigo held his hand and led him into the bedroom. She stopped at the foot of the bed and slid out of her robe, her naked body glowing under the soft amber lighting.

*Exquisite.* Could he really be this fortunate? He sighed and ran his hands slowly over her pure, smooth skin.

She gasped, a shiver rippling through her body.

He recoiled. "Sorry. I'll try and warm them up," he said, rubbing them together.

Indigo stepped in closer to him and grabbed his hands, a blush rising from her gorgeous breasts to the curve of her cheeks. "They're not too cold. It's your touch. It turns me on."

"I know the feeling."

Indigo clutched his face and brought his mouth to hers. She dropped her hands to his chest and unbuttoned his shirt, then undid his pants, their lips remaining locked.

Hugh shrugged out of his clothes and lifted her onto the bed. He lay beside her and held her to him, her red-blooded heat seeping through his skin. She moved her body against his, increasing the friction, her breathing quick and raspy and her skin flushed.

"I want you," she said, and wrapped her leg around his waist.

He stared into her eyes. "I want you too, but we can't."

"Yes, we can. It's safe. I'm not due to ovulate for at least another two weeks."

He touched her face. "Tempting, *very* tempting, but it's not just that. What if I'm too heavy-handed and something happens to you?"

"It would give a new meaning to the phrase 'killer sex'." A devilish spark flashed in her eyes.

"Very funny. But this is serious. Believe me, I *really* wish we could take the risk, but it's not worth it."

"I know…" She went all silent, introspective, then a cheeky grin spread across her face. "There is still that ten out of the fifteen percent we can do, though, right?"

"You're incorrigible," he said and kissed her full, pink lips.

After hours of touching, teasing and exploring, Indigo fell against the bed, breathless, her body glistening with sweat. She looked over at him. "We can continue this when we get home, right?"

Hugh propped himself up on one elbow and drew light lines across the silky skin of her breasts. "I'd be disappointed if we didn't."

"I don't think I can go back to sleeping with clothes on when I'm with you." Her already-erect nipples grew harder beneath the pads of his fingers.

"Me either." He leaned in and kissed her breasts then her lips. "Tonight has been incredible. Perfect. It's only solidified how well suited we are."

"I agree. That last orgasm in particular was" – she sighed – "beyond words. Where did you learn to use your tongue like that?"

He chuckled.

Her skin remained flushed and glowed with sexual satisfaction, amplifying his own gratification. "What I love even more than the pleasure is that I can totally be myself with you. That means everything to me. It's just a bonus that you're such a great lover."

"Thanks. I try my best." He trailed his lips from her neck to her navel. "It helps that you're such a sweet, sexy woman," he said, once again dipping his tongue into her delectable core.

\* \* \* \*

*The big day, August 1997*

Indigo folded her legs up onto the cozy chocolate-brown couch where Hugh had proposed only three months beforehand. "I can't believe we're going to be married tomorrow."

The wind roared and the waves crashed against the nearby shore. Was it tempting fate coming back to Hobart? Hugh looked into her eyes. "I know. I can't wait."

She nestled into him. "How am I going to spend tonight without you?"

"Just think about all the days and nights we'll have together after tomorrow." He kissed the top of her head. "I swore not to say anything yet, but...I've already started looking for a place for us and I think I've found it."

"Really? Do you have any pictures?"

He tapped the tip of her upturned nose. "Uh-uh. No details yet. Be patient, my little angel, or should I say, coquette?"

"Ha-ha. Like you don't enjoy our little trysts."

He chuckled, and glanced at his watch. "It's nearly midnight. I'd better go."

She ran her hand down his chest. "Stay a bit longer. Please."

"Sorry... The groom can't see the bride until the ceremony. It's bad luck. And you need to get a good night's sleep. It's going to be a long day tomorrow...and night." He brushed her lips with his.

"Is that all?" She pretended to be annoyed, but she couldn't hide her cheeky smile. "How about a proper kiss?"

Hugh lifted her onto his lap and pressed his lips to hers in a tender, open-mouthed kiss. Then he travelled across to her ear and gently nibbled and sucked on her earlobe. She moaned and threw her head back, giving him greater access to her neck.

Hugh nuzzled in, planting light kisses along her satiny skin. He reached inside her sexy chiffon dressing gown and caressed her naked breasts, her nipples hardening with his touch. Indigo tightened her arms around him and ground her hip against his growing erection.

"Mmm..." Hugh wanted to take her right then and there, but he couldn't, even if he wasn't short on time.

After they were married, he would revisit his 'no penetrative sex' stipulation and see if he could work out a way around it that would pose less of a risk to her safety.

It could be something as simple as her going on the pill and him using a heavy-duty condom while she straddled him... *Enough!* He'd speak to her about it after the wedding. Right now, he had to get moving.

Hugh ran his fingers along her jaw and brought her mouth back to his, kissing her with an infusion of love and devotion.

"Is that better?" he murmured against her swollen lips.

"Much."

He patted her bottom. "Come on. Up you get."

She crinkled her nose and stood up.

He got to his feet and held her hands. "I'm going to miss you tonight too. But we'll see each other at the church in just a few hours. Now, don't be too late or I'll think you've changed your mind," he teased.

"I'll never change my mind."

Hugh kissed her forehead. "Goodnight, my sweet, beautiful Indigo." Then he turned toward the door.

She touched his arm. "Hey, it's after midnight. Maybe you should just stay now."

He frowned. "Damn it! I wanted to do this right."

"You have. Everything's perfect. Choosing Hobart for our wedding to commemorate your proposal is so romantic."

*And hopefully not my undoing.* "Indigo, I'd love to stay, bu—"

"I know, I know... You want to try to do the whole traditional thing, even though you've kind of stuffed it up." She giggled.

"That's right. Now try to get a good night's sleep. We'll see each other again before you know it." He leaned in, kissed her succulent lips and stepped outside into the blustery, biting wind.

She stood in the open doorway and waved until he went through the gate. Hugh picked up his pace from a brisk walk to a run, the salt-tinged air stinging his windpipe.

Near his Richmond hotel room, he caught a glimpse of vivid violet in the bushes. *Another vampire?* He stopped and surveyed the area, breath puffing from his lungs. Nothing. *I'm imagining things.*

He approached the front door of the stables-conversion accommodation, grabbed the key out of his pocket and looked around. Hopefully he should still be hidden enough, still be safe.

Hugh fed the key into the lock, opened the thick, wooden door and went inside. His open overnight bag sat on the fold-out suitcase rack and his garment bag lay out flat on the bed.

He unzipped it and checked through the contents. *White, French cuffed shirt? Tick. Black fitted jacket, waistcoat and pants? Tick. Black belt? Tick. Violet, black and white paisley tie and antique violet diamond and platinum cufflinks?* Everything seemed in order. *Time for a little nightcap.*

Hugh rifled through his overnight bag, past his underwear and shoes, and pulled out his pewter hip flask. He poured half the contents into a wineglass then topped it up with some complimentary pinot noir. Hugh sculled the special wine blend, put the empty glass on the bedside table and lay on the bed.

If only he could safely get word to Salvator about being in the neighborhood. After the friendship they'd forged and all he'd done, Hugh would have loved for him to share in his special day.

Soon after Hugh had settled in Lake Pedder, he'd had grand intentions to contact Salvator and catch up. But the more he'd thought about it, the more he'd realized it wasn't a great idea.

For one, he didn't know if Salvator had returned from his secondment, and if he sent correspondence to the Hobart office, it might be intercepted. Even if he got on to the researcher, what if Sub Rosa staff saw them together? It would put both of them in danger.

So, he decided the best form of thanks was to keep his friend safe, live well and not undo all his good work.

Hugh closed his eyes, warmth and calm bleeding into his body, though his nerves were still a bit on edge. *Hmmm...pre-wedding jitters. Nothing a second glass won't fix.*

He pushed his lethargic body into standing, got his hip flask, stumbled and grasped the footboard of the bed, his head spinning. It couldn't be too much wine. He'd only had one glass.

He staggered around the side of the bed and fell onto it, drowsiness descending over his brain like a heavy fog. The ensuing rocking motion felt like being tossed around on a boat in a black, merciless ocean.

\* \* \* \*

Hugh woke and snapped his eyes open, the blinding sunlight bars scorching his face. "No!" He howled and sat up. "It can't be."

His overnight and garment bags were thrown in the corner of his cell and lay crumpled on the floor. He buried his face in his hands. *Indigo!* She'd assume he'd had second thoughts, that he couldn't go through with it.

He should have told her about Sub Rosa. He should have reinforced that he'd never change his mind about her. *What must she think of me?* Hugh jumped up and paced, his hands wound into tight, trembling fists. He flopped into his well-worn tapestry couch and cried, his body shaking with each violent sob.

By the time his meal came, his stomach rumbled and he was a wringing wet mess of tears, his cell floor covered with a sea of salty droplets that oozed into the corridor.

One of the guards stopped and inspected his shoe. "Errr! What's this slime?"

"I'd say someone might be a little sad. This one's a crier. Pathetic, isn't it?" the second guard said.

They walked into Hugh's living quarters and dumped his pre-packaged meal on the coffee table.

"How did I get here?" Hugh hissed out his reply through his locked-down jaw.

The second guard's hand hovered over his holster. "Microchipping. It works a treat. As soon as you got within range of Sub Rosa, your signal picked up — and well, here you are."

Hugh rubbed his eyes. "I don't remember anything."

"That would be the IVD," the first guard said.

"What the hell's IVD?"

"Infrared radiation Vitamin D — a newly developed vampire tranquilizer. You've been out for nearly two days," the second guard said.

Hugh shook his head in an attempt to clear the drug-induced cobwebs clogging his mind. "I don't remember taking anything."

"Your hip flask got spiked," the first guard explained.

"When? How?"

"While you were off gallivanting out of range, one of the guys broke into your hotel room," the second guard said.

"But nothing was out of place," Hugh pondered aloud.

The second guard smirked. "Sub Rosa employs excellent, highly skilled staff."

"And what if I hadn't drunk from my flask?"

The second guard tapped his pearl gun handle. "You would have been tasered and had the drug forcibly administered. You had no way out. Just appreciate the time you were on the run, because you're never getting out of here again. Security's been stepped up and now, with IVD, you're all fucked."

A fresh set of tears streamed down Hugh's cheeks.

"Anyway, we'll leave you to it. Enjoy your meal," the second guard said, a mocking smile on his lips.

Hugh's gaze dropped to the fetid food supplement. He sniffled and wiped his eyes with the back of his hand, then guzzled down the vile liquid meal. His face screwed up, sending more salty droplets cascading down his cheeks.

Even though the meal replacement still tasted as revolting as ever, his hunger settled instantly, the methadone to his heroin.

The flood of tears kept flowing into the night. If only he could find a way to get in touch with Indigo and explain, find a way to remedy his broken heart.

# Chapter Twelve

## The Unexpected News

*Hobart, June 2010*

Eden grabbed her cordless phone and rang Grace.

"Eden? Finally. I've been calling you all day! I started to panic. Is everything all right?"

"Yes. Everything's more than all right," Eden said, while her fiancé shuffled around in her bedroom.

"You've been with Rick the whole time, haven't you?"

"Yes."

"And?"

"He's a great guy," Eden said, trying to keep her voice down.

"Obviously. Well, come on. Tell me what happened. You guys have done the deed, haven't you?"

"No! We've been...ah...intimate, but we haven't 'done the deed'...yet. He's a gentleman."

"He's not normal. That's what he is. What guy could resist a gorgeous girl like you?"

Eden sat down on the couch and hugged her legs to her chest. She'd organized for Rick to spend the night with her. Tonight. In her bed. How would she keep her hands to herself? "He's old-fashioned. That's all. He wants to wait until we're married. He wants it to be special. I think it's really sweet."

"I think it's a bit weird. I mean, what if you get married and you're not sexually compatible? Look what happened when you kissed those other guys."

"It's different with Rick. I can't really explain it except to say that when we kiss or even just touch, the feeling is completely opposite to anything I've ever felt before."

"Yeah, but sometimes everything's great until you have sex. Believe me... I know from experience."

"It's not going to be like that with Rick. I can tell."

"I hope you're right. All I care about is that you're happy."

"Thanks, Grace. I am. I'm happier than I've ever been." Eden paused. "Anyway, I'm not just calling to give you an update. I have something to ask you." She got up, peered down the hallway into her bedroom and caught a glimpse of Rick, her pulse rocketing.

"Well, come on. Don't keep me in suspense."

Eden snuck another peek at Rick then wandered into the kitchen. God, he was so handsome and hot. And damn tempting. Like having a plate of rare steak within reach when on a vegetarian detox diet.

"This is probably going to sound a bit...ah...strange..." She braced herself on the kitchen bench. "Rick has asked me to marry him and I've said 'yes'. The wedding's a month from Friday up at Cradle Mountain and I wanted to know if you'll be my Maid of Honor."

"What?"

"Rick and I are engaged and we're getting married…a month from Friday."

"A month from *this* Friday?" Grace said, her tone skeptical.

"Yes. Will you do it?"

"Eden, what the hell are you thinking? You've barely spent five minutes with the guy and you've agreed to marry him?"

"I know it won't make sense to you, but it just feels right, like we're destined to be together." Eden's heart engagement ring glimmered in the dusk light.

"Reality check, please." Grace's voice switched to serious lecture style. "You're in lust, not in love. You've only been out on three dates. You hardly even know him."

Eden placed her hand on her hammering heart. She hadn't realized how much she needed Grace to say 'yes'. She wasn't just a friend. She had become Eden's surrogate family.

"I swear it's not lust. It's so much deeper than that. I know it's quick, but it feels like I've known him forever. I just really want to be with him, more than anything. I really want to be his wife. And no matter what anyone else thinks or believes, we are in love. So even though you don't understand it, will you please, please accept my decision? As my best friend, I'd love for you to be there and support me."

"Of course I will. Just promise me you're not rushing into it because you want to have sex with him."

"You know I wouldn't do that."

Grace's relieved breath swooshed into the receiver. "Okay. Good. Well, congratulations!"

"Thanks."

"So, has Rick asked anyone to be his Best Man?

"Not yet, though he's got a guy in mind."

"Is he good looking?"

"Grace!" Eden rolled her eyes and shook her head.

"Well, is he?"

"I'm not sure. Do you know a guy called Simon? He's a researcher as well and a bit of a computer whiz too." Last light sat on the horizon, letting night sneak in, blanketing Eden's backyard in shimmering shades of silver-gray.

"The name sounds familiar, but I can't place him."

"I've only ever had email contact with the guy. He seems nice."

"If he's even half as hot as Rick, I'll be happy."

"Grace!"

"Well, I wouldn't mind having a bit of fun myself."

"You really are a shocker, you know that?"

"I just like to have a good time. That's all. I'm progressive."

"That's one definition—"

Grace cleared her throat. "Anyway, what's the plan from here? I'll definitely have to organize a girls' night before the big day. Slumber party, cocktails, strippers—"

"No strippers."

"Topless male waiters?"

"No! Seriously, Grace—"

"Just kidding...sort of."

*Yeah, right.* Eden knew her sex-crazed friend—number one admirer of the male form. If Eden had shown any interest in the idea, she'd have had her house full of half-naked men. Speaking of men, Rick had gone quiet. *What is he up to?*

"You're at work tomorrow, yeah?" Grace asked.

"Yeah. I'll see you then."

"Hey, Eden," Rick called out.

"Who's that?" Grace asked.

Eden's heart raced, the hurried beats reverberating all through her on-edge body. "Um... I have to go." Unless she and Rick were having sex, the sleeping arrangements wouldn't make any sense to Grace, and she didn't want to stay on the phone any longer, trying to explain.

"Eden? What's going on?" Suspicion tugged at Grace's tone.

"Nothing. See you tomorrow."

"Sure. Sweet dreams," Grace said, a distinctive grin in her voice.

"Yeah, you too. Goodnight." She hung up before her friend had a chance to ask any more questions.

"Rick, did you need something? Sorry... I was on the phone."

"No, it's all sorted. Thanks."

Eden walked back into the living area and put the phone on its charger, right next to a framed, faded sepia photo of her parents on their wedding day. Rick stood on the far side of the room, reviewing her small, sentimental book collection.

He turned to face her. "Ah...you're back."

"Yes... Find anything you like?"

"Yep." Rick's heated gaze stroked her skin, his tone rife with innuendo.

Eden gulped. "You know, I realize it's only eight-thirty, but I feel like going to bed early tonight...to try and get a good sleep before work tomorrow."

"Sounds like a very good idea." The raw, raspy edge to his voice spoke straight to her sex.

She fingered the rose key pendant around her neck. "I'm just going to have a quick shower first then, okay? Please make yourself at home. I'll be back in a few minutes. Oh, and the TV remote is in the side pocket of the couch."

Eden hurried into her bedroom, dashed to her wardrobe and carefully pulled out her grandmother's wedding dress. She unzipped the garment bag, peeled it back and stared at the only material connection to her family. *Let's see how you look on, shall we?*

She threw off her clothes, slipped into her solitary family heirloom and paraded in front of the full-length mirror. *Wow!* She couldn't believe how well it fit, like it'd been tailor-made for her. She had to wear it. It felt too right not to.

The floorboards squeaked, indicating movement in the living area. Eden stopped dead still and listened. She had to get out of the dress before Rick got a glimpse. Standing in her underwear, she slid the dress back in the garment bag. How would she smuggle it out to get it dry cleaned? *Grace.* She'd come up with something.

The heat of the shower water washed away all the little niggles gnawing at her mind, and nostalgia took over. An image from the far reaches of her memory poked through, commanding her attention.

The special trunk. She smiled. *That's right...* It was what had first put her in touch with her real family. The thoughts continued to flow, reconnecting her with her past. A small wooden chest with brass fastenings, almost like a miniature glory box. And inside, a tarnished, handwritten note sat on top of a mass of off-white silk.

*My sweet little girl,*

*How I wish I could have you with me, but circumstances won't allow us to be together. I hope one day we will be reunited and you will forgive me for my choices.*

*In this chest you will find your grandmother's wedding dress, which your mother wore when we got married, and photos of her and me on our wedding day. I hope you find some comfort in them. I wish I could give you more... I can only hope I will get the opportunity to show you how much I care.*

*You will always be in my heart and thoughts.*

*I love you very much,*

*Your father, Ethan x*

Eden closed her eyes, reliving how her young, eager hands had snatched at the letter and gobbled down every word, like a starving child. She'd tried to find her father, using a range of private investigators — however, none had had any luck.

No records of an Ethan Freberg had been found anywhere. Her father remained a ghost, a concept with no substance, except for the real, tangible letter.

Since the moment she had first read his note and rummaged through the small trunk that had arrived on her seventh birthday, she'd vowed to wear her grandmother's wedding dress for her own marriage. And now, her wish had become a reality. Eden had hardly had any time to arrange anything, and yet everything seemed to be falling into place.

Rick got comfortable on the couch, turned on the TV...and didn't watch it. He became absorbed by the fresh, light and airy vibe of the room. Decorated in a French provincial style, the theme of white and warm honey-toned wood furnishings carried right through the house. The space felt elegant and beautiful, yet quaint, cozy and comfortable. *Very Eden.*

Thornton only took a couple of minutes to size Rick up then jumped onto his lap. He kneaded Rick's thighs and lovingly swished his long black tail in his face. Rick massaged Thornton's head and back until he lay down, then patted his thick, plush coat. Thornton purred, loud and appreciative.

Eden returned with towel-dried hair and wearing a blush-pink dressing gown. "I see you've made a new friend."

"Yep. He's been an excellent host in your absence."

"What can I say? I've brought him up extremely well."

Rick flicked his eyes over her thinly veiled body. "Mmm…come here. I've missed you."

Eden curled up next to him and buried her face into his neck, her shiny, dark cocoa hair falling across his chest. He put his arms around her and kissed her forehead, then tilted her head up and kissed her lips.

She smelled of English roses in full bloom. An image of her lying naked among fresh rose petals commandeered his mind and his cock responded.

"I guess it's my turn," Rick said, needing a cold shower to stop him from succumbing to temptation.

She pressed her hand to his chest. "No, not yet."

He looked into her pleading eyes. "The sooner I'm ready, the sooner we can go to bed." Why had he agreed to this? *A momentary lapse in rational thinking.* Being around her did that to him. How would he restrain himself, lying beside her all night?

Not that he had to hold back. Nothing stopped him from giving in to his craving, including Eden. In fact, she seemed totally up for it. But he wanted to do things properly. Thankfully, their wedding was only a month away. Surely he could hold out until then.

While Rick showered, Eden got comfortable in bed. Waiting. The en suite door finally slid open and she glanced up, her heart hammering. She dumped her book on the bedside table. She'd have to reread those ten pages. She couldn't remember any of the content.

Rick stalked over to the bed, wearing just a pair of jade green and black pajama pants, sitting deliciously low. She licked her lips.

He peeled back the covers, revealing her bare legs, and her jade-green satin and lace slip bunched up around the top of her thighs.

Rick slipped in beside her, his clean skin a heady mix of musk and sandalwood. "Very nice," he said, his words dripping with desire.

Technically, tonight was the first time they'd sleep together, though not by Grace's definition. Heat throbbed in Eden's cheeks. Refraining would be hard.

Rick stroked her hair, sending tingles shimmying down her spine. "I love it when you blush. It's so fucking sexy," he whispered, his breath minty fresh.

He took her in his arms, his bare flesh rubbing against hers, and she sighed. Could a person melt with overwhelming ecstasy? He glided his hands along her curves, his lips never leaving hers. Every one of her nerve endings stood to attention.

She wrapped her leg around his waist, his hard cock pressing against her damp panties. His touch brought out the animal in her, a deep-seated lustful hunger, driving her to behave more like Grace than herself. And she liked it…a lot.

They continued to kiss and make love with their scant clothes on. Desire shone from Rick's eyes, making her feel wanted, adored, and she raced toward orgasm. The familiar tightening took hold, deep in her pelvis, the heat and friction of their bodies threatening to meld them together.

Suddenly, Rick pulled away and laid on his back. "Maybe this wasn't such a good idea." He raked his hands through his hair.

"Oh." *Has he changed his mind?*

Rick looked at her and extended his arm. "Eden, come here."

She hesitated.

"Please."

Eden shifted across and he cradled her against him. "I meant, it's going to be difficult—strike that—almost impossible for me to keep my hands and lips off you."

*Oh.* "I hoped that would be the case."

"How did I know you'd say that?" He teased her lips with a barely-there kiss. How long had that been? Thirty seconds between sexually-charged touches? They really were going to struggle with self-control.

"Hey, how did it go with Grace before?" Rick asked, as though seeking a non-sexual distraction to prevent reigniting their passion.

"Okay."

"She's worried about you, isn't she?"

"Yeah. She thinks I'm rushing into things."

"I suppose you are. We both are."

"It feels right though, so it doesn't feel like we're rushing."

"I agree."

Eden kissed his collar bone and his breath caught. "She just doesn't understand. Thankfully it didn't stop her supporting my decision, even though she thinks it's insane that we're getting married before physically testing things out."

He laughed. "Did you tell her we have engaged in some 'physical testing'?"

"Yes, but she doesn't think it's enough."

Rick caressed her face and she leaned into his hand. "I agree it's not enough, only because I crave more, but it's enough for me to know we're extremely compatible, across the board."

"She'll never get that. Grace needs to know exactly what she's subscribing to before even considering commitment."

"Seems to be the way of the world these days."

Eden shook her head. "Not for us."

"No, we definitely belong to another time."

Rick tipped her chin up and kissed her eyes, nose, lips as though he'd held back long enough, like he had no other choice. He slid his tongue inside her mouth, taunting hers with sensual strokes. Their honeymoon would be amazing. Each time he touched her, every cell in her body lit up like a neon sign, flashing *Take me. Take me now!*

He ended the spectacular kiss and looked into her eyes. "Regarding our honeymoon…"

Being so close to Rick swept her up in a carnal daze. "Mmm…"

"Ah…are we going down the condoms route, 'scuse the pun," he said with a mischievous grin, "or are you already taking something?"

The practicalities of sex. Now that snapped her back into the present. Overcome with excitement at their impending intimacy, she'd forgotten all about the baby side of things.

Heat pulsed in her cheeks. "I'm not taking anything, but we won't need condoms either. Going by the dates, my period's due a few days after the wedding, so we're safe."

He hugged her tighter. "Excellent. I'd really hoped for skin-on-skin, just us. No barriers."

She nestled her head against the curve of his neck. "Me too."

"Good. Now that that's sorted, we should try and get to sleep," he whispered against her hair.

*Damn.* She could kiss and cuddle her alluring fiancé all night. The more they touched, the more she craved. Maybe that would settle down once they'd made love. *Nah.* Who was she kidding? Going by their relationship so far, it would probably enhance rather than detract from her desire.

Eden's pelvic floor clenched in anticipation of their impending encounter. "The sooner we go to sleep, the sooner it will be tomorrow, and I want you here with me as long as possible."

"I will be. I'm not going anywhere."

"But the time will go quicker if we're asleep."

"No it won't, only our perception of it will. Don't get me started on the physics of that...unless you really want me to put you to sleep," he joked.

"You know what I mean."

"Look... I'd much rather lie awake all night just talking and touching..."

She snuggled into him. "Mmmm...me too."

"But we both know where that will lead, and we really have to go in tomorrow if we're planning on taking a few days off in a month."

She groaned. "I know."

They snuggled some more until she eventually drifted off to sleep, and when she next opened her eyes, Rick looked back at her with pure love. *Is he real or a wonderful figment of my imagination?* She reached up and combed her fingers through his hair, flicking it off his forehead. *Definitely not a dream.* Rick, in the flesh, lay right beside her in her bed.

"Good morning," he said, his tone gravelly and sensuous.

"It definitely is." Remnants of sleep clutched her vocal cords, making her voice sound super husky. "What time is it?"

"About quarter past six."

"You were supposed to wake me up fifteen minutes ago!"

"You looked so beautiful and peaceful that I didn't want to disturb you."

She propped herself up on one elbow and stared down at him. "Well, you know what that means. You're going to have to get up fifteen minutes later now. Hope you'll be ready on time."

"I'll be ready. Don't worry. Though, it might mean we have to share the bathroom."

Eden squinted her eyes at him. "You're so naughty!"

"Yep. What are you going to do about it?"

"I thought I'd been pretty clear there'd be a punishment. You have to get up later and get ready in a hurry."

Rick pushed up onto his elbow, leaned in and kissed her. "Hmmm…I might have to be naughty more often. I quite like this sort of punishment…"

They kissed and cuddled some more and finally, but reluctantly, she forced herself to get up. Rick grabbed his gear and went down the hall to the spare bedroom while she finished getting ready.

When Eden entered the kitchen twenty minutes later, she found Rick searching through her cupboards. "Hey, what are you doing?"

He twisted, his guilty gaze meeting hers. "Trying to make us breakfast."

"No, no, no. You're at my place, remember? It's my turn to wait on you."

"That sounds great but, ah-h..."

She put her hands on her hips. "But what?"

"I'll be intrigued to see what you come up with."

Eden strode toward the open cupboard. "I've got bread, Cup-a-Soups and, um..."

He raised his eyebrows.

"Okay, okay. I had planned to go to the supermarket—"

"I think we better leave the grocery shopping to me from now on."

She scrounged up some ingredients and she and Rick sat down to a continental breakfast of Vegemite toast, pineapple juice and coffee.

"What are you going to tell them at work today?" Eden nibbled on her toast, nerves gripping her stomach and making her nauseous.

"The truth."

"No one will understand."

Rick shrugged and grabbed his third piece of bread out of the toaster. "Oh well... We know it's right for us and that's all that matters."

"I guess so."

He spread a thin layer of butter and Vegemite over the top of his toast and took a bite. "I wouldn't worry too much about having to let people know. If Grace beats you in, she'll have told everyone already."

Her shoulders sank. "Ugh. She will too."

Rick's green eyes gleamed. "I can't wait to see people's faces."

She took a sip of her second cup of decaf coffee, and her stomach roiled. "You get a thrill out of shocking people, don't you?"

"I do, actually. I love messing with their sense of equilibrium. It pushes the boundaries of their comfort zone, which I think is important in order to grow as a person."

When they finished eating, they packed their small amount of dishes into the sink and dawdled to the front door.

Eden rested her hands on his chest, his heart beating strong and steady. "I can't believe it's already time to go. How am I going to get through today?"

Rick trailed the tips of his fingers along her jawline and tilted her chin up. "I wish we could spend the day together as well. But seeing we can't, I'll take you out to lunch instead. How does that sound?"

"Really nice. I'm looking forward to it already."

"Me too."

"So…are you going to stay tonight?" She searched his eyes for an answer.

"I really want to —"

"But you can't leave Smokey on his own again. I understand. I'd be the same with Thornton."

After a short, contemplative silence, he said, "How about you stay at my place instead? After work, we can get anything you need from yours and you can put out food for Thornton —"

"You've thought about this." *What a sweet, sweet man. My man. Almost.*

"Absolutely. I've got the whole week planned—and every week, leading up to the wedding. I want to spend as much time with you as possible."

She pressed her lips to his, unable to get enough of his unique flavor—fresh, daring, fun and familiar. "Me too."

They drove into work in under ten minutes and pulled into the car park. The Sub Rosa corporation's thirty-story skyscraper towered over them, the tinted-glass panels shining like a multifaceted black onyx in the morning sunshine. It felt like a thousand shielded eyes were watching them.

Rick opened the passenger-side door and held Eden's hand as she stepped out of the car, then pulled her into his arms and planted a kiss on her unsuspecting lips.

She stumbled back and stared at him, her cheeks ablaze.

He chuckled, low and lusty.

"What are you doing? Everyone can see us down here." Her voice competed with the peak-hour traffic din and won.

He swept away a loose lock of hair that had fallen across her face and tucked it behind her ear. "I'm sure they've got better things to do than watch the car park."

She raised her eyebrows.

"Well, I hope most of them do. But I guess office romances do make interesting gossip…so let's really give them something to talk about." Rick crushed his lips to hers, and they connected like long-lost lovers.

Her mind shouted at her to pull back—however, she got carried away, seduced by his honest, panty-melting passion. Desire sparked and exploded, her whole body lighting up like a fireworks display.

The kiss finally ended, leaving them both breathless, panting and flushed with arousal. Suddenly a month until the wedding felt like an eternity. After a few heart-pounding seconds, Rick slipped his hand around hers, kissed her knuckles and led her toward the entrance of the building.

\* \* \* \*

The Sub Rosa senior managers' meeting was just about to conclude when Andy dropped a bombshell. "I've been reviewing the budgets and we're over half a million dollars in the red. There've been a few additional costs I didn't anticipate, so unfortunately there will need to be some redundancies..."

Their reactions were diverse, in line with their personalities — interest, worry, distress. Interested, the Manager of New Projects, leaned forward and rested his elbows on the table, Worried, the Manager of Organizational Culture, remained frozen in her chair like a bronze statue and Distressed, the Manager of Business Services, stood and strode across to the window. He sucked in his breath, his chest rattling, and shoved his trembling fingers through his salt-and-pepper hair.

"Your jobs are safe...for the time being," Andy added, joining Distressed at the window. He put his hand on the guy's shoulder. "You okay? You look like you're going to have a heart attack." He followed Distressed's gaze to two Sub Rosa employees wrapped in a passionate embrace, locking lips in the car park below.

Distressed stepped away from the window. "I'm fine." His pale blue, speckled eyes, twitched nervously, in contrast to his words.

Interested got up, looked out of the window then glanced at Distressed. "What's the matter? Haven't seen a couple get it on before?"

"Ha-ha. Yeah, it's been a while." Distressed slumped back into his seat, his leg shaking.

"Are you sure our jobs are safe? And what about the Norway compound?" Worried asked, fiddling with her violet diamond-and-platinum ring, her caramel, slicked-back hair glistening under the downlights.

Andy's gaze collided with hers. "Rest assured... Your jobs will not be affected at the moment. And in terms of the running of the compound, nothing will change. The Norway Experiment remains our top priority and I won't let anything or anyone jeopardize that.

"I've got Beauregarde monitoring things. For the moment, the cutbacks will happen in other areas of this site. I need to review the figures again, but it looks like five middle management staff will need to go."

The already cavernous lines in Distressed's forehead grew deeper still. "We can't let things get too out of hand." His hoarse voice quivered.

Andy stared back at him. "And we won't. I promise."

# Chapter Thirteen

The Dark Violet

1231 – 1997

Burning flames shot through Beauregarde's body. He sat up. "Water!"

The woman by his sweat-soaked bed disappeared through the door. When he awoke again, three days later, the heat had gone and his skin was cool and pale. He picked up a small, clouded mirror from the bedside table.

The person staring back at him had black hair and violet eyes. But he was blond with brown eyes. *What the fuck?* His brow crumpled. *That's not me!* What the fuck had happened?

He lay back down and rested until the memories blitzed his brain.

*The 'messenger'. That was what they called him. A warm fuzzy glow saturated his insides. Beauregarde flitted all over the countryside, no errand too big or too small. The town needed him, the crucial link in the chain of communication. Not many people could say they loved their job...but he did.*

*His bulging money pouch lazed on the rough, wooden bedside table, silver coins spilling out like a king gorging himself on a feast. He was just a couple more jobs away from owning his own plot of land.*

*Beauregarde collected his errands for the day from his boss' office in the town center and stuffed them into his reindeer-skin satchel. His third job took him through the forest, but instead of it being lush and green, it grew dim and stark. Leafless trees, tall, spiky and bare loomed above him.*

*The wind gusted through the gaping branches, pushing him forward, his long, blond hair whipping his face. His stomach twisted into strangled knots. When would the morose section end? He scurried along the path, his gaze darting, pulse racing. A gnarled tree root protruded from the ground and he clipped his toe, dropping to the forest floor.*

*Winded, he gasped for air, like a whitefish out of water. Creeaaak...crash! A mammoth black branch slammed onto his back. Crack! His ribs snapped like broken branches. Beauregarde panted and rasped, his lungs punctured, leaking air. A pool of blood gathered under him and he fell into darkness.*

His new family explained he'd now joined the Violet vampire clan. But their lifestyle didn't reflect the stories he'd heard...at all. They had restrictive rules, just like humans. He tried to fit in to their moralistic code — basically, humans were off the menu — but couldn't resist the allure of their blood.

Beauregarde first tried to satiate his craving by having sex with human females. But they were much too messy and fragile. His unintentional heavy-handedness usually killed the women, so instead of letting his conquests go to waste, he made a meal of them.

Bloody Hugh and his puritanical ways got Beauregarde banished from the Violet community. Of all the people that had to see him fuck a human conquest and devour her broken body... So much for brotherly loyalty. But he'd get back at Hugh.

Beauregarde traipsed across the country to Sweden and down into Denmark. Alone, lonely and ravenous, he crawled along the forest floor, searching for food. A rabbit hopped past and he tracked the furry little tidbit, stumbling after it into a labyrinth of caves. Then he collapsed.

His fifth day without red blood... Only two days left to find food or else he'd starve to death...or so the old wives' tale went. Supposedly some vampires expired even earlier. He didn't want to test that theory.

In the blackness, a pair of glistening eyes peeked at him through a tiny gap in the rocks. *A mirage?* He inched over to it. The salty warmth of the hot-blooded creature tantalized his taste buds. It was real all right— close and yet, unreachable. He groaned and thumped his fist onto the damp earth.

The animal's eyes continued their mocking stare— *you can't catch me!* He glowered and shot his hand through the gap. The animal dodged his grasp, but he persisted until the heat of determination radiated through his body and he began to melt. Like raging purple lava, he flowed through the slit, sank his fangs into the unsuspecting rabbit and chugged down its blood.

He sighed, the hunger easing, slid through the opening into the broader cave and transformed back into himself. *What the fuck had just happened?* Although crazy, he couldn't complain. His darkest night had turned into his brightest day.

With no laws to contain him, Beauregarde went berserk, praying on battling communities of humans across Europe. Their deaths would be attributed to the cruelty of war and he could remain hidden.

However, after seven hundred years of nomadic roaming, he became bored and tired. He returned to his hometown, hoping to find new inspiration and possibly even settle, at least for a while. But he got caught in 1939, by humans, of all people.

His stomach roared and he staggered toward a man, the scrumptious scent of blood emanating from his chest. *Zap!* Beauregarde hit the floor, like a massive mosquito in an insect zapper.

Two hulking men dragged him onto a small boat, his body twitching and shuddering. One man rowed while the other stood over Beauregarde, pointing a type of stun gun at his temple.

"One false move and you'll know about it...again," the gunman said with a smirk.

The rower made eye contact with the other man. "You know, I really didn't think that blood lure would work. I mean, there's hardly a thimble full in that test tube."

"He sniffed it out like a dog. And now it's time for the pound."

The two smart-asses laughed.

The rower docked the boat alongside a dingy, jail-looking complex. A double zap shook Beauregarde's body, and he came to inside a dreary, four-walled cell. Drips of water punctuated the silence, like a dysfunctional metronome. His head throbbed in rhythm to the watery timekeeper.

He massaged his temples and leaned his back against the cold, damp wall. He could potentially slip through the small gap under the thick metal door, but then he'd always be on the run. That wouldn't do. His mind ticked over.

*Yes!* He'd found the answer to keep him out of the prison-style place. Now he just had to convince those in charge.

Footsteps echoed down the hallway. Coming closer. *Dinner?*

The door creaked open and his captors entered, both sporting holstered stun guns. "Your food is coming."

Beauregarde threw his hands up into a stop gesture. "Forget about it. I actually have a proposal to make."

The two men glanced at each other, then back at him. "Go ahead."

He rubbed his hands together. "I can get you insider information, Violet secrets, but you have to free me. Permanently."

\* \* \* \*

*1:30 a.m., November 1997*

Beauregarde slithered through the air conditioning vent and emerged in his brother's confined quarters. "Enjoying your time alone?" He smirked.

"What are you doing here?" Hugh said, without looking up.

"I came to confirm my hypothesis that nice guys always finish last."

"All right, you've had your gloat. Now leave."

Beauregarde sat on the couch beside him and crossed his legs. "Come on, Hugh. Can't you take a joke?"

Hugh stared at him, his jaw tight. "Have you ever thought of using your powers and freedom for good?"

"Good is overrated. I tried to live a respectable life. It's just not me."

"You're so self-absorbed and ungrateful. If Mum and Dad hadn't found you in the woods that day, you'd be dead."

Beauregarde shrugged his shoulders. "Maybe, maybe not. How do you know how close I was to death? We can only go off their word. I think they were over-cautious. Yes, they found me sprawled out on the forest floor unconscious, cut and bleeding, but a few stitches would have fixed me up. They could have nursed me back to health and I could have still been human."

"And long dead. You can't tell me you'd have given up all the power and privileges you have now to be full human."

The bastard was right, of course. No way in hell would he admit it to him, though. Not to Hugh. Not ever.

"I might have. No one ever asked me. I had no choice, just like I have no choice about craving human blood. And don't try and tell me it's wrong. Humans justify eating animals for sustenance. It's the same thing."

Hugh shook his head, an exasperated sigh hissing from his lips. "No, it isn't. It's cannibalism. You used to be human, for God's sake!"

Beauregarde wagged his finger at him. "Don't act all high and mighty. Whether you want to admit it or not, you have the cravings too. You just choose to deny them. So who's being more honest, truer to themselves, me or you?"

"Just because you crave something doesn't mean it's right. But go ahead and rationalize your existence if it makes you feel better."

Beauregarde huffed and flopped against the backrest. "You're a close-minded asshole, you know that?"

Hugh rolled his eyes. "Look who's talking."

"At least I didn't leave my bride-to-be at the altar." He stifled a smirk.

Hugh's gaze clamped onto his eyes. "What?"

"Poor thing. Red eyes, sobbing. An inconsolable, blubbering mess."

Hugh glared at him. "You didn't."

"Didn't what?" Beauregarde blinked, acting all ignorant.

"You better not have touched her." Had he heard a hint of threat in his brother's voice? So un-Hugh. Though, knowing his weak-ass brother, any threat was as empty as a puff of smoke.

"And what if I did?" Beauregarde laughed, deep and guttural. Then he straightened his black brocade coat and said, "Relax. As if I'd be interested in a worthless human woman. But she has made an excellent recruit."

Hugh's forehead crumpled. "Recruit?"

"Yes, that's right. She joined Sub Rosa. She's pretty passionate about making sure no one goes through what she did. What did she say? Um…*'vampires are untrustworthy users, charming their way into the hearts of helpless humans, sucking their emotions dry and discarding them to move on to the next gullible, lovesick fool'.*"

Hugh's face scrunched up like he'd just sunk his fangs into a sour lemon. "And what about you?"

"What about me?"

"You're a vampire. She must have figured that out."

Beauregarde sneered. "Yes, but I'm the exception to the rule. You see, I've been there for her. I've stuck by her through the hard times after your desertion."

Hugh's eyes bored into his. "It was you, wasn't it?"

"Excuse me?" He padded his tone full of feigned innocence.

"You were in the forest that night. I saw your violet eyes glowing in the bushes, so don't even try to deny it. You tracked me down and spiked my drink. You're the one behind getting me put back in here. She has no idea, though, does she? She thinks I left her and am roaming free, living it up with a girl in every corner of the world." A film of moisture coated his forlorn, pathetic eyes. "How could you?"

Beauregarde crossed his leg away from Hugh and stretched out his arms across the top of the backrest. "It's easy. I don't like you. I never have and I definitely never will, especially after you got me exiled. What happened to being loyal to your brother? But no, it looks like your loyalty only extends to humans.

"So why should I be loyal to you? I'm ashamed to have you as a brother. Mr. Self-Righteous. Never set a foot wrong. Can't even think let alone utter a swear word. Won't even threaten to punch me after what I've done. I thought you loved this girl?"

Hugh hesitated then took a couple of controlled breaths. "I do—and I always will. And that's something you'll never understand or experience."

Beauregarde clenched his teeth and scowled at his brother while searching his brain for a cutting retort. *Nothing. Blank.*

He couldn't stick around and let Hugh win the verbal upper hand. So he shot up, flew out of the air conditioning vent and into the cold night air. He needed some comfort food.

Slipping in and out of the shadows, he made his way to his favorite Norwegian hunting ground — a small, desolate fishing village that attracted lone fishermen and vagrants. The vagrants weren't as tasty but they were safer, so much safer. No one missed them.

Near the pier, a homeless man rummaged through a bin, condensation bursting out of his mouth, his exposed, goose-pimpled forearms a light shade of purple-blue. Beauregarde salivated. The man wouldn't even know what bit him.

He sped toward the vagrant and a flare shot up, brightening the sky. Beauregarde stopped. A sole, rotund fisherman hung over the side of his agitated boat, violently seasick. Everyone would think he'd fallen overboard. *Perfect.*

Beauregarde ran toward the sea and swooped, plucking the man from his boat and smashing him into the ragged shoreline rocks. He dragged him, unconscious and bleeding, into a cavernous blow hole and sank his teeth into the man's throbbing carotid artery. The blood, deliciously hot and salty, spurted into his mouth and flowed down his gullet.

He sucked and sucked, like a greedy child slurping every last drop of his favorite milkshake. Beauregarde tossed aside the lifeless, almost glowing white man then leaped to his feet.

It was time for dessert, but not of the food variety. He needed to satisfy a different kind hunger. *Which will it be — the Violet or Jade harem?* He curled his lips into a smirk.

After he'd struck up a freedom deal with the Sub Rosa head honcho back in 1939, he'd left the Norway compound and roamed the outskirts of his hometown, hooking up with the party-hard Violet night crew. The sex was otherworldly. Full, three-quarter and even half-castes could go all night with no weariness, no fragility, no restrictions.

The Jade bevy of beauties had been a new thing. Bored with his regular Violet groupies, Beauregarde had needed a challenge. He'd had to sample a forbidden Jade woman if it was the last thing he did. But how could he get his hands on one? Jades and Violets hated each other.

During a mind-numbing Sub Rosa senior management meeting, Beauregarde had begun daydreaming and the kernel of an idea had started to sprout. By the end of the meeting, he had hatched the perfect plan and taken Andy, the CEO, aside to make his pitch.

*'You know how valuable my work has been with the Violets. Ethan has been a great inside contact, so I thought I could try and replicate it with the Jade camp.'*

Andy had stood back and stared at him. *'You've got to be kidding, right? There's no way in hell they'll ever trust you. You're a Violet, their arch enemy!'*

Beauregarde had put his hand on Andy's shoulder. *'Just hear me out. All you need to do is pick a few Jade women to do hardcore testing on and I'll 'save' them from the experiments.'*

*'You really think it's that simple.'*

Beauregarde had tightened his grip. *'Yes, I do. If they see I've put my own life on the line to help, I'll have them right where I want them.'*

Everything had gone as he had hoped. The Jade women had dubbed Beauregarde the hero, the exception to the regular Violet, and they'd welcomed him...

"Thank you, Andy," he murmured as the new, striking blonde took him in her mouth, her deep jade eyes the color of rare jewels. Four others fluttered around him, one sucking on each of his nipples, one licking his balls and one tongue-kissing him, their pallid skin glistening under the dim downlights.

His climax roared through him and the women all migrated to his cock, licking and swallowing the spurts of cum. Then they took turns to kiss his lips and every inch of his body.

*Mmm...now for the juicy cherry on top.* Beauregarde kneeled behind the new blonde and assumed his favorite position—doggy style. He fondled her ample breasts while nipping the snow-white skin of her neck, and thrust his cock right up to the hilt of her tight cunt.

One of the other Jades started making out with the Jade he was fucking, while another lay beneath them and licked her out. He groaned. The last two regulars weaved their fingers through his long hair and massaged his ass and anus.

On the verge of another orgasm, he grabbed the striking blonde's hips and thrust hard. He grunted and came deep inside her, her cunt milking his cock of every last drop. Beauregarde pulled out and sat back on his knees, panting.

As soon as he recovered from his release, he jumped up and redressed in his black, gothic attire. "Thank you, ladies. Until next time."

His new conquest pushed up off the jade-green rug and approached him, still seductively naked. "When will that be?"

*When I choose.* "Soon." He adjusted his lapel. Maybe he could fit in a quick Violet stop on the way to the airport as well. "Right now, I have to go. I'm on a really tight schedule." He turned toward the white timber door.

"Wait!" she called out. "What about Demi?"

*Mmm... Where is that sexy little half-caste?* "What about her?"

She stepped around in front of him. "She's with child."

*Fuck.* "Oh, I see..."

Her intense Jade eyes studied his. "She thought you'd want to know."

"Yes. Thank you." He forced a smile and fled into the dawn.

How many children would that be? Over a hundred? He absolutely met the criteria for a highly sought-after stud. What a fucking impressive effort. Add to that the massive societal benefits... Yeah, the world needed more of him.

He sneered. This kid would be extra special. The first mixed-clan baby. What would it turn out like? *Stop it!* Since when had he ever entertained a thought, let alone a sliver of interest about one of his possible offspring? Maybe he'd gotten soft in his old age. He shook his head. *Not a chance.*

He arrived at the Norway airport, after an express Violet fuck stop, just in time to catch the early flight back to Australia. Beauregarde waited at the gate, reveling in the awe-filled stares and sycophantic blatherings of the other passengers. There was nothing like being seen and treated as a god.

# Chapter Fourteen

## The Living Nightmare

*Hobart, June 2010*

*Andy bit into the blood-red candy layer of his toffee apple. "Today was the best day of my life!" he said from the back seat.*

*He and his parents had arrived home at dinner time, after spending all day at the Royal Hobart Show. While his dad parked the car in the garage, Andy ran up to the front door and tugged at the security door handle. It swung open.*

*"Hang on a min – " His mum's smile morphed into open-mouthed terror. She ran toward him, her jumble of keys smashing to the ground. His dad followed closely behind, loaded up with show bags.*

*His mum grabbed his wrist. "Ouch! That hurts," Andy cried.*

*The main wooden door stood ajar and she pushed it open.*

*In the front foyer stood a handsome blond man and a beautiful young woman, with sparkling jade green eyes...and blood-drenched lips.*

Andy sat up, gasping for breath. Alone, in his own bed. *Thank fuck.* He reached for the glass of water on his bedside table and gulped down a couple of mouthfuls, his pulse still pounding. Always the same recurring nightmare since the incident had happened fifty-six years before. Would it ever stop? How much counseling did a man need?

He switched on the lamp, pulled open the top drawer of his bedside table and grabbed his dog-eared photo album. The first few pictures were of his mum, decked out in fifties fashions, pregnant for the first time...at forty.

Then he flipped to the next page and read the inscription he'd read a thousand times, under his first baby photo — *Our little miracle.* The sting of tears burned his eyes and he packed the album away.

Andy arrived at work by seven a.m. and went straight to his office. He swung the door open and flicked on the light.

"Congratulations, Andy!" Distressed, Worried and Interested said together. Above them hung a big banner — *Happy 30th Anniversary!*

Andy's heart hammered out a rapid, unforgiving tempo. "Fuck! You almost gave me a heart attack!"

"Sorry. We thought it was important to commemorate such a wonderful milestone," Worried said, accessorized with her trademark violet-and-platinum jewelry.

Distressed stepped forward and shook his hand. "Things really progressed when you stepped into the CEO role all those years ago. You've done some great work."

"And shown incredible leadership," Interested chimed in.

Andy smiled, his heart settling into its routine rhythm. "Thanks, everyone. As you know, after what happened to my parents, I'm pretty passionate about the Norway Experiment. I feel confident we're not far from finding the cure. We've got a great research team at the moment."

Distressed fidgeted in his trouser pocket, pulled out a strip of nicotine gum and popped it into his mouth. "See you at morning tea."

"I don't have morning tea," Andy said.

"You will today," Worried replied with a glint in her eye. "The Board has arranged it. They thought it would be a good opportunity to bring everyone together to celebrate and hopefully raise staff morale after the announcement of the redundancies. Act surprised, okay?" With a cheeky grin, she flitted through the doorway, her slicked-back caramel hair catching the light.

Interested sidled up to him. "I just wanted to let you know that I feel really privileged to be working with you. I know you took a big risk hiring me, but although I'm young and inexperienced, I'm a hard worker. Hopefully my results so far speak for themselves."

"They do. The outcome of your All-Weather-Rose portfolio in particular has been groundbreaking."

The new recruit smiled. "Thanks, Andy. Your praise means a lot to me. I really admire your career and share your passion to preserve the sanctity of the human race. My aim is to follow in your footsteps and one day to achieve a similar level of greatness, respect and success."

Interested was a networking schmoozer if he'd ever seen one. *I better keep my eye on him.* "Well, what can I say? Keep up the good work." Andy walked around to the back of his desk and sat in his decadent, black leather office chair.

Interested left his office and Andy logged in and opened Outlook. While he waded through the posts, an email from the Board came through. *No more budget cuts, please!* Andy clicked on it and it opened up.

*July 21, 2010*

*Dear Andy,*

*The Board would like to congratulate you on an outstanding thirty years of service. In this day and age, it is quite an achievement to reach such a milestone. However, you have not only done that but also gone above and beyond expectation. The outstanding quality of your work and excellent leadership has produced incredible results, the most notable listed below —*

*Refinement of the sunlight Taser gun technology*

*Redevelopment of the Norway compound and implementation of the sunlight barricade system.*

*Development of the Infrared Radiation-Vitamin D (IVD) tranquilizer*

*Success of the All-Weather-Rose project and development of an implementation plan from the findings.*

*Your ability to effectively network, liaise and develop rapport with key stakeholders has been essential in securing the required research funds to continue our mission.*

*Going forward, all we ask is for more of the same. We have trust and faith in your work and believe with your ongoing guidance, our vision to improve living conditions across the globe and strengthen the human race will soon be reached.*

*Keep up the excellent work.*

*Regards,*

*The Board*

Andy smiled and leaned back in his office chair. If only they knew the lengths he'd gone to, to get results. On the Norway Experiment in particular, Beauregarde had been a gem. Without him, he wouldn't have known his parents were still alive, if the state they were in could be considered living.

* * * *

*Norway compound, September 1984*

Andy's teeth clenched. "For fuck's sake, Beauregarde. How can they still escape?"

Beauregarde scooped his long black hair over the front of his shoulder, like a dark Rapunzel. "Now that the food's better, they're stronger. It's going to be harder to contain them. The skylights into their cells aren't enough. There are too many hours of darkness overnight to recharge them."

Andy huffed. "You're one of their kind. What do you suggest?"

Beauregarde remained seated. "A system where they're exposed to sunlight twenty-four hours a day."

Andy clamped down his jaw and ground his teeth together. "And where would I get that?"

"I'm sure the research team could invent it or something similar. That's what they're paid for."

"I already have them working overtime on a vampire tranquilizer and eradicating the vampire gene. We don't have enough funds for additional resources." Andy drummed his fingers against the meeting room table. "Though, I may be able to start running both the Australian and Norwegian research departments twenty-four hours a day. I'm sure if I include a bonus or two and reinforce the scientific kudos for those who get results, most staff will be keen to participate." *Yes, that could work.*

"In the meantime, continue hunting for more vampire specimens across the globe, make sure less red blood is included in the captives' meals and have the guards taser them with global solar radiation to keep their energy low."

A smirk slithered onto Beauregarde's lips. "Your wise wish is my command." He studied the split ends in his black mane. "Any updates on the gene eradication research?"

Andy sat in the big black office chair at the head of the table and crossed his legs. "No. But the vampire tranquilizer shouldn't be too far away. The scientists have started tinkering with blood blends. Garlic got trialed first and ruled out. Surprise, surprise."

Beauregarde scoffed. "They would have smelled that coming from miles away."

"They did. Then the researchers tried spraying the clans with garlic instead, but it only acted as a temporary deterrent, like a capsicum spray for vampires, though not as potent.

"Next, the team tried mixing blood with alcohol and sedatives, but they had no effect. Your suggestion of toadstool juice proved limited, as well. Even when the concentrations were increased, the test subjects remained tipsy for no more than a couple of hours."

Beauregarde got up and perched on the edge of the table, encroaching on Andy's personal space. He got his kicks out of intimidating and manipulating people, and Andy got his kicks out of denying Beauregarde the pleasure.

Two could play that dick-measuring game. Andy rolled his chair in closer. "Recently there has been some progress. One new, bright spark suggested distilling elements of sunlight, particularly ultraviolet and infrared radiation, and infusing them, along with Vitamin D, into the blood.

"At the moment, the research team is trialing several different concoctions. Blood laced with Vitamin D, blood laced with ultraviolet radiation, blood laced with infrared radiation and combinations of the three. The finalized formula needs to render full vampires unconscious for at least a full day, long enough to safely transport them."

Andy's watch buzzed and he checked the time. "Thanks for the personalized tour. I need to get going now to make the start of the International Research Summit."

"Don't you want to see the lab?" Beauregarde asked.

Andy snapped his briefcase shut and grabbed the handle. "No time. You'll have to take me through on my next visit. Just keep me up to date with — "

"It will only take a few more minutes." Beauregarde stood in front of him.

Andy hesitated. He should really make the effort. Who knew when he would next have the opportunity to fly over? "Fine."

They power-walked across the complex, past the captives' cells to the experiential lab in the Jade quarters, and stood at the one-way glass. Inside the sterile white room, a gloved-up team of ten scientists paired off and stood parallel to one another, holding clip boards and pens.

Positioned next to them were small metal tables with screw-top sample containers, cotton buds, gauze, scalpels, tweezers and jars filled with rice-sized beads. A steady parade of hunched over, sunlight-tasered Jades, accompanied by guards, trudged through the middle of the researchers, dragging their feet from entry to exit.

"What are they doing?" Andy asked.

"Microchipping, DNA recording and analysis." The glow of Beauregarde's violet eyes reflected in the one-way glass.

"Isn't their DNA already on file?"

Beauregarde turned to him. "The old methods of recording were…ineffective. Plus, a few files have been lost and many of the promising stored DNA samples were depleted when used for experimentation."

The vampires moved along like factory goods in a production line. A Jade reached a pair of the research crew, had a buccal swab or blood sample taken and simultaneously got injected between the scapulae, then continued back to their cell. The researchers recorded notes and repeated the process with the next waiting, taser-subdued Jade.

Andy glanced at his watch again. "I really need to —" He did a double take at a male and female Jade who had just entered the lab. Air stuck in his constricted throat and the blood drained from his clammy skin. "It couldn't be," he choked out. They weren't a day older than when he'd last seen them thirty years ago, but beautiful, so much more beautiful, like their murderers.

Beauregarde stepped closer to him. "Andy?"

"Mum? Dad?" His gaze remained glued to them. "They were dead. Their blood splattered everywhere." All those years of counseling. "I have to talk to them."

"What? Who?"

Andy pointed at the two Jades through the glass. "My parents."

Beauregarde's snicker turned into a dark, twisted belly laugh. "You've got vampire parents?"

Andy shook his head. "No, I didn't. But it's them. I know it's them."

A deeply buried memory broke into his consciousness. A siren wailing, a police car stopping inches from his sobbing, blood-soaked, four-year-old body. Waking up in hospital and being told his parents were dead. He'd never thought they could have survived, that they could have been changed.

The siren must have scared the Jades mid-meal, otherwise he and his parents would have all died. If the police car had come a moment or two later, he could have been a Jade too. He could have been in captivity just like his parents… Things needed to change.

Andy refocused on Beauregarde. "Right… Make sure those two Jades are excluded from any harsh experimentation and anything that might put them in danger. But don't let them escape. We have to concentrate on finding a cure." *So I can get my parents back.*

He took a few steps and stopped. "And the compound living conditions need to improve. When that's done, you're to report to me in Tasmania and give me a full rundown."

Beauregarde's eyes widened and his pale brow lifted, as though he'd been slapped. "Don't you need me here?"

Andy popped open his briefcase. "For part of the time. From now on, you'll be working across the Norwegian and Australian sites. Times have changed. I need you to be more mobile, more flexible." Andy made a quick note in his Filofax, slammed his briefcase shut and looked into Beauregarde's unimpressed Violet eyes. "Expect a detailed memo outlining the implementation plan tomorrow."

"What about the summit?"

Andy grabbed the handle of his briefcase and strode to the door. "I've got more pressing matters to deal with. Find someone and send them in my place."

# Chapter Fifteen

### The Tearful Side Project

*Hobart, July 2010*

*Hi Simon,*

*Forget about finishing up on the All-Weather-Rose project. It's under control. I'd like you to start working full time on vampire DNA body fluid analysis. I've upgraded your security level so you have access to anything you need from downstairs.*

*I expect big things from you. Report directly to me with any updates.*

*Andy Falon*
*CEO*
*Sub Rosa Corporation*

Simon shoved his fingers through his short hair. "No pressure, Mr Big Shot Dictator," he muttered and locked his computer.

Still in his lab coat, he took the stairs to the sample storage area in the bowels of the building, below the basement. He swiped his security pass in the wall-mounted card reader, and the lock on the thick steel door disengaged and swung open into a dark, dusty wilderness.

The stale, musty air stuck to his airways and he coughed. He inched his hand along the wall until he found the light switch and flicked it on. The room spanned the size of a football field, with rows of shelving running from end to end. Above the entrance to each row, a sign indicated what items were stored in that section, like a science supermarket.

He avoided the obvious choice — vampire venom — as many before him had tried to concoct an antidote…and failed. The best outcome achieved had been by using a diluted venom solution, whereby forty percent of rats remained infected and twenty-five percent died, leaving only thirty-five percent cured. Unsurprisingly, the results were deemed too risky to warrant human testing.

Simon made his way down each aisle, checking out the range and quality of the samples before deciding on which bodily fluid to tackle.

"Whoa!" He stopped in front of a tall glass container featuring a full-length torso of a pregnant woman cut into five vertical sections, with a fetus still inside her, though not a regular human baby — a half-caste Violet, going by the ultraviolet tinge to the remnants of the amniotic sac. The information card underneath read *1941 – Female Norway Researcher, twenty weeks pregnant, found dead. Violet father unknown.*

On the waist-high shelf running along either side of the capacious case were smaller glass containers with a range of Jade, and a predominance of Violet, mixed-heritage fetuses dating from 1939 to 1945.

A well-preserved, glowing fluorescent-green and ultra-violet colored specimen pulled his focus and he picked it up, moving it around in his hands to view it from all angles. *Fascinating.* He located the label—1943 – *Sixteen week, aborted, Jade-Violet half-caste.*

In the last aisle, on a dusty shelf, sat twelve vials of a luminous, viscous substance collected between 1939 and 1996 from a single subject. "Full-caste Violet Vampire tears. This is it," Simon said, holding one of the small, glowing ampoules in his hand.

The research department had always been under-resourced, but he couldn't believe the tears had just been left. They were as rare as a full set of hen's teeth. But how robust were they? To be sure of their sturdiness, he'd have to test them against fresher samples.

He took the whole lot back to the lab and organized for fresh samples to be sent across from Norway. Within thirty hours he had a shipment of newer tears to compare to the older specimens. He dipped the sterilized eye dropper into the new batch. "Hmmm…the consistency is different. Let's check the composition."

Simon squeezed the substance into the gas chromatograph and awaited the mass spectrometer reading. Water, mucin, lipids, lysozyme, lactoferrin, lipocalin, lacritin, immunoglobulins, glucose, urea, phosphorescent proteins, sodium and potassium. The same. *That's odd. What changed the consistency?*

During his late lunch break, he ate his sandwich at his desk and scrolled through the electronic research notes accompanying the tear-sample extractions. The most detailed notes were from a researcher named Salvator, during his secondment to the Norway compound during the 1990s.

*There is only one full-caste subject I have found who can produce tears. He is a pure Violet who appears very in tune with his emotions. The first lot of samples were thin and fluidy, though thicker than human tears. However, as the subject became more emotional, the viscosity and luminance of the tears grew and began to glow in the dark, almost pulsating light, like they had a life of their own.*

*When I compared the samples to each other, their composition was the same, but the concentrations were different. From this, I've hypothesized that there is a link between the intensity of the emotion and type of tear produced. The stronger the emotion, the more concentrated the tear…*

Simon's phone vibrated in his pocket and he grabbed it. A text message from Rick.

*Hey mate, just checking that 7:30 still works for you tonight.*

He typed back a response on his state-of-the-art smart phone.

*Yeah. All good. I'll be finishing up here shortly, then all I need to do is pack, have a power nap and I'll be all yours for the long weekend ;-)*

# Chapter Sixteen

## The Pick-Up

Eden held up the skimpy white negligee Grace had given her. "This is so tiny. I may as well wear nothing."

"Uh-uh. Getting Rick revved up to strip it off you is part of the fun. It builds the excitement of the naked action to come," Grace said with a sassy smile, and stuffed the rest of her gift — a colorful set of minuscule lace G-strings — into Eden's overnight bag.

"It's just not me. I'll feel like a stripper." Eden's face grew hotter by the second.

"Believe me, Rick will love it."

"I don't know. Shouldn't I be myself?" *As opposed to a carbon copy of you.*

"Of course. You're just tuning in to your sexy side."

Eden dropped the negligee on top of the rainbow of lace. "He's never going to believe I chose this stuff."

"I don't think he's going to care whether you did or not." Grace plucked a sparkly, jade-green G-string out of Eden's overnight bag. "You have to admit that I chose well. He's not going to be able to keep his hands off you...and not just his hands."

An image of Rick, naked, his mouth between her legs, his green-eyed gaze unwavering, flashed into her mind. "Grace!"

"Well, it is your wedding night. Don't you want it to be special?"

"Of course, but I need to be *me*." Eden squeezed her thighs together, trying to soothe the longing ache in her sex.

"Trust me... As soon as you wear any of these, you'll feel so sexy that you won't think twice about it."

Eden snatched the glittery underwear out of Grace's hand and chucked it on top of the pile of obscene outfits. "Maybe... I hope I can pull this off," she muttered and zipped up her overnight bag.

"You'll be fine. Just don't overthink it."

\* \* \* \*

The driver pulled up in front of the Cradle Mountain accommodation and Eden's mouth dropped open in awe. Two log cabins sat side by side, surrounded by snow, and provided fantastic views of Dove Lake.

The driver informed them that she and Grace were to get ready in the honeymoon suite, and Grace and Simon would spend the night in the two-bedroom cabin next door.

Eden and Grace stood out in the cold, admiring the spectacular views, while the driver took their bags inside.

"Are you sure you're okay sharing with Simon? What if you don't like him?" Eden asked.

"Don't worry about it. If he's a loser, I'll just cut the night short and hang out in my bedroom. I can entertain myself." Grace raised two perfectly-plucked insinuating eyebrows.

Eden shook her head. "You're unbelievable. You know that?"

"I'll take that as a compliment." Grace rubbed her hands together and blew on them. "Let's get inside. It's freezing out here!"

The scent of smoked eucalyptus hit Eden the second she stepped through the front door. In the cast-iron fireplace, burning wood crackled and popped, sending orange and yellow flickers up the cream walls.

"Wow. This is gorgeous," Grace gushed, and continued toward the floor-to-ceiling window overlooking the snow-capped mountain and ink-blue lake.

Eden followed close behind and stopped next to a silver champagne cooler. A note with her name on it, in Rick's handwriting, leaned against it. She unfolded the white paper and read the message aloud.

*Hi, Eden,*

*Welcome to Cradle Mountain! It's beautiful, isn't it? I hope you like it as much as I do.*

*The moment I decided to propose, I thought of this place. I think it's perfect — a beautiful bride and a breathtaking environment... What more could I ask for?*

*If my calculations are correct, you should be reading this about midday, and if all goes to plan, we'll see each other at around 1:30 p.m. And that's right — there are no directions to the wedding ceremony. It's a surprise. All you need to know is you must be ready to leave by 1:15pm. So get cracking! ;-)*

*Looking forward to seeing you soon!*

*Love you,*

*Rick xox*

*PS. Hi, Grace!*

Grace pressed her hand to her heart. "Awww...he's so sweet."

"He is, isn't he?" Eden placed his note on the table, grabbed Grace's hand and dragged her into the bedroom. A carved, mahogany, four-poster bed dominated the room, with creamy white Eden rose petals that transitioned into a blush pink strewn across the white bedding.

While Grace walked to the enormous window, Eden spotted another note from Rick lying on the center of the bed. A poem, penned in Rick's elegant, yet slightly backward-slanted, handwriting.

*Ode to Eden*
*Violet diamonds, brilliant*
*Mysterious and engaging*
*Captivating my mind.*
*Dark cocoa brown locks*
*Long and flowing*
*Drape over me,*
*My heart aching*
*My body craving*
*Your touch*
*A sweet, white dove, fluttering its wings*
*Creating ripples*
*In the deep, still lake,*
*Soaring within my grasp*
*Teasing, tempting*
*Nestling into my chest*
*Into my heart,*
*Captured,*
*I surrender to you*
*Forever changed,*
*An everlasting embrace*
*Eternally united in love.*

Eden squealed and skipped over to join Grace at the window, which boasted similar picturesque views as the living area.

Grace hugged her. "You're so lucky. Rick is perfect."

"He definitely is everything I've ever wanted. You never know, Simon might be great as well."

"I have everything crossed he is. I could do with a good man myself. Okay, maybe not a 'good' man, but you know what I mean," Grace said with a sinful grin.

"I know *exactly* what you mean."

Next, they checked out the en suite. A double shower shared the space with a luxurious spa bath, both bathed in golden, romantic lighting.

"You guys are definitely getting it on tonight. This place is a seduction zone. I hope it's a good omen for me and Simon."

"Grace! He's one of Rick's good friends. Unless you really like him, please don't do anything too...Grace-like."

"I promise I won't pursue him unless I'm interested."

Eden raised her eyebrows.

"Okay, unless I'm interested in him for more than just sex."

"Thank you."

They returned to the living area and Grace cracked open a bottle of champagne, pouring them a glass each.

They sipped and chatted while they got ready, and when Grace finished Eden's makeup, Eden stood up and spun around. "How do I look?"

Her inherited, off-white dress swished and settled against her body. The off-white lace bellbottom sleeves flared out from elbow to wrist, and the upper bodice covered her right up to her neck in exquisite lace. Smooth, off-white silk continued in a figure-hugging design past her hips and fell into an A-line cut with a small train.

In her hair, she wore a garland of violet roses that matched her bouquet, and an off-white chiffon veil cascaded down to her waist. She paraded in front of Grace, picked up her faux, off-white fur wrap from the bridal bed and positioned it over her shoulders.

Grace's eyes teared up. "Beautiful. Just beautiful."

The driver arrived at one-ten p.m. and gave them a five-minute warning.

Digital camera in hand, Grace clicked off a series of shots. "Just one more. Gorgeous. I'm going to call these 'A commemorative journey from single beauty to beautiful bride'."

Part way up the mountain, on the drive to the secret destination, a tiny bluestone church appeared, perched up high and providing an impressive vista of the surrounding snowscape. The sun shone, yet it started drizzling.

Overcome by the stunning views, Eden remained silent for the last five minutes of the trip. She exited the car, holding on to her bouquet of violet roses, the drizzle turning to snowflakes that fluttered around her.

Grace followed, in a short figure-hugging black dress and wrap, carrying a bouquet of colorful wildflowers. She bent down and lifted Eden's train to stop it from dragging on the wet ground.

A spectacular rainbow beamed overhead, with one end streaming down onto the church spire. "Grace, have a look at this."

She stopped fussing and glanced up, following where Eden pointed. "Wow! Let me take a photo. Quick! Stand in front, a bit more to the left. That's it. Okay, smile."

Grace reviewed the picture on the playback screen of the camera. "Breathtaking…" Then, giving the driver her best flirty stare, she said, "Could you please take a shot of us before we go into the church, and then, ah…would you mind taking some more snaps during the ceremony?"

He smiled and accepted the camera that Grace pretty much pushed into his hand.

They traversed the small group of steps into the quaint little church, and inside, stained-glass windows cast a kaleidoscope of colored light. A single aisle ran down the center of the compact space, and two columns of pews lined the walls on either side.

Rick and Simon stood at the altar, alongside the priest, and turned to look at them as the wedding march started. Eden made eye contact with Rick and he smiled, broad and sexy, sending a rush of hot, throbbing lust rolling through her body.

He looked super suave in his black velvet jacket, wide-collared white shirt and cool black with white pin stripe pants. A corsage of white and violet roses poked through the buttonhole of his jacket pocket and he accessorized it with his trademark cross jewelry.

Her husband-to-be looked sexier than decadent, double-chocolate-coated sin. God, she'd so won the magnificent-man jackpot.

"Ooh, Simon's cute. I can't believe I haven't noticed him before." Grace's explicit whisper jolted Eden from her blasphemous thoughts.

"He'll hear you," Eden murmured out of the corner of her mouth.

"I don't mind," she said with a saucy smile and locked her predatory stare on Simon.

He grinned, not seeming to mind either.

Following the ceremony, Rick formally introduced everyone to each other. They'd tried to arrange an intro dinner so they could all meet before the wedding, but with Simon's odd hours and Rick monopolizing Eden's time with the marriage plans, it hadn't happened.

After Simon and Grace congratulated them, Simon kissed Grace hello on the lips, then stepped back, his panicked gray-blue eyes staring into hers, as though to see if he'd breached her socially-acceptable boundary. He had nothing to worry about.

Neither of them had shown much subtlety when it came to their interest in each other. Maybe they too were a match made in heaven... *Hades, more like it.*

Grace smiled, grasped Simon's hand and steered him toward the car.

Eden glanced at Rick and his lips curved up into the sexiest of sexy smiles. Tingles coursed through her hot-and-bothered bloodstream. What did the night have in store...for all of them?

# Chapter Seventeen

## An Intimate Night

Post-ceremony, Rick, Eden, Simon and Grace celebrated at a cozy local pub, reminiscent of a small medieval castle. Rick had really outdone himself in the romance department. Eden couldn't have planned a better wedding herself.

She spotted an empty table near an expansive arch of lattice windows and made a beeline for it. Rick pulled out a chair for her, and Simon followed suit with Grace. Then Rick slipped in beside Eden and held her hand.

Snowflakes fluttered, layering the ground with a powdery white carpet. By late afternoon, the sun started to descend, streaking the sky with gold and purple and pastel pink, transitioning from day into a clear, moonlit night.

Rick went to order their meals, and when he returned, Eden clasped his hand and tugged him closer, encouraging him to sit.

He remained standing, lifted her hand to his lips and kissed the underside of her wrist. "May I have this dance?"

Her pulse punched her skin like hitting the boxing speed bag at the gym. "Oh...um...but no one else is dancing."

"So?"

One thing about Rick—if he really wanted to do something and truly believed in it, he wouldn't let anything or anyone stop him. Eden loved that about him. Although she hated being the center of attention, she couldn't help but indulge her husband. *Husband!*

He led her onto the empty dance floor, and they slow danced to *Hold Me, Thrill Me, Kiss Me* by Mel Carter, attracting both surprised and encouraging looks from the rest of the patrons.

She sighed. "I love this song."

Rick gazed into her eyes and tightened his arms around her. "Me too. I thought it rang true for us."

By the end of the ballad, three older couples had joined them on the dance floor, all offering their congratulations and commenting that they hadn't heard that track for years. A couple in their seventies shared that they'd chosen the tune for their bridal waltz back in 1965.

Rick kissed Eden right as *Baby I'm Yours* by Barbara Lewis started.

She broke away and stared into his eyes. "I love this too!"

"I thought you might, seeing we have so much else in common. It's one of my favorites."

They glided across the floor, Eden's barely contained ecstasy soaring beneath her skin.

"I think we'll have to leave soon," he whispered, tuning into her need, his hot breath stroking her ear.

Arousal swelled in her pelvis. The desire in his voice confirmed that, like her, his stores of self-control and patience were nearing empty and required replenishment. "What about Grace and Simon?"

Rick turned and looked at them, then back at Eden. "I don't think we've got anything to worry about. They probably wish we'd hurry up and go."

Eden snuck a glance, and Rick was right. They sat angled toward each other, gazes interlocked, smiling, chatting and laughing. Their conversation appeared so private that it almost screamed *Do Not Disturb*.

After dinner, Eden and Rick excused themselves and began the short journey back to the cabin. The cold night air pierced her dress and she shivered. Rick put his arm around her and held her close, her temperature rising in seconds — and not just from his body heat.

They strolled along the well-worn honeymooners' path, lined with trees covered in an abundance of sparkling fairy lights, their breath creating spurts of mist against the obsidian, star-filled sky. Could it get any more romantic?

"Tonight, I'll celebrate my love for you…"

"Rick, what are you doing?" Although he had a harmonious voice, he'd attracted too much attention to them…again.

"Serenading my beautiful wife. No one will hear. Don't worry. And even if they do, so what? It doesn't bother me. I'm happy for the whole world to know how much I love you," he said, and started singing again.

How could she deny him when he said things like that? "I can't believe you know an eighties love song. Are you sure you're straight?" she teased.

"That's not quite the response I'd aimed for, but yeah, I'm into women — or at least I'm very much into this woman…or soon will be." Rick stopped, clasped her face between his hands and pressed his mouth to hers, his lips a warm, open invitation.

When they reached the cabin, Rick whisked Eden into his arms and carried her over the threshold. He lowered her onto the couch and planted another tempting kiss on her lips. "Why don't you make yourself comfortable and I'll join you once I get the fire sorted."

"Okay," she said, her voice faint and breathy.

Eden removed her off-white leather and lace shoes and curled up on the comfy black couch. Her husband—*husband, eeeee!*—stood in view, stripped off his jacket, his biceps bulging against his shirt sleeves, and hung it on the back of a dining chair.

He undid his cufflinks, put them in one of the front pockets of his blazer, rolled up his sleeves and walked over to the fireplace. Rick bent down and stoked the flames, the soft glow of the fire highlighting his lean, muscular physique. *Yum!*

Once the fire roared, he popped the cork on a bottle of champagne, poured them both a drink and sat beside her. "To my gorgeous wife."

She accepted a glass from him and held it up to toast him right back. "To my handsome husband."

They chinked glasses and took a sip. Eden placed her drink on the coffee table and Rick lifted her onto his lap. She sucked in a surprised breath. A naughty smile flitted across his face and he dipped his head, teasing her with light, lingering kisses on her parted lips. Eden wound her arms around his neck and they launched into a passionate make-out session.

Things started getting panty-soaking hot and conflicted-emotion heavy and she pulled away. She panted, her nipples pointing into hard, aroused peaks, but her stomach was vacuum-sealed tight with tension. Why did she suddenly feel so nervous? All month she could hardly wait for this moment and now…

It had to be the pressure of the event. Rick had set such high expectations for their wedding night, but what if the sex didn't live up to the hype? Her mind brewed with building anticipation.

What if it turned out to be an anticlimax? What if she couldn't please him? She knew what to do from extensive reading on the subject plus hearing about Grace's exploits in explicit detail, though that wasn't the same as actually doing it.

A huge gap often existed between theory and applying it in practice, something Rick would know all about in his profession. Maybe he felt a bit nervous too. No…unless he hid it extremely well.

The loud pop of fire consuming wood penetrated the static-filled air and she jumped. The weird dream she'd had at Rick's place stormed her head and her stomach clenched to fight the invasion of fear.

He nuzzled her ear and whispered, "Relax…" in stereo with her inner voice. Though, his tone was gentle and calming, unlike hers, which scolded and berated. "We can take things as slow as you like."

Even though his cock jutted into her hip, harder than a rod of steel, she could tell by the sincerity in his voice that he meant it. It was another reason she loved him so goddamn much.

With a shaking hand, she grabbed her glass and gulped a few more fizzy mouthfuls. Rick rubbed her back with slow, sensuous strokes, while delicious smoky eucalyptus scented the air. His magic touch set her skin ablaze with rapture, ramping up her level of anticipation…and anxiety.

Maybe she needed some time out to freshen up and transform herself from virginal bride to sexy wife. If she looked the part, she might just carry it off.

Eden drained the last few drops of champagne and put the empty glass down on the tabletop. "I'll be back in a few minutes. Wait here, okay?"

Rick snuck in another kiss. "Don't be too long — or I'll come in after you."

Eden laughed, the stuttered sound highlighting her nerves, and she climbed off his lap. In the bedroom, her overnight bag sat prim and proper on the luggage rack. She unzipped it, pulled out the skimpy white see-through negligee Grace had given her and held it up to the light.

Part of her wanted to wear it and part of her cringed with embarrassment. What was the worst thing that could happen? *He could hate it.* But whether he liked the outfit or not, the outcome would be the same. It wouldn't stay on for long.

After a quick shower, she stepped out onto the white bathmat and paused to study her naked body in the mirror.

During the week, Grace had convinced her to have a full Brazilian wax, guaranteeing that she wouldn't regret it. *'Your skin will be so smooth and you'll feel really clean and sexy. And believe me, Rick will love it and you will too when you feel his tongue — '*

She blushed. So far, Grace had been right. Her skin did feel super clean and smooth as silk. Was Grace right about the other stuff too?

Eden slipped on the negligee. "Hmmm...not too bad," she murmured, viewing her body from every possible angle. The luxurious material conformed to her figure, a hint of pink nipple pressing against the white lace. Could she really pull this off? Maybe she should walk back out in the complimentary, full length white robe instead?

"Eden, are you okay?" Rick called out.

Her soulmate ring pulsated with heat. "Yes, I'm fine. I'll be there in a minute." She took a couple of deep breaths and tip-toed back into the living area. *Sexy siren, sexy siren, sexy siren*, she repeated over and over like a positive affirmation mantra.

Rick wasn't where she'd left him. She darted her gaze around the room, searching, and found him over by the dining table with his back to her, topping up their glasses with more champagne. Eden edged toward him and a floorboard creaked beneath her feet.

He spun around, nearly dropping the full champagne flutes he had in his hands.

"Too much?" she asked, barely able to breathe.

He shook his head. "No. No way. You look"—he sighed—"mouthwatering. Let me guess—a present from Grace?"

She fingered the flimsy fabric. "Pretty obvious, huh?"

His eyes twinkled like they'd been sprinkled with lust dust. "Yeah...remind me to thank her in the morning."

Rick strode over to her and undid the tie between her heaving breasts, revealing her bare chest and stomach. With a feather-light touch, he slipped the straps over her shoulders, the gauzy garment falling to the floor, then he ran his hands over her skin.

Eden pushed Rick's shirt off his strong arms and it dropped to the ground. She unfastened his pants with trembling, eager hands, and he kicked them off onto the growing pile of clothes. Then he zeroed in on her hips and untied both sides of her panties, leaving her standing nubile and naked.

He breathed out hard. "You're so beautiful."

Eden closed her eyes, her body pulsing with a heady mix of elation and heart-thrumming nerves. Rick trailed his fingers along her jaw, tilted her head up and brought her mouth to his.

And just like that, the mood changed. It felt like coming home — comforting, familiar and exciting — melting away all her anxiety and replacing it with insatiable yearning.

She snaked her arms around his neck, crushed her lips against his and thrust her tongue into his mouth. A small groan rumbled in Rick's throat and he cupped her behind, pressing her navel against his hard cock.

Eden gasped and rubbed against his raging erection. Rick's breath caught and he broke away, making quick work of his black cotton boxers. His heated gaze reconnected with hers and he pulled her to him — skin on skin. Every one of her super-stimulated nerve-endings sparked and tingled and she ached for him to be inside her.

*Take me. Take me now!* She silently implored him, and as though responding to her unspoken request, he swept her up and carried her into the bedroom.

He laid her on the bed, the crisp white sheet against her back contrasting with the heat of his body. He moved his lips along her neck and traveled down, exploring every hill, valley and plane of her virgin landscape.

Rick's mouth and hands were everywhere at once, leaving no area uncharted, bombarding her with earth-shattering pleasure.

When he finally arrived at her core, he glided over the newly discovered bare skin, following every curve and delving into every crevice, setting her nerve-endings alight with need.

The moment he took her swollen nub into his mouth, he instigated an amazing expedition of his own, his tongue ramping up her pleasure to a level beyond euphoria. The pressure, warmth and wetness sent her into an altered dimension, a paradise populated with exquisite sensations, and she came, calling out his name.

"Mmm...you're so delicious." His hot breath caressed between her legs.

With her fingers intertwined in his thick, golden-brown hair, she angled his head up, leaned forward and kissed him.

The giant rose moon's milky rays penetrated the window, bathing them in misty light. With each movement, they created sinuous shadows against the wall, like a sensual, silhouetted art installation.

Rick looked into her eyes, pressed the head of his cock to her slick sex and gently entered her. "Is that okay?"

"Yes," she said, and captured his mouth with hers, surprised that the anticipated sting of first-time penetration hadn't happened. And it wasn't that he lacked in the manhood department either.

In fact, he hit her sweet spot from his first tender thrust. And with each movement, the incredible tingling grew more and more intense. His cock was a pleasure wand, turning on every fuck-this-feels-fantastic switch in her entire body.

Rick picked up the pace and swiveled his hips, further tantalizing her G-spot until she teetered on the edge of exploding.

He groaned and reached climax. "Eden!" The sound of her name on his lips pushed her over.

"Rick!" she cried, coming with hurricane force around him.

They remained joined in connected bliss, riding out their orgasms until they were spent. When their breathing started to settle, Rick stroked Eden's hair and covered her forehead, eyes, nose, cheeks and lips with adoration-infused kisses. Then he untangled the bedclothes, lay on his back and held her against him, tucked under the doona.

They kissed and caressed for quite a while without saying a word. Satiated pleasure radiated from her every pore, like being in a perfect, orgasmic dream. But it was real. Incredibly, mind-blowingly real...and familiar.

"Are you warm enough?" Rick asked.

"Yes. You?"

"Yeah, I'm nice and toasty... I feel pretty good all around, actually."

"Mmm...me too." She kissed his chest. "I know this is going to sound strange, but the way you touch me feels so right, like we've made love before. Everything just flowed like a well-choreographed routine, like you already knew my body."

"Well, I kind of did already know it."

She lifted her head and met his gaze. "No, not intimately like that. This felt different. Do you know what I mean?"

"Actually, I think I do. Touching you, making love to you was amazing. And like you, I sensed the naturalness of our connection.

"It's like I was driven by instinct, by a greater force, something beyond my conscious thoughts. Like you said, it felt almost predetermined, as though I was responding from experience, yet I don't have any.

Everything felt fresh, exciting and new, yet comfortable and familiar.

"I agree. It doesn't make sense and yet it makes perfect sense. We're meant to be together." Rick caressed her cheek. "I love you, Eden, much more than I can ever articulate. Words honestly can't describe my feelings for you, but hopefully my actions can."

She kissed his warm, cushiony lips. "They do. I love you so much."

\* \* \* \*

Simon slotted his key into the front door, and Grace put her hand over his and initiated turning the key in the lock. She pushed the cabin door open and they stepped inside. The flickering embers in the fireplace greeted him with their last remnants of heat.

She switched on the light and adjusted the dimmer until the room glowed with a simmering amber incandescence.

Simon removed his jacket, hung it over the back of the couch, rolled up his shirt sleeves and walked over to the fireplace. He crouched down, prodded the glowing red ashes and steepled a couple of logs on top to reinvigorate the fire.

"Are you hungry?" Grace asked.

He grabbed the poker and repositioned the timber. "No, not really. Are you?"

Within seconds, Grace hovered behind him, her body only millimeters from his. He put the poker down and stood, facing her, his heart galloping.

She slowly ran her fingers along the edge of his shirt collar and looked into his eyes. "Yeah, but not for food."

Simon breathed out hard. It looked like she definitely had the same destination in mind.

Thank fuck for his work friend's intimate Cradle Mountain wedding. He couldn't thank Rick enough for the invitation. Simon had known he'd enjoy the weekend away—the stunning scenery, for starters—however, he hadn't anticipated his mate arranging for Grace, the hot woman he'd been lusting after, to be his roommate bridesmaid.

Simon's crazy work hours and Rick's whirlwind romance hadn't given him a chance to get to know Eden, let alone meet her best friend, Grace...until today. What had he done to deserve this sort of luck? If only he knew, so he could replicate it.

Grace leaned in close to his ear. "I really want you to fuck me. Will you?"

*Yep!* Performance-anxiety adrenaline fused with elation and spiked in his system. Her directness was a massive turn-on. He wanted to get her out of that body-hugging black dress, bend her over the couch and fuck her right then and there.

But he didn't want to rush it. He wanted to explore, savor her body...and mind. *Whoa.* What had gotten into him? *Control yourself.* The Grace seduction virus must have infected his brain and body. Yeah. Had to be.

He gulped as she pulled back and met his gaze.

She put her palm on his chest and his heart just about burst from beneath his ribs. She slid her hand down the front of his body and stopped over his crotch. "Well, that certainly feels like a 'yes'." Then she interlocked her fingers with his and led him into the closest bedroom...

They had sex. No, they made love. Who'd have ever thought he'd use those words, feel that depth of connection — and Simon basked in the afterglow, the air alive with pheromones, unity and soul-deep satisfaction. Grace snuggled into him and it felt good, natural.

Normally he wanted to bolt at the first opportunity. No post-coital cuddles or sleepover. It just complicated things. But not even a twinge of fear registered in his brain with Grace by his side.

"I just want to let you know that you don't have to worry about promising me anything, okay?" she said. "I take total responsibility for what happened and I don't regret it. All that sex talk made me horny and I needed…a physical release. So if our little affair just remains a part of this weekend, that's totally fine with me. Honestly."

He looked at her in disbelief. "Are you kidding? You're so incredibly hot…but I'm sure you know that. As I said earlier, I've had my eye on you for ages."

She grinned. "Just in case you didn't notice, I'm interested in you too. In fact, I wanted you badly…and I had to have you. What do they say? Actions speak louder than words?"

"I don't know — maybe you're just using me for sex? Not that I mind," he said.

She laughed.

"But seriously, you totally took me by surprise."

"Yeah, I could tell. You should have seen your face when I asked if you'd fuck me — priceless!" A triumphant grin pressed into her flushed cheeks.

"Don't get me wrong. I hoped it would go there, but I didn't want to assume. I'm very glad things turned out how they did. The sex was fucking awesome!"

Grace rested her arm on his chest and draped half her body over his. "Mmmm…it was pretty good," she said, her voice a soft, satiated purr.

"I definitely want to keep seeing you when we get back to Hobart. I really like you…a lot. It's not just the sex." Even though she claimed the title for the hottest root he'd ever had — and he'd had quite a few — she had something extra-special…unique.

"Sure," she said with a wry smile.

"Honestly. I wouldn't lie to you." Hopefully the lingering fuck euphoria hadn't shut down his rational brain. Nah, he really did enjoy speaking to her as well.

Grace was gorgeous and skillful, no doubt, but her open mindset made her super sexy. He'd found a sort of a female version of himself.

"If you say so."

He tilted her chin up and looked into her bewitching brown eyes. "What will it take to convince you I'm not one of those guys? If I wanted to leave this as just a weekend fling, I would have said so when you gave me an out a minute ago."

"Hmmm… I guess. All right, I'll take your word for it. You better not disappoint me!"

"So…does that mean you're interested in seeing me when we get back home?" *Please say yes.*

Grace's lips curled into a cheeky grin. "Maybe…"

He flipped her onto her back, pressed her down onto the bed and planted a firm kiss on her mouth. Then he pulled back a little and looked at her. "Do you always get what you want?"

Grace quirked her brow and smiled. "Yeah, pretty much."

They both laughed.

Out of the corner of his eye, he spotted a tiny clump of hot pink lace among their scattered clothes. "Oh, um…sorry about your G-string."

She glanced at the ripped material, then her gaze returned to his. "Don't worry about it. I only wear underwear for special occasions anyway."

"Ooh, you're such a bad girl. I think you need a good spanking."

Grace's scintillating eyes glimmered. "Is that an offer?"

"How did I know that wouldn't be a punishment?"

"Um…because you know a bad girl when you see one?"

He chuckled.

She looked up to the right, then refocused on him, her facial expression turning serious. "Hey, can I ask you something?"

Simon lay back down and wrapped his arms around her voluptuous body. "Of course. Go ahead."

"What do you think about Rick and Eden getting married so quickly? Personally, I think it's a bit weird. To be honest, I'm a little worried about Eden. I know I shouldn't be, because Rick seems like a really nice guy but… I don't get it. I mean, they didn't even have sex to test things out!"

"Yeah, I know. I don't really get it either, except to say that Rick is kind of old-fashioned in that way."

"So is Eden, but she's not the type to rush into anything. It's really unlike her. Normally she overthinks everything. Put it this way… Her nerves paralyzed her so much she couldn't even speak to Rick after six weeks of flirting."

Simon laughed. "They really do make a perfect pair, don't they?"

"Yeah, I guess they do." She rubbed his chest, her silky-smooth hand rousing his libido. "What time are we meeting them tomorrow?"

"I'm pretty sure it's nine-thirty, why?"

"I've been thinking about what we could do to fill in our time until then."

"Oh really? And what did you come up with?" he asked with a suggestive smile.

"Hmmm... How about Monopoly?"

"You do realize that will take us all night."

"No way. Going by our evening so far, I think it's pretty obvious I already have it."

"Monopoly? Over me? Really? We'll see about that!" He pressed her down on the bed again, possessing her smart mouth with a dominant kiss, for the first time looking forward to the ongoing relationship challenge.

*Fuck.* Who would have ever thought he – Mr. Young-Single-and-Free – would consider something more serious at his age? Not him. But he'd found Grace. Fun, open, insightful, spirited Grace, like no other woman he'd ever met.

For the first time, he felt the benefits of a deeper connection. For the first time, he saw the possibility of a joint future.

\* \* \* \*

Eden woke up to a breathtaking view of the emerging dawn. The deep, dark lake reflected the sky's stunning gold, pink and lavender layers. Rick tightened his arms around her, and his brawny chest pressed against her back. Images of their wedding night blasted into her head, lust rushing through her body as she relived every pleasure-filled moment.

"Are you awake?" he whispered into her hair.

Dampness pooled between her legs. "Yes. Isn't the view amazing?"

"Breathtaking…and the sunrise is pretty impressive too."

She sighed. He brushed his lips against her neck, and continued slowly kissing down her spine.

"Did you sleep well?"

"Yes. You?" Her breathing sounded labored, her voice breathy.

"No, not really. It's hard to sleep with such a beautiful, naked woman lying beside me."

Eden exhaled and closed her eyes, tuning in to his hot breath and supple lips traveling along her super-sensitive skin.

Moving back up her body, he kissed her hip, shoulder, the nape of her neck…then his breath stroked her ear. "I want you," he whispered, and went on to explain in explicit detail exactly what he planned to do to her…

They made love twice and finally dragged themselves into the bathroom, unable to stop touching each other. But they had to get ready to meet Simon and Grace. Though right now, with her naked, irresistible husband pressed up against her, commanding her lips and her body, it was hard to think of much else beside him, sex. Again.

Their intimate shower ended up making them half an hour late for breakfast. They entered the dining room of the nearby Highland Restaurant, hand in hand, her system still flooded with delicious endorphins. The waitress directed them to a table near the buffet where Grace and Simon sat cozied up together, deep in conversation.

"You made it," Grace said with a sassy smile as they slid into the booth.

"Barely," Rick replied with a roguish grin.

Heat flared in Eden's cheeks. Now everyone would know Rick was extremely conversant with every fold, cleft, plane and beauty spot on her body. But for once, she didn't mind. They were officially husband and wife. They had a license to touch anytime, anywhere. And she'd happily exclaim to the world the depth of their love.

While the ladies went to stock up their plates, Simon said, "Mate, I can't thank you enough for asking me to be your best man. I mean, I knew I'd have a good time no matter what, but I never, *ever* would have believed it would turn out this good!"

Rick laughed. "You guys hit it off then?"

"You could say that."

"I had a feeling you would."

Simon's inquiring gray-blue eyes stared into his. "So…how was everything with you two?"

"Perfect. I'm the luckiest man alive. Eden is so sweet and beautiful… It's like I've loved her forever."

"I'm really happy for you both. You really do make a great couple."

"Thanks, and thanks for your support too. It means a lot to me." *Especially in the absence of family.*

"No worries. As I said, thank you."

Grace put two pieces of fruit loaf into the toaster. "So how was it?"

"Wonderful!" Eden couldn't contain the dreamy gush in her voice. "He knew exactly how to press all the right buttons, like we'd made love before."

"See? I told you everything would be fine."

Eden took a sip of her pineapple juice. "Thanks, Grace...for everything."

"I should really be thanking you for inviting me up here. Simon's great. Actually, more than great."

Eden searched her eyes. "So you guys..."

"Ah-ha," Grace said with a devilish smile.

"And?"

"Fucking brilliant. We seemed to hit it off really well...on every level. We want to keep seeing each other."

"That's so great." But could Grace keep it going? Long-term relationships weren't her thing. She was more a 'do 'em and dash' type.

"Yeah, it's pretty cool...and unexpected."

*I'll say.* Eden loaded up her plate with extra bacon, cold meats and poached eggs. "Well, as we both know, the unexpected is often the best."

# Chapter Eighteen

Returning Home

With Simon and Grace safely dropped off, Eden and Rick continued driving down the dark street and turned onto the main road. Eden reached over and rubbed Rick's thigh.

He glanced at her with an I-want-you-right-now look, pulled into a quiet spot overlooking the fog-covered Derwent River and shut off the headlights.

"I've been dying to touch you since we reached Great Lake over an hour and a half ago." Rick undid his seatbelt, took off his long-sleeved T-shirt and leaned across to the passenger side.

He grasped her face between his smooth hands and kissed her as though starved for her touch. Things got steamy, literally and figuratively, and he pulled away to wind down his window a touch and adjust his seat back.

Eden left on her mini skirt and long boots, shimmied out of her minuscule G-string and lifted her leg to straddle him.

Rick's green eyes glowed in the close, dark confines of the car. "Let me have a quick taste."

She arched back and he held her hips and brought her shamelessly wet pussy to his mouth. He lapped at her clitoris until it throbbed and swelled with need, then licked along her seam, past her core and continued farther back. Rick spread her butt cheeks, swirled his tongue against her tight little hole, and she bucked with an unexpected explosion of pleasure.

On the verge of climax, he stopped and she mewled in protest. Rick glided her down his body and they kissed, her feminine taste still on his lips, driving her desire higher and higher. He caressed between her legs, ramping up the pre-climactic tingles, and she slid onto his erect cock.

She rode him hard, grinding her clitoris into his pubic bone, and the second his finger prodded her anal opening, she orgasmed.

"Richard!"

"Oh, Eva!" He groaned and came deep inside her.

Eden lay against him, in sensual shock. She'd always deemed anal play a no-no...until now. She hadn't realized how much enjoyment it offered.

After a few minutes Rick pulled back, his forehead furrowed. "Um...did you call me Richard?"

She racked her brain. "I don't know. Did I?"

"Yep."

She stared back at him. "Actually, I'm pretty sure you called me Eva." She fiddled with her rose key pendant. "You know, you could have just told me if you'd been with another woman. It wouldn't have bothered me." *Okay, maybe a bit.* It was probably how he'd learned the benefits of back passage stimulation.

"I swear I haven't been with anyone else. Honestly. I don't even know an Eva." Hmmm…maybe not. But he couldn't have developed that level of skill just through reading. Could he?

"And I don't know a Richard. That's so odd." She shivered.

"Big time. Maybe we tapped into a past life or something."

She laughed. "Yeah, maybe." Though the situation felt eerie rather than funny.

\* \* \* \*

The next morning, Rick hurried along the Sub Rosa passageway to the open-plan office, juggling his coffee in one hand and fumbling for his lanyard with the other.

"Congratulations. I hear you recently got married."

Rick stopped and looked up into the eyes of the senior manager of Business Services, a man who had scarcely spoken two words to him. Why was the guy suddenly so…conversational? "Thanks."

He ran his shaky, nicotine-stained hand through his thick, gray hair. "I've been told the lovely lady is Eden Freberg from upstairs."

"That's right."

The manager coughed, a seasoned-smoker's congestion rattling in his chest. "You're a very lucky man. I'd say nearly every male in the place has had his eye on her since she started. She's very beautiful."

"Thank you. Yes, she is. In every way."

"You haven't known each other long, have you?"

"No. I suppose you could say it's been a whirlwind romance."

Air wheezed out of the guy's windpipe. "Well, that's great. Good on you. It's reassuring to hear this sort of thing really does happen outside of the movies. I wish you both all the best."

"Thanks." Rick continued down the corridor, his mind mulling over possible motives. Management had to have a big, time-consuming project coming up that they planned to spring on him.

The rest of the day flew and, before he knew it, it was home time. *Thank fuck.* Time to see and touch he stunning wife. Eden met him at his car and he kissed her deep and long. He totally had wife withdrawal.

When they finally got into the car, Rick started the engine, pulled out of the Sub Rosa car park and commenced the drive home. "I had the weirdest thing happen to me today."

"Let me guess — all the guys wanted to hear about the sex." Eden rolled her eyes.

"No, that's not weird. I expected that." He grinned. "I did hear, from a rather reliable source, that quite a few guys at work have had their eye on you for a while."

"Well, that's not weird either. I definitely would have expected that."

Rick laughed. "Okay, okay, enough with the mucking around…for the minute. You know the senior manager of Business Services…"

"The distressed-looking older guy?"

"Yeah. He's hardly ever even acknowledged me. Today, though, he was extra friendly, actually stopping me to strike up a conversation. He must want something."

"They've been talking about redundancies. And you're new. Do you think they might cut your position?" Her words were weighed down with worry.

He pressed a reassuring hand to her thigh. "I doubt it. They said job losses would only affect middle management at this stage, and they may also cut the research budget a bit. It's more likely they're planning on dumping more work on me, without overtime."

"That's a relief…though our plan for a string of dirty weekends might have to be put on hold."

He stopped at a red light and looked at her, dead serious. "I hope not."

Within twenty minutes, they arrived home. Rick parked the car, opened her door and held her hand as she stepped out. The moment they were inside, he cuddled her close. "I don't know about you, but I feel like my dessert before dinner tonight."

She pressed into him, making his cock so hard he thought it might split his pants. "Mmmm…tempting…but who's going to cook?"

"I will. You can totally relax and I'll get everything sorted."

She nuzzled her nose against his. "That sounds like an offer I can't refuse."

"Exactly the answer I hoped to hear." Rick scooped her up and charged upstairs to their bedroom.

# Chapter Nineteen

### The Breakthrough

After spending two days on hikes and a marathon three-night fornication fest with Grace in Cradle Mountain, Simon was sleep-deprived and running late for work. Rather than log on to his computer, he went straight to the male change room and opened the combination lock on his designated locker.

He yanked the gray metal door open, and his lab coat and a couple of pairs of protective goggles hung inside. *Where are my protective pants? Oh yeah, that's right…* On Thursday, he'd sent them off for sterilized cleaning and had planned to pick them up before he came in. *Fuck it. No time.*

Normally he was a stickler for following lab protocol, but too bad. If worst came to worst, he'd leave his jeans for sterile washing and go home in his jocks. *Right, that's it. Mind on the job.*

He shoved his arms into the lab coat, and Grace popped into his head, in all manner of dress and positions…and he would see her again later tonight.

Simon shook his head. How would he ever get any sleep?

On the way into the brightly lit lab, he squirted a couple of measures of pink antibacterial solution onto his hands and rubbed them together. He waved them dry and walked to the bench to grab some gloves. He reached into the box and...empty. "Ugh," he huffed.

Simon snatched a vial of vampire tears and strode across to an unopened box on the other side of the room. He placed the vial down and donned the firm, blue, latex-free gloves. When he went to pick it up again, it rolled off the edge of the work bench and smashed onto the floor.

"Fuck!" He couldn't afford to waste such rare samples.

While cleaning up the mess, a shard of glass sliced into his finger and it started bleeding. Just what he needed. Though, in some ways it served him right for overindulging. He obviously needed a bit of pain to balance out the pleasure. Simon chuckled and shook his head.

Using a handkerchief out of his pocket, he went to put pressure on the wound, but the bleeding had ceased and the cut had almost vanished.

"What the fu...?"

His brain flicked through hypotheses. *The tears...* They had to have healing properties. Could they also counteract vampire venom? *I wonder...*

He poured five milliliters of venom into a test tube then added a few drops of the vampire tears. Nothing happened. *Hmmm...* Maybe the conditions were wrong.

Simon filled four test tubes with varying amounts of venom to tears in each one and lined them up in the freezer, then did the same thing but left four at room temperature, four in direct sunlight and four at boiling point.

He stayed, checking on the samples every fifteen minutes over an hour, and was gobsmacked by the results.

The freezer samples turned various shades of aqua and became a fluid, rubber-like consistency. The boiling samples were blood red with a lava-lamp-type viscosity. The room-temperature samples had disintegrated, leaving only a thin, clear, almost-crystalline substance coating the inner curve of the test tubes, and the sunlight samples were varying degrees of gold, with glittery gold speckles scattered through the remaining European-hot-chocolate-consistency substance.

Next, he devised a rat trial to investigate the impact of each compound. Once he had sectioned off a suitable enclosure, he infected sixteen rats with vampire venom and placed each in their allocated space.

Within thirty minutes, they had completely transformed. He administered a different oral serum to each rat and waited. By the time he checked his watch, it was after midnight.

"Fuck! Grace!" He finished up and went straight to the change room. His phone sat on the bottom shelf of his locker, the notification light flashing an insistent green and the screen showing three missed calls. From her. She would be mega pissed.

On the way to his car, he phoned her back, his heart pounding in his mouth.

"Hello?" she answered in a sleepy voice.

"Grace, I'm so sorry. I got totally caught up at work. I think I made a breakthrough!" His words tumbled out of his mouth at breakneck pace.

She yawned. "Great. Are you still coming by?"

"Oh um…yeah sure, if you want me to."

"Of course. The spare key's in a keysafe in the meter box and the combination is six-nine, six-nine. I'll be in bed, waiting…"

He had a great run to Grace's place and after another fucking awesome but sleepless night, Simon returned to work. He logged onto his computer, skipped his routine afternoon coffee and chat in the tearoom and went to the lab to tally up the findings.

His eyes almost bugged out of their sockets at the impressive results. Unable to wait to tell Andy the brilliant news, he raced back to his desk and composed an email update.

*Hi Andy,*

*I've just collated the results of my vampire tear-to-venom-to-temperature rat experiment and thought you should be made aware of the findings.*

*Freezing point vaccine – eighty percent death rate, twenty percent slow and lethargic but still infected.*

*Boiling point vaccine – ninety-three percent death rate, seven percent manic but still infected.*

*Room temperature vaccine – fifty percent death rate, fifty percent still infected but with a reduction in symptoms, moving from full to half-caste.*

*Sunlight vaccine – ninety percent cured and ten percent converted from full to quarter-caste.*

*Out of the twenty-to-eighty, forty-to-sixty, sixty-to-forty and eighty-to-twenty vampire tears-to-venom ratios, the eighty-to-twenty combination yielded the best outcomes across the sample selection.*

*Although the sunlight vaccine results are extremely promising, there is still the ten percent leeway that needs addressing. With your permission, I'd like to have a play around with the vampire tears-to-venom-to-sunlight ratio with the aim to produce a one hundred percent cure rate. In the meantime, I'll store the freezing, boiling and room temperature concoctions for further exploration in the future.*

*Please let me know how you'd like me to proceed.*
*Regards,*
*Simon*

\* \* \* \*

*Due to recent government funding cutbacks, we will regrettably not be able to renew our regular five-million-dollar funding contribution.*

Andy slammed his laptop shut. "Government funding cuts, my arse!" He shoved his high-backed leather chair under his desk and paced in front of his floor-to-ceiling office window.

The Commonwealth government had been the largest and most consistent contributor to Sub Rosa projects for the past ten years. When his mate had retired from the department and the stupid bitch senior manager had become the new decision-maker, the situation had gone to shit. The malicious woman had never liked him.

Andy stopped pacing and stared at the choppy sea through his office window. He could approach his state government co-funders to try and fill the gap — however, without new ground-breaking results, his chances of success were questionable, given the limited bucket of money and competitive market.

The desire for a drag on a cigarette toyed with his willpower. It had been nearly thirty years since he'd last had one and he refused to fuck up all that hard work.

He stalked over to his mini bar, poured a nip of single malt Scotch into his strong espresso coffee and chugged it down. Heat pervaded his throat and the familiar alcohol-induced calm seeped into his brain.

Andy sat in his office chair and tapped his fingers on the desk. How could he resolve the current setback? He flipped his laptop open, clicked into his inbox and a wave of weekly project updates flowed in. He scrolled through the list and stopped on a post from Simon.

A broad smile broke out on his tight lips. "Jackpot."

# Chapter Twenty

## The Birth of a New Era

Rick dropped his black leather man-bag on the couch next to Eden and leaned in.

She put her hand up to stop him making lip contact. "Don't kiss me."

"Eden, this is ridiculous. You need to get over your doctor-needle phobia and have yourself checked. This stomach virus has been lingering for nearly two weeks. That's way, way too long. And you're going to need a medical certificate for work now anyway. Come on. Get ready. I'm taking you to the clinic right now."

She didn't argue. There was no point. She never won when his eyes turned that determined, uncompromising shade of bottle green.

They made it in for the last appointment of the day and after the initial introductory chit chat with the doctor, Eden rattled off her cluster of symptoms. By the time she'd finished, the doctor had a hint of a smile on her face.

Eden glanced quizzically at Rick then back at the doctor. Shouldn't the woman just write a script and send her back home to rest?

"I think I know what's going on here. I just need to do a couple of tests to make sure."

Anxiety and tension sat like an elephant on Eden's chest...until the doctor gave her a small container and directed her into the bathroom for a urine sample. Pure relief washed over her.

When she returned, she handed the sample to the doctor.

"I'll just be a few minutes," she said and left the examination room.

Eden sat next to Rick and he reached for her hand. "She said you'll be fine."

"I hope so. I couldn't stand feeling like this for much longer." She moved her mouth close to his ear and whispered, "Though, I always seem to feel better after we make love."

"Me too." Rick's low, sensual voice caressed her libido.

The doctor stepped back into the room, her face and posture relaxed. So, it couldn't be anything too serious. However, Eden's clenched stomach didn't seem to get the memo.

"It's just as I thought. Hopefully you'll agree this is good news." The doctor pulled up a chair and sat opposite Eden. "You're pregnant. Have you been trying to conceive?"

Eden's mouth dropped open. *Pregnant?* Had she heard right?

Rick squeezed her hand and she looked at him. He beamed with pride.

Eden shook her head, trying to work back to when this surprise could have happened. "No. We've been super careful. We weren't planning to try for a couple of years—"

"But the news is not unwelcome," Rick said.

*Really?* "How far along am I?"

"Going by what you've told me, I'd say about two months. We won't know for sure until you have your ultrasound. I'll book you in for a week's time. Is that okay?"

"Um..." Her mind buzzed like an alarm clock that refused to snooze. She wasn't ready to have a baby, to be a mother. She and Rick had only known each other for five minutes.

Rick cocooned her hand between his. "Eden?"

"Oh, sure."

"Before we go, is it okay for us to continue having sex? Are there any positions we should avoid or anything else we need to be aware of?" Rick asked, his tone unbelievably calm.

A rush of heat bombarded Eden's cheeks.

"No, you can continue with your regular sex life. Just avoid anything too strenuous or rough. Although, Eden, you may find that as you get bigger, certain positions might become uncomfortable, difficult or impossible. You just need to be aware of that and keep communication open with each other."

They left the surgery and Rick escorted Eden to the car, the click of the central lock bringing her back to the present.

He stopped in front of the passenger side door and faced her. "Are you okay?"

"I guess... Are you?"

"I'm ecstatic." Rick wrapped his arms around her waist and hugged her flush against him. "We're having a baby!"

His smile spread so wide it almost split his face in half.

"Don't you think it's a bit soon?"

"I don't care. We did our best to prevent it, yet this little life has come into being. It can only mean one thing. He or she needs to be born. *Now*."

"I suppose…"

"Don't worry. We'll manage. You're going to make a great mum."

Could he read her mind? He'd said just what she needed to hear. Ease trickled through her, dissolving the pent-up anxiety.

"We should celebrate, don't you think? What would you like to do?" he asked.

"I'd love a wine, but I can't. Well, not for the next seven months, anyway."

"How about some celebratory sex then?" His grin turned devilish. "You did say it makes you feel better."

\* \* \* \*

"Twins? What do you mean, twins?" Eden tried to sit up.

"Just relax, Mrs. Hartman. Here you go. Have a look for yourself," the technician said, pointing out the telltale shapes on the ultrasound monitor.

She could just make out the two fetuses. Eden glanced at her husband, who couldn't seem to take his eyes off the screen. She squeezed his hand and he turned to look at her with a great big smile. Joyous tears slid out the corners of her eyes and down her cheeks.

"Everything looks fine, so we'll see you in a couple of months. Just make a booking with reception on the way out," the technician said.

Eden reached for the tissue tucked away in her bra. "Before we go, can you tell me how many weeks along I am?"

"Going by their size, I'd say ten."

Eden wiped the tears from her wet face and blew her nose. "Ten weeks?"

"Will you be able to tell the sex of the babies when we come in for the next scan?" Rick asked.

"We should, though it depends on their positions. Would you like to know?"

Rick looked at Eden.

"I want it to be a surprise. Don't you?"

He smiled at the technician. "I guess that's a 'no' then...for the moment."

The technician removed the ultrasound transducer from Eden's stomach and Rick helped her off the examination table.

Once inside the car, Rick planted an adoring kiss on her lips. "I love you so much."

Another tear rolled down her face and she smiled up at him. He gently kissed it away. "Twins. Can you believe it?"

"I only just started believing I was pregnant, and now this. Can there be any more surprises?"

Rick laughed. "No, I think we've just about covered them all."

Thankfully, over the next couple of weeks, Eden's stomach settled and she finally reached the twelve week 'safe' point. She'd been hanging out to tell her best friend the news but felt compelled to wait until the pregnancy was more...definite.

The last few days, she'd started to show too, so even if she'd wanted to, she couldn't hide it from anyone much longer.

Today was the day. How would her friend react? Knowing Grace, she'd probably give her a lecture about the perils of rushing into things. *Too late now.* Not that it bothered Eden. With each day, she grew more and more attached to and excited about the twins.

They ventured up to Café Destino, and while Grace ordered for them, Eden staked claim to a small, empty booth at the back.

"Ooh, great spot!" Grace wriggled into the booth beside her. "How are you *really* feeling? Is everything okay?"

Eden's morning sickness had been horrendous. It had only recently subsided. "I'm much better now, thanks."

"I'm glad to hear it. I started worrying things weren't right with you and Rick."

Grace's assumption hovered near the truth, but not in the way she thought. "Everything's fine between us, more than fine." Eden subconsciously rubbed her stomach.

"How's Ms. Caramel been with all your leave over the past few months?"

"Pretty understanding, actually." *Though I'm not sure how she'll take my maternity leave application.* "I know most people don't have much time for management, but she's been great so far. I can't complain. How about Mr. Distressed? How's he been treating you?"

"He seems extra-stressed these days. Thankfully, he hasn't taken it out on me. I've been his PA for...no way, seven years! I've pretty much worked out how to keep him happy."

"How do you always manage to make things sound dirty?"

Grace shrugged and that sassy grin of hers slid onto her lips. "Just an innate skill, I guess."

Eden clasped and unclasped her hands. *Just spit it out.* "Um...Grace. I'm pregnant."

She stilled Eden's unsettled hands. "Pregnant? Congratulations?" Her tone sounded hesitant, unsure.

Eden smiled and nodded.

Grace hugged her tight and kissed her cheek. "I'm rapt for you both! I didn't realize you were planning to start a family this soon."

"We weren't. It's a bit of a surprise, but we're both excited about it...now. As you know, neither of us knew our families, so we're looking forward to having our own." Her gaze dropped to her belly. "Um...there's something else."

Grace's forehead wrinkled. "Something else?"

"I'm having twins."

Her friend's chocolate-brown eyes stretched wide. "Twins? Whoa! That's intense. I mean, it's wonderful, but pretty full on." Grace got that lecturing look on her face. "You guys better enjoy yourselves now, because you won't have much time once they come along."

"Grace!"

"Well, it's true! Though, seeing I'm such a good friend," she said with a cheeky lilt in her voice, "I'm more than happy to babysit on the odd weekend so you and Rick can have some *a-lone* time."

"Thank you. Oh, but how about Simon? Actually, what is happening with you and Simon?"

"Don't worry. He won't mind." She shifted in closer and threaded her arm through Eden's. "Just between you and me, we've been talking about moving in together. We see each other every night anyway."

Eden stared at her with disbelief. She'd never expected to hear commitment talk from her free-loving friend.

"Yeah, I know, it's not like me, but I really care about him. It probably helps that the sex is great."

Eden smiled and shook her head. Now *that* sounded more like Grace.

\* \* \* \*

*Access denied* flashed up on Rick's computer monitor. "Argh! Not again," he muttered. How did they expect him to do his job if he couldn't access all the files he needed? Sub Rosa senior management had to be hiding something.

He tapped the desk and stared at the stubborn screen. Out of the corner of his eye, Simon slid into view, hurrying along the passageway. *Providential?*

Rick jumped up and raced to the door. "Hey, mate, can I catch you for a few minutes?"

Simon stopped and made his way back to him. "I wondered when you were going to tell me."

Rick's brow creased. "Tell you what?"

Simon stared him down. "Come on. Don't play dumb. Grace blabbed to me the second she came back from lunch."

*Me and my one-track mind.* He chuckled. "Oh… You mean the twins."

"No, I mean that Eden joined her and ate like a trooper after being off sick with a supposed stomach virus. Of course I mean the twins!" Simon gave him an enthusiastic man hug, thumping him hard on the back. "Congratulations!"

"Thanks."

Simon stepped back and glanced at his watch. "I've just got to finish a couple of things in the lab, then we should grab a drink to celebrate."

"Sounds good. How about I meet you downstairs in half an hour?"

"Done."

They both made it to the front foyer at the designated time, and on the walk up to Café Destino, Simon asked, "Are you guys excited or what?"

"We are now. We were a bit shocked at first."

"That's totally understandable, given you only just got married."

"It was weird, though. We used protection during the unsafe window. In fact, we were careful a bit before and after it too."

Simon's friendly-advice-giving gaze settled on Rick's eyes. "Yeah, but remember no form of contraception offers one hundred percent protection. Obviously, these two little lives need to be born. You might have to search for some double-strength, reinforced condoms once the twins arrive, though, just to be on the safe side."

They reached the café door. "Yeah, I think you might be right."

While Simon bought them both a drink, Rick found a booth seat near the window. Simon returned holding two glasses of Chartreuse on ice, and sat opposite him.

"Is that the seventy percent stuff?" Rick asked.

A mischievous smile crept onto Simon's lips. "Yeah, I thought you could probably do with something strong after that news."

"I'd say I'm still in the easy phase right now. I might need a bottle of this in six months' time," Rick joked.

Simon laughed, and raised his glass. "To you and Eden. May you be blessed with two healthy, happy, well-adjusted children."

"Cheers!" They chinked glasses. "Actually, there is something else I wanted to ask you about."

"Sure. Go ahead."

Rick looked around the cafe, propped his elbows on the table and leaned in. "I'm in the middle of this DNA structures and impact of food research report, but Sub Rosa security settings keep stonewalling me when I try to access some files that could possibly support my findings."

Simon had a sip of his drink. "Have you spoken to Andy?"

"I emailed him about it a few times, but he declined granting me access. Apparently that privilege is for Norway Experiment middle management staff and above only. He tried to convince me the information would be out-of-date anyway, and I should look into more current studies.

"But I'd already checked, and not much up-to-date, conclusive information exists. Plus, I'm interested in the clinical reasoning aspect and how that's impacted on the decisions that were made."

"So, you were wondering if I could weave my awesome computer magic." Simon's eyes flared like a struck match and he tapped his fingers on an imaginary keyboard.

"Something like that. I'll understand if you don't feel comfortable."

Simon moved forward, mirroring Rick. "No, that's fine. I like a challenge. Leave it with me. I'll upgrade your settings and ensure the audit trail is turned off. No one will suspect anything," he whispered.

"Thanks, I owe you one."

* * * *

Two days later, Rick logged on to his work computer and got straight into the restricted area. *Nice work, Simon.* He located the two documents he sought and saved copies onto his USB stick. *What is so special about these files?*

That night, while Eden cooked dinner, he waded through the classified documents in the privacy of his study. The first one outlined the evolution of the vampire meal supplement program, right from its inception in the late 1930s to its full implementation in the mid-1980s.

In the detailed notes section of the report, an alarming statistic jumped out from the page.

*Death by starvation — Jade - 16, Violet - 13.*

*No way.* Sub Rosa had assured everyone on the project there had been no deaths in captivity. He skipped to the second file on Violet and Jade DNA analysis, and the financials section listed glaring funding discrepancies.

The DNA analysis had gone way over budget and Sub Rosa had siphoned allocated funds from the All-Weather Rose and other similar projects into it...without the funders' knowledge or consent.

"You look engrossed."

Rick startled and slammed his laptop shut. He looked up and Eden stood in the doorway.

"Is everything okay? You look at bit freaked out."

"I'm fine." *Sort of.*

She walked over and massaged his shoulders. "Ooh, you're so tight."

"I've been sitting too long on this" — he tapped the lid of his computer — "trying to get my head around the information for my latest research report."

"Good thing I disturbed you then. You need a break. And I thought you might want to know dinner's ready."

Rick stood and held her hand. Something about having her near put him at ease...or turned him on to the max. Both, usually. "You thought right. This can wait until tomorrow."

\* \* \* \*

As Eden's stomach grew, so did the amount of work Rick took home every night. To entertain herself while he slaved away, she browsed through his extensive library to get baby name ideas. Instead, she got sidetracked by titles in the alchemy, archeology, art, literature and particularly the history section.

"What are you up to, young lady? You're very quiet and that usually means trouble." Rick's low, seductive voice never failed to spark a fire in her sex.

"This is fascinating!" She forced her eyes to stay focused on the Nordic Folklore text. She'd had it bad for her husband before, but since the twins, her pregnancy hormones acted like a full-on aphrodisiac.

Rick kissed her on the forehead. "Yeah, my uncle collected an unusual selection of stuff. I'm assuming by the huge interest in Norway, I must have a Norwegian heritage, like you."

Eden placed the book down on the shelf. "Hartman doesn't sound very Norwegian."

"No, it doesn't, smarty pants."

She laughed. If she didn't move away from her husband this second, she'd jump him right between the bookshelves. "I guess I'd better go and make dinner."

"While you do that, I'll finish off a few work things. I shouldn't be too much longer."

It got to nine-thirty p.m. and Eden hadn't seen even a glimpse of Rick, so she put out food for Smokey and Thornton and went to check on him. A multitude of papers were spread across his desk, and he sat, staring at his laptop.

She stopped in the doorway and rested her hands on her heavily rounded stomach. *Hmmm…* How long would it take him to notice her standing there?

Rick looked up and smiled. "Sweetheart, come here."

She waddled over and he gently pulled her onto his lap. "It's getting late…"

"I know, sorry." He held her bulbous belly and nuzzled her neck. "I'll make it up to you. I promise."

Eden placed her hands over his. "That's okay. I understand. I miss you, that's all."

"I miss you too. This workload is getting ridiculous, I know, but—"

"At the same time, we're only going to be bringing in one wage soon and we can't afford to upset Sub Rosa management."

"Exactly."

Rick rubbed her stomach with calming strokes and the babies kicked, as though trying to connect with their dad.

He smiled up at her with wonder.

Glowing warmth and pure love saturated every cell in her body. "Anyway, I wanted to tell you I'm going to bed. I'm feeling pretty tired."

"I'll join you." He waved his hand across the top of the desk. "I've had enough of this for tonight. I'm struggling to keep my eyes open. Help me pack up?"

"Sure." Eden started collecting paperwork but got distracted by a black panel with a red rose design on the front of the gothic desk. She ran her hand over the engraved surface. "This really is a lovely piece of furniture."

Rick shut down the computer. "I agree. It isn't just a desk. It's a work of art."

She traced the carved, painted rose. "Every time I look at it, I notice something new."

"I know what you mean." He collated the remaining paperwork and filed it away in one of the drawers.

A raised nub poked out from the middle of the rose. She pressed it and the panel popped open. "Hey, Rick, look at this."

He reached forward, swung the panel up and it slid into a narrow cavity above, exposing a hidden drawer with a gold lock. She tugged on the drawer. "It won't open."

"Hmmm…there has to be a key here somewhere." He started opening up drawers and feeling the underside of the desk, while she poked through the top compartments.

After a few minutes, she stopped searching. "The key doesn't seem to be up here."

"Or down here."

With eager hands and a determined attitude, she recommenced poking and prodding the desk. "It can't be too far…"

Rick chuckled and held her face in his hands. "I don't think it's worth worrying about at the moment, do you?"

She stopped rummaging around and sighed. "I guess not. All the other drawers open without a problem."

"Then let's go to bed," he said, with an I'm-going-to-make-love-to-you-all-night tone.

And he did, and afterwards she normally fell into a deep, restful sleep. But tonight, she struggled to even doze, her stomach spasming, the pain growing with intensity with each passing minute.

"Rick!" The alarm clock glared three-thirty-two. Eden shook her sound-asleep husband. "Rick!"

"Mmmm..."

"I don't feel very well."

His eyes snapped open and fixed on hers. "What do you mean you don't feel well?"

"I feel funny. I can't sleep. Every way I turn is uncomfortable. My stomach's cramping."

"Cramping? How close are the contractions?" He sat up and pressed his palm to her stomach.

"About fifteen minutes apart."

"I'm taking you to the hospital. Now!"

Within the hour, they were in the hospital elevator, on the way to the maternity ward. Eden doubled over in pain and Rick slid his arm around her, offering support.

"We're nearly there okay, sweetheart," he said, his voice calm, steady.

Eden squished his hand. "I'm scared. They were supposed to be delivered before I went into labor."

His reassuring smile stopped her escalating stress. "Eden, you and the babies will be fine. Everything's under control. I'm going to be right here beside you."

He kissed her clammy forehead, her cracked lips. "I love you so much. We're going to be a family."

"I love you too. I'm so lucky —"

Two nurses arrived, cutting Eden off, sat her in a wheelchair and pushed her into the birthing suite to prepare her for an emergency caesarean.

\* \* \* \*

"It's a boy and...a girl!" the obstetrician announced, just over an hour later.

With tear-filled eyes, Rick rejoined Eden and kissed her. Once her stomach was stitched, she moved into the recovery room and two nurses brought over the twins. She kissed and cuddled both children, then made eye contact with Rick. He bent down to kiss her then the new additions to their little family.

It felt like forever before they were in her private room, alone. Rick shut the door and lay beside her. "You look radiant."

"Rick, please."

"I'm serious."

She tapped his temple. "I think the birth of your children has made you slightly delirious."

He laughed. "I'm ecstatic. It's the most amazing thing, being here with you and our babies." Rick didn't just say the right words. His enthusiasm radiated out of every pore.

"I know what you mean. I'm so glad you can stay."

He propped himself up on one elbow. "So, what do you think we should call them?"

"I'd love Scarlett Rose for our daughter."

"Scarlett Rose…" he repeated, as though testing the texture of the name on his tongue. "I like that too. Now for the little bloke—"

"Yeah, that's a bit harder. I think it's only fair you choose, seeing I chose Scarlett."

"Okay, I thought, Blake. Blake Alexander. I know we haven't discussed it, but it just feels right. What do you reckon?" His light green eyes searched hers.

"That's really nice. I think it suits him." She angled herself more toward her husband. "Hey, have you told everyone I've had the babies?"

Happy crinkles lined his eyes and lips. "Yep. I sent a group text. I'll speak to everyone individually once we're home. Simon and Grace sent their congratulations. They wanted to visit this evening but I asked them to come by tomorrow instead. I told them everything went well, but you're very tired. I hope that's okay."

Such a proud, loving, considerate dad and husband. Even though they'd only been together a short time, he knew her like he lived beneath her skin, like he had direct access to her thoughts, her reactions, her dreams. Rick embodied everything she'd ever desired in a man.

"Absolutely. I just want to be with you and the little ones tonight."

Rick caressed her cheek. "Me too."

Eden fell asleep and woke up in Rick's arms. "How are you feeling?" he asked.

"A bit sore, but okay. I still can't believe we're a family!" She kissed his lips.

He swept loose strands of her free-flowing hair from her face. "Me either. Did you sleep okay?"

"Surprisingly well. Must be the medication…and having you beside me. How did you sleep?"

"Not bad. Scarlett seemed a little unsettled so I got up a couple of times to check on her. She was fine, though."

One of the babies let out a little cry and the other one joined in.

"I'll get up. You stay and rest." He slipped out of her embrace and approached the cradles. "What time are they due for a feed?"

"About four a.m. What's the time now?"

"Nearly four-thirty. I'll bring them over."

Blake and especially Scarlett were so small and fragile-looking that it didn't surprise her Rick chose to carry them one at a time, obviously paranoid about accidentally hurting or possibly dropping them.

Eden adjusted the bed into a supported sitting position, and Rick sat by her, stroking the babies while they fed. Scarlett struggled to latch on, but once she did, she sucked hard. Eden yelped and couldn't stop her face screwing up with pain.

Rick cupped her cheek, his concerned gaze locking onto her eyes. "You okay?"

"Y-es." *Kind of.* "Scarlett's just got a more…aggressive feeding style."

Eden pushed through the feeding discomfort until the twins finished, then Rick helped her burp them, change their nappies and return them to their cradles. Rick slipped his arms around Eden's waist and they stood and watched Blake and Scarlett fall asleep.

Rick nuzzled her ear. "You're so sexy…and delicious… Mmm…"

She sighed. Being intimate with Rick never failed to propel her into a state of pure pleasure that seemed to seep right through to the heart of her every cell. And she didn't just mean the fantastic physical side of their relationship. She was referring to the whole experience — talking, touching, connecting, sharing their hopes and common goals, sharing their life. "You know, in six weeks, we can go back to having unprotected sex…"

"Mmm…as long as you're up for it, I'm there."

She turned within his embrace, and he looked at her as though she didn't just represent the woman of his dreams, but the woman of his reality, like he was the luckiest man alive. "Though we're only safe as long as I keep breastfeeding and don't get my period. The nurse said if I keep up with their feeding demands and don't supplement them with anything, we'll be fine.

"It isn't until the twins reach the six-month mark that we need to start being careful again. Even if I still haven't gotten my period by that point, I can be fertile."

"We should definitely make the most of it while we can, then…as soon as you feel ready." He grabbed her hand, led her back to bed and they lay together, spooning, caressing and chatting until they fell asleep.

* * * *

Grace reached over into Scarlett's crib and lifted her out. "I have to support the head, right?"

"That's right," Eden said.

Grace adjusted Scarlett's pink swaddled blanket. "She's a little cutie, isn't she?"

"She is, though I'm a bit biased," Rick replied. "Simon, why don't you nurse Blake. Then you guys can swap."

Simon hesitated, his face pale, his eyes filled with fear. "I don't know. They're so small. I might hurt them."

"You'll be fine. Here." Rick placed a blue swaddled Blake into Simon's arms.

Grace gently rocked Scarlett. "Have they cried much?"

"Blake's been really good but Scarlett's been a little niggly. The obstetrician said her white blood cell count was up, so they did some tests but didn't find anything, thank goodness. It's usually a sign there's an infection, though I think it might be colic, poor little thing." Eden stared at her sweet little daughter, still not quite believing she'd had a baby — two babies — and was a mother with her own little insta-family.

Scarlett looked sleepy-eyed and settled. Grace seemed relaxed. Who would have thought her good-time-girl friend had such a maternal core? "It's pretty common though, right?"

"Colic? Yeah, it is. They say she should grow out of it. I'm hoping it's sooner rather than later!"

"I hope for your sake that's the case as well."

Grace sat next to Eden and whispered, "Now, on to important stuff. When can you guys have sex again?"

"Grace!"

"I'm curious. I want to know what I'm getting into before I subscribe to this whole kids thing."

Eden laughed. Much more like the girl she knew. "Fair enough. Apparently, we have to wait six weeks...though we can do other stuff."

Grace baulked like she'd been told six months. "Six weeks! That's harsh. But at least there are other fun options. I guess you guys will be extra tired too, huh?"

"I'd say so. Thankfully, they've given Rick a month of paternity leave. It'll be a big help having him home while we get into a routine."

"That's great. Sounds like you'll need it." Grace glanced at Scarlett and caressed her sweet little face. "Hey, little one. Look at your beautiful bright eyes, your adorable button nose and your sweet little mou… Ouch!"

Simon strode over, arms steel-stiff, but Blake stayed sound asleep. "What happened?"

Grace's shocked gaze flicked between Scarlett and her hand. "She bit my finger."

"Yeah right. She's just been born. She wouldn't even have any teeth," Simon said.

Grace pulled her hand away, and sure enough, throbbing redness seethed on the pad of her index finger. "Explain this then."

Eden couldn't. She just sat there, stunned. Maybe Scarlett felt hungry and had confused Grace's finger with a nipple? *Unlikely.* Biting was totally different from sucking.

*Strange.* It must have just been a baby reflex thing. Or new mum over-anxiety. She hoped it didn't indicate something more serious. The last thing she needed was a sick, savage child.

"I think it's time we switched babies," Simon said, an it-could-only-happen-to Grace smile pushing at the corners of his lips.

He picked up Scarlett and she stared straight into his eyes. "She's very alert, isn't she?"

"Yeah, which is kind of amazing seeing the little amount of sleep she's had." Rick rejoined Eden and put his arm around her, taking the edge off her stress.

Grace rubbed her finger. "I wonder what color eyes they'll have?"

"I'm hoping they'll both take after their father," Eden said, trying to keep the worry out of her tone.

Rick looked lovingly into Eden's eyes. "Whereas I'd like Scarlett to be a miniature version of her beautiful mother."

# Chapter Twenty-One

## The Awakening

Nappy change upon nappy change, feed upon feed... The never-ending production line started from the moment Eden got discharged. She had prepared herself for the tiredness, but not the exhaustion.

Having twins wouldn't be too bad if both were like Blake. He'd been a dream child. Scarlett, on the other hand, struggled to settle, no matter what Eden tried.

Each night Eden fell into bed, asleep before her head neared the pillow, then Scarlett woke her every two to four hours, religiously. If Rick had tried to touch her, she didn't remember.

*Poor Rick.* The six weeks post-birth of no sex had extended through to sixteen weeks, and the way things were going, she couldn't see their love life getting back into the swing of things any time soon.

One unusually warm spring afternoon, Eden and Rick sat on their screened-in back porch swing and rocked the babies to sleep. Blake had fed well, his eyelids growing heavy and fluttering with impending sleep, while Scarlett had difficulty feeding and stayed wide awake. The usual routine.

"I'm starting to get worried." Eden's late lunch churned in her stomach. "We've been home for a while and Scarlett is still acting up. Her white blood cell count should have normalized by now and so should the colic. I think there might be something wrong."

"I think we need to stop comparing her to Blake. Some babies take longer than others to adjust. She'll be fine."

Acid reflux rose up and burned the base of her throat. "I hope so." Her gaze dropped to Rick's arms and connected with Scarlett's hyperalert, speckled green eyes.

Rick gently swayed the porch swing. "Hmmm...you don't sound very convinced. We'll ask the doctor for a specialist referral to check her over, just for our peace of mind."

"I think that's a very good idea."

Rick kissed Eden's forehead. "You're exhausted. Go and have a rest and I'll look after these two."

She yawned. "No, it's okay. You've got work tomorrow."

"It's still early. I can manage for a few more hours."

"Are you sure?"

"Absolutely." His confident smile put her at ease. Somewhat. She had to stop being such a control freak. He'd been great with the twins from the moment they had been born.

Eden pressed a grateful kiss on Rick's lips. "You're the best, you know that?" He was a man with incredible restraint, patience and capacity to love. Unconditionally.

He grinned. "I try."

She glanced at Blake. He had nodded off. "Once they're both asleep, I'll go have a nap."

Eden rested her head on Rick's shoulder, and all the pent-up tension melted away. "Is Scarlett asleep yet?"

"Her eyes are heavy. I don't think it'll be too long."

Within ten minutes, Scarlett and Blake were sleeping peacefully. Rick carried both babies upstairs, gently placed them in their cribs and returned downstairs to find Eden, legs curled up on the seat, dozing.

He sat, and she stirred with the rocking of the swing. Rick rested her head on his lap and stroked her long, dark, silky hair, until she too, fell fast asleep.

He leaned his head against the backrest and closed his eyes, but he couldn't sleep. Maybe a bit of poetry would release the worry clogging his mind. For over an hour he tried to compose a poem, but paralyzing writer's block disabled his creativity. *Hmmm…* What about free writing? Maybe it would stimulate his imagination.

*Conflicted, confused, stressed, uncertain, paranoid, worried, distrust, honesty, loyalty, unsure, anxious, tense, in limbo, secret, classified, unknown, danger.*

*So much for a love poem.* He chuckled.

Rick tried to create a flow between the words and craft a dark, moody poem instead. However, his mind kept wandering. Should he tell Eden what was bothering him? He didn't want to stress her out, though if he didn't get it off his chest soon, he'd implode.

Eden shuddered and sat up.

"Are you okay?" he asked.

"Fine." Her ragged breathing said otherwise. "What's the time?"

He squinted at his watch, trying to make out the position of the hands in the dark. "About seven-thirty."

"Seven-thirty! Have I been out for three hours?"

He placed his notepad and pen down on the small side table and turned back to her. "Pretty much."

"Did you have a bit of a rest?"

"Sort of…"

"Have you been out here the whole time?"

"Yep."

"What about Scarlett and Blake? They're probably awake. They're nearly due for a feed." Panic, like sparks of blue-violet fire, blazed in her eyes.

Eden went to get up but Rick pressed a hand to her thigh, keeping her in place. "Relax. They're fine." He reached over his notebook and fountain pen, picked up the baby monitor and showed it to her.

With a relieved smile, she threw her arms around his waist and hugged him.

"Were you doing some writing?" Her voice vibrated against his chest.

"I had planned to, but work is kind of dominating my thoughts at the moment."

She rubbed his back, her hands warm, encouraging. "Is everything okay?"

"Not exactly."

She sat back and searched his eyes. "Has something happened with the project?"

"No. It seems to be on track. It's just—"

"Just?"

He buried his face in his hands and sighed. "I shouldn't have brought this up. You've got enough to deal with."

Eden touched his arm. "What do you mean? Is your job in danger?"

"Not at the moment."

"Rick please, tell me what's going on. You're scaring me."

His eyes met her stare. "Okay. I just need to warn you that this is probably going to be…challenging."

She swallowed hard and loud. "Go on."

"The test subjects in the project aren't voluntary — "

"That's appalling!"

"That's not all. Some are only part-human, and the rest are no longer human at all."

Eden's forehead puckered, like a hemline with a pulled, loose thread. "What? What sort of facility are they running over there? Surely it breaches human rights."

He sighed. "Not technically. There's a bit of a loophole. You see, they capture them already changed."

"Changed to what?"

*Fuck.* He'd run out of ways to ease her in. The V word burned on his tongue until he could no longer stand the heat. "Vampires."

"Vampires? As in, living-dead blood suckers? Come on. That's ridiculous. It's a code name, right?" Hope hung in her eyes.

"I know it's hard to believe. I found it hard too — however, I've seen DNA lab results and video evidence all reinforcing it's true."

She rubbed her forehead as though to scrub the unfathomable notion from her reality. "Vampires don't exist. They're just a fable."

He held her hands in an attempt to ground her, and saw her register the truth in his eyes.

She frowned. "How long have you known this?"

"Since I got recruited to the Norway Experiment. The way management explained it at the start sounded totally reasonable. I naively thought their aims were for everyone's best interests, but not anymore, not after finding out about misuse of research funds, maltreatment of the captive vampires and covered-up deaths."

Rick pressed his forehead to hers. "Sub Rosa doesn't know I've discovered any of this, and I need to keep it that way."

She pulled back and stared at him, disappointment darkening her eyes. "You should have told me."

"And what would that have achieved, except stress you out more?"

"It could have relieved a bit of the burden you've been carrying."

"Hmmm…I guess… The thing is, knowing what I do now, the way Sub Rosa does business — not to mention how the project has been handled — goes against everything I believe in. It's immoral and unethical, and yet I can't afford to leave."

She touched his face. "We'll be able to cope, and with your age and expertise, I'm sure you'll get another job in no time."

His eyes met her intent gaze. "Maybe…if they don't make it difficult for me. Given the high level of secrecy around the Norway Experiment, not to mention the dodginess going on behind the scenes, Sub Rosa won't want to risk any information getting out."

He shook his head, upset at himself for being blinded by possible fame, fortune and power as a result of his research findings. "I should have suspected something was amiss when they made me sign a non-disclosure agreement to be accepted onto the project. But the document isn't foolproof and they know that."

"So what does—?"

He raised his hand in a hang-on gesture. "It's not an issue at the moment, because I plan to stay. Being on the inside will make it easier for me to collect evidence and change things…for the better."

She grabbed his shoulders and shook. "No, Rick, it's too dangerous."

"Not if I'm careful."

"See? Now that makes me more anxious." She dropped her hands in defeat.

He hugged her, determined to do what was right for everyone. "Eden, if I stay and do nothing, I won't be able to live with myself, and if I leave knowing what's going on, I won't be able to, either."

Rick could almost see the frantic thoughts racing through her head. "Is there someone else you can talk to about this, someone who could help?" she asked.

"I'm not sure. I'm still sussing that out. It's hard to know who to trust."

"Have you spoken to Simon about it?"

Rick agitated the porch swing. "Not really. Early on, we spoke about our surprise at finding out vampires exist, but that's it. I'm hesitant to go into my thoughts and feelings on it until I'm certain he feels similarly.

"A lot of the staff justify what Sub Rosa is doing and would turn a blind eye to dodgy practices, because they think vampires are dangerous and it's safer to have them locked up. Most of that thinking is out of ignorance and fear. We all know how vampires are portrayed in folklore, but is that information accurate?

"From what I understand, humans aren't even their main food source. So, are they really as dangerous as people think? I refuse to make assumptions until I know the facts. I guess that's the scientist in me."

Loving acceptance conflicted with apprehension in Eden's watery eyes. "It's not just that. It's your character too. You're the fairest, most honest and non-judgmental person I know."

He wanted to comfort her, to relieve the stress—however, the situation made it impossible. "Thanks. Still, I probably shouldn't have said anything to you yet. At the same time, I couldn't contain it anymore. I know it's probably the last thing you need to hear at the moment, with everything else that's going on."

The tightness in her forehead receded and a sense of reassurance settled on her face. "Rick, it's fine. I'm glad you confided in me. I don't want you to hold anything back, okay? Don't ever assume you can't tell me things, no matter how much pressure you think I'm under. I carry on to you about my crap all the time, and I expect the same in return. We need to support each other. It's not your role to bear the whole burden. It's not the 1960s. Our marriage is an equal partnership."

*Spot on.* He expected openness and trust in their communication but he'd held back. He'd been a hypocrite. Starting now, he had to make it a priority to be upfront with her, no matter how difficult.

A slow and introspective smile crept onto her face, like she'd just gotten some inside joke. "Though, I don't know how much help I can be in this instance. The sleep deprivation isn't making me the most coherent at the moment."

"True."

She elbowed his arm. "Hey, you're not supposed to agree!"

They both laughed, expelling a portion of the pent-up strain.

A conspiratorial sparkle shone in her eyes. "But I know a way I might be able to help you relax a bit."

She shimmied out of her black dress, unhooked her bra and knelt before him, her fingers on the buttons of his jeans, brushing against his growing erection. His breath hitched and held in his throat. Could she possibly grow more and more beautiful with each day?

With his fly spread open, she reached into his boxers, pulled out his cock and took it in her mouth, into hot, heavenly wetness. It had been so long since they'd done, well, anything sexual, that he was trigger-happy, ready to blow.

"Eden..." He groaned and weaved his fingers through her lustrous hair, spurring her on.

She licked and sucked him with such passion that his cock felt coated with MDMA-laced saliva.

Just before he reached the pinnacle she stopped, leaving him teetering on the edge of climax. She stared into his eyes, licked her luscious lips and slid his cock between her swollen breasts.

"Fuck!" He grunted, his ejaculate exploding against her chest.

She slipped out of her black briefs and straddled him. He massaged his cum into her skin and she thrust her tongue deep into his mouth, teasing, exploring. Then she broke away, leaving him panting, lifted his T-shirt over his head and kissed his neck and sucked on his nipples until he grew hard again.

She lowered herself onto his erect cock and rode him, slow and sensually at first, and graded up to hard and fast.

"Eden, fuck!" He groaned, and filled her with a gush of semen.

"Rick!" she cried, her body jolting like a racy rodeo rider on a bucking horse.

She wrung out every last ounce of orgasm and fell against him. Rick held her close and stroked her sexy rose-scented hair, his cock still buried deep inside her. "How did I ever cope with stress before this?"

"I know what you mean." Her voice hummed against his skin. "Sorry that I've been a bit emotionally absent since the babies have been home. I seem to use up all my energy on them, so my motivation for other things—"

"Don't worry about it." Sure, he missed their physical intimacy, but he understood. He'd dealt with Scarlett firsthand and knew how demanding she could be— physically, mentally, emotionally. "The way you're talking, it's as though it's been ages."

She pulled away and looked at him like he'd told her the sky was red. "It has! It's been nearly four months, and that's a long time when you're used to at least once a day."

"I don't expect things to be exactly like before."

Her incredulous eyes stared back at him. "Why not? I'd like them to be. I definitely want to get back to that. I miss it a lot. I miss you."

Relief and joy washed over him. He hadn't realized how much he'd needed to hear her say those words. "I've missed you too. Though it's more important to me you feel up to it. You need to take your time. Please don't feel pressured, okay?"

She nestled back into the crook of his neck, her breath caressing his collar bone. "Thanks. I hope you know I love you more than ever. And my desire for you is as strong as it's ever been."

Loving warmth radiated from his heart right through to his fingertips and toes. "Look... I can't promise I'll stop trying to get a bit, because I find you incredibly irresistible, but just tell me if you're only up for hugs, okay? I'll take any opportunity to touch you."

\* \* \* \*

Eden entered the en suite, baby monitor in hand, and placed it on top of her fluffy, blood-red towel. She turned the shower tap on and undressed, waiting for the water to warm up.

When condensation started filling the room, she regulated the water temperature and stepped under the shower rose. A few quiet, treasured minutes without the little ones... She closed her eyes, the heat of the cascading water clinging to her refreshed skin.

Rick slid his arms around her waist and she shuddered. "You surprised me."

"That was the plan." He kissed the back of her neck, skyrocketing her temperature to scalding.

He trailed his hands over her body and zoned in on her breasts and clitoris, sending her sex drive super high.

"Rick." The sound of his name added to the seduction, and she turned to face him.

"Do you expect me to be good?" A loaded question. If he meant *behave*, then the quirk to the right corner of his mouth, not to mention his massive erection, told her *no*. But if he meant *sexual prowess*, then *yes, yes, yes!*

"No. Yes..." she whispered, giddy with lust and longing. Every time he touched her felt like the first, fevered, unforgettable time.

The intense look in his eyes told her one thing — he wanted her. *Now.* Eden threw her arms around his neck and kissed him so hard that he stumbled back.

Rick righted himself and lifted her, locking his moist lips on hers as she wrapped her legs around his waist. He pressed her against the cool, wet wall tiles and moved his hard cock between her parted legs.

A muffled cry came through the monitor.

She whimpered. "I think it's Scarlett."

"She's fine. She's probably just dreaming," he said and resumed kissing her.

The rubbing of his pubic bone titillated her clitoris and he slipped inside her, filling her fully. He slid nearly all the way out, then slowly in, almost all the way out and in.

"Rick, please," she begged, his thrusts toying with her, holding her on the cusp of coming.

He sped things up, pumping harder, his heart pounding against hers, breathing each other's breath, when a louder, more persistent wail filled the airwaves.

*No!* Eden teetered so close to climax, she didn't want Rick to stop. But Scarlett's persistent cry threw sobering ice over their hot shower. She looked into her husband's lust-hooded eyes. "I really should check on her. Sorry."

He smiled, but the familiar resigned slump of his shoulders showed his disappointment. "That's okay. Maybe we can pick up where we left off a little later?"

"Yes..." Eden stepped out of the shower, quickly dried herself, chucked on her dressing gown and ran into the twins' bedroom.

Scarlett stopped crying and stared at Eden as though silently trying to communicate. The disconcerting look in her eyes suggested she comprehended what was going on, though couldn't express herself verbally…yet.

Eden picked her up just as Rick entered the room with only a low-sitting towel wrapped around his tempting man bits. "She has unbelievable timing," he said, combing his fingers through his wet hair.

"Yeah, I know."

Rick approached them and kissed Scarlett on the head.

"I'll change her nappy and see if she needs a feed. Then maybe later…" Eden hoped rather than believed they could recapture what they'd started in the shower.

"Let's see how tired you are first." His lips quirked up into a teasing smile. "I'd prefer you're awake to enjoy it."

She laughed. Not only funny, but also true. She'd been like a zonked-out zombie since they'd been discharged from hospital. "I'll see what I can do."

"I'm just going to quickly check something. Yell out when you're done," he said and walked through to his study.

Rick sat at his black gothic desk and opened up his laptop, the unresolved work issues crowding his brain and winding his stomach tighter than a cheap-ass watch.

He needed release, the dirty, sweaty, burn-up-the-sheets kind, to make him forget his work woes at least for an hour or two, maybe even trigger a solution. Eden was willing, though she had to be ready. In the interim, he'd have to make do with his hand and imagination.

He tried reviewing his latest research report but just stared at the words on the screen, his mind remaining at an impasse. He picked up a pen off the desk and chewed on the end.

*I know what I can do.* Something physical, mechanical, mindless. Rick rummaged through his desk drawers in an attempt to clean them out and clear his mind. Papers, research journals and a hodge-podge of stationary accumulated on the desk.

He reached the secret panel, popped it open and slid it away, exposing the unopenable top drawer. He stared at the taunting, stubborn lock. *I wonder what secrets you contain.* The answer to his dilemma, perhaps. He chuckled. *If only...*

"Rick, ready when you are."

Eden's sultry voice had him hurrying back into their bedroom. And oh, what a gift. Alone, naked and ready for him on the bed. He discarded his towel, the pulse in his neck thumping, sending his blood south, and slipped in beside her. Rick dove in with ravenous hunger, and they started making out like sex-starved teenagers.

Her soft warmth, the friction of their skin, her hand stroking his cock felt so fucking fantastic that he nearly came. Already. He kissed down her neck, on a mission to make her scream his name. He reached her rose key pendant and stopped. *Could it...*

"What's wrong?" she asked, her voice stripped raw with passion.

He stared into her confused eyes, then kissed her lips. "Come with me. I need to check something."

"Again? Didn't you just do that?"

"Humor me. Please. I won't be able to concentrate until I do this. I'll make it up to you later."

"If the kids don't interrupt," she muttered.

"I promise I'll find a way to get my mouth on that sweet pussy of yours before the end of the night, at the very least."

She squeezed her thighs together. "Okay, if it's that important."

He held her hand, led her to his desk and pointed to the small, locked drawer. "See that lock. It's called a 'rose lock'."

"Yeah and?"

"Look at your necklace."

She glanced down and fingered the rose key pendant. "No way."

"Shall we try it?"

"I don't see how it would work. How and why would I have the key? I'd never even seen that desk before I met you."

"Maybe the key somehow got separated from the desk and got sold as a piece on its own?"

He could just about see her mind working through the probability equations. "Maybe... Though it seems like a massive coincidence that I, out of all people, ended up having it."

"It does. Though think about it—things are often synchronistic, they just fall into place, like you and me finding each other."

"I guess..." Eden didn't look convinced, but he could tell she secretly hoped it would work.

"How about we cut the suspense and try it?"

Eden scrutinized him for a few more moments. Then she undid the clasp on her chain and slid the pendant off the end. With a shaking hand she slotted the red, rose-topped key into the lock, hesitated and gently twisted.

The lock disengaged and the drawer jutted out about an inch, revealing a hint of yellow.

Eden's mouth dropped open and her eyes almost bulged right out of their sockets. "I don't believe it."

Rick pulled open the drawer, took out a faded A4 size envelope and tugged at the flap on the back. It opened easily, the glue seal appearing aged and partially decomposed.

They peered inside. A mix of photos, some handwritten documents... Rick reached into the envelope, selected an item like a lucky dip and pulled out a black-and-white wedding photo...of them — but dated July 1965.

# Chapter Twenty-Two

Piecing It Together

Eden's mind swam in a sea of surreality. "This is a joke, right?"

Rick swallowed, his Adam's apple more like a giant walnut, pressing hard against the pale skin of his neck. "I don't think so."

She couldn't stop staring at the unbelievable photo. It felt like she'd been dropped right in the middle of *The Twilight Zone*. "What the hell is going on then?"

"I have no idea. I'm almost too scared to see what else is inside that envelope, though I won't be able to rest until I do. Is it okay if—?"

She nodded before he finished.

They returned to the bedroom and sat cross-legged on the bed, facing each other. Her heart hammered so hard against her chest that she thought her ribs would crack.

Rick tipped the remaining contents out of the envelope and put the pictures to one side. He picked up one of the hand-written documents. It was a wedding certificate for Richard Hall and Eva Fjelstad, dated 23 July 1965, the exact same date of their 2010 marriage.

"Richard and Eva? Does that sound familiar?" he asked.

One piece of the mind-boggling puzzle fell into place. "The first night we had sex in the car. They were the names we called out."

"Yep." Rick pointed at the happy couple in the picture — them. "I don't know how, but I'm sure it's us." He put the certificate aside and picked up the second document, listing staff working on the Norway Experiment in 1965 and notes for an exposé on it.

"Salvator Aalem," he murmured, then picked up their wedding certificate again. "Look at this." Rick pointed to Salvator's name, noted as a witness. On the other document, it listed him as a researcher involved in the Norway Experiment alongside Richard Hall and a small group of others. "We have to find him, if he's still alive…"

"How do you know you can trust the guy?" Eden's voice vacillated between fear and desperation to know.

"I don't, but I have to find out if he knows something. I have to take the risk. He's our only lead."

While she freaked out, he switched into the seasoned, methodical scientist. She squeezed his hand and looked into his eyes. "Rick, please be careful. We have the twins now and — "

"I know." "He caressed her cheek. I will be. I promise I won't let anything happen to you or our babies."

"Or you… You can't let anything happen to you either. I don't want to lose you, Rick." Her eyes stung, burning like a million bee stings.

He hauled her against him for a hug and kissed the top of her head, his lips firm and reverent. "You won't.

I won't let that happen. I promise I won't do anything reckless. I'll just do some subtle investigating."

Eden looked up at him, her vision blurry from the build-up of hot, unshed tears.

Rick stroked her still-damp hair. "Look... I'll just try to find this Salvator and see what he has to say, and we'll take it from there, okay?"

His mind was set. No way would she win this argument. "Okay."

They packed the documents and pictures back into the envelope and Rick put it on his bedside table. Then they snuggled together and remained silent. Eden attempted to sleep but a barrage of thoughts and possible scenarios preoccupied her mind, trying to make sense of their lives.

# Chapter Twenty-Three

## The Providential Meeting

"Hi, Salvator? We spoke on the phone briefly yesterday."

It was like a portal had opened up and transported Salvator back to 1965. "Rick, yes, come in."

He directed Rick into the living room of his compact, one-bedroom unit and they sat on the solitary three-seater sofa. He'd left the TV on in the background with the volume on low.

An AFL game—Collingwood versus Geelong—played out on the screen. Salvator didn't watch TV much these days. He used it more for company...and distraction.

"You mentioned you wanted to speak to me about a project you're working on?" Salvator asked, his nerves prickling. *Has Rick found out?*

"Yeah, that's right. I noticed in the research files that you were involved in the Norway Experiment in the 1960s and I'm eager to hear more about it. I know the notes are all there, however, it's not the same as talking to someone who worked on it at the time." His smile appeared pleasant but his tone meant business.

Salvator swallowed, swallowed again. "I don't know how much I can help you. It was a long time ago—"

"It's only been three years since you retired." Rick's light jade eyes were friendly yet firm.

"That's true. Though, in my later years, I had a couple of other more important projects that took precedence."

"Oh, I see. Well, anything you can tell me would be really helpful—even just a general overview and history of its origins would be great."

Salvator shouldn't ask, but he'd been dying to know before Rick had even made contact. "How's Eden?" Something about her had always made his pulse race.

Rick's brow furrowed, deep and wary. "You know my wife?"

He smiled, trying to keep his hands still in his lap. "Several years ago, I had the pleasure of meeting her. But she probably wouldn't remember me."

"Sounds like you have an excellent memory."

Hopefully Rick finding him meant his memory wasn't too far behind. "How can anyone forget such a beautiful and enchanting young lady?" Why had he stayed so enamored with her? She'd only ever be Rick's soulmate. He'd tested that out long ago.

Still, just saying her name sent a shiver of excitement up his spine and turned him all hormonal-teenage-boy again. Had he transferred his idealized feelings onto her in the absence of his own soulmate? Or had he just responded to the renowned innate charm her heritage used to suck in unsuspecting prey?

Rick smiled, and it reached his eyes this time. "True. I'm a very lucky man."

"Very."

"Anyway, Eden's doing well, though she's a little tired these days. We have five-month-old twins."

*So they could successfully conceive.* A sliver of regret dropped away, leaving a little less burden of guilt. "Twins? Wow! Congratulations! I'd love to meet them and catch up with Eden again." *Have the children inherited the gene as well?*

"I'm sure that would be fine. Maybe once she sees you, she'll remember."

"I hope so…" Salvator hesitated, and straightened up in his seat. "I guess it's down to business now, then. Before we start, would you like a coffee — or perhaps something alcoholic?"

"A coffee's fine, thanks."

When Salvator returned with their mugs, he handed one to Rick, sat down next to him and launched into the conception of the Norway Experiment. "As you would know, the project was originally designed to eradicate faulty genes in the human race. But in order to proceed, Sub Rosa needed a test group.

"In the 1930s, ethics standards were lax in comparison to now, so it had been easy to convince the board that testing on a small group of people with a supposed 'defective' gene was essential for the good of all.

From the outside, Rick looked the same, though how about the inside? *Have there been permanent molecular changes to his cells, to his personality?* "Things really got into full swing around the time of the Second World War.

"Sub Rosa board members and some of the executive management group had ties with the German army and found out about experimentation they were doing that fit with their aims — to eradicate faulty genes and strengthen the human race.

"However, instead of focusing on existing human populations, as the Germans were doing, Sub Rosa had another target group in mind. Vampires. They were seen to be the biggest threat, and with effective use of fear propaganda — another thing they learned from the Germans — the study easily got ratified."

Salvator had a sip of his coffee, holding the cup with both hands to steady their shaking. "Still young and eager and ambitious when I first got involved, I believed the project would benefit the human race as a whole, so I participated without question.

"It only took a little while before I realized things weren't that simple and black-and-white. There were a myriad of variables. Who has the right to decide what's normal? Who's good? Who should live or die? What is worth preserving?"

Rick's jade eyes glowed in the same intense way they always had. "Exactly."

"I probably should have left at that point. I probably should have at least got myself off the project. I had a conscience, though, so I justified staying by telling myself someone had to be there to make sure things were as fair as possible, that experiments were done in the most humane way."

Salvator gulped down the remainder of his steaming black coffee, burning his tongue. "I don't know whether I made the right decision. I think about it every day. Maybe I should have tried to shut down the project instead. But on my own, it seemed impossible. I saw what happened to someone who tried."

*What is Rick thinking?* He'd sat like a Rodin sculpture and had hardly blinked, let alone uttered a word.

Salvator waited, leaving Rick some more space to speak. However, he just sat and stared, silently encouraging Salvator to continue. "Sub Rosa has thrown millions into it over the years and they're still trying to recoup as much as they can."

*Time to test him.* Salvator edged closer to Rick. "I know for a fact they've censored information, and where required, adjusted findings to ensure recurrent government funding."

A sudden knowing sparked in Rick's eyes, and he finished his coffee. He didn't say anything, just returned his empty mug to the table and resumed his statue-still listening position.

"Just before I left, the research department was pushing to try to extend the ethics approval to also include quarter-caste vampires and even those with no presenting symptoms but who were known carriers.

"They thought that by increasing the parameters, they might increase their results and possibly attract more research dollars. However, as far as I know, their proposal still hasn't been accepted, thank God.

"The technology keeps getting better, though, and I'm concerned if these researchers get into positions of power, they'll prevent individuals from making informed choices. Prospective mothers will be told something's wrong with their child and abortion cited as the only option."

Salvator crossed his leg toward Rick and leaned in closer. "From what I've seen, the 'questionable' gene isn't necessarily bad or defective. Like with anything, there are positives and negatives. Like with any group of people, there are good and bad, and I don't believe any of us have the right to decide what that is—do you?"

Rick sat up tall in his seat, his eyes full of conviction. "Definitely not. It's way too subjective."

His sincere statement was the first strong hint that Rick's insides were still true to his essence. "I thought you might agree." Salvator had hoped, wished, prayed for that exact reaction...even though he didn't have a religious strand of DNA in his body.

Rick stretched his arms above his head, as though to limber up, then rested his elbows on his knees, the late afternoon sun highlighting the natural golden streaks in his hair. "I've actually been questioning things for a while. Then I came across information reinforcing my concerns, but I didn't know where to go with it."

Salvator's eyes filled with relieved tears. "Richard, it's still you. I'm so glad."

"Sorry?"

*Shit!* Every muscle in Salvator's wound-tight frame started twitching, shaking, like he had early-stage Huntington's disease. "How do I explain?"

Rick produced a black and white wedding photo of him and Eden dated July, 1965. "Just start at the beginning."

# Chapter Twenty-Four

## The Unreal Explanation

Salvator unhooked his glasses from his inside jacket pocket and put them on, moved forward in his seat and studied the photo. "You found it...the envelope."

"The one I'd hidden away back then, yes."

*In the secret locked drawer of the black gothic desk.* "You were always two steps ahead."

Rick's jade eyes bored into him like a high speed, electric drill. "Not always. What happened?"

Salvator swallowed the large lump of anxiety in his throat. How would Rick react to his explanation? "It's a long story."

"I've got all the time in the world," Rick said, and settled back into the couch.

Salvator lifted his glasses onto his head and scrubbed his face with his hands. *Where to begin?* Over the years he'd often thought about this very moment, trying to prepare himself as best he could. Now, all his planning went out the blasted-open window.

Salvator re-established eye contact with Rick, his lungs strangled with escalating stress until he could barely breathe. He coughed, trying to free up his constricted airway, but the weight of anxiety still pressed on his chest. "It all started when I undertook some research for the Norway Experiment and came across alchemic potions from a Norwegian missionary in the Middle Ages.

"His documented results fascinated me and I became obsessed with one formula in particular — a soulmate serum. It claimed to identify a person's soulmate through touch, and I decided to try and recreate it.

"So, I began a little side project in my own time and successfully trialed it on rats. However, I needed to know whether the results translated to humans. I tried the serum on myself first, but it backfired. I had to break off my engagement and I never found anyone else."

Salvator plucked his glasses off his head and placed them on the table. "I didn't lose interest, though, determined to find volunteers to see if it worked and on what percentage of people.

"Anyway, I'd met you briefly and mentioned I needed test subjects. Soon after, you and Eva contacted me. You came in separately but it didn't take long to realize you were a couple.

"Before administering the red, rose-flavored oral serum, I explained that if you weren't each other's soulmates, you would be attracted upon sight but would feel nothing when you touched.

"I had no antidote, so once you'd taken it, you had to live with the outcome. Whether positive or negative. You were confident, though, and you were right to be. You two are perfect for each other, a perfect match." A nervous smile twitched at the corners of Salvator's lips.

"Within a few days I received a wedding invitation from you and was surprised and honored that you asked me to be your witness. Over the next three months, our friendship blossomed. Then, in October, everything changed. I'll never forget being called into the basement and asked to 'manage the situation'.

"I'd been told a couple of employees had taken steps to expose Sub Rosa and needed to be…silenced. When I saw you two, I didn't know what to do, but I had to do something, and quickly. I had to find a way to justify keeping you alive."

All Salvator's stores of saliva had dried up and he struggled to swallow, his tongue dry-vacuum sealed to the roof of his mouth. He managed to force it free and said, "I came up with a proposal."

Salvator closed his eyes, tried to extract the key components of his tumultuous thoughts and did the second hardest thing he'd ever had to do — look Rick in the eye and tell him the horrible truth. "To use you as test subjects in two cutting-edge Sub Rosa research streams that desperately needed human trials — cryogenics and memory modification. It wasn't the ideal solution, far from it, but the best I could come up with under the circumstances."

Rick stared, motionless, his face an unreadable mask, as though trying to absorb, process and fully comprehend the unbelievable story. Was he in shock? Catatonic with information overload? On the edge of exploding? Salvator's pulse sped up to pre-heart-attack pace.

"Soon after you were both sedated, you were given the memory eraser drug, and once your minds were 'clean', I administered a memory filler drug to increase your brain's receptiveness and allow it to 'fill in the gaps' with artificial but believable memories.

"This included altering your names so no one, not even you or Eden, could connect you to your previous selves. I wanted to prevent any complications."

Salvator sucked in a long, deep breath, the air quaking in his windpipe. "In between sessions, you were taken to the cryogenics storage unit and frozen—"

Rick's mobile phone rang and he fumbled for it in the back pocket of his jeans.

"I need to take this," Rick said, his voice clipped, and answered his phone. "Yes, everything's fine, sweetheart. Salvator just *enlightened* me about a few things. As soon as he's finished, I'll head straight home, okay? How are the kids?" He paused. "I promise I won't be long. Love you."

Rick shoved his mobile back into his jeans. "So, you were saying we were frozen? I never realized Sub Rosa had cryogenics funding." His voice sounded calm, measured, but restrained anger flared in his eyes.

Salvator tried to clear his dry throat, but it felt like sandpaper scraping his gullet. "They don't anymore, though they did for many years. All the research would be archived now. They lost a lot of money on their foray into cryogenics, so I think they like to try and pretend it never happened.

"Unfortunately, the testing wasn't very successful, except on both of you and a very small percentage of monkeys, so the government funding bodies withdrew their recurrent funding.

"As soon as I heard, I used the opportunity to push for the release of you and Eden—however, I only got permission to choose one of you, on the proviso that the other remained stored and would be freed after five years, assuming reintegration proved successful."

Hostility clearly grew in Rick's eyes and a muscle in his jaw twitched.

*Keep going. You can get through this.* What was the worst thing that could happen? Murder? Heart attack? No matter what the risk, he owed Rick honesty, the facts. "I freed Eva first, and two years after she left the facility, the remaining cryogenic 'samples' were deemed too expensive to store and earmarked for disposal. I panicked.

"I barged into Andy's office and managed to convince him to release you early and see if you could mimic the success of Eden's reintegration. Then, just like with Eden, I gave you a memory solidifier to consolidate the implanted memories and doctored a range of physical evidence, such as photos and memorabilia to support the false memories.

"I couldn't risk you remembering what had happened straight away. It would have had very detrimental effects on your mental and emotional health, not to mention the success of your re-assimilation.

"However, when I pulled together your exit wardrobes, I couldn't help but include some original items as well, like the rose key pendant to go with the black gothic desk I had given you and Eden for your 1965 wedding gift."

"So you knew the key opened the hidden desk drawer?" Rick asked.

"Of course. And so did you. I explained the clever idea at the time and liked that it gave you somewhere safe to keep the key if you decided to hold any important documents hidden away in the secret compartment, which you did."

Rick seemed to be searching internally, as though trying to locate the lost memories. Hopefully his genetics would be the key to unlocking the chemical divide to retrieve them. "Yes…"

"I had to include Eden's black-and-white polka dot dress too. She wore it the night you came in for the soulmate serum trial. I wanted to see if it would jog her memory…or yours.

"I always hoped your memories would return eventually, when it was safer. I'd like to believe the dress, combined with some of the other material objects, triggered something, because you connected with each other again.

"The researcher in me wanted to stay involved with you somehow, to find out, but it was too dangerous. So, once you were safely released, I resigned and severed all contact."

Rick's brow creased, like one of Salvator's rumpled suits. "I thought they were still waiting on ethics approval for the memory drugs."

Salvator smoothed out the crinkled material of his slacks. "They are."

Rick got in his face and glowered at him. "Our brains could have been fried! We could have died!" Then he shot up and started to pace, shoving his hands through his hair, once, twice.

"If I hadn't done what I did, you definitely would have." What were those de-escalation techniques he'd learned? Keep the voice calm, controlled. "It seemed the safest option." *For all of us.*

Rick stopped and turned back to him, his jade eyes seething. "Are there any side effects?"

"Not that I'm aware of."

"Not that you're aware of... Great." Each of Rick's words stung with sarcasm.

"I know it's difficult to hear and a lot to come to terms with. Although you might not believe it, I am truly sorry for putting you through all of this. I had the best intentions, but very limited options."

Rick sat back down and glared at Salvator, silent, stewing. "I believe you," he said through gritted teeth. He raked one hand through his hair, once, twice, three times. "It's just...infuriating, overwhelming." Rick shifted in his seat and took several steadying breaths. "I can't believe something like this could happen, has happened. It's unreal, surreal, like something out of a sci-fi book. I'm still trying to get my head around it all."

"That's totally understandable." His response was a lot better than anticipated. Salvator hadn't been sure what to expect. Anything from a slog to the jaw right through to a hospital-worthy beating.

It was nothing he didn't deserve. His heart rate slowed. He should have known Rick was too sensible and enlightened for any primal, physical outburst.

The nervous *tap tap tap* of Rick's foot hitting the timber floor added a new tension to the air. "So...what's happening now? There's no way they'd release me and Eden without some safeguards."

"You'd be surprised. Your detainment happened before Andy started and the circumstances were kept hush-hush, which means he wouldn't have any idea of who you really are or that you tried to expose Sub Rosa in the past.

"There's only one employee left that started in 1965, close to when you and Eden were apprehended, but I wouldn't worry about him. He worked as an accountant back then, and is the senior manager of Business Services these days, so removed from the research area. Given that, combined with the fact a lot of time has passed and your names are different, I doubt he or any other current Sub Rosa staff would make the connection. I don't think you've got anything to worry about...at this stage."

"Management haven't recruited any staff to watch us, then, even just to check if the memory drugs were successful?"

Now Rick knew what Sub Rosa was capable of, his concern was understandable. "I doubt it. They have my reports on the success of Eden's reintegration and, when I left, Andy explained he couldn't justify spending the insufficient budget on unnecessary surveillance, except in the instance of a perceived threat.

"However, just to be on the safe side, for any future contact, use your mobile to ring mine. If you're anything like me, you have it with you all the time, so it's unlikely they could've tampered with it. Then once you've rung or I've rung you, make sure you erase your call history and I'll do the same, in case they somehow get hold of our phones."

*Better stop there for today.* Not the full truth, but now wasn't the time to burden Rick with the rest.

* * * *

Rick hadn't even reached the top step when Eden threw open the front door, her face contorted with concern. She nursed a dozing Scarlett in her arms. "I thought you weren't going to be long. It's nearly eleven," she whispered, her voice rough, shaky.

"I'm sorry. Time got away from me." He kissed Scarlett's cheek and she stirred, though didn't rouse.

Eden's blue-violet eyes searched his. "You look drained. Is everything all right?"

*Not even close.* He'd spent the whole drive home trying to find the right words to tell her, but there were none. He just had to be honest and upfront as he'd promised and hope for the best.

Rick mustered his most reassuring smile and caressed Eden's cheek. "Let's put Scarlett to bed and I'll explain everything."

# Chapter Twenty-Five

## Business as Usual

Eden discarded her violet satin robe and joined Rick in bed. "I feel stagnant, almost frozen, like we literally were for forty-odd years. How do we move forward from this?"

"By changing things…for the better."

"How?"

"I have something in mind."

*Oh no. That unmistakable determination in his tone again.* "This is *not* something that can be done by one person. Look at what happened when you last tried…" A sob-like breath highjacked her speech.

"Sub Rosa has been playing with people's lives for far too long. I can't let it go on, and I know a group approach won't be viable. The more links in the chain, the more chance for error." Rick stroked her cheek, his touch comforting in contrast to his troubling words.

"Plus, I don't want to put others at risk. I wish I could tell you otherwise, but it has to be done alone and I'm the best person to do it. I already have access to incriminating information. I just have to collect as much evidence as I can, work out who to get it to and how to do it without arousing suspicion."

"But, Rick—"

"Please hear me out." His light green gaze pleaded along with his words.

She gave one short, sharp nod.

"As you know, I've been feeling pressured and unsettled for months. Now something has clicked into place and I feel realigned with my path, my destiny. I feel really focused and driven. It's like I've found my purpose again. And I'm wiser this time around. I really believe if I think things through properly and don't let my emotions get in the way, I can do it."

The steel fist of fear gripped her stomach. "If you go ahead with this, do you realize what's at stake? Are you willing to risk everything? Because that's what you'll be doing."

Rick held her face between his hands. "You know me. I need to do what's best for everyone. I can't compartmentalize my life and delude myself into believing that because everything's great with us, the world is wonderful. I can't live happily knowing others are suffering and being mistreated, especially when I'm in a position to try to stop it. If I continue working at Sub Rosa, knowing what I do and do nothing, then I'm passively condoning their actions. I couldn't live with myself."

"Then leave," she begged. "Let's move away, somewhere safe, and we can start over."

He dropped his hands to her shoulders, steadying, preparing her for the inevitable outcome. "We've already spoken about this, and as I explained, I can't run away, not when I'm perfectly situated to make a difference."

Eden didn't want to cry. She wanted to talk. She wanted to appeal to his logical and rational mind and convince him another, safer way existed. But no matter how hard she tried, she couldn't think of a less risky alternative.

The last thing she wanted to do was use emotions to guilt him into inaction. She swallowed back the mounting tears burning her eyes, and one escaped, sending a flood streaming down her cheeks.

His face filled with anguish. "Eden?"

"The thing is." Sobs punctuated her speech. "I respect and admire how you feel about this and what you want to do. I agree that someone has to do something. I just don't want that someone to be you. I know it sounds selfish, but I don't want anything to happen to us, to our family. And I'm so worried it will, given what happened in the past. I couldn't bear for us to be torn apart, to lose you and the twins."

Rick embraced her, his warmth seeping through her chilled skin. "You know I wouldn't jeopardize our family. I've lived a life without parents, as you have, and I would never inflict that on Blake and Scarlett.

"I want them to know and respect us, to be guided by us. I want us to be a positive influence in their lives so they grow up confident and driven to make the world a better place."

She sniffled into his shoulder. "I want that too, but I'm scared. If you pursue this, it puts us in danger. You can't deny it."

He rubbed her back with long, slow, soothing strokes. "The truth is we're already in danger and have been since 1965. Unless this is resolved, we won't ever be truly safe. We're balancing on a knife's edge. Now that we know the truth, it would only take the smallest slip and we'll be cut to ribbons…and I don't just mean that metaphorically. But I promise I won't act until I work out the safest way to proceed. I don't want to escalate things through being impulsive or careless."

Rick pressed his forehead to hers. "I wish more than anything I could tell you I'll drop this and move on, but you know I can't. Even if I could, it won't make us any safer."

He pulled back and peered into her eyes. "And just so you know, I don't think you're being selfish. You're just trying to protect our family. I totally get that." He cuddled her close, leaving no space between their bodies. "You're a wonderful mother and wife. I'm so lucky to have you."

"I'm lucky to have you too. I couldn't ask for a better husband or father to my children." Her voice sounded muffled against his chest.

Up until they'd found those locked-away documents, Eden had thought they had all the time in the world, that Rick would always be around. It suddenly struck her how complacent she'd been, especially since she'd had the twins.

Without realizing it, she'd put her relationship with Rick on the back burner. She'd wasted too much precious time. And now time was of the essence, a prized commodity. She wanted to make the most of every minute.

Eden traced the outline of Rick's defined abs, as though touching and really seeing him for the first time. She kissed his sternum, the sprinkling of hair soft and downy against her lips. Her soulmate ring heated up and, in seconds, her desire for him peaked at a heart-throbbing fifteen out of ten.

A desperate need to relish every inch of him overtook her and she started to lick and suck on his nipples. He caressed her hair and worked his hands over her back and bottom, arousing every cell in her body.

She threw off the doona and moved between his legs, trailing her lips down his taut stomach and along the inside of his thighs. He closed his eyes and breathed out hard. When she reached his feet, she ran her tongue along each sole, took his little toe into her mouth and sucked on it as though it were his cock.

He shifted against the bed, his breathing loud and heavy. "Eden," he said, her name almost a groan.

She moved from one toe to the next, licking, sucking, nibbling, until his cock strained against his washboard stomach. Then she stopped, flashed Rick a mischievous smile and assumed the sixty-nine position.

He delved his warm tongue between her legs, sending a tidal wave of ecstasy from her pelvis right through to the tips of her toes.

Eden closed her eyes, savoring the muscle-melting sensation. "Rick..." She moaned and took the full length of his shaft into her mouth.

His hot breath burst against her skin and he picked up the pace with his tongue. Eden sucked on his balls, then tantalized the head of his cock with soft, saliva-filled licks. She had never wanted him so badly.

"My sexy, delicious wife," he murmured, and she shot straight to climax.

Rick lapped up her juices like she was the best thing he'd ever tasted and filled her mouth with his own release. She swallowed his hot cum, covered his cock with gentle, loving kisses, then turned around and kissed his wet lips.

His green eyes glowed with insatiable longing, and he rolled onto his side, taking Eden with him, so they faced each other. He hooked her top leg over his hip, grasped her butt and pulled her in super tight. She gasped. His pelvis pressed into hers, sending a surge of anticipation through her.

She wound her arms around his neck and they kissed, deep and long, rubbing their naked bodies against each other. His growing hardness stroked her clitoris over and over and over, and just when she came close to losing herself again, he slowly entered her dripping-wet sex.

"Uh-h," she moaned against his lips, his slow, sensual thrusts, filling and stretching. The dreamy, intense closeness felt so exquisite, she almost liquefied in his arms.

They'd had plenty of long, passionate sessions but had never done it like this before...not in their Rick and Eden incarnation. It took their connection to another level, a level she'd never imagined existed. The pleasure, passion, lust and love were all amplified a hundredfold, like reaching utopia.

They moved toward orgasm, though instead of speeding things up, Rick held the rhythm, plunging steady and deep. Part of her wished they could stay like this forever.

The love-filled look in his eyes combined with his incredible touch finally pushed her to climax and he followed straight after. She gave herself wholly to him and him to her. The sex between them had always been amazing, but this was...beyond words.

"What brought that on?" Rick asked, still breathing hard, a huge, satiated smile on his face.

"Just appreciating my husband." *For as long as I can.*

\* \* \* \*

When Eden woke the next morning, Rick had already left for work. *Damn!* She had hoped for a special morning wake up call. Nothing like the threat of loss to put things back into perspective.

She stretched, her aching muscles a welcome reminder of their extraordinary sexcapade the night before, and glanced at the alarm clock — nine-thirty a.m. already! The pull of motherly duties snapped her into the present.

Eden rushed into the twins' room, and they were both still asleep. She tip-toed down to the kitchen, and in the sink were two empty bottles of her expressed milk. Rick had topped them up before leaving. *What a sweetie.*

While eating her breakfast in the conservatory with Thornton and Smokey curled up next to her and the baby monitor at her side, the serious conversation she had had with Rick the previous night invaded her mind. There had to be a safer, workable solution that didn't involve Rick, a strong, infallible idea he could only agree to.

One of the babies stirred.

*Scarlett.* Eden gobbled down a cold slice of Vegemite toast and ascended the stairs to the babies' bedroom. By the time she reached it, Scarlett wouldn't stop wailing.

Eden picked her up, took her downstairs and began breastfeeding her on the conservatory couch. In usual Scarlett style, she struggled to get going, though once she did, she sucked like an industrial vacuum cleaner.

After she fed, Eden always felt sore, whereas Blake was a sedate feeder, leaving her almost serene. When on paternity leave, Rick had gotten her cabbage leaves to place over her inflamed, tender breasts and followed up with a full body massage. She missed that...a lot.

The doorbell rang and the cats scattered.

Eden pulled Scarlett off her breast and her little face scrunched up. "Sorry, honey. You'll have to finish feeding in a minute."

She did up her bra, hurried to the door and eased it open. "Grace! What a lovely surprise!"

"I had the day off so I had to come and see you guys."

Eden led her into the conservatory. "Take a seat. How about I grab us a coffee? Is decaf, Swiss chocolate espresso okay?"

Grace sat on the off-white lounge chair by the window, bathed in morning sunlight. "Mmm...yes, thanks."

"Would you like to hold Scarlett? I won't be too long."

"Sure, I'd love to."

Eden handed Scarlett over and she squinted and started screaming.

"First she gums my finger and now this. Do you think she's trying to tell me something?" Grace said with a wry smile.

"Don't be silly. It looks like the sun is in her eyes. Maybe try sitting over here instead." Eden pointed to where she'd been sitting earlier.

Grace relocated to the darker spot and Scarlett settled. "I can't believe how much she's grown."

"If you think she's grown, wait until you see Blake."

Eden returned holding a tray with two cups and a selection of chocolate and shortbread biscuits, and placed it down on the coffee table.

"Mmm....smells delicious! I bet you'd like a taste, huh?" Grace said, touching Scarlett's little rosebud lips.

"Ouch!" Grace jolted her hand away from Scarlett's mouth and examined her finger. "Did you bite me again, you little bugger?"

Eden hurried over. Blood dripped from Grace's index finger and a hint of blood smeared across Scarlett's mouth. "I'm so sorry, Grace. When you arrived, I hadn't finished feeding her...I think she's still hungry." Though that didn't entirely explain the strange behavior. Eden picked up her misbehaving baby. "I'll get you a bandage."

"No, that's fine. I've got one in my bag."

"You're a very naughty girl," Eden said to Scarlett, and sat down to recommence breastfeeding her. She guided Scarlett's mouth to her nipple and Eden's eyes widened in horror. Instead of Scarlett being unsettled, she sucked on her lips as though to lap up every last trace of blood, as though she enjoyed the taste of it.

*What the hell is going on?* Eden's heart rate went ballistic and her gaze darted over to Grace. Thank God, her friend was focused on trying to fasten the bandage to her finger. Whatever Eden did, she couldn't let on to Grace that anything was wrong. She'd just have to wait out the visit, then try and find an explanation.

When Grace left, Eden reached for the cordless phone and called Rick.

Within twenty minutes he arrived home and, after a brief chat, went into their library to look up possible solutions. Eden had already undertaken a preliminary Google search, but it had just brought up references to *Twilight* and vampires in general.

A couple hours later, Rick stormed back into the conservatory and pinned Eden with his frustrated stare. "This is ridiculous! I'm going to ring Salvator. I have a feeling he might know exactly what's going on."

# Chapter Twenty-Six

## Just One Other Thing...

Rick opened the front door, his steely glare freezing Salvator to the spot. "You didn't tell me everything."

"No. I thought it might be too much all at once."

"You know what I'm talking about then." Rick's jaw ticked, as taut as a high-tension spring.

"I think I've got a pretty good idea."

With a stiff arm, Rick gestured for Salvator to step inside then led him into the conservatory. Storm clouds gathered in the sky, dimming the room with charcoal-gray light.

"Take a seat. Eden will be down in a minute. Can I get you a drink?" Rick's cold tone seemed to suck all the warmth from the room.

Salvator sat on a puffy, off-white lounge chair. "No, I'm fine at the moment." His hands shook and his legs were like half-set jelly. He'd be seeing Eden any second. *Pull yourself together!*

Rick sat on a matching two-seater lounge chair opposite and stared at him, a muscle jerking in his jaw. A fluffy gray cat appeared and jumped onto Rick's lap.

He began patting the feline without breaking eye contact.

Footsteps echoed on the timber floor and Salvator turned toward the doorway.

Eden swept into the room, holding one of the babies. She looked as elegant and breathtaking as the day he'd met her, forty-six years ago. *Don't stare. Don't stare. Don't stare!* But he couldn't stop.

"Eden, Scarlett, this is Salvator," Rick said, snapping Salvator's brain back into line.

"Hi, Salvator. Thanks for coming at such short notice."

Her friendly yet wary facial expression confirmed she didn't remember him. Hopefully she didn't think he was a sleazy old scientist. "No problem. It's the least I could do. It's good to see you again. You look as lovely as ever."

"Thank you." A hesitant smile flickered on her lips and she went and sat beside her husband. Rick put his arm around her, a very distinct, protective 'mine' gesture.

"We weren't sure who else to speak to about this." Her voice sounded nervous yet gentle. It didn't hold anger like Rick's, more curiosity. "We thought you might know—"

A clap of thunder boomed and a bolt of lightning flashed into the room. The rain started to fall, the large drops splashing the vast, rear window and trickling to the ground.

A baby's shriek split the air and the cat jumped off Rick's lap. Not Scarlett. Had to be the other twin.

Eden's eyes were apologetic. "Sorry... I'll be back in a minute." She handed Scarlett over to Rick and ran out of the door.

For a few uncomfortable moments, Salvator sat in silence with Rick, then Eden returned, holding the second baby. "You've already met Scarlett, and this is Blake."

He gurgled and flapped his arms, a big smile pushing into his chubby cheeks.

Salvator's eyes stung with years of bottled-up emotion. He couldn't be happier for them. Not that the positive outcome made up for all the anguish he'd put them through, but it was something. "You have a beautiful family."

"Thank you," Rick and Eden said in stereo.

"Now…" He blinked back the prickling threat of tears. "Having seen both twins, I can tell you only one carries the gene."

Eden's brows knitted together and she clutched Blake to her chest. "What gene? And how can you diagnose anything from just looking at them? Don't you need to do some tests?"

Salvator fiddled with the collar of his jacket. "No. The tests are just a formality." He clasped his hands in his lap and looked up at them. "Before I put you both into storage, all those years ago, I took blood samples. It's standard procedure for anyone less than three-quarter vampire. For full vampires, buccal swabs, skin or hair samples are used, because they have no red blood to take.

"In your case, not just agency procedure drove me to test your blood. Some anomalies I'd observed made me curious. When the results came back, I can't say it surprised me to find out that you both carry the vampire gene."

"What?" Rick and Eden said in unison, their eyes wide, like they'd been slapped with shock and disbelief.

"You're both quarter vampires and descend from rival clans. Eden, your family has Violet origins, and Rick, yours has Jade. As you'd know, Rick, different clan members' eyes come in various shades. The stronger the vampire gene, the deeper the eye color.

"You both have pale, yet distinctive eyes, though not identifying enough on their own to make anyone question your humanness. However, coupled with other characteristics, like your flawless fair skin, aversion to garlic and love of rare meat, an annoyingly observant scientist like me might start asking questions."

Rick shot up off the couch and started pacing, a hyperalert Scarlett in his arms. "This is impossible. How can we be part vampire? How did I not realize? Did we ever even know?"

"I don't think so. When I originally met you, you told me you were both brought up in boarding school and didn't know much about your biological families."

Eden sat silently, her arms wrapped tight around a wriggly Blake, tears streaming down her face.

First the experimentation revelation and now this. Their minds had to be in overdrive trying to get a grasp on everything, trying to put it all in perspective. They had to be angry, fearful, sad.

Salvator's heart lurched, his eyes on the verge of tears at their torment and grief. But he had to forge on. They had a right to know the full truth.

"Once I had your DNA, I correlated it with those living in the Norway compound, just out of curiosity, and found that, Rick, you have a half-vampire relative living there.

"It wasn't until I traveled to the Norway site for a six-month secondment, about fifteen years ago, that I met a subject named Rhoda. Your mother. She wanted me to pass on some cross jewelry as a way for her to be close to you, to offer protection. She'd be really happy to see you wearing it so proudly."

Rick stopped, and he and Scarlett touched the cross around his neck, a flicker of awe shining through the rage and sorrow.

"During our meetings, she told me your father was full human and they had managed to correspond by letter over the years. I finally met up with him right before your release in 2007. Unfortunately, he passed away before I could reunite you. I wanted to tell your mum, but I couldn't. Making further contact would have endangered both of us." He shifted to the edge of his seat and leaned forward.

"Your dad's name was Abe and, up until he died in his early nineties, he had always been a strong, determined, selfless man. I only got to speak to him once before he left this world, but he told me some amazing stories about the vampires he'd hidden in this house over the years to help save them from persecution. He also explained that in order to avoid suspicion and prevent any harm coming to you, he'd passed himself off as your uncle, Bram."

Rick dropped back down onto the couch next to his stunned wife. "My uncle..." he murmured, his eyes focusing internally, as though grasping for a just-out-of-reach memory.

"You actually did know him once. You lived with him before you got married, and he gave you this house as a wedding gift. Then, after you disappeared later that year, he spent the rest of his life searching for you, while continuing to hide and protect the vampire community.

"Hopefully one day you'll remember him..." Salvator's gaze shifted to Eden. "You also have a half-vampire relative living in the Norway compound. Unfortunately, that's all I know. Sorry."

Eden stared at him, her mouth moving but unable to produce sound. The bombardment of information seemed to have overwhelmed her brain and used up all its thinking capacity.

Her non-response was more disconcerting than full-blown anger and hysteria. And that reaction had occurred just from hearing about their true identities. How would she be when he related the news about Scarlett? No matter how hard, he had to tell Rick and Eden everything.

Salvator levered himself off the couch and approached Eden. He crouched before her and directed his attention to Blake. "Hey, little feller," Salvator said, pinching the little boy's cherub-like cheek. "You're so handsome."

Blake responded with a dribbly grin.

Salvator glanced at Rick then at Eden. "He has lovely gray eyes, so he definitely hasn't inherited the gene. He's full human." Then he moved across to Scarlett, who sat on Rick's lap. "Hey there, young lady. You're beautiful, just like your mother."

A proud smile beamed on Scarlett's lips.

Salvator's gaze flipped back to Rick, then Eden. "Have you ever noticed her eyes? They're an amazing jade green with violet flecks. She has inherited the vampire gene from each of you, making her a half vampire with mixed clan origin. She's the first of her type that I've met. It's a rare combination, given the longstanding bad blood between the clans. Though, as I mentioned, I've met single clan, half vampires such as your mum, Rick, and in order to thrive, they need a human-vampire diet. I imagine Scarlett is the same."

Eden's face twisted with terror. "What the hell is a human-vampire diet?"

*Thank God! A response.* "A mix of human nutritional requirements and red blood. That's the reason she's not doing as well as Blake. She can get by on a full human diet, though it won't fully satisfy her and she'll feel weak, exhausted and unsettled."

Eden recoiled. "How am I supposed to give her blood? And where am I supposed to get it from?"

"Wherever you can. I'd suggest raw mince as a starting point or collect the bloody run-off from steak before cooking it then warm it up for her to drink."

Panic filled Eden's eyes, like a blocked pressure hose on high. "They can't know about her...or us. No one can."

"I agree. We can only trust each other." Salvator reached for her right hand, as though to be reassuring. He had to touch her again. Things were getting serious and he needed to think straight. He needed to make sure his emotions wouldn't get in the way.

The skin-on-skin contact shut down his raging teenage hormones. All the pent-up feelings he'd rebuilt for her over the last few years dissolved, thanks to the effects of his soulmate serum.

Strangely, he didn't feel sad, more relieved and he still had a pure respect and platonic caring for her...and the ever-present desire to find his own soulmate.

The drained, shattered look in her and her husband's eyes gave away their total exhaustion. They'd stayed physically present while their minds had hit saturation point. "I think I should go. You both need time to absorb everything.

"Then, when you're ready, give me a call and we'll discuss the specifics around how best to proceed. I want to help you make things right." Salvator smiled at the twins. "Bye, Blake. Bye, Scarlett. It's been a pleasure to meet you."

Hesitant smiles stagnated on their lips, as though they'd picked up on the gravity of the situation.

Salvator stood and adjusted his suit. "Bye, Eden. Really lovely seeing you again. I just wish it was under better circumstances."

She tightened her grasp around Blake and kissed him on the top of his head. "Yes, me too. Bye, Salvator."

Rick escorted him to the front door, still holding Scarlett in his arms. "You have told us everything now, right? I'm assuming there'll be no other surprises," he gritted out through clenched teeth.

They stopped in the foyer, facing each other. "There are no other surprises. I promise." A black cat sauntered over to Salvator and bunted his legs, then retreated behind Rick. Salvator smiled at Scarlett and she raised her little hand and waved goodbye to him, a troubled look in her eyes.

Rick made his way back to the conservatory, Eden's sobs reverberating down the hallway. She cried over Blake's shoulder and he patted her head with his plump little hand, as though trying to calm her.

Rick bent down and stared into her blue-violet eyes, which were now red-rimmed and bloodshot. How had he not seen their Violet and Jade connection? Their eyes had held the biggest clue. Usually he didn't miss anything, especially a scientific link like that. He was supposed to be a high-end, renowned researcher, for God's sake.

He and Eden were so human, though, except for a few small things that now stood out like large, hairy dogs' balls. It highlighted that the mind, with its lifetime of rules, constructed boundaries and resulting frame of reference, only allowed a person to perceive within its limitations.

"I'm just going to take the twins upstairs, okay? I'll be right back."

She nodded and sniffled.

Rick collected Blake in his arms and carried him and Scarlett up to their bedroom. He put them in their cots and said, "Now, try to sleep. I'm going to talk to Mummy."

A fretful expression descended over Scarlett's face, as though she fully understood, as though she could tune in to people's emotions. From now on, he and Eden had to be careful around her when things were worrying them.

They couldn't afford to stress her and Blake out as well. They had to create a safe home environment for the twins, while educating them on recognizing danger and how to keep out of it.

Rick re-joined Eden on the couch and embraced her. "I know this has been extremely difficult to comprehend and put into any sort of perspective — however, we really need to try and get a handle on it. The kids are getting stressed."

Eden looked up, streams of sadness trickling down her wet cheeks. "Getting a handle on it is easier said than done. It's like a rug's been pulled from under us and we're still floundering somewhere in space. I don't know about you, but my mind is all over the place trying to work out who I am, who you are, while trying to come to terms with the increased threat to our lives. We're even greater targets now…" Her eyes swelled with the growing bulge of fresh tears.

Rick wanted to comfort her, to take all her pain away, all *his* pain away, but he felt helpless. He imagined both of them did. They'd need to pick through the exploded bomb representing their life. Only time would help them sort out the pieces and promote healing.

More tears tumbled down her cheeks. "Finding out about our past was dangerous enough, let alone that we're part vampire and Scarlett is a rare breed. If Sub Rosa find out any of this, we're…we're… We'll be collected and experimented on again, though as a family this time. We can't let that happen, especially to the children."

Rick pulled her onto his lap and cradled her against him. "I agree. If it's any consolation, I'm struggling with this as much as you. But I have faith we'll come up with a way to keep us all safe. However, right now, we need to focus on processing everything."

He needed to buy more time. She wasn't ready to hear his proposition yet, and he still needed to work out the finer details. Hopefully in the meantime he'd think of something better, safer.

Eden's alarmed gaze met his. "What happens if, while we do that, we put ourselves at more risk, in more danger?"

"We could, but if we don't get our heads around the facts first, we might make a stupid mistake…like before."

She stared at him as though weighing up his words. "The problem is, I'm so full of grief, sadness and rage at the loss of the life we had, at the life we were prevented from having, and for who I thought I was, that it's hard to think straight. Now I'm even questioning what memories are actually mine."

He stroked her back, trying to ease the built-up tension in her muscles. "I know. It's all very confusing and stressful. Though once the emotion settles and we organize our thoughts, we'll be able to come up with a strong plan."

She squinted her eyes at him. "Something tells me you already have one." Did he detect the hint of a smile on her lips? With all the chaos going on, a plan provided a sort of refuge, a strategy to restore some order. Obviously, she could see that too. However, if he revealed his Norway secondment idea, she definitely wouldn't be too enthusiastic.

So far, it seemed the only viable option. It would give him the best opportunity to release their captive vampire relatives and the other test subjects, as well as collect all the evidence he needed to bring down Sub Rosa and ensure that he, Eden and the twins were finally safe.

"You know me too well. I've got the beginnings of one gaining momentum in my head and now just need it to germinate. Once we've regained a sense of equilibrium, I think we need to sit down with Salvator again and nut things out some more."

\* \* \* \*

"Andy, it's me." Beauregarde's cultured, cocky voice broke into the silence.

"This better be important," Andy slurred, still half asleep. He turned and squinted at his alarm clock—two-thirteen a.m.

"It is."

Andy propped himself up in bed. "Spit it out."

Beauregarde's vibrant, violet eyes pierced the darkness. "Salvator's been trying to access Norway Experiment files remotely."

"What?" Andy sat bolt upright. "I need to get on to IT to strengthen the firewall, then reset and heighten security settings both internally and remotely." He shook his head. "You'd think after having worked here so many years he'd realize we'd be monitoring things like that."

Beauregarde stepped out of the shadows. "Obviously not."

"Have you *spoken* to him about it?"

"No, I—"

"Then what the fuck are you doing wasting your time talking to me?" Frustration seethed in Andy's veins. "Find out what he's after, then dispose of him."

"What if he won't tell me?"

*Do I have to spell out every fucking detail?* "Get rid of him anyway. He's an unknown quantity, a liability we can't afford."

# Chapter Twenty-Seven

The Truth, the Whole Truth
and Nothing but the Truth?

Rick took the lift to the top level, his thoughts flying at the speed of light. The ping of arrival jolted his mind to the present. The metal doors opened and he gulped.

"Rick, come in and have a seat," Andy called from his office at the end of the hall.

*Something is wrong. Very wrong.* His heart pounded, the blood gushing in his ears. Andy never invited grass-roots staff into his office for anything. Well, not for anything good, anyway, or he'd have heard about it.

Rick sat in a low chair on the other side of the CEO's massive desk. It looked like the type of furniture featured in one of those sleek Italian designer magazines—all shiny and black and angular.

Andy stared down at him from his luxurious black throne, a menacing smile on his lips. "You're probably wondering why I've called you up here. Concerning information has come to hand and I believe you might be able to make some sense of it."

"What sort of concerning information?" Rick's thunderous heartbeat thumped, loud and unrelenting, like it had been blasted through a loudspeaker.

"About a security breach."

*He knows about me accessing the classified files? Fuck fuck fuck!* How would he explain his way out of this one? "Security breach?" Rick repeated, with his best I-don't-know-what-you're-talking-about tone.

"Yes. Someone tried to access files remotely."

*O-kay...* "Did they?" Definitely not him. So why had Andy pulled him aside for one-on-one questioning?

"Yes." Andy scrutinized him with his beady blue eyes. "I remember you asked, a little while back, to read some restricted files."

*Oh...* "I did. After several attempts, putting my argument forward, you denied my request and I moved on." *And got what I needed with the help of Simon's awesome hacker skills.*

"Did you? You were pretty persistent at the time. It didn't seem like you were going to take no for an answer."

Rick tried to calm his accelerated breathing. "It was frustrating, but I got over it. Where are you going with this?"

"You'll see in a moment. And, hopefully, so will I."

A flash of violet shot through the air vent and a sharp sting tore through the main vein of Rick's left arm. "What's going on?" Rick could hardly recognize his own voice, his words slurring like he'd had a stroke. Whatever he'd been injected with was super-fast-acting.

"I don't have time for games. This way, I'll be sure to get a straight answer." Andy sounded like he was speaking under water, his face a nasty, gray blur.

Lethargy descended over Rick like a dense cloud.

"Has it kicked in yet?" Andy whispered to a dark shape in the corner of the room. "Great, thanks."

He came around the side of his desk and pulled up a chair opposite Rick. "Are you employed as a researcher at Sub Rosa?"

Rick fought to keep his eyes open and his breathing steady. "Yes."

"Are you married to Eden Freberg?"

"Yes." *What the fuck? He knows all this stuff?*

"Did you try and remotely log in to Norway Experiment files?"

"No." The answer shot out of his mouth before he had time to think. *Oh shit. Truth serum. Don't ask about Salvator. Don't ask about Salvator. Don't ask about Salvator.*

"Do you know a Salvator Aalem?"

*Fuck.* His breath halted in his chest. "I know of him." *Good work.*

Andy shifted forward, crowding his personal space. "How?"

Rick's pulse points pounded like a fast-paced piston. "I saw his name on Norway Experiment research notes. He did some great work." *So far, so good.*

"Did you know he recently tried to remotely log in to Norway Experiment files?" Andy's stale coffee breath slammed against his face.

"No."

"Do you know what his interest might have been?"

*I could have a guess…* "No."

Andy leaned in closer. "Had you enlisted his help to gain access to classified documents?"

"No." Though he had been hoping to. Rick tried to move back but the chair wouldn't budge.

Andy loomed over him. "Do you know of any other Sub Rosa staff that might have been in contact with him?"

Perspiration broke out of Rick's pores. Eden remained on maternity leave, which technically meant she didn't meet active-staff criteria. "No."

Andy shoved his face right in his. "Did you know he was found dead this morning?"

*What the fuck?* "No." *Poker face. Breathe. Calm. Breathe.*

Andy pulled back and stared at him, as though awaiting an incriminating response.

Rick returned his stare in the long, spine-shuddering silence. *Have I convinced him?* A drop of sweat trickled down his back.

Andy returned to his throne. "Yes, horrible situation. Looks like he had a fall at home and hit his head."

*Hang on.* How did Andy find out about Salvator's demise so quickly? And how convenient that Salvator happened to die soon after attempting to access Norway Experiment files.

A film of clammy coldness settled over Rick's skin. Fuck, this guy would stop at nothing to keep things quiet. It seemed that trait had been a prerequisite for Sub Rosa CEOs since the commencement of the company.

Andy started tapping on his computer keyboard, his face now hidden behind the computer screen. "Thanks for your time, Rick."

Rick stayed slumped in his seat, his limbs still lead-like, and tried to settle his body's traitorous behavior. Andy had made his fate clear, if he were found out. Thank God he'd avoided succumbing to the serum. But how? He'd given eighty percent of the truth and it seemed to be good enough. What about the remaining twenty percent? Could it be his vampire genetics provided a buffer?

"You can go." Andy's abrasive voice scratched Rick's tender brain.

Rick rubbed his sleepy eyes and tried to straighten up. "Um—"

"It'll wear off shortly."

Sub Rosa didn't have the right to subject him to drugged-up, interrogation-like questioning—definitely not without his consent. Would he have enough time to get a tox screen done? That in itself would give him evidence of the organization's immoral practices.

While contemplating his options, the lethargy started to lift. They'd worked it out perfectly. *Of course they had.* Just like with everything else, they knew exactly how to stay a step ahead, to ensure no trace evidence. Maybe Rick could use the opportunity to get his brewing plan into action instead.

"You can get up," Andy barked, like an impatient, egocentric tyrant.

Rick stood and steadied himself on the edge of the desk, the drug almost dissipated from his system. "Before I go, Eden and I never got to have a proper honeymoon and we've even been considering a bit of a...change. If I submit a request for time off and follow up my holiday with a secondment to the Norway site, would you approve it? The Norway Experiment fascinates me and I'd love to get firsthand experience of the facility."

Andy studied him for a few moments. "Sure. We need passionate, dedicated researchers like you onboard. When would you like to leave?"

# Chapter Twenty-Eight

The Best Laid Plans...

"Salvator's dead."

Goosebumps pricked up all over Eden's body. "Dead? What do you mean?"

Rick ran his hand through his ruffled hair. "According to Andy, someone found Salvator in his unit this morning. Apparently, he died of natural causes."

"Really? He seemed fine when he visited us yesterday." Her voice shook in sympathy with her hands.

"Supposedly he had a fall and fatally hit his head."

Her eyes searched his. "You don't believe it."

"Do you?"

"No."

Rick joined Eden at the kitchen bench and embraced her, her silent tears pooling over his heart. "The funeral is this Friday."

Eden tried to stifle a sob. "I want to go."

"Me too. But we can't. It's too dangerous. Andy's already questioned me about Salvator..."

She jerked her head up, her heart and mind racing. "What?"

He smiled—however, his dilated pupils told an I'm-still-rattled story. "Don't worry. He seemed to believe no link existed between us...for now. But you, me and the twins are getting out of here and quickly, just to be on the safe side."

Her stomach clamped down. Leave their home? Their one source of stability? "Where would we go?"

Rick's determined jade eyes stared into hers. "To Norway. I need to find a way to sort this out, once and for all."

# Want to see more like this?
## Here's a taster for you to enjoy!

# Vamp Hunters: Hunt Her
## Elle Q. Sabine

### *Excerpt*

"Since you weren't active sexually prior to starting the antidepressant, you may notice increased ease in sexual arousal and achieving orgasm now that you're discontinuing sertraline. I wouldn't want you to be concerned or worried. Orgasm dysfunction and sexual arousal disorder are known side effects of the drug, and you have been taking it since you were a teenager."

"I'm not a virgin, Dr. Freud," Meghan returned dryly, studying the literature in front of her. Discontinuing the antidepressant was a major step for her, and she needed time to adjust to it before tackling the more worrisome problem of the sleeping medication she'd relied on for more than a decade. It was time she took control of her life again, while her reliable psychiatrist was still practicing.

He'd begun to make noises about retiring to a warm climate, and the thought of making the transition to a strange doctor worried her more than life without antidepressants and sleeping pills. Meghan wasn't afraid of changes or challenges, but she freely admitted she was rather dependent on the older man she alternately called Freud and Miracle Man in her mind. She felt as if she were important to him, and that was an intimacy she didn't share with anyone else. Certainly she wouldn't have the same familiarity with a new psychiatrist.

He snorted at the moniker. "No, but you reported a rather lukewarm interest in those pursuits, which is uncommon in healthy young women but not necessarily abnormal. I trust that even then you were being honest about your sexual activity. I believe we even discussed the medical side effects of the pharmaceuticals as a possible cause of your lackluster response, as well as the theoretical possibilities of your inadequate lover, the difficulties of time and place as a college student and the possibility of a naturally low sexual function. It's been several years since you've made any effort at sexual activity, perhaps driven by your similar lack of interest in a committed relationship. Since there's no history of sexual trauma in your past, I just want you to keep in mind that things might be different now that you've discontinued this particular medication."

"I'll remember, Doctor." Meghan glanced at the clock then stood. "And that's my cue. You must have dinner plans, and I'd like to walk home before dark."

"Of course." Freud pinched his nose beneath his glasses in a familiar gesture and stood as well, reaching out to shake Meghan's hand. "And, Meghan, please call if you have any concerns at all about the process for discontinuing the prazosin. Your transition off the antidepressant went well, but I'm concerned you may not adjust to life without the sleeping medication nearly so easily. Don't jump ahead of the process I've outlined, and that means keep taking it for another week at least, while the sertraline finishes exiting your body. If you begin to have nightmares again and we don't address them correctly, you could start an unhealthy downward spiral of insomnia and depression that trigger your anxiety and panic attacks associated with the post-traumatic stress syndrome. It's important that we keep a close eye on any possible changes before they become problematic."

Meghan accepted the handshake and smiled naturally as Freud's lecture concluded. Perhaps his age was why she'd always felt comfortable with him, when so many men felt overbearing and overtly sexual. Or perhaps it was because he was simply an excellent physician, who was honestly concerned about her.

"Thank you for seeing me today." She walked away easily with a friendly smile to the receptionist, who was already packing up her belongings for the day.

Meghan slipped into the street, still thinking of the doctor's final warnings. There was a way to find out, of course. She walked directly home to her small apartment. When she arrived, she locked and chained the door behind her then left her purse in the closet with her jacket and walking boots. She still had the heels in her arm bag she'd worn at the office, and she carried those into the bedroom with her, before dumping the bag on the floor with her gym clothes, running shoes and the dirty laundry that she always left piled in the closet. Meghan rustled in the top drawer of her bureau for several minutes before unearthing the silicone beauty that she'd invested in prior to convincing herself she was more asexual than not, and she gave a disgusted snort when she pushed the buttons for nothing more than a faint wiggle.

"Damn it," Meghan grumbled, feeling around in the drawer a second time as she searched for the charging station. It took only a minute to plug in the stand and set the burgundy-shaped vibrator in place.

"Now what?" she asked herself, glancing around the room, then down at herself. With a grimace, she stripped off her clothes. On her way to the shower, she turned off the overhead light and switched on the nightstand lamp, wondering what on earth she would think about when she finally turned on the vibrator in the secluded room.

Her college housemates had once advised her that a visual aid helped, but Meghan wasn't convinced. Josh Hutcherson always looked too young. Heath Ledger was dead. Once upon a time, she'd thought maybe David Beckham might have done it for her, but then there had been that photo of him in his tattoos and underwear, and whenever she saw an image of him now, she just wanted to laugh. Her first attempt eight years earlier, with a poster of Brad Pitt on the wall opposite the bed, had gone horribly wrong, and she'd burned the grinning image two days later. She'd always liked Orlando Bloom best as an elf, but the pointy ears were a distraction. Ian Somerhalder was probably her favorite eye candy at the moment, but she still couldn't imagine staring at him while touching herself.

Meghan paused while washing herself and she shuddered. "There must be a better way," she muttered, as the water coursed down her back. She closed her eyes, letting the steam soak into her skin. She washed mechanically with gel and a washcloth, wondering why she couldn't lust after distant celebrities or her work colleagues with the same narrow, eager focus other women her age exhibited. It wasn't that she found men — or women — unattractive. It was simply that they didn't incite any level of desire, whether dressed in a power suit and silk tie, a tuxedo or nothing at all. Was it truly a side effect of medication, or could it be something more fundamental to her personhood?

She hadn't always been dependent on a psychiatrist for a primary relationship. Like other girls her age, she'd yearned for a boyfriend, though she'd never actually found a boy she liked enough to bother to try to attract. She had a brother. Her parents had loved her, and if—

No. She couldn't think of that, or she'd spend the night on the floor of the closet crying, instead of experimenting with her long-lost, battery-operated friend.

The dreams hadn't all been nightmares. Once upon a time, they'd featured a hero instead of a villain. In her earliest dreams, he'd been something conjured from the legends of films—dark and striking, his beard scruffy, his eyes always a vibrant sky-blue. As time passed, he'd taken on the costume or hairstyle of her favorite movie character of the moment. He'd worn the black combat gear of elven archers and carried a sword that gleamed as brightly as a lost prince's blade or dragon slayer's shining harpoon. Fearsome power had rolled from his hands as he'd fought beside wizards. He'd walked beside her as a man and again as a wolf, her guard and her guide through an adventurous, fantastical landscape of ice, water, mountains, majestic castles, lush forests and wide, golden grazing lands. He'd stood on the deck of a ship, the wind whipping around him as he'd shouted orders to the crew, his cape flying majestically. He'd urged a horse across the plains, chasing her as she laughed gleefully, tailed by dimmer apparitions that had tried to emulate him but simply couldn't, because they weren't him.

The same hands that were so fierce in battle had also cradled an injured eagle with infinite patience and had brushed her cheek and chin ever so gently. In her dreams, it had been a fleeting sensation, one that had sent a tingle through her nervous system. Then, she'd been too innocent to spin out those fantasies into explicit detail, but now she was twenty-eight years old, and her hands were already stroking down her sides, over her hips and onto the silky skin at the front of her thighs.

*They were alone when he finally trapped her steed near the corner of a paddock fence. How and why they'd left the others behind didn't matter, but he dragged her from the horse and onto the saddle of the giant horse in front of him, wrapping her inside of the great cape that hung around him. He grumbled something against her cheek, but Meghan only smiled and slid her hands up and under his shirt, rubbing her palms over the hard muscles and hair until she found his nipples and pressed each of her palms to one.*

He tightened his hold on her, rubbing her through the cotton garments she wore, even as Meghan dried herself off with a soft, thick towel. When she wrapped herself in the comfort of the old quilt on her bed, she grasped the contoured silicone device and imagined him taking them both to the grassy paddock while their horses moved obediently aside. Beside her, he brushed his hand over her pubis, pressing firmly and rubbing in a circle against the sensitive upper edges of her labia, as the blunt, flat-tipped vibrator eased against her wet skin.

Meghan shuddered. When had she ever been so wet? Her fingers ran over the buttons on the control pad, and the device buzzed pleasantly in her fist. Obligingly, his finger slipped between those same wet labia lips and pressed against her clitoral hood, even as he murmured to her about how she would always belong to him, how she could always rely on him, how she could always trust him.

She didn't know if it was him, her imagination or the vibrator, but in the end, it didn't matter who or what was responsible. The low vibrations spread from her clitoris to her lower back, thrummed through her vagina and finally sped up her spine into her mind.

When the bliss faded, she was alone with a silicone massager in her hands, naked, wrapped in an old quilt. He was gone, just as he'd been gone since the day she'd needed a hero. But she'd done it herself. If she could do this for herself, what else could she accomplish on her own?

*Everything*, she told herself. She'd start by finding Red.

Sparring could be vicious, especially when the battle-honed fighter Atlas faced off against his brother, the master. The other warriors watched, leaning against the outer walls of the basement training facility. Built to their specifications with noise-muffling technology, earthquake-resistant resonance, high ceilings and floors covered with durable matting, the space still sustained damage when the most powerful among them took to the ring. Already a crack in the mirror on the north wall reached a span of six feet, because, at full strength, the master had thrown Atlas against it. Blood pooled near the west corner where Atlas had thrown a knife that had grazed his brother's right shoulder. The knife had pierced the master's shoulder, but the blade was presently lodged deep into the west wall. Spatter across the mat stained their feet and had transferred to their bodies, though it was mostly invisible against the basic black outfits both wore.

These two were unquestionably among the most powerful beings of their kind. Still, his sparring partner executed a powerful kick that hit Atlas in the center of his chest and sent him sprawling across the floor. The impact into the east wall caused the entire building to shake.

"The man's going to lose it if his vamp doesn't show up soon."

Enna kept his eye on the two men on the mat and grunted in response. 'The man' was an innocuous term to describe the master, Atlas' brother and sparring partner, also the lord's heir. Enna had elevated his brother to the title 'lord' more than two decades ago, though the master was still the heir and not yet the lord. The master's name meant something when spoken, particularly when a blood bond existed between the two, so the warriors avoided using his name as much as possible. It was a courtesy, but also a matter of privacy — if they didn't want the master's attention.

Still, 'the man' held Enna's loyalty and affection, in addition to being Atlas and Enna's brother. Referring to him by that casual term grated on Enna's notion of respect, though he understood Jeb intended nothing sinister by the comment. In fact, Jeb was making an effort not to distract the pair on the mat. Distraction during battle led to mistakes that could have generations of consequences, particularly in this world.

None knew such effects more intimately than General Enna himself.

The thought of that ancient history reminded Enna that the master needed to be prepared for any complication, even distraction. Certainly his lord was a superior warrior — born powerful and trained to use his skills ruthlessly. "Lord Valor would indeed represent us well in a true battle," he replied graciously, quite aware that everyone in the training room would hear him, no matter the volume of his voice. Enna shared a blood bond with his brothers that had endured since their youngest years, and he'd fought and defeated all of the warriors repeatedly, creating bonds with each of them. Even without those bonds, the warriors' senses were much more developed than a human's would have been, especially with the enhanced gifts that had come to them with their rebirths. "Lord Valor and our warriors can indeed defend us against any raiding parties trying to enter through the portal. But what of a human army of soldiers carrying guns — or helicopters or planes with fighters dropping into our fortress? What ought we do then?"

"Follow the general's battle strategy, of course," the master spat out, before spinning to avoid the side kick of his opponent. "And utilize my shielding gift to give us all time to retreat into the fortifications and through the portal. It can be sealed from the other side." He used his momentum from the spin, throwing a solid punch into Atlas' stomach. Atlas grunted and stepped back, letting the master's hit propel him into a backflip. His left foot caught the master's chin as he went over. Valor didn't hesitate, delivering a direct front kick that landed squarely on Atlas' ass and sent him sprawling onto the mat. Atlas rolled and jumped smoothly into a low spin, his leg stretching in a beautiful roundhouse kick that caught the master in the back of his knee.

With a wild roar — a battle-cry of old — Valor sprang out of the way, performed two forward handsprings and landed two feet in the air on a balance beam, a long wooden staff racing across the room to slap into the master's grip.

Atlas' eyes sparkled and gleamed bright blue with the master's use of telekinesis. Casually, he lifted a hand and drew a staff identical to the lord's toward his own hand. It streaked across the room from the wall of practice weapons then landed in his palm with a smack as he, too, answered Enna. "For my money, if guns are in play, the general's battle strategy ought to be to run and hide, just as the master says. I'm all for it too. Bullets hurt."

"Surviving bullets while still standing on your feet would reveal our true nature, as surely as telekinesis," Enna murmured, aware that both the master and Atlas could hear him. "It's a lesson the pair of you have not learned, despite living here for hundreds of years."

"'Tis better to live to see another day in another world than to die foolishly in this one," the master said calmly, his eyes on Atlas' graceful movements as the man twirled the staff in a ballet of motion. With hardly an effort, the master lifted his staff and threw it, knocking Atlas' weapon cleanly from his lieutenant's hands. "As for Jeb, he's correct. I feel the separation keenly, and I sense inwardly that I have begun to age as she ages. 'Tis a dangerous thing for all of you. It is right and proper that you should all practice to defeat me, to keep me restrained, if my sanity comes into question."

Atlas snorted then smacked his hands on the front of his thighs. "Your sanity is safe. It's your temper we guard against."

Home of Erotic Romance

Sign up for our newsletter and find out about all our romance book releases, eBook sales and promotions, sneak peeks and FREE romance books!

# About the Author

Sandra Carmel is an Australian-based author of engaging, thought-provoking romance novels, novellas, short stories and poetry, who writes for the pleasure of stimulating herself and others with words. An obsession with classic romance novels, particularly *Jane Eyre*, combined with marrying her own Mr Rochester were key motivators in commencing her romance writing journey. So far, she has taken the scenic route from contemporary to paranormal to erotic, creating provocative stories that delve beneath the surface of desire. She reads and writes a lot, frequently disrupted by her ever-attentive, cheeky cats, and sinfully amorous husband.

Sandra loves to hear from readers. You can find her contact information, website details and author profile page at https://www.totallybound.com